NORTH SOMERSET LIBRARIES

WITHDRAWN AND OFFERED

FOR SALE

ALL ITEMS SOLD AS SEEN

I NS

1 2 0593399 1

First Time Hard

Colin Holcombe

This book is dedicated to my three beautiful
granddaughters – Chloe, Beth and Amy.

CV

I would like to acknowledge and thank Jan Hartnell
and Stephen Foulkes for their interest and advice.

This novel is entirely a work of fiction. Any resemblance to actual persons, living or dead, is entirely coincidental.

First published by Completely Novel in 2012

Copyright : Colin Holcombe 2012

Printed in the UK by CPI

ISBN   9781 8491 42991

All rights reserved: No part of this publication may be reproduced, stored in a retrieval system, or transmitted, in any form or by any means, electronic, mechanical, photocopying, recording or otherwise, without the prior permission of the publishers.

Front Cover by
Christos Trivizas

Prologue

The three of them were taking turns with the air rifle, trying to hit one of the glass bottles that they had placed on top of the low brick wall, separating the lush green lawn from the raised flowerbed. The twins, who lived at the house, were well-practiced with the gun, which had been a recent present from their father, the Christmas before. The other boy, whom the twins knew from school, had cycled out to the house on his new bike. It was his birthday, and his parents had bought the bike for him, because he had outgrown his previous one by a country mile. It would have been a mistake to call the three of them friends, because the twins didn't really have friends; they just had people that they knew and, often, used. They didn't need friends, because they always had each other. Sometimes, they allowed other boys to think that they were their friends, but that was only if they wanted them to do something, or get something for them. Once that was done, the pretence of friendship would end abruptly, and the contempt would begin in earnest. Many of the boys at school desperately wanted to be friends with the siblings, because they were clever and charismatic and clearly had money and possessions, amply provided by well-off parents. Everyone seemed to respect the twins; certainly, nobody messed with them ... there were vague warnings and rumours of boys being badly beaten who dared to cross them.

The day had started off normally enough; with the twins' father going in to work, as usual, around seven a.m. in order to beat the worst of the morning traffic. Just before midday, their mother had gone out in the car to visit a friend and do some shopping. She had told the boys to amuse themselves in the garden, as it was such a mild day for December, and she felt there was less chance of them causing any substantial damage outdoors in the garden. She would be back to start dinner around five, so that it would be ready for their father's return from work.

The boys had played football on the lawn for a bit, taking turns in goal, but they had soon tired of it, so they set the bottles up to shoot at with their air rifle. Many parents would have bought the boys a gun each, fearing heated arguments over whose turn it was to use it. But the twins' father had known that it wouldn't be a problem; they had always shared everything they had, no matter which of them the object actually belonged to. Unlike other siblings, his boys never argued. There were times when he wished that they would fall out and have a proper fight, like normal brothers. Their total lack of brotherly squabbles was singularly unnatural and slightly disquieting.

Stephen Potter had turned up unexpectedly, just after the football had become a bore and the target shooting had begun. He was a tall, slightly awkward lad, but quite clever academically. He was very popular with the teaching staff at the school they all attended, unlike the twins, who the staff rightly regarded as arrogant and conceited bullies. He lived with his parents, about five miles away from the twins, and had been recently hanging around them at school, trying to make it look, to others, that he was friendly with them, but few were fooled by his behaviour. They knew that the twins didn't want, or need, friends. They would make fun of him in front of his real friends one minute, ask him if he wanted to play football the next and then dare him to do something stupid, like stealing from the local tuck-shop.

They were not really surprised when he turned up, out of the blue, to show them his new bike, and they were pleased that they now had something else to play with, something that didn't really matter if it got broken.

'Hi, Stephen,' one shouted, 'nice bike ... you're just in time for target practice. Have you ever fired a rifle before?'

There was more of a spring in the twins' steps now, as they showed him the bottle targets and how to load and fire the gun.

It turned out that, as well as being good at math and English at school, Stephen Potter was also a crack shot with an air rifle, better, even than the twins, and, needless to say, they didn't like that very much.

'I've got an air rifle of my own at home,' declared Stephen, proudly. 'My friend Nathaniel and I shoot all the time; we love it,' he said, enthusiastically, as yet another bottle bit the dust.

The siblings eyed each other, with grim, irritated expressions. They had hoped to humiliate Stephen with the target practice, but now found themselves searching the house for more bottles, he had hit so many, despite the fact that they appeared to be rather smaller than the ones that the brothers had fired at. The fact was that the brothers were now becoming annoyed with Stephen. He was tolerated there, as long as they could manipulate and humiliate him for their own purposes, not the other way round, so that would have to change, pretty damn quick. He would have to be taken down a peg or two.

The last visit into the house to search for more targets had resulted in one twin returning with something quite different. 'Look what I've found,' he said, proudly, holding aloft a very impressive-looking pistol. 'It must be Dad's old service revolver. It was in a box on one of the shelves in his wardrobe. There are bullets, as well ... look!'

Although, to Stephen, it was made to look as if the gun had only just been discovered during the search for more targets, the fact was that both boys not only knew of its existence, but had handled it many times before and were very familiar with it, had even fired it, once, unbeknown to their parents.

'What shall we do with it?' asked the other brother, grinning, but unsure as to why. 'How many bullets are there?'

'Only six ... not enough for target shooting, but I've thought of a brilliant game we could play.'

'What game?' It was Stephen who asked, rather timidly.

'Well, Stephen, have you ever heard of a game called ... Russian roulette?'

Stephen felt a little uneasy. He desperately wanted to be friends with these two boys, and he didn't really believe any of the foolish stories that he'd heard about them, but they seemed serious about playing Russian roulette with a real gun. That had to be extremely dangerous. Then, he saw them smile at one another and cottoned on. It was all a set-up; they were taking the mickey out of him, yet again. It wasn't a real gun at all, but one of those replicas that you can buy. Of course, there was no way that their parents would be careless enough to let them have access to a real gun. They were always playing rather unpleasant tricks on people ... so, OK ... he'd go along with it; perhaps it would even be fun.

'How do we play?' he asked.

'I think there are two ways you can do it,' one twin explained, eagerly, 'you can put one bullet in the chamber ... spin it...and then we each take a turn holding it to our own heads and pulling the trigger, until someone chickens out or is shot dead, or you can put one in and spin the chamber around every time. What do you think?' he asked his brother, playfully.

'I think, for the first game, we should put one bullet in and spin the chamber each time, and I think we should do it three times each,' he declared, boldly.

'That sounds good to me. How about you, Stephen? Have you got the bottle for it?' he sneered.

Stephen's legs felt a little wobbly at the prospect, but he was determined to put on a brave face and impress them, and, in any case, he was sure that it was all some kind of ruse; even though, he had to admit, the gun looked very real and so did the bullets. Then he reasoned: if the gun didn't look real, then it wouldn't be a very good replica, would it? He was still afraid at what was unfolding, though. The air suddenly felt much colder, but he was determined not to let his fear show.

The twin who had discovered the gun now loaded a bullet into the chamber and spun it. The gun was very heavy, and he had to hold on to it with both hands. As he pulled the hammer back to cock the pistol, he held it so that the barrel pointed almost straight up, and so he was able to see the front of the revolving chamber. He reasoned that if the bullet could be seen from the front, when the weapon was fully cocked, then it wasn't under the hammer, and it wouldn't fire when the trigger was pulled. On the first occasion, the bullet was clearly visible after he had cocked it, so he pointed the gun at his own head ... and ... with his heart pounding heavily in his chest ... he pulled the trigger. The hammer made such a loud crack as it descended on the empty chamber, that, for a brief moment, the boy thought that he had miscalculated and had actually shot himself. It had taken nerves of steel to pull the trigger, even when knowing the round that was loaded was not under the firing pin. But he had been up to the task, so he consequently thought of himself as The Boy Who Laughed in the Face of Danger, and, his brother, who hadn't worked out what his sibling had done, was very impressed.

Even though he was unaware of how his brother was doing it, the other twin knew, beyond any shadow of a doubt, that when his brother handed him the gun, his life was not in any danger. He steadily pointed the gun at his head and pulled the trigger. His brother would never do anything to endanger him. Even so, he was mightily pleased with himself. It had still taken real courage to pull the trigger. The twins exchanged knowing, satisfied glances; their mutual respect for each other having just grown immeasurably.

The third time that the twin spun the cylinder, the bullet was not visible as the gun was cocked; there were six chambers in all, and four were clearly visible and empty. This meant there was a real chance that the gun was poised to fire this time.

'Your turn, Stephen,' he said ... his voice trembling, just a little.

He knew that if the gun fired, Stephen would probably be killed. And he knew that there would be terrible consequences if this occurred. The only thing he didn't understand was why he just..... didn't care.

He casually handed the gun over to Stephen, who, having seen the gun aimed and fired at both the other boys' heads, was now doubly sure the that whole thing was a well-planned joke that was being staged and was determined to play his part confidently.

'What are we actually playing for?' asked Stephen, cockily. 'Surely we should be staking something on the outcome?'

The twin who had passed him the gun stared back at him, earnestly. 'Oh, but we are, Stephen – our lives!'

Stephen dutifully raised the pistol to his head, the way he had seen the other two do so, but hesitated, looking searchingly from one twin to the other, trying, unsuccessfully, to pick up some small sign that would confirm his suspicion that the whole thing was an elaborate ruse, designed to test him. But trick or not, there was no way that he could back out now.

As he pulled the trigger, he closed his eyes, somehow half-expecting the flash and horrendous *bang!* that resulted, but, in fact, he experienced nothing.

To the twins, the piercing sound of the explosion seemed infinitely worse than when they had both fired the gun before. Perhaps the sound was intensified by the knowledge that the gun was aimed, this time, not at the silver birch at the far edge of their parent's grounds ... but at a boy's head.

Stephen fell dead on the spot, without uttering a single sound. The two brothers watched the gruesome spectacle, with a mixture of fear, horror ... and exhilaration.

Chapter 1

As Mrs Gladys Harper began her unconventional descent of the nineteenth-century oak staircase, she was mentally alert enough to reflect on the brutal fact that, having celebrated her seventieth birthday only two months earlier, she would probably, now, never celebrate her seventy-first. With her right foot still in direct contact with the top step, and her head well on its way to making intimate contact with the tread, seventh from the top, she briefly wondered how her two sons, Kevin and Craig, would take the news of her death. There had been no real contact with either of her sons for a good many years, so she doubted that there would be a great deal of sadness or grief at the events that were unfolding. After all, she reasoned, they hadn't shed a tear when their father had died, and they'd only been small boys then.

As she continued her involuntary descent of the stairs, she had expected a certain degree of pain and was pleasantly surprised when there wasn't any. Everything had started happening in slow motion, from the moment she had realised that she was falling. She knew that her head had hit the stair tread with some force and that this had somehow resulted in the rest of her body, and then her legs, overtaking it on the journey down. As her body travelled over the top of her head, she reflected that she hadn't done a somersault since she was a little girl in gym class and she passed out. She was, therefore, unaware that it was actually the final impact – that of her head, once again, but, this time, with the less forgiving surface of the stone wall at the bottom of the stairs – that actually caused her death. The final impact also made a noise that was loud enough to be heard by the shadowy figure standing at the top of the stairs, and stomach-churning enough to make a quiet night's sleep, for this man, a thing of the past.

There were two men in the house – one standing at the top of the stairs, watching Gladys' descent with mounting dread, and his friend, business partner and, now, accomplice, standing at the bottom. They stared at the body of the motionless woman crumpled against the stone wall with heavy hearts. It had not been their intention to kill anyone.

Jack Simmons and Alan Salter had called at Mrs Harper's house only fifteen minutes earlier, when Alan had cheerfully introduced himself as, 'Richard Drake... I'm very early, I'm afraid, Mrs Harper. I hope that's not too much of a problem, but I had forgotten that I have another appointment close by at three. This is my associate, by the way, Steven Brown,' he continued, indicating Jack, standing beside him.

Mrs Harper was rather annoyed and said as much. 'It would have been better if you had rung back to let me know that you would be coming early. I don't like people turning up unexpectedly ... but as you're here now, I suppose it will be all right, this one time. Come in.'

Grumbling, she showed them into the front lounge, which was just on the other side of the small porch that she had been standing in. The lounge was much bigger than Alan had expected, from viewing the cottage's exterior, and full of antique furniture, paintings, china – all sorts of valuable objects. Also contrary to expectation, the room was remarkably light and airy, with the bulk of the furniture being of delicate Sheraton and Hepplewhite design. The best piece in the room was, undoubtedly, the serpentine-fronted chest, standing flush against the opposite wall. The chest was an excellent example of nineteenth-century marquetry, with a beautiful smooth marble top that had a distinctive pink grain. Proudly sitting on this marble top was a large bronze, easily a foot-and-a-half tall, of an American cowboy on horseback, holding the reins of his beautifully sculptured horse in one hand and an iconic Winchester rifle in the other, with its stock resting against his thigh and the barrel pointing skyward. It looked, for all the world, as if the figure was standing guard over the contents of the room and eyeing the new arrivals with suspicion. Alan surmised that it was worth several thousand pounds, having his own modest collection of bronzes, although nothing remotely as good this piece. However, it was unlikely that the old girl would part with it, even for a fair price, he surmised, and, besides, there were plenty of other things of interest. They soon realized that the usual sort of con-tricks that they played would not work with this particular lady, who was, obviously, a knowledgeable collector and had no pressing financial reason to sell anything. Obviously, she wasn't short of a bob or two. No ... even with no husband on the scene, getting out of the house with anything cheap would be next to impossible. Their best option was to lift something small, when the old girl wasn't watching.

To this end, Jack was already making his way up the stairs. 'You don't mind if I use your bathroom, do you, Mrs Harper?' he said, as she watched him ascend the stairs.

'Well ... I ... ah ... no, go ahead. It's to your right when you walk down the landing,' she said, uneasily.

She was reluctant to have them split up; there was no way that she could keep an eye on them both, and she had so many valuable things in the house - upstairs and down - but what could she do? Other than refusing to let him go upstairs - there was, after all, a perfectly good downstairs cloakroom -but he was practically up there now. She felt trapped. Richard Drake had been recommended to her - he had a good reputation for honesty and fair dealing, she'd heard, but something didn't feel quite right about these two.

'What was it you wanted me to value for you, Mrs Harper?' enquired Alan, hoping the item, or items, in question were not upstairs. The more time he could keep her occupied downstairs, the more time Jack would have to nose around the bedrooms.

'It's these four miniatures,' she began, indicating the items on the table, but she froze, suddenly, mid-sentence.

Mrs Harper and Alan stared at each other, having both heard the loud and unmistakable squeak of a door opening, above. They both turned instinctively and looked towards the stairs.

Mrs Harper was furious.

'What's he doing in my bedroom?' she demanded, angrily, and flew towards the stairs, like a sprinter out of the starting blocks. She was up the stairs, before Alan had even registered the fact that she had left his side. She certainly was a sprightly old girl, he thought.

Upstairs, Jack had opened the bedroom door carefully and quietly and, having not found a jewellery box on hand, was going through the top drawer of a Victorian chest, which was situated up against the wall, just inside the bedroom door. However, after a while, the weight of the door, which had been fitted with rising butt hinges, slowly began to close it again, causing the betraying squeak.

Jack had not heard the woman's cry of anger from below, nor her hurried ascent up the stairs. He had just located a pair of rather elegant, solid gold cuff-links in a box and was in the act of pocketing them, when Mrs Harper entered the room. She instantly recognised the box in Jack's hand as the one containing her late husband's cuff-links and was so incensed, that she rushed towards him, grabbed hold of the box with one hand and made to slap his face with the other.

'Give me those!' she shouted. 'What do you think you're playing at? Get out of my house this minute.'

Jack had been slapped in the face by women more times than he could remember, and so he recognised the signs of one coming. He tried to hold onto the box with one hand, whilst grabbing her wrist tightly with the other. Gladys was so incensed by this impudent man's behaviour, that she was determined to cause him some harm. Letting go of the box, she brought her hand up quickly to his other cheek and scratched him as hard and as deep as her strength would allow. His resulting howl of pain gave her great satisfaction.

Jack felt as if a hot poker had been placed against his left cheek, as he cried out in anguish. The bitch had scratched him! Gripping even more tightly onto the small box in his right hand, he brought it up over his left shoulder and backhanded her across the face with it, causing her to cry out in pain and stagger backwards into the half-open doorway. When a shocked, and somewhat disorientated, Mrs Harper looked back at Jack's face, she recognised rage and knew that she was now in danger, not just of losing possessions, but of physical harm. She made quickly for the top of the stairs, still a little woozy from the blow she had just received.

Jack followed her, still fuming. As he did so, he put his hand up to his smarting cheek, then held it out and saw that it was streaked with blood. My God! She'll pay for that, he decided, vengefully.

On reaching the top of the stairs, Mrs Harper had to steady herself, by holding onto the newel post, and it was here that Jack caught up with her. She turned her head towards him, to see what he was doing, and he struck her again, with brute force. He had aimed his blow at her face, where a bruise from his first strike was already beginning to show just below her eye, but she raised her arm defensively to fend him off, and the blow landed, instead, on her raised forearm. It was this blow that had dispatched her on her last-ever trip down the stairs.

As Jack and Alan stared mutely at the lifeless body at their feet, their first thoughts were not ones of pity or regret for the senseless loss of life, but of self-preservation and escape.

What had started out as a promising business call had now turned into the worst day of their lives.

Jack came slowly down the stairs, gripping tightly to the wooden banister rail and unable to tear his eyes from the crumpled heap at the bottom that had once been a loving wife and mother. He eased his way past the inert body and joined Alan in the lounge, where he was struggling to control his anger at Jack.

'My God, what the hell are we going to do?' Jack exclaimed.

'Well, stay calm and not panic, for a start,' said Alan, exasperated by the sudden turn of events. 'What the hell happened up there?'

Jack could see the condemnation in Alan's face. 'I didn't do it on purpose, for Christ's sake! The bitch attacked me.'

'Yeah, well...she's not the first woman to have done that, is she? You didn't have to throw her down the bloody stairs.'

'I didn't ... throw her down the stairs. She fell,' he said, defensively, then turned back to look at the body. 'She looks dead. Do you think she's dead?' he asked, as if the very act of questioning would alter the fact.

Alan approached the body cautiously, but even without feeling for her pulse, it was quite obvious that she was dead – very dead, about as dead as it was possible to be – and Jack had killed her ... that bloody temper of his! Alan had sometimes considered getting a different partner, because of Jack's unpredictable nature and his almost pathological hatred of women, but he'd not done so, because Jack had an uncanny knack for spotting the worthwhile amongst the worthless, and thus he was a master at what they did together, which had made Alan a lot of money over the years, and that was what was important, at the end of the day – money.

'Your fingerprints are on record, same as mine,' said Alan, trying to keep the anger out of his voice. 'We'll have to wipe over everything you can remember touching. Make a start upstairs. Try to re-enact everything you did. Wipe things over, even if there is just a chance you may have touched it. I'll do the same down here, and, for God's sake, don't touch anything new, unless it's with a clean handkerchief.'

After they were sure that they had wiped down everything they might have touched, they, once again, stood side-by-side together in the lounge.

Alan said, thoughtfully, 'I suggest we leave as quietly as we came, but I'm damned if I'm leaving empty-handed, after all this. Be quick, and see if there is anything we can sell for good money that isn't too big to carry. Was there any jewellery?'

'I was still looking when the old witch came upstairs and caught me at it. I'll go back and quickly finish searching.'

'Don't leave prints!'

'I won't,' Jack replied, angrily.

Although Alan had suggested to Jack that he take only small items, he was not going to follow this suggestion to the letter. He knew exactly what he wanted to take, and it definitely wasn't that small. He walked over to the marquetry chest and tested the weight of the bronze cowboy ... heavy, yes, but not too heavy. It was going with him, no question about it.

They hurriedly loaded the car with several worthwhile pieces from the house, including the woman's extensive collection of jewellery, which turned out to be in her bedside cabinet, and the large bronze cowboy. They quietly closed the door behind them, wiped it down afterwards and drove off, greatly relieved to be away, at last, from the house and the memory of the disastrous events that had unfolded inside.

Alan informed Jack that he wanted to keep the bronze for himself, but Jack was dead set against it, reminding him that they had always had an agreement on that score. They could only keep something for themselves on the condition that they both agreed, and, in this case, Jack most certainly did not agree.

He reminded Alan of what had just taken place, saying, in frustration, 'For Christ's sake, Alan, that thing can link us to a woman's death. We need to offload it today, and I mean all of it. Maybe we should have just left and not taken anything at all.'

Alan was angry and more than a little disappointed, but he knew that Jack was right this time. Although he was as mad as hell with him for getting them both into a situation that could potentially lose them their liberty, he was talking sense, for once. Perhaps, in hindsight, it had been a mistake to bring incriminating stuff away from the house, but it was done now. There was no going back.

Jack and Alan always carried with them a useful little book, *The Antique Shops of Britain*. Updated regularly every year, it is, basically, an extensive list of all the antique shops in the country that were worthy of the name, with most of the entries being adverts for various shops, stating what they specialised in and supplying addresses and telephone numbers. The book stated that there was a shop in Bath that bought and sold antiques, including figurines and bronzes of all shapes and sizes. They punched the postcode of the shop into their Sat Nav and headed for Bath.

The shop in question was called, simply, *Bath Antiques* and was run by a very knowledgeable, though, to some, rather disagreeable, man in his early sixties, Simon White. Simon loved the bronze as soon as his eyes fell on it and immediately offered the sum of eight hundred pounds for it. He was trying it on, of course. He could tell that Alan and Jack were very anxious to sell it and probably even surmised that the bronze might be stolen. But he was prepared to take that chance. The men appeared to be a bit on edge, and one had some fresh scratches on his face, which he was trying, unsuccessfully, to conceal behind a turned-up collar.

Not everything in Simon's shop had a complete and unbroken line of ownership. Simon wasn't a fence, exactly, but if he saw a good profit in something worthwhile, he didn't ask too many questions as to precisely how the vendor had come by it.

Jack and Alan were very anxious to sell, that was true, but they were not willing to accept a silly price for anything. They spent most of their own time ripping people off, but that didn't mean that somebody could do the same to them, regardless of the circumstances. There was still time left in the day to sell it elsewhere or there was even tomorrow to look for a buyer, if it was necessary to wait.

Alan looked Simon squarely in the face, with a stern expression, and replied, 'Don't take the bloody piss mate. It's worth nearer eight grand than eight hundred, you know that. We're here to do a deal, not get done over.'

Simon had acted shocked by Alan's attitude, but, in the end, said, coolly, 'OK ... OK ... don't blow a gasket. Let's be upfront with each other, yeah? You're obviously keen for a quick sale, and I want it. I've got four grand in cash in the safe. It's all the money on the premises. Take it or leave it.'

Alan stroked his chin, as if considering the offer, and returned, 'I'll agree on four for the bronze, but we have other stuff in the car. Are you still up for a deal?'

'What sort of deal do you have in mind?' Simon asked, cautiously.

After viewing the rest of Alan and Jack's ill-gotten gains and some more fraught negotiations, Simon agreed to buy all the items that they had with them, including the bronze and the jewellery, for a total of ten grand. It was agreed that Simon would give them the four thousand in cash from the safe and then an additional six thousand pounds worth of stock from his shop. Jack and Alan could pick what they wanted, but it would be at the marked price, with no negotiations. It was a good deal for Simon, selling a large chunk of stock at the marked price, and some of the things Jack and Alan had were very saleable, as long as they weren't too hot, and, besides, the bronze was just out of this world.

Jack and Alan were also happy with the deal, having secured a good price in cash for the bronze and exchanged all the other items that could possibly tie them in with the unfortunate events of earlier in the day. They were, however, still quite unnerved by everything that had happened and decided, soon after leaving *Bath Antiques*, that they would head home to Newcastle early. They had been on the road for only four weeks, but, in addition to the now totally clean goods in the car and about fifteen-and-a-half grand they had with them, they had already banked the satisfying sum of eighteen thousand. So, all in all, it had been a very profitable four weeks, seeing as they had started out with just five thousand in cash and a tank full of petrol.

The events of the day had driven a wedge between them. But they had been in a very profitable partnership for some years, and a couple of weeks of r-and-r would soon have them back on top form and raring to go, with all the hassle of this day forgotten. In the meantime, they both thought it would be a good idea to keep their heads down for a while. Both men shared the desire for the 'good' life and working together had given them the resources to enjoy just that. So they loaded up the car and headed back towards Bristol to pick up the M5, stopping only to fill up with petrol at the nearest filling station.

* * * * * * * * * * *

Richard Drake turned his two-year-old Volvo Estate into the driveway of Hilltop Cottage and drove the relatively short distance up to the house. When he turned off the engine, he glanced at his watch. It was spot on three o'clock. He loved being punctual. Few things annoyed him more than waiting for people to turn up when they had an appointment and were running late; in Richard's opinion, it was the height of bad manners.

Getting out of the car, he strolled over to the front door and rang the bell. While waiting for the door to be answered, he looked around with mild interest at the large and beautifully maintained grounds. The driveway curved easily up to the house, which was set at right angles to the main road, so if you had been able to see the house from the road, you would have been looking at only one side of it. Standing at right angles to the main entrance, there was a large double garage set back to the left; stone built at a much later date, to match the main property, which was decidedly Victorian in era.

Richard had been so absorbed in contemplating the beauty of the property, that it must have been a full two minutes before he realised that the door should have been answered by now. He rang again, and, this time, to make sure that the bell was working, he put his ear to the door to see if he could hear it ringing inside. Sure enough, the familiar sound of the Westminster chime was clearly audible. Why was no one answering? Had Mrs Harper forgotten their appointment? Or had she gone out, intending to be back in time for their three o'clock appointment, and been held up? Richard got back in his car and rang Margaret at the shop, to confirm that both the time and the address were correct. Having confirmed that he was not in error, Richard decided to wait for half an hour to see if Mrs Harper would turn up. He hoped that it wasn't all going to be a terrible waste of time.

Half an hour had gone by and there was still no sign of the mysterious Mrs Harper. Richard was frustrated and not a little annoyed. The double garage was closed, so there was no way of knowing if her vehicle was inside or not. He got out of his car again and posted one of his business cards through the letterbox, having first written quickly on the back, 'Called, as arranged, at three. Sorry to have missed you.' He was irritated and a little angry at the situation that had unfolded. The afternoon looked to be a waste of both time and petrol.

Nothing could be gained from staying at the house any longer, so he reluctantly got back into his car and, after turning around outside the double garage, headed back down the drive. At the end of the driveway, he was just about to turn back in the direction that he had come and return to the shop, when he made the split-second decision to turn the other way and pay a visit to a few antique shops in Bath. If he could manage to find something for one of his clients, the afternoon wouldn't be a total waste, after all.

Mrs Harper's house was on an almost-direct line between Bristol and Bath, so it wasn't very long before Richard pulled up outside *Bath Antiques.*

Richard didn't particularly take to Simon White, whose shop it was, but he had to admit that he did seem to get hold of some very worthwhile objects from time to time. As Richard hadn't been into his shop or spoken to him for a little while, there was bound to be something new that he hadn't seen. No matter what he thought of the man on a personal level, he was a useful contact and, therefore, had to be cultivated. It was a pleasant, summery day, and Richard had enjoyed the short drive to Bath.

Simon White was not as lucky as Richard with the parking arrangements outside his shop - having double yellow lines along virtually the whole length of the road -something which the traders were constantly complaining about to the Council. The dealers who called at Simon's shop pulled up outside, slightly on the pavement, and often left the tailgates of estate cars, or the rear doors of vans, wide open, as if in the act of loading or unloading goods. Richard did the same.

Unlike Richard's shop, where you could walk amongst the furniture with ease, and surfaces had maybe two or three items arranged on them with the utmost care, Simon's was more like a rather haphazard box room or loft. It was piled high with ornaments and interesting artefacts, intermingled with some more common household items and cheap pictures. To view the entirety of Simon's stock would take at least a week of delving and foraging, and it was possible to speculate the length of time an item had been in stock, by examining the thickness of dust on its surface.

As Richard approached the small desk at the rear of the shop where Simon normally hung out, his attention became focused on one thing. The object of Richard's attention was a large bronze of a mounted cowboy, which was sat squarely on the front of Simon's desk, and in which Simon was engrossed, studying it in detail.

'Hi, Simon, how are you keeping? How's the family?' enquired Richard, in his usual friendly manner.

'Richard!' cried Simon, looking up. 'I'm fine. How's yourself? You haven't been seen in these parts for a while. Not getting too grand for us, are you?'

Simon always felt that Richard was a little bit stuck-up and superior – but, to his credit, he knew his stuff and was always willing to pay a fair price, so Simon was genuinely pleased to see him.

'Nothing could be further from the truth, Simon. It's just that the fates haven't pulled me this way for a while. How is your wife getting on with that new kitchen, by the way? Has it improved her cooking at all?'

Simon grimaced.

'Chance would be a fine thing. I spend eleven grand on a new kitchen, and I'm still stuck eating takeaways four nights a week. I'd have been better off spending the money on cooking lessons for myself.'

His wife's cooking was always a source of frustrated complaint for Simon, as all his customers were well aware. He leaned back casually in his chair, and held his arms out wide in an all-embracing gesture, smiled broadly from ear-to-ear and said, 'Well, what do you reckon?' as he unnecessarily indicated the imposing bronze.

Richard smiled and proceeded to examine the bronze in minute detail, picking it up with some difficulty and carefully turning it over in his arms to look underneath.

'A fine piece, Simon, no doubt about that, but no signature, that I can see, and that's disappointing,' he acknowledged, returning the bronze to its upright position on the desk.

'How did you come by it? Has it got any provenance?'

'It's, literally, just this minute, come in, swear to God. I don't know a thing about it, except how much it has bankrupted me, and I've not had a chance to research it, yet. So, we are both in the dark, Richard. It's obvious from your expression that you like it, so make me an offer.'

'I'm not going to be both a buyer and a seller for you, Simon. You're the vendor – you tell me what you want for it.'

'Oh ... you're a wily one, Richard, and no mistake. Look ... no bullshit, we're both blindly guessing at its value, so my uninformed guess is ... it's gotta be worth ten grand of anyone's money.'

'Ten grand!' Richard exclaimed, doing a pirouette on one foot for dramatic effect. 'What have you been taking, Simon? You're not on the happy pills again, are you? Five grand is much nearer the mark, if you ask me.'

'I don't need happy pills, when people bring me in things like this, Richard, but I suppose I could do a deal, as it's you. How about I let you have it for eight grand?'

Richard was deep in thought for a moment and then he responded, 'It's a really good piece, Simon, we both know that, but there's no signature, which is going to affect the value considerably, and I can't attribute it to anyone, can you? Let's call it five-and-a-half grand and shake hands.'

'Looks to me like we've settled on six,' said Simon, holding his hand out, expectantly.

Richard hesitated for only a moment, and then shook Simon's hand, and the deal was done; both men very pleased with the outcome.

'Remember me to your wife, Simon, and why not spend some of the six grand on cooking lessons for her? You never know ... she could end up with a Michelin star.'

'I'll think on it, Richard. Now mind you don't drop that on your way out,' said Simon, smiling cheekily.

Richard carried the bronze carefully out to his waiting car, after the briefest of looks around the rest of Simon's disorganized shop, to discover a traffic warden in the process of writing down the license-plate number of his car.

'Sorry about that,' called Richard, smiling and indicating the bronze in his arms, as he visibly struggled to his car, 'but it's awfully heavy.'

The warden was sympathetic to Richard's plight, after seeing him struggling with the bronze, he smiled warmly and moved on, without comment. As Richard carefully placed the statue in the back of his Estate, he was thinking that even though Elizabeth wouldn't be overjoyed with it, the bronze was destined for his home, rather than the shop. Elizabeth would probably consign it to live in his den, where several other pieces he particularly liked were forced to reside, but he could live with that. He looked at his watch – it was five thirty-five; Margaret would lock up at six, so there was little point in returning to the shop now. He called her quickly on his mobile and filled her in on the events of the afternoon, then told her that if there were no remaining customers in the shop, she could call it a day and lock up early. Richard was now feeling good about the day, as he set off for home.

When he got home, Elizabeth was sitting comfortably in the lounge reading a book, which was unusual, as her book reading was normally confined to bedtime. The anomaly, however, was soon explained. Their only daughter, Rebecca, had recently applied for the position of events manager at the hotel where she currently worked as bar manager and that afternoon, she had just heard the good news that she had been given the job. She would start in a few weeks' time, when a new bar manager could be appointed. She was thrilled and had insisted on cooking the evening meal, so that they could all celebrate together. Richard was, naturally, very pleased for his daughter, who emerged excitedly from the kitchen to greet him.

'Hi, Dad,' she said, kissing him on the cheek, 'Did Mum tell you I got the job?'

'She did, indeed. I think we should all go out for a family meal on the weekend – to celebrate properly.'

As neither Elizabeth nor Rebecca were ones to turn down a chance to dine out, they readily agreed. As everyone was in such a good mood, Richard thought it was an ideal moment to introduce 'Tex', so he returned to his car and carried the bronze into the house. On the way home, he had decided that if the bronze was to be adopted into the family, it had better have a name. 'Tex' seemed an appropriate name for a cowboy, Richard thought, happily, totally unaware that it had already been christened, twice before.

Richard was both surprised and delighted to discover that both his wife and daughter, who now joined them in the lounge, thought that 'Tex' was beautiful; well, to be honest, Elizabeth had used the word beautiful, Rebecca had said, 'He's quite cute', which amounted to the same thing. Elizabeth even suggested that Tex would look good on the sofa table – a location that would put the statue almost in the centre of the room and was an honour, indeed. Richard positioned the bronze on the spot where his wife had suggested. He had to admit that it looked as if it had been made for just that location; he was, to use the vernacular, well chuffed.

Rebecca jumped suddenly at the sound of a timer ringing in the kitchen, and, as she dashed for the door, she yelled back, 'Dad, I'll have a white wine. Can you get you and Mum one?' Richard smiled happily to himself. From a rather disappointing beginning, the day had turned out remarkably well, after all.

Chapter 2

The day following the purchase of the bronze passed uneventfully for the members of the Drake family. Not so, for George Green. George was sixty-two years old and had been a gardener for forty-two of those years. He had taken early retirement from his position of Assistant Head Gardener at one of Her Majesty's estates. He now thoroughly enjoyed his retirement, but liked to keep his hand in, as it were, by maintaining one or two local gardens, such as Mrs Harper's garden at Hilltop Cottage.

As he stopped his little van outside the large double garage, he sensed that something was wrong. Even though he had a set of keys for the garage and for the iron gate to the rear garden, where all of the gardening implements were kept, he was surprised that the gates were closed. Mrs Harper was an early riser and normally had the garage already open for him. Either she had had to go out early or she was having an uncharacteristic lie-in.

George opened the garage door and surmised, reasonably, that it must be a lie-in that Mrs Harper was indulging in, as both of the cars were in place – her little Audi A3 and her late husband's Granada GL. He opened the door at the rear of the garage, which had been enlarged to allow the sit-on mower to be driven in and out, and checked the mower engine for sufficient petrol. There was enough in the tank to do the back lawn, at least. The front would have to wait until one of the cars was moved, as the mower wouldn't go through the iron gate that separated the front garden from back, and the other side of the house had a substantial number of bushes and shrubs in the way.

An hour later, he finished mowing the back lawn. As he got down from the mower, he reflected that the smell of freshly cut grass was something that he would never tire of. He was going to make a start weeding the borders and flower beds, all, that is, except the rose beds. Mrs Harper always insisted on doing them herself.

He had often wondered about the rose beds. Mrs Harper took a keen interest in the garden and only employed a gardener because it was too big for her to manage completely on her own. She was always altering things. Some years, there would be a big project, like the year they created the pond and waterfall. Other years, it would be simply altering shrubberies or borders, but, surprisingly, never the rose beds –they were never touched. He had always felt that the rose beds were out of place where they were, but Mrs Harper was adamant that they were not to be moved or altered in any way. He had never asked why, always assuming that there was some sentimental reason behind her reluctance to discuss even the possibility of their repositioning.

His mind kept wondering where Gladys Harper was. Even if she was ill and in bed, she would have heard him; she would have come down to make him his cup of tea with honey or at least have let him have access to the kitchen and downstairs toilet or 'cloakroom', as she called it.

George was growing quite concerned about Gladys now, and so he peered cautiously through the kitchen window. That, too, was odd, he thought – there was unwashed china on the kitchen worktop, and the calendar on the wall facing the window had yesterday's date showing. Gladys would never leave dirty crockery out overnight, and she was meticulous in her habits – one of which was setting the calendar to the right date each morning, first thing. Something was definitely wrong.

What should he do? If he broke in, and it turned out that Gladys had gone out in a friend's car this morning, he would look a right fool and would likely get a bill for any damages. If he called the police – again – he would look a fool if she suddenly arrived home. He doubted that the police would turn up, anyway. As far as he was concerned, they were a useless bunch to rely on these days; too busy catching law-abiding motorists to do any real police work – six miles an hour over the limit, that's all he'd been doing. He called her number on his mobile for the second time that morning. This time, being nearer a window, he could hear the phone ringing in the house, but there was still no reply. There were only two scenarios, as he saw it, either she was out in a friend's car or she was in the house, but unable to answer the phone or the door.

As he was standing in the back garden making the phone call, his eyes wandered to the upper floor and that clinched it – one of the bedroom windows was ever so slightly ajar. There was no way on this earth that Gladys would go out, leaving a window open. Also, he surmised that the open window meant that the alarm wasn't set.

George decided that he had to do something, so he quickly retrieved the extension ladder that was kept hanging on the back wall of the garage and put it up to the open window. Fortunately, there were paving slabs underneath the window, so he didn't have to rest it on the newly mown lawn. He knew that Gladys would throw a blue fit if her precious lawn was damaged in any way. He ascended the ladder rather shakily – it had been a while since he had last climbed one, and he had to keep telling himself not to look down. The window in question was one of the old sash types, and it was the top section that was slightly open, but he somehow managed to lift the bottom part sufficiently to get his fingers underneath, so that he could open it up fully. He clambered carefully off the ladder and in through the now-open bedroom window, scraping his knees in the process.

He found himself standing in the master bedroom, and, to his immense relief, Gladys was not lying dead in the bed. He called her name, loudly, but there was still no sign of anyone in the house. His heart was beating fast, and he was mortified to realize that he felt like a burglar or intruder. Before venturing any further into the house, he looked down at his muddy shoes and decided that it would be prudent to remove them, which he quickly did. If Gladys returned to find him in the house, whatever the reason, she would not be pleased; if he traipsed mud across her carpet into the bargain, he thought his life could likely be forfeit.

He crept, slightly hunched over, rather than walked, towards the bedroom door, feeling more than a bit like a burglar in a silent film and thinking that he really should be wearing a striped jersey with a bag of swag over his shoulder to complete the picture. He had no reasonable idea why the act of entering someone else's house, uninvited and through a window should result in him acting in such a bizarre manner; he felt rather silly. Nonetheless, he could not shake off the deep feeling of unease that continued to grip him.

The top drawer of one of her chests had been left wide open, and he was tempted to close it as he went by, but decided against it. He proceeded out onto the landing and was just about to descend the stairs, when he was stopped in his tracks.

The staircase that led down into the lounge was L-shaped. Anyone ascending from the lounge would go up three steps onto a half-landing, before turning right and continuing the climb upstairs. To their left, when standing on the half-landing, was a very substantial stone wall, which had previously been the front wall of the house, before the porch had been added. It was this stone wall, and the sad sight before it, that held George transfixed.

Gladys Harper was lying in a crumpled heap on the half-landing, with her normally-tidy hair askew across her bloodstained face, her skirt in disarray and her legs at a very improbable angle. Just above her, on the thick stone wall, was an ugly, dark red stain that George had no doubt was blood, deposited there by Gladys' head. He could tell, from where he was standing, that she was dead; there was no doubt in his mind. He sat down heavily on the top step, not wanting to descend any further, and held his head in his hands. Gladys had not been a close friend, he had never socialised with her, other than the cups of tea they had shared when he worked in her garden, but he had known her for some time and had liked her, even though she was a bit pompous and bad-tempered on occasion. He was very upset and shaken at finding her that way, and it must have been a good ten minutes before he was able to bring himself to go down the stairs, stepping cautiously past her body and call the police. He thought, ruefully, that they would have to come now; a death would certainly rank above the crime of speeding. He automatically dialled 999 and asked carefully for both the police and an ambulance. Why he asked for an ambulance, he wasn't quite sure; no emergency treatment was going to bring her back; he just didn't know who else to ring. He then recalled that Gladys had once mentioned to him that they shared the same doctor, so he looked through her address book and, finding that that was, indeed, the case, he quickly called him, as well, recalling from somewhere that you have to have a doctor to certify a death.

Paul Manley had been a police inspector for less than six months, and, at thirty two, he was young to hold such a rank. At just over six foot in height, with smooth, dark hair and piercing green eyes, most women considered him good-looking. Constable June Kelly had not been a police woman for much longer. Five foot seven in her stockinged feet, with black hair, she was a little heavier for her height than she should be – at least, according to the graphs at her local health centre – but she was happy enough with her figure to feel comfortable wearing a bikini on the beach, and she was blessed with a pretty face and a winning smile. They were both new to their current positions and were both keen to make the right kind of impression. There were already local police officers on the scene, by the time that they arrived, and it was one of them – a Sergeant Brown – who had called in for a more senior officer. Sergeant Brown introduced himself to the new arrivals and gave them the general gist of what had happened at Hilltop.

'The gardener – George Green – found the body, sir,' Sergeant Brown explained. 'He called the police, saying that his employer, Mrs Harper, had fallen down the stairs. I arrived at the same time as both an ambulance and Mrs Harper's doctor, who the gardener also called,' he continued.

'How did the gardener know who her doctor was?' asked Inspector Manley, confused, 'and why did he call an ambulance? Was she still alive when he found her?'

'Apparently, they both share the same doctor, sir, and he'd looked in her telephone book to make sure. The gardener is local, and, it would seem that Mrs Harper, her gardener and the good doctor are all on friendly terms, along with everyone else in a five mile radius, if you ask me. As for calling the ambulance, I think he was just in shock and not really sure who to call.'

'I see. And what made you call us, Sergeant? You don't think she fell?'

'I don't know, sir. She could have fallen ... but I had a look around upstairs, and a drawer is left open; it looks like someone was searching for something in it. It could have been the old girl, of course, but, then, why leave the drawer open? Unless she was disturbed, of course ... it just looked kind of odd to me, Inspector. I hope I haven't wasted your time, sir?'

Inspector Manley replied, quickly and reassuringly, "Nothing is a waste of time when someone has died, Sergeant,' although he knew the sentiment wouldn't be shared by his superiors, if Mrs Harper did turn out to have accidentally fallen.

He surveyed the scene in front of him and then turned back to Sergeant Brown, 'Can you prevent anybody else from entering the house, Sergeant, and, please get one of your men to stop people trampling about everywhere. If a crime has been committed here, the scene needs to be preserved, intact.'

'I'll see to it right away, sir.'

Sergeant Brown turned to walk away, but stopped suddenly and turned back, having just remembered something.

'I'm sorry, sir,' he apologised, 'but I forgot this – perhaps I shouldn't have touched it, but I picked it up instinctively, just inside the front door.'

He apologised profusely a second time and handed the business card that he was holding to the inspector.

The Sergeant continued, 'It looks as if someone put it though the letterbox, after missing an appointment, sir.'

Inspector Manley examined the card, on the front of which was the name – Richard Drake – and the inscription, 'Antique Dealer and Valuer'. On the reverse was briefly scrawled, 'Called, as arranged, at three. Sorry to have missed you.'

'OK, Sergeant, leave this with me and just make sure nobody else goes into the house or tramples unnecessarily over the garden, will you?'

Paul Manley confirmed the sergeant's findings inside the house and, only after this, did he then call the Detective Chief Inspector, the divisional doctor and SOCO, or 'Scenes of Crime Officers'. After making the necessary calls, he suddenly remembered that there was an ambulance and Mrs Harper's doctor on scene, so he asked Constable Kelly to thank them for attending and to explain to them that their presence was no longer required.

'Oh, and, Constable, ask them if they have touched or moved anything while they've been here, will you?'

'Will do, Guv,' replied June Kelly, thinking that the doctor was not going to be pleased, having been called out and then sent away without being needed; the ambulance, she knew, had already left.

Inspector Manley informed Sergeant Brown that he could now go, but to leave his constable on the front door to secure the scene, and added, 'You were right to call us, Sergeant.'

Sergeant Brown seemed relieved, 'Thank you, sir. So you think it looks odd, as well?'

'Who knows what's odd and what's not, Sergeant? But most people who fall on the stairs simply trip and fall backwards or to the side, not many go head-over-heels, as Mrs Harper appears to have done. We'll see what SOCO have to say.'

The SOCO team arrived forty minutes later, and it wasn't long before the place looked like a real crime scene, with areas securely taped off, men and women walking around in protective overalls and caps and a photographer intent on capturing every scene from every possible angle. The divisional doctor, who had arrived with the SOCO team, confirmed that Mrs Harper had, apparently, died as a result of the fall down the stairs, but he couldn't rule out anything until he had her 'on the slab', as he put it. He also pointed out that she had a bruised cheek, which might not have been caused in the fall, and he couldn't confirm it yet, but it looked as if she might have some skin and blood under her nails.

Inspector Manley asked, expectantly, 'You think she scratched someone?'

To which, the enigmatic reply was, 'Maybe ... I'll let you know for sure after the PM, although that is certainly my first impression, but don't blame me if she was a messy eater and it turns out to be the remains of something she had for lunch.'

Inspector Manley, whilst obviously regretting that a woman had died, was, nevertheless, enthused by the possibility of his first murder enquiry as an inspector. He would be sort of in charge of the operation. Obviously, a Senior Investigating Officer would be appointed and that would, in all probability, be his DCI, William Blake, known affectionately, but only behind his back, as 'Blakey' – the bus inspector from the British seventies sitcom *On the Buses*. Paul racked his brains to think if there was anything else he should do whilst at the scene. He looked again at the business card the sergeant had given him and kicked himself for not having put it into an evidence bag – a mistake that he now quickly rectified.

Back at the police station, he put one of his men in charge of finding out all he could about the victim, Gladys Harper. The gardener and the doctor both said that they thought she had sons, but what their names were, or even where they worked, neither had any idea.

He told his sergeant – Reginald Evans – that tracing the dead woman's next of kin was a priority; in the meantime, there was little they could do, until they had the post mortem report and heard the results from SOCO. After all, as things were at the moment, evidence-wise, it could still simply be a tragic accident. It was late afternoon, but Paul's adrenaline was flowing, and he needed to do something. The business card found at the scene contained not just a name and number, but also the address of the shop. Paul decided that now was as good a time as any to go and visit it.

Constable Kelly suggested that she drive him, but he replied, 'No, it's OK, June. I think you would be better employed helping to trace Mrs Harper's next of kin – that's our top priority at the moment. We need to have the body formally identified, and we need to know if anything is missing from the house.'

Forty-five minutes after leaving the station, Paul pulled up outside Richard Drake's shop, locked his car, gave the shop a once-over from the outside – thinking that he would have to earn a lot more than police inspector wages, in order to shop there – and finally entered.

The woman who approached him introduced herself as Margaret and politely asked if she could help him with anything. She appeared to be in her early to mid-twenties and was very attractive – thick, chestnut-brown hair with golden highlights and piercing hazel-green eyes that seemed to smile at you even when her mouth didn't. She was neatly dressed in a conservative knee-length skirt and a simple white blouse. Paul was finding it very difficult not to stare at her. As he was there on police business, it was just as well that he wasn't aware that Margaret had been having similar thoughts about him. He looked, to her, to be in his early to mid-thirties – a little older than the men she would normally be attracted to – six foot or six one in height and with an air of authority about him that would have been attractive in itself, even if he hadn't been. She also noticed that there was no tell-tale sign of a ring on his finger. The absence of a ring didn't mean that he wasn't spoken for, of course, or even that he wasn't married, but Margaret took heart from this small clue. She was attracted to this man, and, it was obvious, from the nervous way that he was trying not to openly stare, that he found her attractive, as well.

Paul introduced himself as Inspector Paul Manley and smiled warmly at her, delighted to see her smile back in response. When her mouth broke into a smile, her whole face lit up.

'I wonder if I could have a word with Mr Richard Drake?' he enquired, politely.

'Mr Drake's not here at the moment, I'm afraid. He's been at an auction all day, and I'm not expecting him back until much later. Is there anything I can help you with, Inspector?'

'The rest of my life,' thought Paul, but simply replied, 'No, it's Mr Drake that I need to speak to. Would it possible to get his home address from you, so that I can contact him there?'

'Well, I wouldn't normally give Mr Drake's address out. Is it police business? Nobody's been hurt, I hope? It's nothing like that, is it?' asked Margaret, suddenly concerned.

'No, no, it's nothing like that. I was just hoping that Mr Drake could answer a few questions concerning a Mrs Harper, who, I believe, he had an appointment with a few days ago.'

'Oh ... well, I can tell you about that, Inspector.'

'Paul ... please.'

'Well ... Paul, I was the one who made the appointment for Richard with Mrs Harper. She rang the shop and asked if Mr Drake could value some items for her, but she wasn't at home when he turned up for the appointment, so he never got to meet her in the end.'

'OK, thank you, Margaret. You don't mind if I call you Margaret ... do you? I always prefer to be on first name terms with people,' he lied.

He had loved hearing her speak his name.

'No, that's fine, and, of course, I'll let you have Richard's home address. I'm sure he won't mind, as it's the police. Actually ... I was just about to make myself a cup of tea. Would you like one?' she asked, politely, but hopefully.

Paul was not really a tea drinker at all, but, in this instance, he readily accepted. It would give him the opportunity to spend some more time in Margaret's company and possibly get to know her a little. He was standing quite close to her as she spoke, and he caught the aroma of her perfume as it wafted towards him. It was a long time since he'd had a friendly conversation with an attractive woman that he wasn't actually interviewing.

He stayed chatting amiably with Margaret, until she eventually closed up the shop at six o'clock. The more that they spoke to each other, the more they discovered that they liked each other; they both happily realised that they had a lot in common. They both enjoyed listening to jazz piano and relished reading murder mysteries in their spare time. Paul helped Margaret to securely lock up the shop, after drying the cups that they had just used for their tea, and then enquired as to how she was getting home. Margaret owned a six-year-old Ford Fiesta, but as both her house and Richard's shop were on an unusually efficient bus route, with bus stops within a few minutes' walk of both, she normally caught the bus, only using her car if the weather was particularly inclement. Having explained all this to the inspector, quite unnecessarily in her nervousness, Paul offered to drive her home.

'Oh! That would be lovely,' she said, and immediately regretted sounding quite so keen. She was normally quite wary of men that she didn't know, but this young man, Paul, really was 'very cute' – an expression she thought she must have inadvertently picked up from Becky, Richard's daughter, and she silently promised herself that she would never use it out loud.

'I hope you don't think I'm in the habit of accepting lifts from men I've only just met?'

'Of course not,' he replied, excited by the prospect of driving her home, 'but, anyway, you can trust me ... I am a policeman, after all,' he quipped 'Now, where is it that you live?'

After a fifteen minute drive, during which Margaret interrogated him about his career in the police force, he dropped her outside the small house that the inheritance from her parents had enabled her to buy. Her parents, John and

Freda Collins, had been tragically killed in a coach crash three years earlier, while on holiday in Spain. They had been best friends with Richard and Elizabeth Drake for many years, and Rebecca – the Drake's daughter – and Margaret were very close, with both of them being only children. Rebecca was nineteen and Margaret was twenty-four, and they were like sisters. They kept in constant contact by phone, and there were no secrets between them; they told each other everything. When John and Freda had died so tragically, Margaret didn't think she would have coped, if it hadn't been for the loving emotional support of Richard and his family. She had started working for him at the shop soon after. Richard's previous assistant had become pregnant and so had left to raise a family. Meanwhile, Margaret was rather unhappy in her existing job at the bank, and, therefore, the arrangement had suited them both.

Paul and Margaret said their goodbyes as she got out of the car just outside her house, but as Margaret was turning to leave, he called her back.

'Look ... Margaret ... I don't suppose you would like to go out some time? You know, to the cinema or, perhaps, out for a meal somewhere, ah, would you?' he asked, hesitantly, half expecting her to come up with some vague excuse, like she had a boyfriend or was planning to become a nun or something.

It had been a while since he had asked a woman out, and he felt quite awkward about it. Coupled with the fact that he had met this woman whilst investigating a case, and he felt that it was very unprofessional of him to ask her out, but he desperately wanted to see her again. It had been a couple of years, at least, since Paul had been on a proper date; work had pretty much taken over his life, and he had no desire to date a policewoman. The only people that he met these days were police, witnesses or suspects, so his social life had dwindled into near non-existence. With Margaret, he had felt some kind of connection straight away, maybe because he found her physically attractive, but he instinctively felt that it was much more than simply that. He was a man, after all, and he found a great many young women physically attractive, but he didn't feel any connection with them. Also, but he could easily be wrong here, he knew, he had the distinct feeling that she felt the same way about him and that excited him more than anything that he could remember in a long time. But, he reasoned, she was probably about to turn him down, at least, she was certainly taking her time about answering him; he braced himself, ready for rejection.

Margaret wondered nervously just how long she should pretend to be making up her mind, before accepting Paul's invitation, and decided thirty seconds would have to suffice.

'I'd love to. Give me a call,' she said, and, once again, regretted sounding too keen, so she immediately turned around and walked quickly towards her front door.

'I haven't got your home number ... or your mobile,' he called after her, expectantly.

She turned her head back, smiling broadly, but continuing to walk away. 'I thought you were some kind of detective?' she joked, cheekily, wondering if he would be put off by a woman with a sense of humour.

'I'll call you tomorrow, then,' he replied, smiling, happier than he'd been in a very long time.

She almost blew him a flirtatious kiss as she turned away again, having finally reached her front door. She then kicked herself, mentally. What on earth was she playing at? Did she have no self-control at all? She felt almost intoxicated; she couldn't ever remember being so attracted to a man so quickly.

Paul watched her until she entered her house and then set off for the Drake residence, wondering whether Margaret was going to feature as much in the rest of his life, as he hoped.

Inside, Margaret kicked off her shoes and slumped down comfortably on the sofa, wondering what on earth had happened to her; she never behaved like that, especially with a man that she had only just met. But, oddly, she felt as if she had known him for years. She couldn't wait for him to ring her, and she hoped that she hadn't blown it, by not giving him her number.

Richard Drake had been born in Bristol. He loved Bristol as a child and had always been happy there. He had met and married his wife, Elizabeth – a nurse at the Bristol Royal Infirmary – and it was here that they had raised their only child, Rebecca, now nineteen years of age. Bristol held only good memories for Richard. There was no way that he could know that it was all about to change, dramatically.

He had first started trading in antiques when he left university, having studied Fine Arts. His father had lent him the money to put a deposit on a small shop, and he had done well, almost straight away, but soon realised that he would never make a fortune buying and selling the contents of a small shop, no matter how good the margins. So Richard had begun widening his client base and the service that he offered. He knew that if he moved to London, he could double his takings overnight, but his turnover and profits were growing, and, last year, his business had given him a net profit of close to a hundred thousand pounds, and he decided that he could happily live a good life on that with his family. The thought of living in London, of bringing his daughter up in London, filled him with nothing but horror.

The shop he owned now only accounted for a small amount of the business he did – less than five per cent, maybe – the bulk of his work was done on the phone, on the internet, by word of mouth and by meeting clients at their home or place of work. The shop was simply a base to work from and acted as a warehouse for his stock. His clients were busy people, who furnished their lavish homes with antiques and fine art, but who had no time or interest in searching for what they wanted themselves. They would rely on, and trust, Richard to do that for them. Richard knew where to look for the specific things that they wanted; he knew what dealers would be likely to have the items his clients were looking for and his clients trusted him to acquire it for them at a fair price.

His customer base was large and varied and, amongst them, he had some famous actors and actresses, a footballer – who probably earned more than Richard's yearly profit every week – many company directors and some corporate firms. There was even a film studio that paid Richard for help and advice on period settings and furnishings, when they were filming historical pieces. All in all, Richard's life was interesting, successful and fulfilling.

The shop premises that Richard owned were not in the centre of Bristol, but neither were they on the outskirts. It was in one of those places in-between, which had, at one time, been a completely separate community or village and had been swallowed up by the big city's expansion, now just a district within the sprawling metropolis. It was located in a small road, numbering only one hundred and forty properties consisting mostly of shops – small, single-fronted at one end of the road and larger, double-fronted ones, like Richard's, at the other end. There were some residential properties intermingled with the shops, and the road itself stretched between a moderately busy main road at one end to a wide avenue at the other, which ran across a huge expanse of inner city park – The Downs. The city council had obviously overlooked this particular part of the city, as there are no yellow lines to impede parking, which made it very popular with shoppers. In addition to this, the shops in Richard's rank possessed back entrances leading out onto a large piece of vacant land, with two allocated parking places for each shop and a number of privately owned garages.

His home was a detached four-bedroom house, six miles outside central Bristol and to the north of the city.

Paul rang the bell at the Drake's residence. The door was answered by an attractive-looking woman in her late thirties or early forties, that he rightly assumed was Elizabeth Drake.

'Good evening, Mrs Drake?' he began, politely.

'Yes, that's right. Can I help you?'

Paul showed her his warrant card and introduced himself. Then he asked if he could speak to her husband.

'Yes, of course, he's in the lounge,' Elizabeth gestured for him to follow her in and proceeded to show Paul into the lounge, where she introduced him to her husband.

The furniture, at this end of the large room, consisted of two comfortable sofas facing each other, with a large coffee table between them, obviously intended for entertaining and conversation, and it was in one of these that Richard was sat. At the far end of the lounge were two more sofas, this time arranged almost at right angles to each other, but pointed towards the large television in the corner. Between the two middle sofas was the regency sofa table, on which 'Tex' now sat, watching serenely over his new surroundings and completely oblivious to the fact that he had been both abducted and re-christened.

Richard quickly offered his unexpected guest a seat, and Elizabeth said that she had just made a pot of tea and asked if he'd like one. Paul had consumed his full year's quota of tea while chatting to the lovely Margaret earlier and couldn't face any more, so he politely declined. Richard pressed him, good-naturedly, asking if he fancied a coffee instead or perhaps something stronger, and Paul, noticing Richard's drink and against his better judgment, replied that a small whisky would be very welcome.

Elizabeth looked quizzically at her husband for an indication of whether he knew what the inspector wanted, but Richard looked as puzzled as she was at the recent arrival, so she fetched the inspector a neat whisky and sat perched on the sofa next to her husband, wondering what on earth the police could want with him.

Paul made himself comfortable on the sofa and, after thanking Elizabeth for the drink, explained about the unfortunate death of Mrs Harper. Richard felt a pang of guilt that he'd not done any more than ask Margaret to ring a couple of times after his aborted visit, but she wasn't a regular client, indeed, he had never met her.

Paul sipped his whisky thoughtfully and went on to say, 'We found your business card at the cottage, Mr Drake. Can you tell me what happened when you saw Mrs Harper?'

'Well, the thing is, Inspector, I didn't see her. There was no reply when I knocked on the door, that's why I left the card. I waited a good half an hour to see if she would turn up, but there was no sign of her at all. My God! Do you think she was lying dead in the house when I was standing there waiting?'

'That would seem likely, I'm afraid ... but there's nothing you could have done ... and no way that you could have known. Did you notice anything unusual when you were waiting? Was there any signs that anybody else had been there?'

'No ... not that I can recall.'

'What did you do when you left the cottage?'

Richard went over the rest of his day with Paul, filling him in on not just the short visit to Mrs Harper's and leaving the business card, but even telling him about his successful business trip to Bath and showing him the bronze he'd purchased.

Paul put down his now-empty glass and examined the bronze; Richard Drake was obviously thrilled with it. He was, at first, unable to see what Richard was so excited about when he spoke of it. He certainly wouldn't have wanted it in his house, standing there mutely and collecting dust, although it started him thinking, for the first time in ages, about his father, who was a big cowboy fan. When a lad, his father had constantly gone on at Paul about Westerns, or 'Horse Operas', as he called them, which had been on the television when he was growing up. *Bonanza, Wells Fargo, The Man from Laramie, Bronco* – the list had seemed endless. His father, he realised, would love it, so, slowly, he began to see what the attraction might be for others, even though he failed to share it himself.

Paul had just re-seated himself when Rebecca Drake flounced into the room to pick up her mobile phone, which she was constantly leaving all over the house.

Noticing her parent's guest, she offered her hand to Paul and said, 'Hello, I'm Becky. Who are you?'

'Inspector Paul Manley,' replied Paul, rising to greet her.

'Oh, don't bother getting up ... a police inspector, eh? That's cool. Have you come to arrest my dad for something? How exciting is that?'

She plonked herself down on the sofa next to the inspector and said, 'Can I listen in? Or better still ... can I read him his rights? Would that be allowed?' Then, noticing the now-empty glass, she continued, 'Are you allowed to drink on duty, Inspector?'

Paul couldn't hide a grin, listening to Rebecca's excited ramblings.

Richard threw up his hands in mock despair and asked Paul whether he had any kids.

'No ... not married, I'm afraid.'

'Wow! Dishy and single,' said Rebecca, 'how old are you, Inspector?'

'Rebecca!' her mother cried, 'stop embarrassing our guest.'

'Oh, you don't call them guests when they've come to arrest someone, Mummy. Isn't that right, Inspector?' asked Rebecca, turning to Paul for confirmation.

'Well, I'm way too old for you, young lady, and, as much as I hate to disappoint anyone as charming as yourself, I'm afraid I don't intend arresting anyone tonight.'

'Not enough evidence, eh? I understand.'

Richard closed his eyes in mock despair for a second, 'Rebecca, why don't you stop harassing our guest and go and play in your room for a while, like a good little girl? Go and play with your dolls or something.' Then, to the inspector, he apologized, 'I'm sorry about this, Inspector, but she's never been a very well-behaved daughter.'

Rebecca got up to leave, poking out her tongue at her dad as she disappeared.

'I know when I'm not wanted,' she called back over her shoulder. 'Don't expect a character reference from me when whatever this is about goes to court. I know you love Margaret more than you love me.'

For a moment, the reference to Margaret caught Paul off guard. He wondered if the last remark had been for real, but he turned in time to see Rebecca laughing heartily as she exited the room.

'And with good reason!' her father called after her, equally tongue-in-cheek.

Rebecca came back into the room straight away, writing something on a piece of paper that she then handed to the inspector.

'Just for that,' she said, grinning from ear-to-ear, 'this is my number, Inspector, if you want the dirt on my Dad – call me, I know everything,' and out she flounced.

Elizabeth Drake had stayed out of the cheeky exchange between her husband and daughter; the light-hearted banter between them was something that she always felt excluded from, but she didn't resent being excluded, because she enjoyed witnessing it so much. Rebecca had always been a 'Daddy's girl'. It had been in Richard's arms that she had ceased crying as a baby, and it had always been Daddy that had to read her the bedtime story and tuck her in at night. But, from Elizabeth's point of view, their relationship was wonderful. Richard was more than just a caring husband and father to them both. It was as if he was some kind of guardian angel to them, who would do, or sacrifice, anything to keep them from harm.

Paul found himself liking these people a great deal, in the same way that he had really liked Margaret at the antique shop, earlier in the afternoon. They were a welcome change to the low-lives he spent so much of his time with these days. He was sure that none of them were in any way involved in the death of Mrs Harper – directly or indirectly. He envied them their relationships with each other; it made him realise, suddenly, just how lonely his own life had become. He stood to leave, and, then, out of the blue, he thought of another question – one he thought, at the time, had no connection at all to the case, but was just idle, polite chit-chat.

'If you don't mind me asking, Mr Drake, how much did you pay for the bronze cowboy?'

Richard looked sheepishly at his wife, who had tactfully refrained from asking that very same question. Paul looked from one to the other and, seeing Richard's hesitation, thought that he may have accidentally initiated a family row. Richard lowered his head and cringed, fully expecting his wife to be shocked.

'Six grand,' he whispered.

'Oh, thank God for that!' Elizabeth exclaimed, smiling at her husband's unease, 'I was afraid you might have paid over the odds for it, Richard.'

Richard was so surprised and relieved at his wife's reaction that he started laughing, and, Paul, relieved that his question hadn't been the trigger for a family row, started laughing with him, with Elizabeth soon joining in.

Rebecca, who had now returned, and was standing in the doorway with her hands on her hips, exclaimed 'Six grand! Six thousand pounds! Have you any idea what I could do with that kind of money?'

'Yes, I do,' said Elizabeth, 'and that's why I'm glad your dad has spent it on something far more worthwhile.'

Paul left them all still smiling, and, when he got back into his car, he found that he was in high spirits; his thoughts were of the beautiful Margaret and the domestic bliss of the Drake family – all of which was a very long way from sudden death and police investigations. He decided that he would ring his parents or his sister in the next few days – he hadn't spoken to them in a while and a catch-up was well overdue.

* * * * * * * * * * *

Jack Simmons and Alan Salter were not particularly violent men, although neither was afraid to use his fists if he happened to be threatened or angered. But it would be difficult to justify describing them as good or honest men either, simply because they were unscrupulous in the way that they made their living. They had no empathy for the people that they cheated out of their belongings or robbed of their hard-earned money. It was true that Alan could be quite charming, if he needed to be, but it was only superficial. If you scratched the surface of his character, you would quickly find a man who would happily cheat you out of house and home and expect you to thank him for it. Jack was similar in many ways, but found it difficult, if not downright impossible, to be charming in any way, unless he was cheating you out of something, and his deplorable attitude to the fairer sex was frequently landing him in trouble. They called themselves antique dealers; the antique trade called them knockers.

Knockers earn a living by making cold-calls: knocking on the doors of houses and asking if the occupants have anything they wish to sell. They present themselves as antique dealers looking to purchase stock, saying that they are in the area for a few days to that end and that they have a great deal of money that they wish to spend. They offer to come in and complete a free valuation of your belongings and to pay cash for anything that you wish to sell. This is how Jack and Alan had successfully made a living, since the mid-seventies.

Driving a respectable-looking, black, three-year-old Ford Mondeo Estate, with a large flat roof-rack – the type favoured by antique dealers the world over – they parked today towards the middle of the street. Their intention was to call at all the houses in the street, one at a time.

'Good morning,' chirped Alan, as the fifty-something woman answered the door. She was Marge to her friends, although there were precious few of those these days.

Alan was always the one to speak first, rather than Jack. He seemed to have the ability to charm even the most hostile victim or, as they liked to optimistically think of them, client. He once had a door opened by a giant of a man wearing tracksuit bottoms and a string vest, who was obviously in the middle of a heated row with his wife and looked as if he was primed and ready to pull someone's head off. Most people in his position would have apologised for calling and left as quickly as possible, but Alan stayed for an hour and left having paid thirty pounds for a pocket watch, which he later sold for one hundred and eighty pounds to a jeweller, no more than two miles away.

Offering a rather posh-looking business card, which presented himself as Alex Smyth of *The Mall Antiques*, London, Alan explained, 'We are covering the local area, looking for interesting items to buy for *The Mall Antiques*. Perhaps you have heard of us?'

The woman looked puzzled and shook her head, as Alan continued, cheerfully, 'We offer to come in and do a free valuation of items in your house, and, if you decide you would like to sell an item, we pay cash for it on the spot. The lady at forty-six has just had eight hundred pounds from us for a picture that she was thinking of throwing away.'

'Really? Mavis at forty-six? Eight hundred pounds? She must be thrilled.'

Damn! That was bad luck – she knows the woman at forty-six, Alan cringed. But cool as a cucumber, he continued, 'I don't think her name was Mavis. Now, was it forty-six or forty-four? We've called at so many houses today, I simply can't remember. But you're right – whoever the woman was, she was thrilled. Would you like us to take a quick look to see if you have anything valuable?'

Marge Stevens was a divorcee, trying to bring up two children on her own. Her ex-husband paid her a small sum of money to help with living costs, if she badgered him enough or if he'd had a good win on the horses, which wasn't too often. She didn't think, for one moment, that there was really anything of interest or value left in the house. Anything decent, her good-for-nothing husband had taken with him when he left. All except for the few bits and pieces that had been her mother's, that is; he wasn't having those. But, who knows, even a few quid would be handy. She just managed, at present, now that the kids were at school, and she had the part-time job on the check-out at the local Co-op, but there was never anything left over for treats at the end of the week. Even a few quid would be a nice change.

Marge was just about to say they could come in and look if they wanted, when she realised that they were already inside the front door. How had that happened? She must have instinctively stepped back as the man was talking to her, and they must have followed her in. Well, what did it matter? She had made up her mind to let them in anyway.

As soon as Jack was past Marge in the hall, he opened the door to the lounge and, bold as brass, walked straight in, as if he'd been invited.

If Alan was the one with the gift of the gab, Jack was the expert who could spot something of interest from yards away, within seconds of entering a room. Neither Alan nor Jack were above simply slipping a small item into their pocket when their victim wasn't looking, but they would only do that if the item in question wouldn't be easily missed. For instance, they would usually try to separate, once inside a house, with one going upstairs, saying casually, 'You don't mind if I use the loo, do you? We've been on the road for hours.' Once upstairs, as long as the householder stayed with the other safely downstairs and didn't immediately follow him up, he would head for the main bedroom. There would normally be a jewellery box somewhere, often lying on the dressing table. He would have a quick look in to see if there was anything of even moderate value that didn't look like it was worn very often and, therefore, would be unlikely to be missed for some time. Taking wedding or engagement rings was never done. This wasn't because of any moral consideration, but was purely because they were too easily and quickly missed. If the householder was suspicious of them at all, the first thing they would do is check their jewellery, and a phone call to the police could be taking place, even before Jack and Alan had time to get into their car.

On this occasion, events took a different tack. As soon as Jack entered the lounge, his trained eye had gone straight to the china cabinet against the far wall – a factory-produced, burr-walnut veneered cabinet of questionable quality, it would probably realise between thirty to forty pounds in an auction house general sale. Inside the cabinet, however, was the unmistakable shape of a small, brass carriage clock in its original, green leather carry case.

Jack approached the cabinet at once, declaring, in a loud voice, so that Alan would overhear, 'Oh! What a beautiful cabinet.'

From the tone and volume of Jack's voice, Alan knew to accompany Jack and Marge into the lounge, rather than venture upstairs alone and, possibly, spoil whatever scenario Jack had planned. He was also anxious to see what little gem had caught Jack's eye. Alan couldn't help getting a little excited at these crucial moments.

He dutifully followed Marge into the lounge to see Jack, apparently engrossed in examining the cabinet in minute detail.

'Well, there you are, Mrs ... ah ... sorry, I didn't catch your name? I'm John, by the way, and this is my colleague, Alex. Would you ever consider selling this beautiful cabinet?'

'Well, I don't know. Is it worth very much? Oh, and, please, call me Marge,' she replied, with a slightly excited, flushed look on her face, which she was trying her best not to show.

Jack threw a questioning look at Alan. 'I think we would be inclined to go to ... say ... fifteen hundred for it. What do you think, Alex?'

A small muffled exclamation of excitement escaped Marge's lips, much to her annoyance.

Jack deliberately interpreted the exclamation of excitement as reluctance and continued, smoothly, 'Well ...

maybe we could even go to two thousand for it, but no more than that.'

Marge couldn't believe her ears – two thousand pounds? She had never really liked the thing, anyway. It could have been slung out, for all she cared. She only kept it so as to have somewhere to keep her old mum's bits and pieces and the things that the kids had brought back from various holidays.

She tried to stay calm. 'Well, yes, I certainly would sell it for two thousand pounds.'

Just think what you could do with that amount of money, she pondered, excitedly. This was turning into the luckiest day of her life.

'There are a couple of little bits in the cabinet, as well, that we would be interested in,' continued Jack, 'Say, forty pounds for the little clock, and thirty pounds for the silver-plated set of spoons?'

Marge was now definitely in selling mode. 'Yes, OK, that seems fine,' she said, although a little surprised that the set of spoons were only silver-plated; her mum had always insisted that they were made of solid silver. Still, these boys obviously knew their stuff. That made it two thousand and seventy pounds – wow! A celebration drink was in order tonight, for sure.

Alan and Jack were escorted around the rest of the house, as if they were royalty. They had to keep up the pretence, whilst being shown the most mundane and boring contents of cupboard after cupboard, but they had to be polite, as the most important card of the scam was still to be played.

'Well, I'm sorry we didn't manage to find any other treasures, Marge, but, still, two thousand and seventy pounds that you didn't know you had – that's not bad, is it?'

'No, no, I'm very glad you called,' Marge replied, now anxious to have the money in her hands.

Alan took a large wallet out of his coat pocket and began removing money as Marge eagerly watched, her eyes growing larger at the sight of crisp, new notes.

'Of course, Marge, we haven't got room in the car for the cabinet now. We'll have to come back in the morning with the van for that. Would, say, nine o'clock be all right for you?'

'Yes, nine o'clock will be fine. I'm always up well before then,' said Marge, just a little disappointed at the delay.

'That's excellent, Marge. We'll just take the clock and the spoons now.'

Jack already had the items in his hands and was swiftly heading for the front door.

'Here's the seventy for the spoons and the clock that we're taking now, and we'll be back with two thousand more in the morning, when we pick up the cabinet.'

Alan handed over seventy pounds in crisp new notes to Marge, and they were on their way. Marge gave them a tentative farewell wave from her front door and hoped that they wouldn't be late in the morning. The crisp, new notes felt good in her hand, and she couldn't wait to have two thousand pounds' worth there; it was so exciting to have come into some money. Even at noon on the following day, Marge was still convincing herself that either traffic had unfortunately held them up or that the van had broken down. Still, they were such gentlemen, you would have thought that they would ring to let her know they were going to be that late.

So, June the first, 2010, had been a very profitable day for Jack Simmons and Alan Salter. The carriage clock, purchased from Marge for forty pounds, had, on closer inspection, not only a beautiful enamel dial, but turned out to have been made by a very well-respected London maker. It was, therefore, even more valuable that Jack had initially hoped. After stopping for coffee at a roadside pub, they examined their ill-gotten gains and decided that the clock would certainly fetch upwards of four grand; luckily, the spoons were also by a good maker and of solid silver and would fetch upwards of eight hundred.

The second of June, 2010, in contrast, was turning into a nightmare. Things had started off well enough, even though the pompous excuse for a dealer had refused to buy the carriage clock and other items, without some form of proof of ownership. But it had been a stroke of luck being in the shop when he took the old lady's call.

Jack and Alan had called into the posh-looking antique shop, with a view to selling some, or maybe even all, of the ill-gotten contents of their Estate car. It was their first time in the West Country, and Bristol, and then Bath, was as far as they were intending to go. Devon and Cornwall were full of tourists and narrow roads, which didn't appeal to either of them. After visiting Bath, they would head back up north to Newcastle, via the Lake District. The journey could take four to eight weeks, depending on how many places looked worth knocking, how lucky they got and, strangely, how homesick they felt. Both men were childless and separated from their partners, or wife, in Jack's case. Neither had any family to get back to, but both men somehow felt out of place down south and longed for what they saw as the more agreeable and easy-going lifestyle of their native north.

Richard Drake Antiques, the sign had read outside the shop, and there were a couple of valuable-looking clocks in the window. When they entered the shop, they were greeted by a woman in her early to mid-twenties, five-six, five-seven, maybe, and quite a looker.

Jack wondered if she was Mrs Richard Drake and said, 'Hello. Mrs Drake, I presume?'

'Oh no, I'm not Mrs Drake. My name is Margaret. I'm Richard Drake's assistant and book-keeper,' explained

Margaret, suppressing a shudder at the way the customer looked at her.

Oh, yeah, I bet he's shagging you, though, thought Jack, as he, not too discreetly, gave her the once-over.

Alan heaved a sigh of exasperation when he saw Jack unashamedly eyeing the woman up. Jack was good as gold with people when he was doing them over, but, generally, his manner with women left much to be desired and had caused them problems on more than one occasion.

'Hi, my name's Alex,' he said, as he intervened. Alan rarely used his real name.

He went on to explain that they had some items for sale that they hoped Mr Drake would be interested in, amongst which was a rather splendid little carriage clock.

'If you would like to bring them in, I'll fetch Mr Drake for you,' Margaret replied, a little uneasily.

She waited until they were outside the shop, before she moved towards the little office at the back where Richard was researching the details of some recent purchases. She didn't like the look of them, especially the one that had spoken to her first.

She put her head round the door.

'Some men are bringing in a carriage clock and some other items for you to take a look at, Richard, but I didn't like the look of them at all – one of them positively gives me the creeps.'

Richard entered the shop from the back office, just as the two men were coming back in, carrying a large cardboard box and various small items. They arranged everything on a Regency card table at the front of the shop, as Richard approached, having already spotted the stunning little carriage clock. It was beautiful, and Richard could tell, at once, that it was both genuine and valuable, but he was on his guard. Margaret had indicated that she didn't like the look of them, and Richard had high regard for both Margaret and her instincts about people.

'It's a lovely clock,' said Richard, as he examined it in detail. 'How much do you want for it?'

The phone rang shrilly at the back of the shop, and Margaret moved to answer it, glad to be away from the two men.

"We think five thousand five hundred is a fair price," replied Alan.

Richard was about to start negotiating, but Margaret suddenly called over to him from the back of the shop.

'I'm sorry to interrupt, Mr Drake, but I've got a Mrs Harper on the phone. She wants to know if you could value some items for her later today? She said she's about six miles out of town.'

Margaret always called Richard Mr Drake in front of clients or other dealers, even though she was not just an employee, but a close family friend; she felt it was much more professional.

'Sure. Check the diary, will you, Margaret? But I'm pretty certain I don't have anything else on today. Get her address, and tell her I'll be there at three o'clock, if that's convenient?'

Margaret wrote Mrs Harpers' address on the notepad that was always kept beside the phone, and, after getting some cursory directions to the house, she hung up. She then began entering Mrs Harper's details into the work diary, together with the appointment time. She put her details on their database and then made out a client card to go in the filing cabinet, as was her normal practice with a new contact.

Richard had resumed negotiations with Alan Salter, while Jack, with the pretense of looking at items for sale in the rest of the shop, slowly meandered over to the desk at the rear of the shop. Margaret instinctively moved away, as she felt uncomfortable being close to the man, and, as Jack passed the desk, he surreptitiously made a mental note of the address that Margaret had written down for Mrs Harper. He reasoned that if she wanted Richard to value items for her, then she was definitely worth a call.

Meanwhile, Richard was marvelling at the sheer variety of items that the two men had brought in. Most dealers had expertise in certain areas and tended to buy what they knew most about, whereas these two seemed to specialise in anything small and expensive. There were snuff boxes, card cases, watches, jewellery, an ivory chess set and even a stamp album. After carefully examining everything, Richard negotiated a price of eight thousand pounds for all of the items that Alan and Jack had spread on the table; some of which, like the little carriage clock and a beautiful solid gold vinaigrette, were very desirable. However, it was a large sum of money to pay to complete strangers who called in unannounced off the street, so Richard wanted to see some identification and proof of ownership.

Some years ago, he had purchased several early cameras. The cameras had been brought in by a young couple, who had explained that the girl's grandfather had just died, and she was his only heir. They had said that they were clearing out the house he had left to her and had found the cameras in a case under the bed. They convincingly went on to explain that they were trying to save up enough money to be able to get married. Richard was no expert on cameras, early or otherwise, and they were not the sort of thing he would normally have bought, but he had wanted to help the couple out. He had paid them four hundred pounds, honestly believing it to be a good price, as nothing had stood out to him as being anything particularly special. Indeed, he was fully prepared to just get his money back with no profit, and he had bought them, purely because he wanted to help the young couple. Unfortunately, the cameras turned out to have been stolen during a house burglary and one or two were, in fact, quite rare and valuable. Because Richard had bought them for well under their true value – although out of ignorance, not intent – and because he had no proof of purchase, the police had been intent on charging him with receiving stolen property. It was only because he had a good reputation, no previous convictions and a good solicitor that Richard had managed to avoid being arrested and charged. The whole experience had taught Richard a valuable lesson.

'It's not stolen or anything, if that's what you think,' sneered Alan, with spurious offence at Richard's request.

He began gathering the items together to leave, knowing that there was no deal to be done here and having had the nod from Jack that something of interest had come up that required their immediate attention.

When they left the shop, Richard felt somewhat relieved. True, he would have dearly loved to have bought some of the items, especially the little carriage clock, as he had a client who would pay top price for it. But he had shared Margaret's dislike for the two men, and he did wonder if the items were really theirs to sell, especially as they hadn't produced any paperwork or ID.

Once back in the car, Jack filled Alan in on how he was now in possession of the name and address of a woman who obviously had a number of valuable antiques.

'She is expecting Richard Drake to call at three o'clock,' Jack said, looking at his Rolex.

Technically, the watch still belonged to a man in Manchester, who had first missed it after his wife had sold a little silver box of her mother's, but, to Jack, it was now his pride and joy. Just gone noon – plenty of time to find the address and arrive there long before that sorry excuse for a dealer.

It turned out that Mrs Harper lived in a comfortable, secluded property called Hilltop Cottage, set back in its own grounds off the main road between Bristol and Bath. It was quite lucky, really, as Bath was next on their list of places to visit, anyway. The house itself could not be seen from the road, because of a sharp bend in the drive. Added to which, several trees and a tall hedge all served to conceal it from view. The garden was beautifully tended and well maintained. Jack reasoned, maliciously, that Mrs Harper probably employed a gardener, in which case, she would be a stuck-up bitch, who deserved to be taken advantage of. In Jack's narrow worldview, women were only good for one thing, and when they were too old for that, they should stick to washing and ironing.

Jack and Alan looked at each other to check that each was ready. Assured, Alan reached over and rang the bell.

Chapter 3

The morning of the fourth of June was slowly turning into yet another clear, sunny day. Richard arrived at the shop at nine-thirty to find Margaret busy arranging flowers.

'Good morning, Richard,' she beamed, as he came through the door.

Richard had two parking spaces at the rear of his shop, but because Margaret nearly always got the bus to work, one was left mostly unused. The flower shop, four doors up, also had two spaces, but the owner had a small delivery van, as well as a car. His two assistants – a woman with a most unfortunate laugh that could be heard two streets away and a young girl of about eighteen – also drove to work. The tacit arrangement that had grown up between them was that if Margaret wasn't using her car, the flower shop could use her space, and, in return, they often supplied Richard's shop with fresh flowers. They had obviously just popped some in, and it was these that Margaret was joyfully arranging.

'How are you this morning, Margaret? You seem remarkably cheerful for a workday.'

'Just happy to be breathing, I guess,' said Margaret, taking a deep breath and enjoying the combined aromas of the new flowers and the familiar furniture polish that was ever-present in the shop.

'Did that inspector chappy get in touch with you last night?' she enquired. 'I hope you didn't mind me giving him your address? What was it he wanted?'

Margaret suddenly realised that in spite of the time that they had spent chatting together the evening before, Paul had not confided in her why it was that he wanted to speak to Richard, other than it had something to do with the aborted appointment with Mrs Harper. Margaret was amazed that she hadn't thought to delve any deeper on the subject.

Richard explained, 'It would seem that the reason I didn't get a reply when I called at Mrs Harper's was that she had fallen down the stairs. I wish, now, that I had done more, but the inspector did say that she died in the fall, and I wouldn't have been able to save her or anything like that. But it's horrible to think that she was lying there, just on the other side of the door, when I rang the bell.'

'Oh, Richard, I'm so sorry. That's really awful. But if Paul said there was nothing you could have done about it ...'

'That's right, he did. But I still feel bad about it, nevertheless. Oh, and after I left there, I went to see Simon over at *Bath Antiques*. I bought the most wonderful bronze of a mounted cowboy; we've got it in our lounge now. It's not signed or anything, but whoever sculpted it was certainly extremely talented.'

Margaret was intrigued and replied that she couldn't wait to see it. She didn't seem at all surprised that Elizabeth had liked it. Casually, she asked, 'Do you think you will be seeing the inspector again?'

'I wouldn't have thought so,' he replied, 'I don't see how I can be of any more help, not that I was any last night either ... Paul ... you called him Paul just now. How did you know his name was Paul?'

'He must have introduced himself that way, I suppose,' Margaret replied, somewhat sheepishly.

Richard plonked himself down in the chair behind the shop desk, frowning.

'Right ... he seems a nice chap, though, this Paul. Rebecca was quite taken with him.'

'Becky met him? You tell Becky to keep her hands off. He's mine. I saw him first.'

Richard stared at her, his frown changing into a broad grin.

'Yeah, Rebecca hit it off with him straight away. He liked her, as well, I think.'

'Fibber!' Margaret stuck her nose in the air and turned away, as if the conversation was now boring her.

'You'd better put the kettle on and tell me what's been happening in your life,' said Richard, soothingly. 'There are some biscuits in the cupboard.'

Almost as soon as Margaret had put the kettle on, one of the dealers who regularly called on Richard came stumbling through the shop door, carrying a large cardboard box and a full carrier bag. The dealer's name was Sidney Shaw, known to his friends as Sandy, not because of the colour of his hair, which was grey, but because he shared his name with Sandy Shaw – the sixties pop singer.

Sandy was struggling a little with his load, and Margaret hastened to help him.

'Good morning, Richard. Good morning, Margaret,' said Sandy, cheerfully. 'It's a lovely day for the race.'

'What race is that?' Margaret asked, relieving him of the heavy bag in his right hand.

'The human race, of course, Margaret. Is the kettle on?'

Margaret rolled her eyes, 'One of these days, I'm going to slap you, Sandy,' she said, grinning. 'Human race, indeed.'

'I'll look forward to that, Margaret,' said Sandy, grinning back at her. 'I haven't been slapped by a beautiful woman in years. In the meantime, though, I've got a box of goodies for you to go through, Richard.'

He placed the box down on the seat of a convenient chair.

'Tell me if there's anything in there for any of your posh clients and get your wallet out.'

Richard smiled and looked over at Margaret, 'Better make that three teas, then, Margaret, but don't let Sandy have any biscuits, unless there's something in that box worth buying.'

Sandy started removing items from the box and placing them carefully on one of the many tables. Richard took his time going through them. When Margaret had finished making them all tea, she brought over a plate of biscuits as well, despite Richard's comment. In her book, Sandy was definitely one of the good guys. He was always in a good mood and regularly had a silly story or a joke ready to tell; she enjoyed his visits a great deal.

While Margaret and Sandy gossiped, Richard selected six items from the assortment of china figures, silver candlesticks and other objets d'arte that made up the contents of Sandy's box, including one item that was just what he was looking for. Elizabeth had been complaining that the paperknife she currently had was next to useless. It was made of ivory, for a start, and she was uncomfortable about using anything made of ivory these days, even though it was made long before ivory poaching had become an issue. It was also quite blunt, so not only could you not insert it into envelopes without first tearing a corner by hand, and, thus, defeating the object of using a knife, but when you did get the knife in, it tore the paper, rather than cut it smoothly. In Sidney's box was a miniature dress sword, about one hundred and forty millimetres long, with a silver handle and scabbard and steel blade, double-edged and sharp. It may, or may not, have been made as a paperknife. It could just as easily have been a presentation piece of some kind that had had, at some point in time, a little stand to rest on and a plaque showing the name of the recipient and the reason for the award. But, either way, it would fulfill the function of a paper knife extremely well, and he was sure that Elizabeth would love it, even though it did look quite lethal, as well as beautiful.

'I've got some sporting memorabilia in the car, as well, if you're interested, Richard – a couple of quite early golf clubs and a nineteenth-century cricket bat, probably a bit like the one you used to play with in your day.'

Margaret laughed.

'Don't be so bloody cheeky, you,' admonished Richard, 'it wasn't that long ago that I hung up my bat.'

Margaret became interested.

'Did you know Richard when he used to play cricket, then, Sandy?'

'Oh yeah, he was something of a local legend back then. He used to score the odd run or two, but he was best known for running the opposition out. He would be onto a ball with the speed of a cheetah, and he could turn and throw it at the stumps with the accuracy of a sniper. It was said that he could hit the wicket, end on, even from the boundary. Now, who was it that used to say that? Oh, yeah, I remember. It was you, wasn't it, Richard?'

Margaret loved the witty exchange between the two of them.

'So he used to blow his own trumpet a bit in those days, did he, Sandy?'

'Oh, you couldn't shut him up some Saturdays. Did he ever tell you about the time he was taken to hospital? A ball just missed his left ear by 4 inches.'

'No ... but why would he be taken to hospital if the ball missed him?'

'I said it missed his left ear by 4 inches ... it hit him right between the eyes.'

Margaret cracked up, almost spilling her tea, and she remembered, once again, why it was that she enjoyed Sandy's visits so much.

'OK, OK, that's enough, you two. You can put the biscuits away now, Margaret,' interrupted Richard, 'and no thank you, Sandy, sporting memorabilia is not my thing, as you well know, but there are a couple of pieces in here that I could do with, as long as your prices aren't a joke, as well.'

'Money is the one thing I never joke about, Richard. Show me the pieces you want.'

Richard concluded his business with Sandy in no time at all and shook his hand genially, having purchased the paperknife, a silver table snuff box and two silver-and-glass inkwells. Sandy was one of the old school– a handshake to him was as good as a signed contract, and Richard had great respect for that philosophy. He didn't need any proof of ownership with Sandy, he trusted him implicitly. Sandy said his farewells and was rewarded with a kiss on the cheek from Margaret, which caused him to be heard blissfully chanting to himself, 'Ah ... tea ... biscuits ... and a kiss from a fair maiden – my life is complete,' as he walked to his car. Margaret was laughing out loud as she closed the door behind him.

When he left the shop that afternoon, Richard put the miniature sword safely in the map pocket of his car, behind the driving seat. He didn't want it on show if Elizabeth had occasion to get into the car, but he did want it on hand, in case the opportunity arose to smuggle it into the house unseen. He intended to give it to his wife on her birthday, which was in four weeks' time.

* * * * * * * * * *

Long before Sidney Shaw had arrived at Richard's shop, Inspector Paul Manley had been sitting at his desk, carefully reading the **PM** report on Mrs Harper. It confirmed that she had died as a result of falling down the stairs and hitting her head hard against the stone wall at the bottom. It also stated that the bruising to her cheek did not appear to have come from contact with any surface of the staircase, but was more likely the result of a strong punch or slap with the back of a hand. Furthermore, the tissue under the victim's nails was human skin and blood, so it would appear that the victim had scratched her assailant very hard, and whoever it was would have very deep scratches, most probably on the face or the back of their hand or forearm. In short, it was now definitely a murder inquiry.

As he finished reading the report, Constable Kelly stuck her head round the door, which was almost always left open, and announced that she had traced the next-of-kin. The gardener had been right – there were two boys, Kevin and Craig Harper, non-identical twins. The Constable had some interesting facts about Kevin and Craig.

'They have form, Guv – a stretch for armed robbery, some years back. I dug a bit deeper and found that there had apparently been some controversy concerning the shortness of their sentence; they both served less than two years.'

'Two years? For armed robbery?'

'Apparently so, Guv. They were sentenced to seven, initially, but it was reduced at their Appeal, and then there was time off for good behaviour and so on, and there's more.'

'Go on, June, I can't wait.'

Constable Kelly continued, 'Well, I discovered that, a couple of years ago, Craig was arrested for rape. A young office girl, called Alice Jones, claimed that after a night out, Craig had given her a lift home in his car and wouldn't take no for an answer. She had, by all accounts, been quite badly bruised and knocked about, but it never got to trial, because a week after she made the complaint, it seems that she was involved in some kind of accident at home, with a kettle of boiling water. She was badly scalded and disfigured, and she dropped the charges against Craig, saying that she had made the whole thing up out of spite. Then, after being advised that she faced years of operations and skin grafts, she somehow managed to gain access to the hospital roof, and, presumably not wanting to face a life of permanent disfigurement, she ended it all by jumping off and killing herself.'

Paul grimaced, 'Was there any evidence to point to this Craig being involved in her accident or the suicide?'

'No evidence, Guv. But that's what was suspected at the time. Before the accident, she had been, by all accounts, well up for testifying against him, couldn't wait to get into court, whereas, afterwards, she just cried whenever his name was mentioned and adamantly claimed that she had made it all up.'

Paul shook his head in disbelief. 'I take it you have informed these lovely gentlemen of their mother's demise?'

'Yeah ... but the one I spoke to, Kevin, seemed to take it quite well, considering. He didn't break down in tears or anything, and I don't think either of them will need counselling, somehow.'

'No, I guess not, June. They sound like a lovely pair. Did you tell them that we need them to call in and formally identify their mum's body?'

'Didn't need to, Guv, Kevin said they would be here before midday. They're coming from London ... and get this...'

Paul continued to listen with interest, wondering not only what other information June had managed to dig up on Mrs Harper's offspring, but just how, and where, she had acquired it so quickly. There was more to Constable Kelly than met the eye, he mused, thoughtfully.

June Kelly was standing directly in front of Paul's desk. She placed her two hands on the front edge for support and leaned in, as if she was going to divulge a long-kept secret and didn't want anyone else to hear.

'Well,' she began, almost at a whisper, 'the armed robbery they went down for involved the theft of diamonds that were never recovered, and, although our friends in the Met.

suspect that they make most of their money these days from extortion and protection, they do have a legitimate business.'

Constable Kelly paused for effect. Paul was impatient, but he indulged her, because he was intrigued.

'They run a nightclub called .... wait for it, Guv ... *Sparklers.* Can you believe the audacity of these guys? *Sparklers.* They're actually telling us that the club was funded by the sale of the diamonds.'

Paul Manley was incredulous and shook his head in disbelief.

'And this pair did less than two years for the armed robbery. How is that possible?'

'That's a bit more difficult to discover, Guv. But my source is still digging.'

'What source is that?' asked Paul, frowning.

June Kelly placed her right index finger against the side of her nose to indicate that her source was a secret and quickly walked away, before Paul could push her further on the matter.

He watched her go, thinking, 'I'm going to have to keep my eye on that one,' then called after her, 'let me know the minute you get any more details.'

'Will do, Guv.'

If Constable June Kelly could have asked the late Mrs Harper for information about her two sons, she still wouldn't have heard anything to cause her to alter her low opinion of them. If truth were told, both of her sons had been a disappointment to Gladys and her late husband, Fred – both in childhood and as mature adults. It would be wrong to blame it on falling in with a bad lot at school, simply because they *were* the bad lot at school. Non-identical twins, they were getting into trouble from the time that they could walk – hitting and biting other children as toddlers, gradually developing into more serious fights and stealing as they grew older and the inevitable shop-lifting and petty crime as teenagers. Then there had been the unpleasantness that she and her husband had to sort out; thank God that had never come to light. But, probably, God wasn't the right entity to thank for that. The boys had been inseparable from birth, sharing a bedroom by choice, rather than necessity, they were together morning, noon and night. They would have been easier to part if they had been Siamese twins, but because there was no physical join between them, which could be severed by the surgeon's knife, the bond was impossible to break. Some time in their early twenties, they had moved to London and, consequently, got involved with more serious crime and more dangerous criminals. The eventual stretch in prison for armed robbery, when it came, was long overdue.

They had both inherited her husband's aggressive and, sometimes, violent nature, but neither had even his scant morals or conscience. From her, they had acquired their love of beautiful things, and they both appreciated fine art and good food. From him, they had inherited their aggressive determination. Everything else in their make-up seemed to come from some dark place, unknown to her or her husband. Perhaps, unbeknown to them, their ancestry contained some dark soul, whose genes had skipped a generation or two and had now resurfaced in their sons.

Soon after the boys moved to London, they had stopped coming home to visit their parents; they stopped ringing, even. Gladys and Fred had realised, years before, that they had lost any influence over the boys, and, if truth be told, any love, which they might, at one time, have held for the fruit of their loins. That was just how it was; there was nothing to be done about it. When she and Fred had first married, they had talked of having three, or even four, children, but the way the twins turned out soon put them off that idea. When the twins were grown up and had flown the nest, they resolved to get on with their own full and, really, quite privileged lives. The boys were men now, and they had made their own beds, so to speak, so they could lie in them and accept whatever consequences their chosen careers had in store. They seemed to be making good money, from whatever unpleasant business they were involved with in the capital. They made no demands on their parents for financial aid or any other kind of help. They dutifully sent cards at Christmas, but they had obviously forgotten their parent's birth dates or couldn't be bothered or were too busy to ask or care when these might be, so birthday cards never appeared. As for Gladys and Fred sending cards, this was very difficult. Of course, they could remember their offsprings' birthdays well enough, but they had no idea where to send a card to; indeed, they had little idea of how to contact their sons at all. For some reason best not investigated, Kevin and Craig liked to keep their whereabouts on a strict need-to-know basis.

Antiques, fine jewellery and works of art had always been Gladys' passion, and, fortunately, her husband's small, though very successful, engineering business had provided them with enough money to indulge her in collecting such items, while still enjoying a very comfortable, relaxed lifestyle. That lifestyle included holidays in more up-market resorts, a holiday cottage in France – regularly let out when they were not using it – and the nineteenth-century cottage with five acres of land, whose staircase she had descended in such a dramatic and final manner.

Her husband, Frederick Reginald Harper, had come from a comfortable middle-class background, had been well-educated and had gone to college, where he had learnt about design and engineering. Despite his somewhat aggressive nature, he had made a lot of useful friends and contacts at college and was soon able to set up in business, designing and manufacturing various components for the engineering industry. Fred had always been too busy with the business to help with raising the kids. Raising children was women's work, anyway, in his mind, and he had the responsibility of running the all-important business that provided their income. The business supplied the holidays and the little luxuries that they all took for granted. He did, however, have occasion to discipline the boys, now and then. Spare the rod and spoil the child was his faithful motto. His father's belt had taught him a useful lesson or two during his childhood, and his would, no doubt, do the same for his two boys. As things turned out, in the end, he lived just long enough to discover that the motto was sadly inaccurate, as far as his own sons were concerned.

Fred had died at the relatively early age of sixty. He had smoked heavily from the age of twenty and succumbed to the almost inevitable cancer, after narrowly surviving a serious heart attack, but he had left his wife very well provided for. The five-bedroom cottage, in which they had spent the last thirty years of their married life, was paid for, as was all their other possessions – the two cars and the holiday home in France, which was now managed and let-out on a year-round basis. Gladys didn't feel the need for holidays abroad anymore, even though she was more than able to afford them. Collecting beautiful things and playing bridge and Mah-jongg twice a week with friends kept her mind active and her life full.

Her two dreadful sons could go to hell, for all she cared, and they probably would, she often thought, eventually.

It was nearly midday when Detective Chief Inspector Blake called Paul into his office and announced that, as Paul had suspected would be the case, he was to be the SIO., or Senior Investigating Officer, on the case. They had been allocated an incident room on the third floor, and DCI Blake had already decided that Paul would be the inspector leading the team. He could pick a Sergeant and three Constables to make up that team. Paul had begun to protest, but the DCI had cut him short and indicated that he should sit down.

'I know it's not a very big team, Paul ... well, hardly a team at all, you'll be well understaffed, but we're really short on manpower all over. There are two other ongoing murders at the moment besides this one, and, as you know, I'm also the SIO on the shopkeeper murder, so I shall be heading two. It's bad timing for your first murder as an inspector, I know, but, as SIO., I will give you all the support and advice I can; it's just that I may not be able to put in the time that I would, ideally, have hoped to, because of the other case. I should be running the whole show, of course, but, instead, I'm going to be relying on you to, effectively, run it for me, to do all the work and keep me up-to-date on a daily basis, not just about what's happening, but about what you're thinking, as well. Sergeant Derrick Jacobs is retiring in six months' time. I know you two haven't had much contact with each other, but I think he would make an excellent office manager. Of course, as I'm expecting you to virtually do my job for me on this occasion, if there is someone else you have in mind... anyway, I'll leave the decision to you.'

'As a matter of fact, sir, I was going to ask your advice about appointing an office manager, so Derrick will be fine. Let's hope we get a result before he retires, and thank-you for your confidence in me, sir.'

'It's not how the investigation should be run, Paul, we both know that, and I'm putting a lot on your relatively inexperienced shoulders, but we just don't have the men, and, if you look at it this way, a quick result on this one will do us both a bit of good. At your tender age, this would make you 'Inspector of the Year', for sure; at least, it will in my book.'

Paul left the DCI's office deep in thought and a little worried – could he really run a murder enquiry with less than half a team? He had an office manager, in the shape of Derrick Jacobs, a very experienced Sergeant, in Reg Evans, and one constable at the moment, June Kelly, who was still new to the job, despite already having useful sources. He needed six more detective constables, at least, but could only appoint another two. They were certainly going to be stretched to the limit.

The Harper twins turned up at the station at just after one o'clock, so the briefing that Paul was giving to June, Reg and Derrick had to be cut short. The twins were both six feet tall, with upright postures and physiques that made it seem probable that they worked out on a regular basis. Their skins was tanned, but whether this was from time spent abroad or sessions under a lamp was anybody's guess, and they both looked and dressed more like successful executives, than vicious gangsters.

Constable Kelly took them to identify their mum's body, which they did with no visible show of emotion, according to her report. She accompanied them into the small clinical room, where their mum's body was lying on a hospital trolley, covered with a pale white sheet that looked as if it had been laundered almost out of existence. The mortician uncovered Mrs Harper's face.

The brothers looked at their mother's body, and Kevin confirmed, 'Yeah, that's the old girl, all right.'

After the formal identification, Inspector Manley and Constable Kelly asked them to accompany them to Hilltop Cottage to see if they could tell what, if anything, was missing from their mum's home.

'Yes, of course, Inspector, anything to help the police. How exactly did our mother die?' asked Kevin, who seemed to be the brothers' spokesperson.

'We believe she either fell or was pushed down the stairs during a confrontation of some sort.'

'I see. And do you know who this confrontation of some sort was with?'

'Not at the moment. That's why it would be helpful if we knew what, if anything, is missing from the house.'

'Of course, we'll do all we can to help, Inspector, but if you don't mind, my brother and I will take our own car to Hilltop. We'll meet you there.'

Constable Kelly drove Paul's car out of the police station car park, just in front of the brothers' car.

'They're probably allergic to the inside of police cars, Guv.' said June, speculating aloud as to why the brothers had decided to take their own vehicle.

'Yeah, perhaps that's it, maybe a bad experience in one when they were young. What do you make of our friends, June?'

'Very smoothly spoken, aren't they, Guv? And good-looking, too, I suppose, if you like the rugged type. You could almost take them home to meet your mother, couldn't you?'

'Yeah, maybe, if you didn't know their history. Have we checked their whereabouts for the day of the murder? ..... And what are these sources of yours?'

June Kelly smiled at her inspector's frustration, not yet ready to let on that she had an elder brother in the Met., who seemed to have access to all sorts of useful information.

'They said that they were at their club all day, and, of course, they have lots of witnesses to vouch for it. They agreed to make a formal statement, when we get back from the house. But you don't think they had anything to do with their mum's death, do you, Guv?'

'No ... no motive that I can think of. They seem pretty well-off, money-wise, judging by the silver Mercedes. That must have set one of them back a pretty penny, and, don't forget, whoever killed Mrs Harper will have an almighty scratch somewhere fairly obvious. It's a shame though ... The scumbags should go down for what happened to that poor girl who killed herself. I don't suppose we could frame them for something, could we?'

June glanced sideways and frowned at the inspector. It was taking her a little while to get used to him and his particular sense of humour, but she would get there in the end. She thought Paul had a very sharp mind and would make a very good detective inspector; she was looking forward to working the case and learning from him. Constable Kelly was ambitious; she intended to end up at least a chief inspector, if not higher.

Both cars pulled up outside the entrance to Hilltop Cottage, and Paul was slightly annoyed when Kevin beat them to the front door and let himself into the crime scene with his own key, breaking the string of police tape that criss-crossed the front door.

Paul and June exchanged knowing glances, and Paul thought to himself, 'That's bloody typical – no contact with his mum for years, but he can put his hand on a front door key to her house when he wants one.'

As they all followed Kevin into the house, Paul politely asked the brothers not to touch anything, but to have a thorough look around and see if anything obvious was missing or out of place.

As soon as he entered the lounge, Kevin announced, more to his brother than to the police, 'Roy Rogers is gone!'

Paul looked at him, puzzled, waiting for an explanation.

Kevin sighed heavily, seemingly regarding the police presence as an unwelcome interference, but, eventually, explained, 'Mum and Dad had a bronze statue of a cowboy on horseback sitting on the chest over there.'

Kevin indicated the marquetry chest against the far wall.

'Mum would never have parted with it.'

Paul experienced an unpleasant feeling growing in the pit of his stomach.

'Could you describe this statue for me in a little more detail?' Paul asked, afraid that he already knew exactly what it looked like.

'Sure. It was about a foot-and-a-half tall, and, like I said, the cowboy was on horseback – he was holding the reins of his horse in one hand and a rifle in the other, with the rifle stock resting on his hip. It was an impressive-looking thing, Inspector. Craig and I loved it as kids.'

Paul's heart sunk. There was no doubt in his mind that 'Roy Rogers' was the same bronze that he had seen at Richard Drake's house the night before. It would be too much of a coincidence for there to be two similar bronze statues floating about.

He asked June to take the brothers upstairs to see if there was anything missing up there.

'I have a quick call to make,' he explained to her.

June and the two brothers ascended the stairs, and, as they were going into the main bedroom, Kevin suddenly announced that he needed the toilet and hung back, allowing June and Craig to enter the room alone. He wanted to know who the inspector was calling and why; he could have been mistaken, but he had the distinct impression that the description he had given of 'Roy Rogers' had struck a chord of recognition with the inspector.

Paul took out his mobile and called Sergeant Evans back at the station.

'Reg,' he began, 'go to my desk, would you? Written in my diary is the address for *Richard Drake Antiques*; his home address is there, as well. You know where I keep it in the bottom drawer. I want him brought in. Get it done right away, will you? And, also, at Mr Drake's house is a large bronze statue of a cowboy on horseback – get that brought in, as well, and have it thoroughly dusted for prints. It seems the cowboy's name is Roy Rogers, and he belonged to Mrs Harper.'

Richard hung up, and Kevin quickly rejoined Craig and Constable Kelly inspecting the bedrooms, having listened with interest to Paul's side of the phone call.

After the tour of the house, Kevin and Craig announced that they couldn't identify anything else that was missing, although they couldn't find any jewellery at all, and they were sure that their mum would have had an extensive collection.

'To be honest, Inspector, neither of us have been home in some time, so there could be all sorts missing, and we wouldn't know. But, in terms of jewellery, Mum would have had some good pieces, for sure.'

Yeah, not been home in some time, but kept a key, Paul thought, suspiciously. The more time that he spent in the twins' company, the more he actively disliked them.

'Why are you so sure your mum wouldn't have parted with the bronze?' he asked, carefully, 'as you've been out of touch for so long. She could have sold it, surely?'

Kevin explained, 'Her father made the bronze, Inspector. He was an undertaker by profession, but a painter and sculptor at heart. We were too young to remember him when he died, but, apparently, he loved reading about the old West. He sculpted the cowboy in clay and had it cast by a firm of church-bell makers in 1918. It was our dad who christened it 'Roy Rogers'. Kevin continued , 'Our grandfather hadn't put a title on it, but, according to Mum, he always referred to it as 'The Night Watchman'. Apparently, the figure is supposed to be watching over a herd of cows at night, keeping them safe from predators and rustlers. I think the old boy copied it from an illustration in one of his books.'

'I see ... Well, thank-you for your help so far. Now, we just need you to come back to the station and make a statement about your whereabouts on the day. Just routine, you understand, and I think we should have 'The Night Watchman', or 'Roy Rogers', at the station later today. I would appreciate it if you could identify it before you leave. Are you staying here or travelling back to London?'

'Sure, we'll call back now and make the statement that you want, and I promise we won't go anywhere, until we've seen the bronze.' It was Kevin who spoke, once again. 'Then we'll be getting back to London, Inspector. There's nothing else to be done here, until you release Mum's body.'

Paul Manley was slightly puzzled by Kevin's casual reply. Having only just informed the police about Roy Rogers, he would have thought that he might have asked how they expected to have it at the station so quickly, but, instead, he had just accepted that they would. Paul felt that he had missed something important, and it worried him.

As they drove away from Hilltop, Kevin turned to Craig and said, 'We have to locate an antique dealer by the name of Richard Drake.'

'Oh ... why is that?' Craig enquired, intrigued.

'Because it would seem that he is now in possession of Roy Rogers.'

'Is he, indeed? We'll have to introduce ourselves and find out how he came by it, won't we? I'll ask him the questions, if you like?' said Craig, smiling. He liked asking people questions or, to be more precise, he enjoyed making them answer.

'Patience, brother ... all in good time,' said Kevin, 'I told the inspector we would be heading home to London, but I think we need to stay and keep an eye on things for a while. Do they have any decent hotels in Bristol?'

Paul contemplated his next meeting with Richard Drake, as he watched the two brothers drive away from Hilltop. Was Richard lying about how he came by the bronze? Was he doing a bit of fencing on the side? None of it made any sense to him. If Richard was involved in the murder in some way, why had he left his business card at the scene, and, more than that, why had he invited a policeman into a room with such an obvious clue as to his involvement so proudly exhibited? He was still deep in thought as June Kelly gently pulled the car into the station car park. There was a large silver birch tree overhanging the far end of the park, and, although there were spaces nearer the entrance, she decided to park under it, so that Paul's car would be in some shade. The Chief Constable was away at some strategy meeting or other, but Paul noticed, as they drove past, that his designated parking space, which had a large, imposing sign over it, saying, 'Chief Constable Only', was occupied by the Harper brothers' Mercedes, even though there were lots of other spaces available. He found the brothers quite detestable ... but he had to smile at their cheek.

'I don't know about you, Sir, but I'm famished. Do you mind if I go to the canteen for my lunch now? It's nearly three o'clock,' asked Constable Kelly, with her hands pressed together, as if in prayer.

'Yes, you go on, June. I want to see if Reg has come up with anything.'

'Thank you, Guv.'

As he walked into the incident room, he noticed at once that Reg was sitting waiting for him.

'Richard Drake is in interview room two, Guv, and the bronze is being dusted, as we speak. How was your morning? Remarkably fruitful, by the sounds of it.'

'You could say that, Reg. Have the brothers identified the bronze yet? I noticed their car in the car park.'

'Yes, they've seen it and confirmed that it is definitely their mum's bronze. It's nice, Guv. I wouldn't mind it myself. Has it got a name?'

'Oh, not you as well, Reg. What is it about cowboys that I'm not getting? Apparently, it's called 'The Night Watchman', alias 'Roy Rogers', so take your pick.'

'The Night Watchman, eh?' repeated Reg, scratching his head. 'Oh, I get it, Guv. He's watching over the herd, right?'

Paul shook his head in disbelief and brought his sergeant up-to-speed with events, as they walked together to the interview room to interview Richard Drake.

As they entered the room, Richard stood up to shake Paul's hand and greeted him cheerfully. The greeting was in stark contrast to the gloomy surroundings of the room itself, which consisted of a table and four chairs, at one end of which was a recording device. One of the plain, and rather dirty, walls had a large two-way window in the centre of it, which allowed interviews to be observed from outside. Paul bade Richard sit down and explained that there had been some developments in the case that they had spoken of the night before.

He explained, carefully, 'We've established that Mrs Harper was definitely murdered, and it would seem that the bronze sculpture, which you said that you bought in Bath, was most probably taken from the house at the time of the murder.'

Richard was clearly shocked; Paul watched his reactions, closely.

'No, no ... that's not right. I bought the bronze from *Bath Antiques*; ask Simon White, he'll tell you. It must be a different bronze.'

Richard was struggling to try and understand, to grasp the implications of what Paul had just told him. He sat back down on the hard wooden chair, put his elbows on the table and rested his head in his hands, completely confused and a little scared by the events that were unfolding.

'OK, Richard, I'm going to leave you to make a formal statement with Sergeant Evans, here. He will write down everything you tell him, both about your visit to Hilltop Cottage and about the purchase of the bronze. He will go through it all with you and then get you to sign it, when you're happy with it. Then you are free to go, but, mind, don't leave town, as they say. I'm going to check your account of things with Simon White at *Bath Antiques*, and, if he confirms that you bought the bronze from him, then I see no reason why you should be involved any further. The only other thing is that we would like a sample of saliva to check your DNA, if that's all right? And Sergeant Evans will also need to check your forearms and neck to make sure you don't have any scratches. Is that all OK, Richard?'

Richard was still trying to absorb what he had been told and was in a daze.

'Yes, yes, that's fine. I had nothing to do with any of this, Paul ... honestly, you have to believe that.'

Paul had interviewed a lot of guilty men, and Richard Drake just didn't fit the bill. He was convinced that Richard's explanation of events was the truth, no matter how unlikely it seemed.

'Actually, I do believe you, Richard. I can't believe you would have been stupid enough to let me see the bronze at your house if you were involved, but it's my job to check everything. You understand that, don't you?'

'Yes, of course. You do what you have to do ... Simon is ...' Richard stopped, mid-sentence, 'no, it doesn't matter.'

'Tell me what you were going to say, Richard. I'll decide whether it matters or not.'

'Well, it's just that Simon isn't always that careful about ownership, when he buys things for the shop.'

'You mean, he sometimes buys stolen property?'

'Not knowingly, I'm sure. Look, Paul, I don't think Simon is dishonest, not in the true sense of the word. The fact of the matter is that he just doesn't always engage his brain when he sees something he likes or something with a good profit in it.'

'OK ... I understand what you're saying, Richard.'

Paul left the interview room, collected Constable Kelly, who was now back from her three o'clock lunch, and had her drive him to Bath – a journey that was completed in almost complete silence. June concentrated on navigating the busy main road, while Paul silently wondered if he could possibly be wrong about Richard. Could it really be a coincidence that Richard had bought a bronze that had been stolen from the very house he had just visited? It seemed implausible and yet ...?

When Simon saw the police woman and her companion enter the shop, he was a worried man. The two dealers that he had bought the bronze cowboy from had done a deal that left him in possession of a lot of gear that he suspected was dodgy, but, fortunately, the police only seemed interested in the bronze.

Simon confirmed that he had sold Richard Drake the bronze statue, having bought it only hours earlier from two men that he had never seen, or bought from, before. He gave a very sketchy and uncertain description of the two men and said he hadn't noticed what sort of car they were driving, although he did mention that one of them had some nasty scratches low on his cheek, which he had tried, unsuccessfully, to keep covered. Simon White wasn't the most helpful or co-operative witness that Paul had ever dealt with. He couldn't make up his mind whether the man was being deliberately evasive or if he was just incredibly unobservant and disorganised. Certainly, the state of his shop would indicate the latter, as it was a mystery how he ever managed to keep track of any stock. The place was a shoplifter's paradise; if something was stolen, it could be days before it was missed.

'Did these men sell you anything else?' asked June.

'No, just the bronze,' Simon lied. He didn't want the police confiscating thousands of pounds worth of his stock. If the bronze was stolen, the police would have that already, and Richard would probably want his money back; at the end of the day, he had to try to contain the damage, as much as he could.

Paul said, 'I'd like you to come up to Bristol and work with a facial composite artist, so we can have a better idea of what these men look like, and to sign a written statement confirming that you sold the bronze to Richard Drake.'

'I'm a busy man with a shop to run, Inspector. I can't spare the time to go swanning off to Bristol to make statements. I've told you all I know about the bronze, and the men that I bought it from.'

'Well, that's all right, Simon. If you can't make it up to Bristol, I'll have Constable Kelly, here, come back down and get your statement from you at the shop. She can bring our list of stolen goods with her and check your entire stock against it. That way it'll put your mind at rest that you haven't inadvertently bought anything else dodgy. Is later today OK with you?'

'All right, all right, you win. I'll call up in the morning – always happy to help the police.'

'Thank you, Simon, that's very co-operative of you.'

As they left the disorganized shop, Paul and June heard the unmistakable sound of a small china object smashing against a wall. They looked at each other, smiling, and June said, 'Oh, dear, I hope that wasn't too valuable.'

Paul replied, 'I just hope it was his'.'

They were both laughing out loud when they got to the car.

'I take it you want his stock checked anyway, Guv?'

'I think it would be a good idea, June. Mrs Harper's jewellery has to be somewhere, but we haven't got the resources to search for it. It will take forever with the manpower we've got. We'll pass it on to uniform and get them to keep us informed.'

At least Paul was, once again, certain that Richard was in no way connected to the murder or the theft, which pleased him no end, not only because he really liked Richard and his family, but because it made his life easier, with regards to seeing Margaret again. By the time that they arrived back at the station, Richard had made his statement and left. Paul rang Richard's shop, rather than his home, to let him know that his version of events had been corroborated by Simon White, in the hope that it would be Margaret, rather than Richard, who would answer. Even just talking to her on the telephone lifted his spirits immeasurably.

Elizabeth had the following day off work, so Richard decided to spend the day with her. There were no local auctions that day, and Margaret could easily manage the shop. They spent the day at the city docks visiting Brunel's *SS Great Britain* – the first ship to combine an iron hull and a screw propeller. Neither of them had seen her since she'd been returned to Bristol as a rusting hulk, back in 1970. They both marvelled at the transformation that the restorers had achieved, as she now looked as good as new and ready to put to sea once more. They had a hearty lunch in one of the many cafés along the dock and generally had a pleasant time enjoying one another's company, forgetting about the unpleasant business of the last few days and the fact that Richard had spent six thousand pounds, that he would probably have all sorts of trouble recovering on an item he loved, but would be unable to keep.

Elizabeth enquired, tactfully, 'If Simon refuses to reimburse you the money for the bronze, what will you do?"

'I think it's unlikely to be worthwhile taking him to court, because lawyers' fees will swallow six grand in no time, and, even if I win, there is no guarantee that I would be awarded costs. Adding to the fact that suing a fellow dealer is not going to win me any friends or inspire trust in others. No ... I'll just have to put it all down to being one of the pitfalls of the business.'

'Perhaps you can convince Simon to, at least, refund any profit he made out of it.'

'I'll speak to him about it, of course, and there's good reason for him to do that. I've spent a lot of money with him in the past, and I expect to do so in the future. I don't think he'll want to fall out over this, any more than I do. The trouble is that I have no idea how much he paid for it. If he tells me he only made twenty quid profit out of it, I have no way of knowing otherwise.'

Elizabeth decided to change the subject, hoping that Richard wouldn't dwell too much on the loss of the bronze, which she knew he had really wanted to keep.

'Peggy said her husband has finally agreed to the two of them going on a cruise. She said he's booked for them to have two weeks in the Med. I'm so pleased for her. Peggy's wanted to go on a cruise for years; she's forever talking about cruises their friends have been on.'

Peggy Holmes was the Drake's cleaning lady, who came in for two hours on Mondays, Wednesdays and Fridays to give Elizabeth a hand with the day-to-day household chores – a job that she had been doing for them for the past seven years. She and her niece, Louise Brown, ran a little family business called *Dusters*, and they were becoming so successful that they had been recently talking about taking somebody on.

'When is she going?' asked Richard, worriedly 'and who is going to replace her and give you a hand on those weeks?'

'Apparently, it's all been taken care of. Her niece, Louise, is going to cover for her. I've met Louise before, and she's a lovely girl, about the same age as Rebecca, I would say.'

Richard's only concern was that, whereas Peggy was well-acquainted with the way that Richard liked his antique furniture cleaned and looked after, her niece certainly wouldn't be. The use of spray polishes or anything containing silicon was strictly banned in the Drake residence or, at least, those areas where there were antiques.

'It's all right, Richard, don't panic,' comforted Elizabeth, smiling, 'apparently, Peggy has given Louise detailed instructions on how you like things done, so there is no need to worry.'

'Well, that's OK, then, I'm pleased for her, anyway. When did you say they are going?'

'I can't remember the exact date she said, but it's soon. Her husband obtained a late booking, apparently, at a very good price.'

After finishing lunch, they took a short stroll around the old docks. Richard's dad had often told him stories of when he was young, and the docks were still in use.

'It must have been exciting for a young boy back then, with all the ships unloading goods from all over the world, well, the Commonwealth, anyway,' said Richard.

'The Commonwealth would have been most of the world back then,' Elizabeth said, 'but I think I prefer the docks as they are now – still full of hustle and bustle, but with the people enjoying themselves, rather than working. I love all the different aromas in the docks now – the coffee and hot bread smells from the cafés, the diesel engine smells from the ferry boats and the little craft. Much better than a working dock,' she argued, and Richard happily conceded.

* * * * * * * * * * *

Rebecca Drake wasn't due to start her new job as events manager for another month and was training the new bar manager, Tom, who would take over her role. That night, she was lending a hand behind the bar in the cabaret lounge, because two staff had called in sick. She was bored, and it was late. The cabaret had finished for the evening, and the magician was having a drink in the bar and chatting to Rebecca. He had shown her a couple of close-up tricks with coins, and she was intrigued; she'd always liked to watch magic shows, but this was the first time she had seen magic performed close-up, and this guy was really good – she couldn't believe some of the things that he'd done. After he had her hooked, he asked her if she wanted to see something really astounding, and she bit.

'Is there a fifty pound note in the till?' he asked.

'Probably ... why?' she enquired, a little on guard.

'Because if I'm to show you a sensation, a fifty pound note is required. Can you get one for me? I assure you, it won't get lost or anything. You'll have it back in no time.'

Rebecca opened the till, took out the required fifty pound note and asked – more out of a need to speak, than interest – 'What made you decide to take up magic as a career?'

'Oh ... I've always known I was going to be a magician,' he replied, 'because when I was born, I came out of the woman in the next bed!'

Rebecca, who had still been dubious about handing over such a large sum of money for some trick, laughed at his joke and thought, what the hell, as she handed him the fifty pound note from the till.

The magician, who was billed, simply, 'Carl', was in his forties and wore a wig that only he thought was inconspicuous. His assistant had changed out of her costume and came in to see where he was. Rebecca thought that they were probably a couple, even though they had different surnames and separate rooms. Perhaps one or both of them were married.

Carl asked Rebecca to sign the note she'd taken from the till in one corner, which she did. He then proceeded to wrap the note in a piece of tissue paper that he produced from his pocket and placed it in a small wooden box, also from his pocket; at which point, his assistant appeared bored and wandered off. After waving his hand mysteriously over the box a couple of times, he asked Rebecca to retrieve the note from it. But, to her horror, when she opened it and searched in the tissue paper, ... the note was gone.

'Hey! This is no joke,' she protested, suddenly a little uneasy. 'If the till is down fifty quid, I'm going to be for it.'

Carl played along for a while, smiling broadly and explaining that the trick had never gone wrong before, and he couldn't understand it, but, after a while, he told Rebecca to calm down and have more faith in his magical abilities. He then suggested that she go and look in the till again.

Wow!! There was the fifty pound note, right back in the till where it belonged. And there was her signature in the corner, so there could be no mistake – it was definitely the same note.

Rebecca was suitably impressed.

'How on earth did you do that?' she exclaimed. 'That was brilliant! That's impossible. Tell me how you did that.'

'Maybe another night,' he said, 'but I think it's time for bed now.'

His assistant had returned, and they left together, arm-in-arm, chatting softly to each other, like conspirators. An hour later, when they closed the bar, Rebecca was still trying to figure out how the trick could possibly have been done – he'd been standing in front of her the whole time ... nowhere near the till.

The next morning, Rebecca was in work early, and her first job was to cash-up the bar takings from the previous night.

'Bloody hell.'

It was rare for Rebecca to swear out loud, but the till was down. She couldn't believe it. And not just down by a pound or two, either – it was down by forty-eight pounds and ten pence. She and Tom, the soon-to-be Manager, checked the takings three times. There was be no mistake; the till was forty-eight pounds and ten pence short.

A few times in the past, the till had been down, but seldom by more than a pound or two, and it could always be easily explained by instances of incompetent addition or carelessness when giving change. Once or twice, it had been down by five pounds, and, in these cases, it was easily explained by someone taking a five pound note and giving change for a ten, but it had never been this much down – nearly fifty pounds. If it couldn't be accounted for, it would come out of Rebecca's pay cheque, and she was mad as hell, as it probably meant that one of the staff was stealing. But it was Tom who had been working the bar with her last night, and she couldn't believe it was him – he wouldn't be stupid enough to jeopardise his new job, and it was such an odd amount. If someone was taking money from the till, you would expect it to be down by an amount of notes, either fives or tens or a combination of the two. OK, she reasoned, the ten pence could have just been given in change by mistake, but that didn't explain the odd eight pound. It was a mystery. She kept thinking about Carl and the trick with the fifty pound note, but the till wasn't down by fifty, so that didn't seem to be an issue, and, anyway, she'd seen the note in the till with her own eyes, and it was still there this morning.

That night, Richard and Elizabeth could tell from her manner that something was wrong; their daughter was normally a bubbly and highly-charged individual. Tonight, she was very quiet and deep in thought. When she explained to him what it was that was wrong, Richard suggested that they speak to their new friend, Paul, who seemed to have taken a shine to Margaret and vice versa. He was a detective, so he might have some ideas about how they could unmask whoever it was that, quite literally, had their fingers in the till.

'Good idea,' said Rebecca, brightening up, 'I'll speak to him about it. I need to find out what his intentions are towards Margaret, anyway. I don't want him taking advantage of her innocent nature and then swanning off or something.'

'Oh ... you be careful what you say to him, Rebecca,' cautioned her mother, 'you're not going to interfere or anything are you?'

'Oh, really, mother. I'm Margaret's best friend, for goodness sake, of course, I'm going to interfere –that's what best friends are for.'

* * * * * * * * * * * *

Graham Edwards pulled his Ford Focus onto the drive of Hilltop Cottage at 7am and let Chewbacca out of the back door. The large German Shepherd sat and looked at his handler excitedly, wondering if he was going to be given the instruction 'go play', which meant that he could run and hunt and do his own thing, in order to get exercise and stay fit enough to perform his duties as a clever and well-trained police dog. Or whether the instruction would be 'harness', which meant he was going to work and had to sit still, until his lead was attached to his harness, and he was told what he had to do.

Today was a little confusing, because Graham – his handler of three years – wasn't wearing his uniform. Although Chewbacca was wearing his harness, as if he was going to work, they had arrived in Graham's own car and not in the little, white police van, in which they usually travelled to work.

Graham knew that it was a long shot, but he was hoping that the gold lighter his wife had given him for their fifteenth wedding anniversary, and that he was now missing, had been lost when he attended the call-out at Hilltop Cottage the other night.

Chewbacca was good at sniffing out drugs or dead bodies, but whether he could find his lighter for him was another thing altogether. But he was the best dog he'd had, and it was worth a shot. The trick would be in what scent to give him. It was Graham's day off, and he had decided that before he took the dog for his morning walk, he would see if he could locate his lighter for him.

Graham had been first on the scene with his sergeant, when the gardener had called to say that the old girl who lived in Hilltop Cottage had been found dead at the bottom of her stairs. He had entered the house with his sergeant, but he was sure that the lighter was in his pocket when he had taken his handkerchief out to sneeze; the hay fever tablets he was currently taking were next to useless. That had been after his excursion inside the cottage. So if his lighter was still at Hilltop, it was on the grounds and not inside the house. After he had been in the house, he'd taken a brief, initial statement of events from the gardener. They had begun their talk in the front garden, but had gone around to the back of the property, when the gardener had explained how he had gained access to the house.

Graham could tell that Chewbacca was a little uncertain about what was expected of him, but, after he had sniffed at the lighter-fuel that Graham held out for him and had received the command 'seek', Chewbacca had been off at a pace, now certain of what he was expected to do.

Graham decided to have a cigarette while the dog was doing his thing, but he realised that he had left his matches on the dashboard of the car, at the top of the drive. He looked at the dog that was now intent on the task of finding something, sniffing backwards and forwards across the lawn, and decided that he could get his matches from the car and be back before the dog missed him. As he slowly wandered back up the gravel drive to the car, he thought, for the hundredth time that week, about how much money he could save, and how much healthier he would be, if only he could give up the disgusting habit. He lit his cigarette and took a few drags on it, before he began strolling back to the house. He was almost back at the iron gate, when he heard the familiar bark that meant Chewbacca had found something of interest.

Graham quickened his step expectantly and called out to his dog, 'Good boy. Leave now, good boy,' as he hurried through the gate into the back garden.

'Oh no!' thought Graham, seeing his dog digging furiously in the rose beds, 'what's he found in there? It can't be my lighter. I didn't venture into that part of the garden.'

He rushed over to his dog, concerned about the damage that he appeared to be doing, and saw that he had been intent on digging a large hole. Chewbacca had unearthed some old bones. He had to pull the dog back by his harness, but then patted him and told him again that he was a good dog, making him sit. At first, Graham thought that Chewbacca had unearthed the grave of a large family pet, probably a big dog, by the size of the bone he was looking at, but something made him look closer. Sticking out of the hole, beside the bone, was the end of another – one with the characteristic bulbous end of a joint. There appeared to be an awful lot of bone sticking out and only one end in sight.

'How long is this bone?' Graham wondered, 'how big a dog had it been?'

He went down on one knee and had to hold back an excited Chewbacca, as he pulled the rest of the bone free of the porous earth. He stared at it for some time, trying to think if he could possibly be mistaken, but he was reasonably familiar with the human skeleton, and if that wasn't a human femur he was looking at, then he was a Dutchman. He put Chewbacca back into the car and then called his friend, Constable Mike Walker, who he knew was on duty.

'Mike, you had better get over to Hilltop Cottage – you know, the place where they found that woman at the bottom of the stairs the other day; the one they think was murdered. Well, I'm there at the moment, and Chewbacca's just dug up some human remains in the garden. I'm going to pop up to Bristol and explain, in person, why I was there, and how I came to find them, but I don't want to leave a second possible crime scene unattended.'

Graham waited until Mike had arrived and explained that he wanted to report in at the police station in person, so that he could better explain his presence at the Harpers' on his day off, and precisely why his dog was running loose at a crime scene, digging up old bones.

Chapter 4

Kevin and Craig Harper pulled their Mercedes up directly outside *The Contender* café, totally ignoring the yellow lines and the fact that a traffic warden was walking slowly towards them, with a gleam in his eye.

'I hope you don't intend leaving your vehicle there, sir?' asked the warden, wondering with frustration why it was that people with expensive cars always seemed to think that parking restrictions didn't apply to them.

Kevin loved traffic wardens.

'Well, not as a permanent feature, since you asked so politely,' he replied. 'We shall be visiting this eating establishment to ascertain just how good their meals are and perhaps partake of a cup ...' Kevin stopped for a moment, turned to look at the café, as if studying it, and then continued, 'sorry ... mug of tea, before returning to our vehicle and leaving, possibly never to return. Does that answer your question, Mr Warden?'

Both Kevin and Craig were grinning, maniacally, from ear to ear. It had been years since they had been accosted by a traffic warden. All the wardens around their patch were well aware of the fact that the Harpers were entitled to park wherever they wanted and for as long as they liked.

Andrew Parks, the warden, was new to the area. In fact, this was only his sixth day there. He had met some characters in his fifteen years in the job, but he had to admit that these two took the biscuit. They obviously had money, not just because of the Mercedes car – which could easily be a hire job – but Andrew was an observant man, and he had noticed the hand-made suits, the gold watch and the manicures, as well, when he got up close. But none of that made them any better than him. Well, if they wanted to flout the law and be sarcastic to him into the bargain, now, that was up to them. But it was also up to him if he walked away now and returned, a minute or two later, to place a well-deserved ticket on their swanky car, when they were happily ensconced in the café.

'I'm only doing my job, sir,' said Andrew, as politely as he could, 'in pointing out to you that you will be eligible for a ticket if you leave your car there.'

Andrew was now standing right next to the car and only six or eight feet from Kevin, who pointed his key at the car and pressed the button to lock it. There was a loud bleep from the car and the indicators flashed, announcing that the vehicle was now secure.

Two youths in hooded tops, who had been stood close by and had observed the exchange from its inception, were eager to see how it would turn out. They'd not seen this warden before or the two strangers in the Merc, but they knew the area, and they knew the café. It was owned by Dave (no last name) – a one-time boxer, who now made his money dealing drugs and lending money out of the café. It might look like a shit establishment and be situated in a pretty shit part of the city, but Dave also drove a Merc, and you spoke to him with respect, if you didn't want to find yourself in Casualty.

This new warden needed to watch himself, anyone turning up to see Dave in an expensive suit and car, and with the kind of confidence these two had, could only be big time heavies or maybe even crime bosses. You had to be pretty dim to get on the wrong side of these guys. Anyone with any sense could see that they weren't the type to be messed with. This warden was going to learn things the hard way if he didn't back off, and the lads were keen to see how this scene would unfold. They knew, of course, that if anything did happen, and the sap got hurt, to keep their mouths firmly closed.

'I commend you for your diligence in carrying out your duties, Mr Warden, and, if you're contemplating giving me a ticket, I have a preference for *Chicago*, if that is still showing. If, however, you should be referring to a parking ticket, then I feel it only fair to warn you – that would upset me a great deal,' Kevin had approached the man as he spoke and was now standing very close, facing him, eye-to-eye, 'and I'm not a nice man to know when I'm upset.'

The two youths who were watching felt like they had won ring-side seats to a big event. One of them took a packet of cigarettes from his breast pocket, removed one from it and tossed the packet casually to his companion, who did the same. They weren't going anywhere until this was over, so they might as well have a fag.

Andrew was beginning to feel that perhaps he had bitten off more than he could chew and was anxious for the confrontation to be resolved, but he was reluctant to back down and lose face, especially as a small crowd of locals had begun to congregate, obviously expecting something to kick off. There was no way that he was going to back down to this ignorant tosser in his big, fancy car. Andrew really didn't like people with money, especially if they liked to show it off, and he was never one to back down from a confrontation, even though this man looked a handful. Andrew had done some boxing in his day; he could handle himself, if need be.

The large glass door to the café opened, and Dave emerged, wondering why a crowd – which now, collectively, took a step back – was congregating outside his 'eatery', as he liked to think of it. Dave was tall and well-built and, apart from the fact that his nose had quite obviously been badly broken more than once, he was good-looking for an ex-boxer. He surveyed the developing scene with interest, and his face registered recognition, as he spotted the Harper twins. He knew them from way back, when they were teenagers, and he had been told that they were in the area, something to do with their mum dying? He managed to recall their first names, just in time.

'Kevin, Craig, what brings you slumming? London getting you down, is it?' asked Dave, cheerfully.

Dave greeted both Kevin and Craig with a firm handshake, followed by a hug. The twins were happy to shake Dave's hand, but gave no indication of whether they were pleased to see him or not; Kevin always said this lack of emotion kept people on their toes.

The small crowd which had collected – numbering maybe fourteen people – were amazed at what had happened. Everybody there knew Dave, but not one of them had seen him greet anybody like that before. He only shook hands to cement a deal and that meant you owed him money, and he never hugged anyone, unless he intended cracking a rib or two in the process.

With the greetings over, the crowd's attention was, once again, drawn back to the ill-fated traffic warden; they were all a little surprised that he hadn't taken the opportunity to slip away. Didn't he know who Dave was?

It was Dave who finally broke the silence, looking from one to the other and enquiring of his friends, 'Is there a problem here?'

'No, no problem, Dave,' said Kevin, 'This nice traffic warden was, I think, going to offer to look after our car, while we have a quick bite to eat.'

He turned to face the warden, who was still stood, stubbornly, beside the car, 'Isn't that right?'

Andrew looked around him at the crowd, trying to gauge if he had any support amongst them, but he didn't see anything hopeful. However, he decided to stay firm and stand his ground; he was in the right, after all, and he had his job to do. He could handle himself, he thought again, if the need arose.

'I'm sorry, sir, but if you insist on leaving your car there, I will have to issue you a ticket.'

The small crowd was hushed.

Dave stared at the warden in disbelief, wondering if he could really be that stupid.

Kevin sighed; he was annoyed that things had developed the way that they had, especially with a crowd collecting. What had started out as a little bit of harmless fun with the warden had somehow gotten out of hand. Their visit to Dave was supposed to be discreet, but now that some of Dave's neighbours were witnesses to a confrontation outside his business, this stupid little official would have to be taught a lesson or it could reflect badly on them.

'I am going to give you one more chance to walk away and come out of this without any pain,' said Kevin, 'but it's your last chance. Walk away ... now.'

Kevin genuinely hoped that the warden would do just that, as he and his brother had other, more pressing, business to attend to.

Andrew took out his book to begin writing a ticket.

Dave looked over at Craig, who was now speaking casually to someone in the crowd and, with sham concern on his face, asked, 'Do you think I should call an ambulance for him now? Or shall I give it a minute?'

'I'd give it a minute,' replied Craig, grinning broadly. Unlike his brother, he was still enjoying the situation.

Kevin, once again, used the car's remote – this time, to unlock the vehicle. He walked over to it and opened the driver's door. Andrew thought, for a minute, that he had triumphed and that the man was going to move his car, but he was forced to swiftly re-evaluate the situation, when Kevin reached inside for the button to remotely open the car boot.

This done, he closed the front door again gently, strolled casually to the rear of the car and removed a large baseball bat from the boot. He held the bat almost lovingly in his right hand and tapped it lightly, a few times, into the open palm of his left, as if testing the weight.

Andrew watched the proceedings in horror and hurriedly reviewed his options, deciding that he only really had one option left that would leave him unscathed. Finally acquiring some common sense at seeing a well-built, immaculately dressed man wielding a baseball bat, Andrew began to run as fast as he could to the sound of jeers and cat-calls from the assembled crowd and one or two upstairs' windows.

Damn! Why hadn't he done that earlier? Kevin would now have to decide if the crowd thought the warden had gone too far, broaching Dave's patch – in which case, they would have to punish him in such a way that the locals would be aware of it – or if they would think the humiliation of running away was enough. Kevin didn't want to take it any further; it would be a distraction from their main task and would use up valuable time and resources.

As Dave, Kevin and Craig finally entered the café, several people were already parking an assortment of cars, some hardly roadworthy, outside on the double yellow lines.

'I hope that's not going to be the cause of any bother for you, Dave,' enquired Kevin, with genuine concern. 'If he needs to be taught a lesson, we can oblige.'

'Nah, the guy must be new. I've not seen him before, and if he's got the bottle to turn up again for a shift here, he'll have his work cut out. I guarantee there won't be an inch of unoccupied yellow line in his entire area. If he tries to write a ticket, he'll be in Casualty before it's finished. Actually, we haven't had this much fun round here since the local nick was fire-bombed. Don't give it another thought. Have a seat, you two, can I get you anything?'

Kevin and Craig both had good palates for food and wine and enjoyed fine dining, but they didn't want to upset Dave, as they were about to ask for his help, so they each ordered a toasted sandwich and a lager.

'Good choice, my cook does a mean toasty,' beamed Dave, with obvious pride.

The twins exchanged judgmental glances, but made no comment. There was total understanding, between the three men, of exactly what their relationship was, and, although they were both in similar lines of work, Dave was very much the small fish in the equation. It would have been possible for the Harpers to simply demand his help, and they would get it, but the façade of friendship made things more agreeable.

'Well, now, you two didn't come all this way just for lunch. There must be something I can help you with?'

Dave was apprehensive. A visit from the Harpers could go one of two ways. They obviously wanted something, and if you let them down, it could be bad, but, on the other hand, if you were of help to them, they were known to be generous, and they were handy people to have on-side, as they had influence all over.

'We need to locate a local antique dealer, by the name of Richard Drake – home and shop address will do – and we need a couple of lads to carry out a few tasks. You know the score – no druggies, they may need their wits about them, and we may need them more than once.'

'It's good as done. How do I contact you?'

Kevin wrote a mobile number on a piece of paper and slipped it across the table to Dave, together with a mobile phone.

'Just text Drake's details to us on that number and give that phone to the two lads you select for us. Tell them to keep it charged and to keep it with them at all times. We'll contact them on it when we're ready. Make sure they know to be discreet.'

'OK, no problem. I've got just the lads for you – their names are Mark and John, they like to call themselves 'The Apostles', would you believe, but don't be put off by it, they're reliable lads, who know the score. They can handle themselves to – both are good boxers, and they've both done a bit of martial arts shit.'

Kevin took a brown envelope out of his pocket and passed it over towards Dave.

'There's six grand in there – it should be more than enough for what we have in mind.'

Dave took the envelope, without checking the contents. 'That's generous,' he said, 'nobody can accuse the Harpers of not paying their way.'

Just as Dave had finished speaking, the door opened, and a boy of about sixteen, with a shaved head and an armful of tattoos, put his head though and shouted in their direction.

'Dave! You betta come an' 'av a butchers at this, ba. You ain't gunna b'lief it!'

All three quickly got up from their seats and went outside, where an even bigger crowd than before had collected to witness the towing of Kevin and Craig's car.

The three of them were truly stunned by the traffic warden's actions. Was he suicidal?

The driver of the tow-truck looked over at them, anxiously, expecting trouble, but neither Kevin nor Craig showed the least sign of emotion. Kevin casually took his car keys out of his pocket and tossed them across to the tow-truck driver, who caught them nimbly in his cupped hands.

'Take good care of it!' ordered Kevin, 'I'll inspect it for scratches on its return.'

The implication in Kevin's remark was not lost on the driver, who was wishing he could be somewhere else.

Kevin looked at Dave and said, 'I'm sorry about all this, Dave. It would seem our traffic warden is tired of living. Find out who he is and where he lives. Text us that information, along with Drake's details, and we'll sort it out – it's of our making. When we know more, we'll let you know what day he'll have his lesson, and you can arrange to be seen somewhere at the time, in case you need an alibi.'

'You guys are going to be busy boys while you're down here. Why not let the apostles sort him out?'

'No, we'll see to it. It's our mess, and it's a job that needs doing properly.'

'If you'd prefer, of course. What's brought you to our neck of the woods, anyway, if you don't mind my asking.'

'Our mum died.'

'I'm sorry to hear that. I'll arrange for some flowers to be sent. When is the funeral?'

'We'll let you know. The police haven't released her body yet.'

'Released her body? Are you saying somebody killed her?'

'Yeah.'

'Do you know who?'

'We will soon.'

'My God ... the poor bastards.'

'Yeah.'

Andrew Parks, who was now accompanied by two large policemen, smiled as he watched the car being towed away. He strolled over to Kevin, with what could only be described as a swagger, and gave him a document explaining where the car was being taken and how it could be retrieved.

As Kevin took the document from him, still showing no sign of any emotion, he looked him in the eye and asked, casually, 'left or right?'

Andrew was puzzled, and his forehead furrowed, as he replied, 'What do mean, left or right? Left or right what?'

Kevin smiled, sweetly, 'I haven't made my mind up yet. I'll let you know when we see you next.'

At this point, Dave, who had gone back inside unnoticed, returned and said quietly, 'I've arranged a car and driver for you both. He should only be a minute.'

Kevin watched as Andrew Parks and the police bodyguard walked away from the scene and said, 'Thanks, Dave, that was thoughtful. We'll be in touch.'

He then turned to Craig and said, 'Life's never dull, brother. Have you noticed that?'

Early the next day, Kevin and Craig retrieved their car from the compound and returned to the Marriott Hotel they were staying in. After enjoying a swim and a sauna in the hotel's leisure facility, they headed to the bar to relax, with a coffee and the morning papers.

'What are we going to do about this bloody traffic warden?' asked Craig. 'Do you think I should kill the little shit?'

Kevin smiled at his brother.

'You really don't have any sense of proportion, do you, brother? He was only doing his job. The man's conscientious ... cut him some slack.'

'Yeah, you're right,' Craig said, thoughtfully, 'I admit ... I sometimes go a bit too far. I'll just cut his legs off instead, shall I? Did you see his face when you got the bat out of the car boot?'

'No, I missed that. But I did see him run – he looked bloody fast. Do you think he's in training?'

'Yeah, you'd have had a job catching him, if you'd gone after him.'

'Not in the car, I wouldn't.'

'Oh, no, that's true. You could have run him down – would've saved us a lot of trouble.' They both laughed. The light-hearted banter between them had always been a feature of their relationship, even when they were kids.

The mobile phone in Kevin's pocket bleeped, telling him there was a message. Removing the phone, Kevin held it up and read the text, with Craig looking on, expectedly.

'It's from Dave,' he explained. 'The details of Richard Drake's house and shop, and, apparently, our warden friend is a Mr Andrew Parks, and he lives local to his patch. I'll tell Dave to make sure he has witnesses for his whereabouts this evening. Might as well get it over and done with, and then we can get on with contacting our antique dealer. This whole bloody traffic warden business is an inconvenient diversion, and I want it out of the way.'

Craig nodded in agreement with his brother, although, personally, he was looking forward to seeing Andrew again.

* * * * * * * * * * * *

The sixth of December, 1980, was a warm ten degrees. But as Mrs Harper loaded the last of her shopping into the back of her brand new Vauxhall Viva, she wished she had worn a coat. She wondered if she had time to look for a present for Mr Harper's birthday in two weeks' time. She wanted to get him something special, as a thank-you for the new car, but decided it would have to wait until another day, because she had left the boys playing on their own and that often meant trouble these days.

Kevin and Craig had always been a handful, but now they were getting older, the kind of mischief they got up to was much more serious. Only a few weeks ago, Craig had got into a fight with a classmate in the playground, over some remark that had been made, and Kevin had joined in. The boy in question had been taken to Casualty and had received three stitches to his face and had been very badly bruised. His parents had threatened to go straight to the police with the matter, but the staff had gently persuaded them against it, not wanting the school to acquire a reputation for bullying. The parents eventually begrudgingly agreed not to involve the authorities on the advice of the school head, although Gladys had thought it was more likely that it was the two hundred pounds compensation which her husband had paid to them that was the deciding factor. She really was at her wit's end with the boys. Even when her husband took a belt to them, it didn't seem to do any good. In fact, there were times when she thought it actually made them worse.

When she got home, she parked the car outside the double garage and carried the shopping though the open lounge and into the kitchen. It took her three trips from the car to the kitchen, and it was only after the third trip, that she glanced casually out of the kitchen window and saw the two boys sitting on the grass, talking quietly to each other. Something about their demeanour made her feel very uneasy. It was then that she noticed the other boy lying nearby on the grass, apparently asleep, but, no, not asleep, there was something not quite right about his posture and ... Oh my God! There was blood – lots of blood. She rushed out of the back door, frantically, and found, to her horror, that the boy was not asleep, but dead. On one side of his head, there was a gaping, bloody hole.

Unlike the scenes in movies when a woman discovers a body, Mrs Harper didn't scream, instead, she stood back numbly and stared in horror and disbelief at the spectacle before her; both hands held up to her face, trembling uncontrollably. She was unable to make any kind of sound at all.

The boys came running over, shouting, simultaneously, 'It wasn't our fault! It was an accident! We didn't know the gun was loaded! We found it when we were looking for bottles to shoot at. Stephen said we should play Russian roulette, and he put the gun to his head, and it just went off. We didn't mean to hurt him. Honestly, we didn't know it was loaded.'

Only now did she see the gun lying on the lawn beside the dead boy; it was her husband's gun, it had been his father's revolver when he was in the army. She had told him to get rid of it on numerous occasions, or to hand it in when the police had one of their amnesties, but he wouldn't listen. Now look what had happened – the boys had found it, and what do you expect boys to do if they find a gun? They're bound to play with it. They're boys, for God's sake! And, dear God, why was it kept loaded?

The boys appeared to be calm and seemed oblivious to the enormity of what had happened. She supposed they must be in shock, so she took them into the house and made them drink sweet tea, while she phoned her husband, to tell him to come home and sort the mess out. She was still shaking while she was talking to her husband, and she could no longer hold back the tears.

Gladys had been pacing up and down the lounge wondering what to do for the greater part of an hour before her husband finally arrived home.

'What are we going to do?' she cried. 'The boy's dead, for Christ's sake! The twins might be arrested. They are bound to be blamed. It will be in all the papers and on the television – we will be pariahs in the eyes of the village. It might even affect your business! My God, Fred ... do something!'

Frederick Harper was thinking hard.

'Who knows the boy was here?' he asked.

'Well ... just us, I think. Apparently, he just told his parents he was going for a ride on his new bike, but not where he was going. Why?'

Sometimes, Fred wondered about his wife. She seemed to be in a blind panic, not knowing what to do, but she had obviously questioned her sons about who knew the boy was there, so she had already been thinking about covering things up, even a boy's death.

'Because if nobody knows he was here, we could make this thing go away,' her husband replied. 'I know it sounds awful, but the boy is dead, and nothing we can do is going to bring him back. We have to think about our boys, now, and us, about what will it do to our lives if they get arrested. And what good will it do, really? It won't bring the boy back, and it was just an accident, after all ... just a bloody awful accident. Didn't the boy shoot himself, after all?'

Frederick Harper spoke of it as an accident to his wife, but he knew damn well that the gun hadn't been loaded when they found it. He always kept the ammunition in a different place from the gun; the boys must have loaded it, before giving it to the boy. His sons were quite well informed on the subject of guns. They were obsessed with them and had piles of books and magazines on them in their room. ... No, this had been no accident, he was sure of it. His boys were a bad lot, and they frightened even him sometimes. He couldn't help but think that they had somehow managed to get the boy shot on purpose. But he dared not share his suspicions with his wife – it would break her, without a doubt. Not that she had false illusions about their offspring, but deliberate murder? She would never believe that, and she would turn against him, for sure, if he even so much as suggested the possibility.

He was thinking on his feet. The house wasn't overlooked at all. In fact, the nearest house was 400 yards away, so no-one will have seen the events unfold, and, if anyone had heard the shot, they would have naturally assumed that it was a car back-firing. The boys were certainly capable of keeping secrets, and Gladys would keep her end up, for appearances' sake, if for nothing else. After all, what other people thought meant everything to her. They could bury the body in the garden. It would be easy enough. But he wasn't sure that he could manage to dig two large holes on his own, so the bike would have to be disposed of in a different way.

He decided to let Gladys deal with the boys – to give them a good talking-to, tell them how much trouble they had caused the family, that they are lucky their dad doesn't call the police straight away and have them dealt with by the law, lucky that they don't end up in prison.

Gladys had suggested that he deal with the boys.

'They need a damn good thrashing for what they've done,' she cried, forcefully.

Fred was angry with her, for the first time in years.

'Me? Why do I have to deal with the discipline all the time? You're their mother, for Christ's sake! Why don't you take a turn? They don't listen to me...never have. It's probably your fault that they're so bad, anyway –you've been far too easy on them over the years, and if I deal with them now, what are you going to do? Will you dig a grave for the body? No, I didn't think so. Will you get rid of the bike? No. So damn well sort your kids out!'

Gladys had been shocked by her husband's outburst and fled, in tears, to their bedroom, more upset by her husband's anger, than she had been at finding a dead boy on their property.

It took him three long hours of hard work to dig a hole that was deep enough and wide enough for the job at hand. He was tired, sweating and still angry with his wife when it was finally complete. He hadn't eaten anything since breakfast, so he was hungry, as well as everything else. To top it all off, he had a nagging pain in his chest from all the digging; he must have pulled a muscle or something, he thought, rubbing his chest.

He made the boys search the garden for anything that could connect Stephen with a visit to the house. Then he had them carefully clean anything that Stephen may have touched, including the air rifle and the bike, after which, he burnt the clothes that they had been wearing. There was blood on the grass where the boy had fallen, but that was easily dealt with.

When he was satisfied that there was nothing that could place Stephen at the house, Fred put Stephen's body in the ground and covered it over. He knew he was doing something wrong, of course. He knew that hiding the body would cause Stephen's family even more grief, because they would never know what had happened to their boy. They could never have proper closure, because of his actions, but he had his own family and his own life to consider.

Frederick Harper told his wife, who had, by then, stopped crying and returned to the garden, that she would have to plant something special on the grave, something that would last and not have to be changed every other year. She was always tinkering with the damn garden.

After the grave was covered over, although neither of them were church-goers or particularly religious, they felt compelled to say a few words over it. Gladys had cried again, not so much for Stephen and his family, but for the way their sons had turned out and the trouble they had caused, and because now they had turned their parents into law-breakers, as well. When the four of them stood over the grave with their heads bowed, the twins looked sideways at each other and shrugged their shoulders, as if to say, 'What's this all about?', grinning at one another.

By the time Fred had finished covering over the grave and clearing away his tools, it was after six o'clock. His foreman would have shut the workshop half an hour ago and left for home. Fred reasoned that if he took the wheels off the bike, he could get it into his car and take it to the workshop, where he could cut it up and dispose of it, along with the scrap metal. Then he realised that he had forgotten about the gun. It had been his father's, and he didn't really want to part with it, despite the damage it has caused. He remembered that there was a loose floorboard in the far corner of the bedroom, so he quickly took the gun upstairs, pulled back the carpet just far enough so that he could lift the board and, after unloading it, placed the gun and the bullets under the floor. He would nail the board down when he had more time, but, at the moment, he was anxious to get the bike safely to his workshop without anyone seeing it. The pain in his chest was driving him mad, so he went to the medicine cabinet in the bathroom and took some painkillers.

Fred put the bike and its wheels in the back of his car and covered it with a blanket, in case anyone happened to see it. An hour after leaving Hilltop Cottage, he pulled up outside the wooden gates to his workshop. It was located on a small industrial estate, and all the little workshops were now closed for the night. The premises in that part of the estate were self-contained, detached properties in their own yards, and Fred's premises had a container in the yard for scrap metal, which was emptied once a week by two men with a lorry. They were due the next day. Fred took the bike frame and the wheels into the main workshop, where he stood the frame against a bench and placed the wheels on top. He started to walk towards the large tool cabinet on the back wall of the main workshop, intending to get one of the large hack-saws and cut the bike up, so that he could put in with the rest of the scrap metal.

Halfway over to the cabinet, he became suddenly breathless, and the pain in his chest became ten times worse, extending down both his arms, making him clutch dramatically at his chest. It was as if someone had put the top half of his body in a huge vice and was tightening it slowly, inch by inch.

He knew he had to act fast, in order to summon help, realising, with rising panic, that he was probably having a heart attack. So Fred grabbed the phone from the wall as he fell to his knees in agony and managed to dial 999. When the operator answered, he only managed to gasp out his workshop address, before doubling up with the pain, and slipping into unconsciousness. The operator on the line was unsure of the type of emergency that Fred had called in. He had sounded breathless and in a lot of pain, but he could have been caught in a fire, assaulted by youths or just taken ill, so she alerted all three services, to be safe. The police had the name of a key-holder for the workshop and called Fred's foreman, Alan West, who was in the middle of his evening meal and not pleased to be called out.

The ambulance was first on the scene and, discovering that the workshop was not ablaze, the crew radioed in to cancel the fire appliance that was en-route. The police were next to arrive, but, having checked over the building and finding nothing amiss, they checked that the ambulance team didn't need any assistance and promptly left, when the foreman showed up with his keys. As far as they were concerned, it was just a case of someone collapsing while working late – no reason for police involvement.

Alan West had been Fred's foreman for six years, and, although their relationship was strictly that of employer and employee, Alan was dismayed and a little puzzled to find Fred in the condition he was in and equally confused at finding him in the workshop at that time of night. Fred had left early after receiving a call from his wife, and, when he left, he looked concerned about something.

While the ambulance team worked on Fred, Alan took a look around the workshop to make sure all was well, and it was then that he spotted the bike at Fred's bench. Thinking that Fred had brought it in to work on it in some way – maybe customise it for one of his boys, perhaps – he took it into the storeroom and stowed it away safely for when Fred could get back to work on it.

Fred was 44 years old on that fateful day. He had suffered a massive heart attack that he was lucky to survive. Just to make his misery complete, it was during his lengthy stay in hospital, after his coronary, that he was diagnosed with lung cancer, and, from that day on, he resigned himself to despair. In a strange quirk of fate, it was probable that the heart attack was the reason he enjoyed, or, rather, endured, a further sixteen years of life. For, if he had not suffered the heart attack, the cancer would probably not have been discovered until it was too late. But the fact was that Fred was never a well or happy man again, and he never returned to his workshop or his unfinished business there. The foreman, Alan, ran the business for the next five years, but without Fred's drive, it went into rapid decline, and, when he left to start up on his own, Fred closed the business and the workshop, once and for all.

* * * * * * * * * * * *

Michael Pegler was an arms' dealer. Not the kind who sells rocket launchers and grenades to mercenaries, but one who sells flintlock muskets, cavalry sabres and suits-of-armour to avid collectors. Normally a lively and charismatic figure, today – the 12th of September, 2009 – he was the most wretched man on the planet.

He was sitting next to his wife's sister, Elizabeth, and opposite her husband, Richard, and their daughter, Rebecca, in the back of the first funeral car, watching the hearse they were following turn into the driveway that led up towards the crematorium. Inside the coffin, in the back of the hearse, lay the body of his wife, Mavis. He wondered how he was ever going to cope without her. Their union had not been blessed with children, but Mavis had enriched his life for the last thirty-one years.

He was angry with her now, for the first time in his life, because she had left him on his own, and the pain and the sense of loss that he felt was intolerable. Dying was such an uncharacteristic thing for Mavis to do – she had never really been ill in all the time he had known her. Oh, she had had the odd cold or flu once or twice, but the symptoms were never very severe, and they certainly never stopped her working.

He, on the other hand, had had his fair share of illness – chest infections, ear infections, gastric problems, mumps, you name it, but he had never passed any of it on to Mavis. It was as if illness purposely stayed well away from her, in case it got more than it bargained for in return. She could be a formidable woman. Then, less than a year ago, she had suddenly begun to complain of pain in her back. They both thought that she had overdone it and hurt her back by lifting or carrying something too heavy, but the pain had got steadily worse, and, eventually, she had given in and seen a doctor. At first, they could find nothing wrong, but, eventually, after Michael had kept insisting that they carry out more tests, they discovered a tumour on her lung. It turned out to be a secondary cancer, and they discovered that she had the dreadful thing in her bones and her liver, as well. The last few months of Mavis' life were not what she deserved. Michael had cared for her, as well as it was possible to do so, but nothing seemed to ease her pain, not even the morphine, and it had been a kind of blessing when she had passed on. The one thing that Michael could cling to was the knowledge that she was no longer suffering.

Elizabeth and Richard had been a huge help during her illness, sitting with her when he had needed sleep and doing most of the household chores, so that he could be constantly by her side. He hoped that they realised just how grateful he was, because, at the moment, he was too upset to let them know himself.

Mavis had been the most caring person that Michael had ever known; she had worked full-time for a small charity that helped victims of domestic violence. She was never happier than when she was helping someone else, and, as she was always helping someone, she was always happy, until the end, that is. Michael had promised himself that he wouldn't cry in front of anyone, but he was finding it very hard, especially as Elizabeth had succumbed to a little weep on the car journey.

The cars pulled up outside the crematorium, amidst a throng of people. Richard was the first to alight from the vehicle, holding the door for his wife and for Michael. As Michael looked about, he was astonished by the sheer number of people who were attending Mavis' cremation. Had her life really touched the lives of all these souls? Richard and Elizabeth were also amazed by the number of people present and realised that they would not all be able to get inside, some people would have to remain outside the building. At least the sun was shining, and there were plenty of places to sit in the beautiful grounds.

They took their places in the front pews, and, as they did so, Michael finally lost his battle against the tears, as the coffin was brought in and placed in position at the front of the congregation. Elizabeth held his hand to try and give him what meagre support she could.

The service itself was one of which Mavis would have said, 'It was a good service.' The vicar who took it had known Mavis personally and was well aware of the numbers of people she had helped, although he, too, had been unprepared for the number that had actually turned up. He had lots of stories and anecdotes about her life, some of which made Michael and Elizabeth smile through their tears.

After the service, everybody gathered outside to view the myriad of floral tributes, and Michael began to mix with the crowd, enquiring of people he didn't know, and learning just how they had known Mavis, discovering, as he did so, that a large number were young wives and mothers, who Mavis had helped to extricate from violent relationships. He began to wish that he had taken more interest in Mavis' work, but she had always been very discreet about it, even to him.

Mavis and Elizabeth had often helped with the cricket teas, when Michael and Richard played, which was every Saturday in the summer time, for several years. Although Richard had given up playing six or seven years previously, Michael still umpired on occasion and had been on the club committee for some years. It was for this reason that the wives had insisted on Mavis' wake being held at the cricket pavilion, where they would lay on a spread that would do Mavis proud. It was there that they all headed, after leaving the crematorium.

Richard carried two coffees across to the table where his wife and daughter were sitting and set them on the table quickly, having spotted one of his clients – a film director, by the name of Robert Powers – talking with Michael.

Surprised to see him present, Richard walked over and interrupted them, by saying, 'Robert Powers, what are you doing here? Did you know Mavis?'

Surprised to see him, Robert turned and greeted Richard, holding out his hand, 'Richard, how nice to see you again. I was just introducing myself to Michael, here. Are you two friends?'

'Oh, Michael and I go back a long way, and Mavis was my wife's sister. So if you're introducing yourself to Michael, I assume you knew Mavis in some way, then?'

'It was actually my daughter who knew Mavis,' said Robert, 'I never had the privilege, personally, and that is something I regret. I would have liked to have been able to thank her for all the help she gave my daughter, Helen. It's not widely known, thank goodness, but my daughter was in a very unhappy and unhealthy relationship and only managed to get away and settle in America with a great deal of help and support from Mavis. I had my suspicions about the marriage from the start, but Helen, at first, tried to keep it from me. I'm pleased to be able to say that she is now in a good relationship with a doctor in America and that she has never been happier, due, in no small part, to Mavis.'

'Thank you, Mr Powers,' said Michael, a little tearful once again, 'I am glad to hear your daughter has her life back now. It must have been horrible to cope with at the time.'

'It was, indeed. Helen would have liked to have been here in person; she was extremely upset when she heard that Mavis had died. They kept in touch, you see, via e-mail, I believe, and Mavis had mentioned that she was off work, because of ill health, but she never even hinted that it was in any way serious. It was someone at the charity who broke the sad news to us.'

Robert put a supportive hand on Michael's shoulder and continued, 'I have since been in contact with the charity, by the way, and informed them that I shall be making a substantial contribution, as a mark of our respect and admiration for Mavis and the work she did.'

'Well, that's very kind of you, Robert,' said Michael, holding back the tears, 'Mavis would be delighted, I know.'

Robert shook Richard's and Michael's hands and said that he really ought to be leaving, then turned again to Richard and said, 'It's odd ... bumping into you like this. We will be in contact soon, actually. My wife wants to make some changes at our house in California, and she wants you to track down some items for us. We're staying there, at the moment. I just popped over for the funeral, so I'll ring you in few weeks,' and, with that cursory promise, Robert Powers left.

'Well, that was a turn-up,' said Michael, after Robert had gone, 'apparently he's some kind of film producer.'

Richard's daughter, Rebecca, had come over to join them and said, 'Where have you been for the past decade, Michael? That was Robert Powers, and he's a film director, not producer, and a very good one – he must have at least three Oscars by now. Mum and I love his films, but I had no idea my dad knew him.' Then, to her dad, she said, 'Next time you see him, I want an introduction.'

'And why would that be? He's much too old for you, and he's married.'

'Oh, Dad, you know I've always wanted to be an actress,' she replied, 'he could get me a part in his next film.'

'But I thought you wanted to be a fashion model?'

'No, don't be silly, not any more. That was when you had that famous photographer client, don't you remember? Honestly! Any good father would keep up with his daughter's ambitions,' she admonished.

Elizabeth came over and joined them, pointing out that everybody had left, except them and one or two of the cricket wives, who were still clearing away. Elizabeth had not been inside the pavilion since Richard stopped playing, and she was remembering all the hard work she and Mavis – and many of the other wives – had put in, while the men played their silly game. She and Mavis had not got on very well as children, while they were growing up, but had become the greatest of friends in adulthood, and Elizabeth was going to miss her sister desperately.

Rebecca had left her car overnight at the pavilion car park, so that she could drive them home, and they could all have a drink in Mavis' memory. She now suggested that it was probably time to leave, as most of the mourners had left.

As they all walked to the car, Elizabeth said to Michael, 'Are you sure you wouldn't like to stay with us, Michael? At least for one night?'

'No,' he replied, 'I'd rather be on my own, but thanks for the offer, anyway. I'm not going to do anything stupid, you know, Liz. Mavis would never approve of that, and I'm not going to let her down now.'

He put his hand on her shoulder, by way of reassurance, and Elizabeth gave him a tight hug, before getting into the car.

Rebecca dropped Michael at his house, before getting the rest of them home, and, so, one of the worst days of their lives ... *so far* ... drew to a close.

* * * * * * * * * * * *

Andrew Parks was a man who was down on his luck. At thirty-two years of age, his life had been a downwards spiral. His parents had been quite well-off, but his dad had died when Andrew was still in school, and, although he had left his son a sum of money in his will, Andrew had blown the lot on a car, when he passed his driving test at the tender age of seventeen. His mother had begun to drink heavily after her husband's death and so had passed on two years ago, bequeathing the remaining money and the house to the local church, leaving Andrew with nothing.

Not long after the funeral, he had gone around to the church and asked the vicar whether he thought it was the Christian thing to do – to accept all that money and leave him with nothing. It was his inheritance, after all – she'd been his mother. The vicar had been very sympathetic, but said that the church was duty-bound to carry out his mother's wishes.

The condescending, smug little bastard ... calls himself a man of the church, thought Andrew, at the time. He had come very close to punching the man in the face.

He had, fortunately, managed to get onto the housing ladder, by purchasing a small terraced house in the run-down area of the city where he now worked, but the mortgage left him with little to live on. His brief, childless marriage had lasted only five years, and his social life was non-existent.

Yesterday had been a particularly bad day for Andrew. He'd only been working the area for a few days and a large group of people had seen him humiliated and forced to run away from a confrontation with a motorist who had parked illegally. Today, he had patrolled the same road, only to find there were six cars parked on the yellow lines outside the café. One car had a youth leaning against it, and, when he saw Andrew coming, he had made a call on his mobile phone. Five others had turned up, in no time at all. By the time Andrew got there, each car had someone leaning against it, and each person was holding either a baseball bat or a short scaffolding pole.

Andrew didn't normally walk away from trouble –until yesterday, that is – but even he realised that it would be stupid to confront six youths, armed with clubs. No job and no amount of self-esteem was worth that, so he had simply ignored them and made to walk right past. What else could he do?

The café owner, Dave, who had also swiftly appeared after the phone call, called him over, 'Andrew, isn't it?' he said,

'Look, I've told the lads here not to touch you, as long as you don't get your little book out. So, from now on, you and me have an understanding ... right? If anybody wants to visit my café, they can park outside for as long as they like, and, if they get a ticket, you get a hiding – that's the way it works.'

Dave put a supporting hand on Andrew's shoulder.

'Now, you look as if you could do with a big mug of hot tea and a breakfast inside you. It'll make you feel a lot better about things. It's on the house, Andrew. Come on in. Nobody's going to get hurt today.'

Andrew had gone in and gulped down his mug of tea, basically capitulating to this man and the mob. He felt wretched about it, but as he had to work and live in the area, he had no choice. He was a beaten man.

Returning home from his shift, he picked up a pint of milk at the corner shop, together with yet another frozen meal for his dinner, wondering how long it would be before he was asked to do a favour for someone or get a hiding. He thought it would be prudent to transfer to another area, if he could.

He unlocked the front door of his house, put his evening meal and the pint of milk down on the small hall table, closed the door and automatically attached the security chain. He took off the coat that he was wearing, carelessly draping it over the newel post at the bottom of the stairs. Picking up his shopping once again, he went straight into the kitchen to brew a much-needed cup of tea. It wasn't until he had filled and switched on the kettle that he noticed the back door was ajar.

He was puzzled, at first, trying to think if he could possibly have left it open when he left for work that morning, but he was sure that he hadn't. Then, he noticed the broken glass, and the fact that the key – which was always in the lock on the inside – was gone. His former wife had always warned him of the dangers of leaving keys in the lock. Well, now it had happened – he'd been burgled. Why was he not surprised? It was the perfect ending to his day. How much had they taken, he wondered, and did it really matter? He thought it was a sad reflection on the state of his life that there was nothing in his house which was worth stealing.

'Oh, God, I hope they haven't done anything nasty, because they couldn't find anything worth taking,' he thought, 'that really would round the day off nicely.'

He went to check the front room, half expecting to find it trashed. As he pushed the door inwards, still holding onto the handle, he put one foot in the room and poked his head cautiously around the door. He almost leaped out of his skin. One of the easy chairs had been pulled around so that it faced the door ... and sitting in it, holding a gun that was pointed at Andrew's head was Kevin.

As he was not fully in the room and still had hold of the door handle, Andrew's instincts for survival took over, and he hastened to take flight. Stepping quickly back into the hallway and dragging the door rapidly shut behind him, he made quickly for the front door and escape. He half expected to hear the sound of the gun being fired behind him as he fled, but, instead, he came to a sudden halt, just in time to avoid colliding head-on with Craig, also with a gun in his hand, who must have come down the stairs as Andrew had opened the lounge door, and now stood proudly in front of the main entrance, blocking Andrew's escape route.

'Whoa! Not so fast, my friend. You'll do us both an injury,' said Craig, smiling.

Kevin casually emerged from the lounge, and all three men stood silently in the hall, until Kevin said, simply, 'upstairs, Andrew', gesturing with the gun.

Their footsteps echoed hollowly on the bare, uncarpeted treads as they ascended, and Kevin remarked, 'You really ought to get a shade for that,', as he pointed to the bare 60-Watt bulb that barely lit the landing and stairs, 'and a bit of carpet wouldn't go amiss; have a little pride in your surroundings, Andrew.'

'Look ... everything has been sorted out now,' Andrew protested, 'Dave and I have an understanding. We sorted it all out today ... didn't he tell you? Ring him ... you'll see.'

Craig gestured, to the still-protesting Andrew, to enter the back bedroom, where they made him sit in a chair that they had previously placed there.

Again, Andrew explained to them that he had sorted everything out with Dave, as Craig started securing him in the chair with a piece of cord. Kevin pulled a small bedroom stool across to the middle of the floor and sat facing Andrew, close-up, the gun still held casually in his hand.

After securing Andrew in the chair, Craig sat on the edge of the single bed, produced a clean rag from his pocket and began casually cleaning the gun he held, as if his part in the proceedings was at an end. Andrew watched him carefully, with mounting dread.

'I keep telling you that this has all been sorted out. Why don't you believe me?' Andrew said, with just a hint of pleading in his voice.

Kevin stared Andrew in the face, long and hard.

'I don't ... not believe you, Andrew. It's simply that whatever arrangements you may have come to with Dave, are exactly that – an arrangement between you and Dave. It has nothing, whatsoever, to do with any issues between us.'

'Oh, right ... OK ... I see that. I'm sorry I had your car towed away. It was stupid of me ... I see that now. I'll give you the money back that it cost you. What else can I do? I'm truly sorry!' he repeated, frantically.

'Firstly,' said Kevin, in his usual, calm manner, completely unmoved by Andrew's obvious distress, 'the money is unimportant ... it's less than three hundred pounds. I'll spend more than that on a tie. It's the principle; it's a matter of keeping face. Towing my car away is an inconvenience. Towing my car away in front of a crowd? That's a matter of face. You do see the difference ... don't you, Andrew?'

'What can I do to make it right? You tell me, and I'll do it ... honestly.'

Andrew was afraid. He kept looking at the gun in Craig's hands; surely they weren't going to shoot him?

'You have to be punished, I'm afraid, Andrew. So just take it like a man. You showed some balls yesterday, before you ran. Show some now, and we can all get on with our lives.'

'What are you going to do?' Andrew was shaking uncontrollably, and small beads of perspiration had broken out on his forehead.

'Well, now, Andrew, my brother and I have discussed exactly what your punishment should be, at some length. It's difficult, you see. If, for instance, we say that the most severe punishment is a bullet in the head, and the most lenient is having a finger broken, where should yours come on that scale? And bear in mind the fact that, whatever it is, it has to be visible, so that people know you have been punished. That is ... after all, the whole point.'

Andrew's voice trembled, as he asked, 'What did you decide?'

'Do you remember what I asked you yesterday?'

'Oh my God!' Andrew remembered, all right, 'left or right.'

Andrew was closer to tears than at any time he could remember, since he was a child.

'That's right, Andrew. Did you make a choice?'

'How can I make a choice, when I don't know what I'm choosing?'

He began to cry, but, shocked by the fact, he brought himself under control and started to take deep breaths instead.

Kevin was impressed.

'Well done, Andrew. I told my brother you had bottle. We decided an ear would do it. Nothing too drastic or life-threatening about losing an ear, but it's visible ... and that's what we want to achieve, isn't it?'

'If you do this, I will go to the police, I swear to God, I will.'

Kevin sighed and rolled his eyes, 'You do have balls, Andrew, I'll give you that, but you have to be one of the most stupid men that I have ever come across. Just take your punishment and get on with your life. If you don't, you'll have to be punished yet again, and, next time, we'll cut off something more important than an ear, something you will miss a lot more. Please tell me you understand how this works, Andrew, because, believe me, my brother here wants to do all sorts of nasty things to you.'

Craig looked up from his cleaning and nodded in agreement, smiling.

Andrew sighed, closed his eyes, and shouted, 'Just do it, then,' and gritted his teeth.

'Left or right?'

'Left! Just get on with it.'

He didn't have to wait long, although it felt like a hundred years, and he didn't feel a great deal of pain, either, just a sharp stinging sensation. However, when he opened his eyes, he couldn't believe the amount of blood – it was everywhere.

Kevin had moved out of the way before the deed was done, and, Craig, who had put down his gun and donned a clear plastic apron – the type nurses use, when doing dirty jobs in hospital – actually performed the surgery. Kevin fetched a towel from the bathroom and handed it to Andrew, as Craig cut the cords that were holding him and began cleaning the cut-throat razor that he had used.

Andrew held the towel close to his ear, hoping it was clean and not likely to cause an infection.

As they left, Kevin stopped in the doorway and said to Andrew, 'I hope this is the last time we have reason to meet, for your sake. And, if you want my advice, I would get to Casualty pretty quick – that's going to need stitches.'

It was almost a week later that a still heavily bandaged and emotionally weary Andrew Parks walked into his manager's office and handed in his notice.

Chapter 5

Margaret turned the key to lock the shop door and went through her normal routine of ticking things off in her head – back door locked and bolted, windows closed and locked, filing cabinets locked, lights out, alarm on and, now, front door locked. There was so much of value in Richard's shop; she always took her responsibility of locking up very seriously. It had rained in the night, and the day had started out rather gloomy and overcast, but it had brightened up as the day progressed, and it was now a pleasant evening. So Margaret enjoyed the short walk to the bus stop. The bus was running on time, and, thanks to the bus lane that followed most of her route home, the journey seldom took more than forty-five minutes, even in heavy, rush-hour traffic.

Hopping off the bus, Margaret headed straight for her house, instead of calling in at the fish-and-chip shop, as she usually did on a Friday evening. Her house was only an easy ten minute walk away, and she was anxious to get home and have a shower and change. Paul was taking her out for a meal this evening, and she was eagerly looking forward to it. She walked briskly up Pine Drive, heading for the first corner, Maple Way, and then into her road, Ash Croft. When she turned into Maple Way, she saw two youths with hooded tops skulking about on the pavement, just before the turning into her road. One was leaning back against a wall, and the other was standing on the pavement facing him, apparently in conversation. Margaret felt a little intimidated by the pair and debated as to whether she should cross the road, so as to pass them on the other side, but she decided that she was being silly; just because they were wearing hoods, it didn't mean that they were up to no good.

As she approached the two youths, the one nearest the curb stepped back, as if to make way for her to pass, effectively forcing her to walk between them, which she reluctantly did. Just as she moved past them, she felt a short, sharp tug on the thin strap of her handbag, and, as she turned towards the offending youth, who now had a firm grip on her strap, his accomplice pushed her hard between the shoulder blades, knocking her completely off-balance and causing her to fall forward, heavily. She instinctively put out both of her hands to save herself, letting go of the bag. The youth who had hold of the strap pulled hard as she let go, wrenching it off her arm and causing her to twist and fall slightly sideways. As the Apostles made off with her handbag, Margaret's left knee impacted heavily with the pavement, and she continued to fall, hitting the concrete twice more – once with her shoulder blade and then with the side of her head, creating a crescendo of pain.

She lay stunned and bleeding on the concrete pavement, vaguely aware that a silver car had slowed down to look at her and had then driven away in the same direction that the youths had fled. She sat up, crying; her knee hurt so badly that she was convinced that it was broken, and her shoulder felt as if it was on fire. Her head was positively pounding, and there was blood on her suit top and running down her face.

'Damn them!' she cried.

She'd been looking forward to her evening with Paul, but there was no way that she would be going out now; she felt utterly dreadful. She sat on the pavement, crying, unable to get up.

After a couple of minutes, a car pulled up beside her, and a middle-aged couple got out and ministered to her.

'Are you all right, my dear?' asked the man, looking very concerned.

'What happened? Would you like me to call someone? I have a mobile – my daughter bought it for me,' he said, helpfully, as his wife dabbed at the cut on Margaret's head, with a handkerchief that Margaret prayed was clean.

Instead of waiting for Margaret to reply to his question, the elderly man kindly dialled 999 for an ambulance and gave their location.

'Could you ring the police for me, please?' asked Margaret, 'and get a message to Inspector Paul Manley, telling him what's happened. I haven't got his number, I'm afraid. It was in my bag, and they've taken it.'

The couple – Mr and Mrs Evens – who, it turned out, were neighbours of Margaret, stayed with her until the ambulance arrived and managed to leave the requested message for Paul.

* * * * * * * * * * * *

The morning of June the ninth was bright and sunny. After they had returned, rather late, from their short visit to the city docks and Brunel's ship, Elizabeth and Richard had ordered a take-away Chinese meal, watched a couple of old films that they remembered from their courting days and got ever-so-slightly drunk. So, that morning, Richard had a bit of a lie-in with his wife – something they hadn't done for a long time. Elizabeth didn't have to be at work until midday, so they had a relaxing breakfast in bed, as they listened to the morning news on the radio. Later, after getting up and showering, Richard quickly skipped through the morning paper and *The Antiques Trade Gazette* and still managed to get to the shop by ten-thirty.

But, almost immediately, he registered that something was wrong. The shop was still closed; where was Margaret? He rang her mobile, but there was no reply from this or from her home number, either. Richard was worried. It wasn't like Margaret not to call if there was a problem, and why wasn't she answering her mobile? He was forced to park at the front of the shop, because the flower shop's delivery van was occupying one of his spaces, and there was a silver-grey Mercedes in the other.

Who did that belong to? he wondered.

Just as he got into the shop, his mobile rang. It was Inspector Paul Manley.

'Richard, it's Paul Manley. I'm sorry I haven't rung earlier, but this is the first real opportunity I've had. Margaret's been mugged; she's OK, just cut and bruised where they knocked her to the ground, but, obviously, she's very shaken. I'm at the hospital with her now. She rang me last night from here. It all happened on her way home from work.'

'Hospital?' exclaimed Richard, 'I thought you said she was all right? Tell her, I'm coming down. Which hospital is she at?'

'No, listen, Richard, wait. They kept her in overnight for observation, because she has a nasty bump on her head, but they are going to send her home after the doctor has looked at her today. She's in the Bristol Royal Infirmary, where Liz works. She said to tell you that she's sorry for not calling you last night, but she didn't want to spoil your day with Liz. She says she thinks Liz will be in soon, anyway, as this is her ward. How lucky is that? She'll have her own nurse to look after her.'

'Let me speak to her.'

'I can't, Richard. I had to come out of the hospital to make this call, but, listen to me, this is important...'

Richard wondered what was coming; his concern for Margaret was making him anxious.

'The two youths who mugged her took her handbag with all her cards. I have already cancelled all of them for her, but, more worryingly, the keys to her house, your house and the shop were in her bag. You need to get all your locks changed, as soon as possible, and, I mean now, today, Richard. Her address book was also in there, so, whoever they are, they've got keys and addresses. I'll sort Margaret's locks out and keep you up-to-date. No doubt Liz will ring you when she gets in.'

Richard was still a bit taken aback, and, if he was completely honest with himself, he was a little upset that Margaret had rung Paul, rather than him, and, now, there he was, offering to get her locks sorted for her, as well. No ... Richard suddenly realised that he wasn't so much upset, as jealous. Well, no, not jealous, exactly ... but ... oh, he didn't know what he was, just a bit put-out, he supposed, that Margaret had rung Inspector Manley, instead of him. The important thing was that Margaret wasn't too badly hurt. Now he had to sort things out.

'Listen, Paul,' he said, 'don't worry about Margaret's locks. I'll arrange to have them all changed – hers and mine. I'll get it done through the business. Give Margaret my love, and tell her not to worry about anything, and I'll see her as soon as possible.'

'I will, Richard. Keep in touch, yes?'

'You'd better believe it.'

He said goodbye and hung up, still wrestling with his feelings.

Richard walked over to the two filing cabinets that inhabited the back office – one of which contained all the normal office files associated with running a business, including details of contractors they had used. Amongst these was a security firm that supplied and fitted locks. It was details of this firm – Thornton Security – that he was looking for.

The other filing cabinet was always kept locked, because it contained the personal details of all Richard's clients – the footballers, the actors, the managing directors, the firms – they were all in there. Each file had a name and address, private phone numbers, names of family members and anything else that Richard felt he should know. Sometimes it was months or even years between dealings, and Richard needed to be able to remember family members and the like; his clients needed to believe that Richard was a friend, who took an interest in their lives, and he couldn't remember everything about all of them, so it went on file for when it was needed – hobbies, birthdays, that kind of thing. He stared at it, with a funny feeling building in the pit of his stomach. One drawer was slightly open. Both he and Margaret were meticulous about keeping it locked. He checked its contents quickly, but nothing appeared to be out of place.

Richard sat down to think for a moment. Someone had been in the shop, they must have been; Margaret wouldn't have left the cabinet open like that. He got up again straight away and did a tour of the premises. Nothing appeared to be missing or out of place. When he has established this, he sat down again, his head spinning. It had to be the louts who mugged Margaret – they had used her keys. He had recently installed a burglar alarm, and both he and Margaret were in the habit of keeping the code with them, in case they forgot it, so they must have had that, as well. But it made no sense. Why would they mug somebody, steal their keys, use them to gain access to a shop full of valuable items and, yet, not take anything? The only thing he was sure that they had touched was the filing cabinet, but although it contained details of some rich and influential people, there was nothing of any value to muggers. There was no information that could be used to blackmail anyone, and, although there were addresses, all of these people would have strong security in place – state-of-the-art alarms, the works.

Richard did wonder, briefly, whether he should ring his clients and let them know that his security had been breached, but he wisely decided that it would do more harm than good.

Ignorance would be bliss, from the point of view of his clients, because they would just worry unnecessarily if they knew what had happened. He did, however, think twice about letting Robert Powel know, simply because he had spoken to his wife the other day in California, so he knew they were still out of the country and that their house near Bath was standing empty. But, again, he thought it would do more harm than good. And, anyway, Robert's house was famous for its lavish interiors; it had been featured in several magazines and, consequently, would be more difficult to get into than Fort Knox. So there was no point in ringing anyone, he concluded.

That decided, he picked up the phone and rang Thornton Security. They assured him that they would be at the shop within the hour, and, when it was made secure again, they would follow him, first to Margaret's house and then to his. That done, he rang Paul, to keep him abreast of matters and to get the latest on Margaret.

Margaret was doing all right, considering the horrible ordeal that she had been through, and she *was* on Elizabeth's ward, so she was being well looked after. The doctor, however, had still not been in to give her the all-clear to go home. Elizabeth had asked Paul to pass on the message that she would be too tied-up at work to ring, so she would update him on matters that night and that Margaret had agreed to stay with them to convalesce.

Paul said that as Richard was tied-up with getting new locks fitted, he had arranged for Margaret to call him when she was to be discharged and that he would take her to Richard's home, letting themselves in with Elizabeth's keys. That way, they could pick the new keys up when Richard arrived with the locksmiths, unless, of course, he was already there, and Richard agreed that it sounded like a good plan.

'Are you one hundred percent sure that they haven't taken anything from the shop?' Paul continued.

'As sure as I can be, without doing a full inventory. There's certainly nothing missing that I can see, but it does look as if someone has been through my files – a drawer that is always kept locked was open this morning. Do you want to come and look for fingerprints or anything?'

Paul explained, 'I don't think there's any point, Richard. Anybody that would gain access to an antique shop and not steal anything obviously had a purpose and would, therefore, be organised enough to wear gloves. In any case, as far as my superiors are concerned, it was just a mugging, so they are unlikely to sanction the expense of a fingerprint search, when the drawer could just simply have been left open. This whole thing is bizarre, though, Richard. When you get to Margaret's, check to see if there are any signs of them having been in there, and check your place thoroughly. We'll talk when I get there with Margaret.'

The men from Thornton Security arrived at eleven-thirty in a large brown van that was a sort of mini-warehouse for locks. They had locks to fit everything, it seemed to Richard, and so he also got them to change the locks on the disturbed filing cabinets. The older of the two appeared to be in his forties, with glasses and a small beard. They both wore a uniform consisting of brown work trousers and a lighter brown short-sleeved shirt, with 'Thornton Security' emblazoned across the shoulders. Somehow, the younger one – who Richard took to be nineteen or twenty and who sported a beard and a pony tail – still managed to look like a member of a rock band, despite the uniform.

They were quick and efficient and had soon replaced all the locks, including some window locks, for which Margaret had no keys.

This accomplished, the locksmiths followed Richard to Margaret's house. It took them no more than a couple of minutes to drill out the lock in her front door and gain access to the property. Richard had often said to her that someone should hold a spare set of keys to her place, in case she lost hers, and Margaret had agreed with him, but had never got around to having any cut.

While the men from Thornton Security went about their work, Richard did a tour of Margaret's house. He had only been inside a couple of times in the past and had never been upstairs, so he felt a little as if he was intruding, but he did it to make sure there was no damage or anything unpleasant that he wouldn't want Margaret to discover on her return. Everything looked fine, as far as he could tell – at least, there were no nasty surprises lurking – so he re-joined the locksmiths downstairs. There was a deadlock on the back door, as well as the front, so that had to be drilled out, as well, but all the locks were soon replaced, and they arrived at Richard's, in less than ninety minutes.

Richard did a complete tour of the house, while they worked on his locks and, as had been the case at Margaret's, could find no trace of anything untoward. When the men had finished, Richard thanked them for their professionalism, wrote them a cheque to cover the bill, gave them a ten pound tip, for which they were suitably grateful, and bade them farewell.

He poured himself a whiskey, sat down facing the sofa-table that had briefly been home to 'Tex' and awaited the arrival of Paul and Margaret. Elizabeth still hadn't put anything back onto the sofa-table, and he found himself staring vacantly at it, as he sat thinking over the strange events of the last few hours and days. He wondered whether there could be any connection between being taken in by the police for questioning about the bronze, Margaret's mugging and the strange non-burglary of his shop. However, apart from the obvious connection between the mugging and the invasion of the shop, he could not think of anything that would tie-in his being questioned by the police and the mugging. But with both events being so out-of-the-ordinary and happening so close together, he, nevertheless, felt, in his bones, that there had to be a common denominator – there had to be something that linked the mysterious events.

He was still pondering these things an hour later, when the doorbell rang, and he heard someone trying a key in the door. He got up from his seat to answer the door and found that it was, as expected, Paul and Margaret, but their mood and demeanour was not what Richard had expected. Paul looked very concerned, and he had his arm around Margaret's shoulders, trying, in vain, to prevent the terrible shaking that racked her frame.

My God! thought Richard, what is the doctor thinking of sending her home in that condition? It was a very anxious Richard that led them into the lounge, sat them on one of the sofas and mixed them both stiff drinks.

He was just about to ask if he should ring the hospital, when he caught sight of the handbag that Paul was holding out to him, dangling from one finger.

'Don't touch it more than you have to, Richard. Can you put it in a plastic carrier bag or something for safe-keeping?' instructed Paul, reluctantly leaving Margaret's side.

Richard instinctively knew the answer to his question, but asked it anyway, 'What is it?'

'It's Margaret's handbag – the one the muggers took. It was on your doorstep. I've checked inside it, and everything is still there – credit cards, cash, her address book and all the keys.'

'I don't understand,' said Richard, carefully substituting his finger for Paul's under the strap of the bag.

'Join the club, Richard, neither do I. How long ago did the locksmiths leave?'

'About an hour or so, I think ... why?'

'Somebody must have placed it outside your door between the time that they left and we turned up, which means that either they were lucky with their timing or they were watching the house.'

'Why would they do that?'

'You keep coming up with questions that I don't know the answers to, Richard.'

Richard did as requested and put Margaret's bag into a plastic carrier bag from the local supermarket, leaving it on the worktop in the kitchen. He noticed his hand was shaking as he did so and realised how much worse Margaret must be feeling.

Re-joining the other two in the lounge, he asked, 'What does it all mean, Paul?'

'There you go again. I really don't know, Richard, it's a mystery to me ... Look, I hate to leave Margaret on her own at the moment, so can she stay with you? I need to get back to the nick and see if I can make sense of all this. Is that OK?'

'Yes, of course. I think she's staying the night with us, anyway, aren't you, Margaret?'

Then, to Paul, he said, 'The bag's on the worktop in the kitchen.'

Paul retrieved the bag, then walked over to the sofa and gave Margaret a kiss goodbye.

'Look after her for me, Richard, and I'll let you know if I figure any of this out.'

Then, to Margaret, he said, as cheerfully as he could, 'I'll ring you tonight, and we'll fix up another date.' Then he headed off to the police station, deep in thought.

Richard felt the resentment rising inside him again. 'He's asking me to look after her,' he fumed, 'what does he think I've *been* doing?'

He acknowledged to himself that, although he liked Paul, he felt that he was, in some way, usurping his position with Margaret. What on earth would his feelings be like when Rebecca finally found the love of her life? He mixed Margaret another drink, and this one she took upstairs with her, so that she could have a lie down in the spare bedroom. She was still trembling a little and was incredibly grateful that she wasn't on her own.

Paul handed the supermarket carrier with the handbag inside to Constable Kelly to be checked for prints and explained the circumstances of its recovery to the team, which now had two more additions – Detective Constables' Clive Pascoe and John Campbell, both experienced police officers, although John had only been in plain clothes for a couple of months. Paul formally welcomed them to the team and made sure that they had been properly introduced to everyone.

Sergeant Reginald Evans put down the phone he'd been holding and asked for everyone's attention. He stood before one of the notice boards and pointed to the rather ugly face that someone had drawn to represent Simon White.

'Simon White has spent some time with the composite artist, and we now have an idea of what the two men look like, who sold him the bronze and who are, of course, our prime suspects in the murder of Mrs Gladys Harper.'

Paul had been about to ask if there was anything new from the rest of the team, but the Sergeant continued.

'We have also received complaints from some local home owners, who have discovered items missing, after having two antique dealers call around. Now, we have checked the various descriptions of the antique dealers with the composite picture sketched from Simon White's description, and they appear to be very similar.'

'Thanks, Reg, that's good work,' said Paul, who was very pleased with the turn of events. 'So we will work on the assumption that Mrs Harper may also have been visited by these two dealers and that something went wrong, resulting in a fatal struggle.'

'That's right, but there's more, Guv,' Reg interrupted, and, once again, he had everyone's attention. 'One of the individuals who have complained about the dealers happened to notice that they were driving a Ford Mondeo Estate ... black or dark blue ... with a large, flat roof rack.'

'Well, that's excellent news!' exclaimed Paul, 'Life just keeps getting better and better. If you were good-looking, Reg ... I'd give you a kiss.'

The team laughed at Paul's remark, and June elicited more, by saying, 'Wow, Guv, I know people who'd pay good money to see that.'

'Well, they can keep their money, June, it's not going to happen, is it? Because, as everyone can all see ... Reg is as ugly as sin.'

Even more laughter ensued after that remark, but Paul raised his arms to quieten them all down and shouted, 'Listen up, everyone. Quiet! I know it's a long shot, but get someone to check all the filling stations on the roads leading to Mrs Harper's from Bristol and all the ones from Mrs Harper's to Bath, check their CCTV cameras for the day of the murder and see if any black or dark blue Mondeo Estates with roof racks called in for fuel. Perhaps we can get a number plate. We deserve some luck.'

'I'll get someone on it straight away, Guv,' said Reg, 'let's hope they were low on fuel.'

June shouted from across the room, 'I'll do it, Reg! And I wouldn't say you were as ugly as sin.'

'Thanks, June,' replied Reg, with a grin that soon disappeared.

'Ugly? Yes. But not as sin.'

Clive, one of the new boys on the team, spoke up, 'There's news about the bronze, as well, Guv. They've managed to lift some recent prints off it that don't belong to Mrs Harper, Richard Drake or Simon White.'

'Wow, what idiots,' said Paul, smiling, 'you mean to tell me that they spent time wiping their grubby little fingerprints off everything in the house, but didn't wipe the bits they took and sold.'

'Looks that way, Guv.'

'We need to get these guys off the streets for their own good, before they hurt themselves.'

'They were probably quite shaken up, Guv,' said June, 'and got careless, having just killed the old girl.'

The team was still laughing at Reg's expense, but it was all friendly, and Reg was smiling with them. Paul was pleased; it was a sign that they were not only gelling as a team, but also accepting his leadership, even though he was actually younger than some of them. He looked around the incident room and noted, happily, that everyone was not just busy, but talking and working together, as if the team had been together for years. They seemed a good bunch.

Constable Kelly popped her head around the door to Paul's office.

'DCI wants to see you, Guv.'

Paul groaned, 'Why now? We've been keeping him updated.'

June just shrugged her shoulders and slipped away.

Paul knocked on the door of Detective Chief Inspector Blake's office, straightened his tie and shined each of his shoes on the back of his trouser legs.

'Come in.'

Paul opened the door and entered his DCI's office, marvelling, as he often did, at the array of trophies and awards adorning the walls. Looking at the man now sitting behind his desk, it was difficult to believe that the white hair and lined face belonged to the same man who had won them all. There were awards and medals for running, cycling and fencing. Paul hoped that the line of work they were both in wasn't the reason his DCI was clearly ageing so badly.

'What's the latest, Paul?' The DCI asked, looking up from the pile of paperwork in front of him.

Paul was thankful he had a good team and that timing was on his side. An hour ago, he would have had precious little to say, but now, he had plenty to report.

'As you know, sir, after eliminating our first suspect very quickly, we concentrated on the identity of the two men who sold Mrs Harper's bronze to *Bath Antiques*. We have now established that the descriptions of these men closely match the descriptions of two antique dealers, who are suspected of stealing from other homes in the area. At the moment, we are checking to see if any garages in the area have a car on CCTV that matches the one the men were known to be driving. In addition to this, we have lifted prints from the bronze statue, and Clive is currently checking them to see if there is a match on the system.'

'Well, you certainly seem to be on top of things, Paul. I'm very pleased, especially pleased that this Margaret Collins doesn't seem to be involved in any way.'

'No, sir.' Paul's brow furrowed.

Who the hell had been wagging their tongue to the Chief about that? Margaret had never even been interviewed, so what business was it of anyone's that he was seeing her? In fact, he didn't think anyone on the team was aware of his interest in Margaret, so what the hell was going on? He was furious.

'Will that be all, sir?'

'Yes, that's it, Paul. Good work, so far. Keep it up, and keep me informed; let me know the minute you're close to an arrest.'

'Will do, sir.'

Paul left the office, pleased that he had something positive to report, but mad as hell that someone had been blabbing about Margaret and him and puzzled as to who it could be.

He returned to the incident room to find everyone listening intently to a uniformed constable that he didn't recognise. Reg saw him enter the room and immediately called him over.

'You need to hear this, Guv. You're not going to believe it. I'll let Constable Edwards, here, give you the news.'

Constable Edwards explained that he was one of the first officers to arrive at Mrs Harper's when the gardener had rung, and he also briefly explained that he was an experienced dog handler.

'Well, after I left the scene that night, I discovered that I had lost the gold lighter my wife had bought me for our anniversary, and I knew I had it with me at the house.' He continued, carefully, 'So I went back to the house earlier today. It's my day off, you see – the first chance I've had to see if I happened to drop it when I was searching the back garden. As it's my day off, I decided to do it at the same time that I took my dog, Chewbacca, for his walk. Well, I parked the car at the top of the drive and let the dog off the lead to have a sniff round the garden to see if he could pick up on the lighter. I knew it was a long shot, but Chewbacca is a very good search dog, the best I've had. After a few minutes, Chewbacca was going bananas in the rose beds, and I thought he had found the lighter, but, by the time I got there, he had dug up some bones.

Now, I'm not an expert, but they looked like human bones to me, and I've seen a few. So here I am.'

Paul and the rest of the team had listened intently to the constable's story, and Paul was dumbfounded.

'What? Why didn't you call it in? Don't tell me you've just left the place unattended?'

'Oh, no, sir. I called the on-duty bobby, Mike Walker. He's at the scene looking after things. But I wanted to explain in person, you know, how I came to be there and found them.'

Paul scratched his head in disbelief.

'How sure are you that they are human remains? Say, on a scale of one to ten?'

'Nine point nine, sir, unless they're gorilla bones or something, but Chewbacca and I have found human remains before, sir – we know them when we see them. Sir?'

Paul was deep in thought for a moment, and then he turned to his sergeant.

'Reg, you arrange for SOCO to get down there? And it's probably best to go yourself, as well. You know what to do at the scene. Oh, and take Clive with you. I'll be down as soon as I've broken the good news to Blakey.'

He then turned to Constable Edwards.

'These bones had better be human, constable, or I'm going to bury you in the garden for your dog to find! You got that?'

'I've got the gist of it, sir. Do you want me there, sir?'

'Oh, yes, Constable, I want you there all right. I don't care if it is your bloody day off. If these turn out to be animal bones, then you can explain to the DCI why SOCO was called out, and then I'll dig another hole and put you in the ground. Have you got the gist of that, Constable?'

'I have, sir,' said Constable Edwards, who was quietly relieved. He thought it could have gone a lot worse.

Paul made his way along the corridor to the DCI's office, once again, knocked on the door, entered and, after heaving a big sigh, said, 'Have you got a minute, sir? There's been a development in the case.'

When Paul arrived back at Hilltop Cottage, SOCO were also just arriving, so he parked on the road, next to his sergeant's car. He briefly explained the situation to the head of the SOCO team, Mark Lovejoy, who Paul had met the other night. He accompanied him into the back garden, where Constable Mike Walker was standing beside what remained of the rose beds and was casually chatting to Reg. Mark Lovejoy confirmed very quickly that the bones were, indeed, human and appeared to belong to a juvenile male, probably between the ages of twelve and twenty. Paul stayed at the scene for another hour, but gleaned little more information, other than that the body had been in the ground longer than the roses, which he thought he could have probably worked out for himself, but he tactfully made no such comment.

At this point in the proceedings, he turned to Reg and said 'Carry on and look after things here, will you, Reg?'

'Sure thing, Guv. Where will you be?'

'Well ... after I've told Blakey that we definitely have another body at Hilltop Cottage, I think I need to find a dark room to sit in, so that I can try and get my head around what's happening and what to do next. In other words, Reg, I'll see you in the morning.'

'OK, Guv, give Margaret my love.'

'What?' Paul snapped, 'who the hell told you about Margaret? And who else knows?'

'Can't remember who told me, Guv, but everyone knows.'

'You mean, everyone in the team?'

'No, Guv ... I mean, everyone in the nick.'

'Oh, shit!'

After work, Paul called in to collect Margaret from the Drake's and take her home, if she felt up to it. Both Elizabeth and Rebecca – who had asked her to stay with them –repeated their offer for her to stay overnight, but Margaret was feeling more herself now and was anxious for things to return to normal. She insisted that Paul take her home.

Before they left, Richard asked how things were going with the case, and Paul told him about the discovery of the body in the garden, but that he was not to mention it to a living soul on pain of death; life was complicated enough as it was. Richard appreciated the confidence. If nothing else, it showed that Paul no longer had any doubts about him having any involvement in the theft of the bronze.

Rebecca, who had insisted on hearing every gory detail about the body being found, now said, 'Tea before you go, you two. I need to speak to Paul about another case I'm working on.'

Margaret and Paul frowned, and Paul said, 'What's this? Have you set yourself up as a private investigator or something?'

'Something like that.'

'What's the case?'

Elizabeth made coffee for Paul and tea for everyone else, while Rebecca told Paul about the shortfall in her till, the other night.

'I need a Sherlock Holmes,' she said.

Margaret found the situation rather amusing and said, with a smile, 'I don't understand, Becky. If you need a Sherlock Holmes, why do you want to speak to Paul? Or do you think he might know of one?'

Paul put on a hurt expression and clutched at his chest as if he'd been shot in the heart, causing everyone to laugh, and Elizabeth to reflect upon the fact that everyone seemed to be laughing a lot more since Paul had come on the scene or, at least, Margaret and Rebecca did. She wasn't sure how her husband felt about Paul's arrival. They got on well enough, she would even say that they seemed to like each other, but, sometimes, she felt that Richard resented Paul's influence over Margaret. But, as far as she was concerned, he was a welcome addition to their circle of friends.

Paul listened with some interest, as Rebecca explained about her till being down, and he insisted that she describe, in detail, everything that had happened that night. He seemed particularly interested in her encounter with the magician at the bar.

Paul sat back in the chair, drew on an imaginary pipe in his best Sherlock Holmes pose and asked, 'Tell me, was his assistant there at the time?'

'On and off,' replied Rebecca. 'She put in an appearance halfway through and then wandered off somewhere. I think they might be a couple, even though they have separate rooms.'

'And I think you're a gossip, Rebecca Drake,' said Margaret.

Paul asked, 'Was anyone else working behind the bar with you?'

'Yes, Tom was there. I'm training him up to take over as the bar manager, but he wouldn't have done anything like this.'

'Maybe not, Watson,' said Paul, pulling on his imaginary pipe again, 'but we have to bear everything in mind. This could well be a two-pipe problem. How much were you down? Did you say forty-eight pounds and ten pence?'

'That's right.'

'That's a difference of one pound and ninety pence between the shortfall in the till and the fifty pound note you borrowed for the magic trick.'

'So? I mean ... what's the significance of that, Mr Holmes?'

'Well, let's see ... what do you sell that costs one pound ninety?'

Rebecca thought for a moment and then announced, 'We sell a bottled fruit juice for one ninety. Why?'

'Well, that's it, then ... case solved.'

Everybody looked at Paul, expectantly.

'Well, that's it, then ... what?' asked Rebecca, clearly flummoxed.

'That's how they did it. Elementary, my dear Watson.'

'I'm going to thump you in a minute if you don't explain it right now,' joined in Margaret, who was intrigued with the way the conversation was going.

Paul began, 'Look ... you took a note out of the till and signed it, so that you could identify it again as the same note, right?'

'Right.'

'But this Carl never actually wrapped it in tissue paper or put it in a box. He palmed the note and kept it in his hand, just pretending to wrap it up and box it. All that went into the box was the tissue paper.'

'Oh, brilliant, Holmes! Even I could have managed to work that bit out,' sighed an increasingly frustrated Rebecca, 'but how on earth did he get it back in the till? Tell me that. I was watching him all the time.'

'Oh, come on, Watson, think. How does any money go in the till? When his assistant was standing beside him, he must have slipped the note to her without you seeing.'

Rebecca was now quite worked up, and, although nobody else had worked it out yet, they were all enjoying Paul stringing her along.

'Well, how did *she* get it back into the till, then?'

Paul stayed silent for a moment to build up the tension and then announced, calmly, 'She took it to whoever else was serving and bought a one pound ninety bottle of fruit juice with it.'

There was stunned silence from everyone for a moment, as they absorbed the significance of what Paul had said.

'That way,' Paul continued, 'the note went back in the till, and the assistant walked off with forty eight pounds and ten pence in change, from a fifty pound note that was already in the till and accounted for.'

'The bastards!' screamed Rebecca.

'Language, Rebecca,' cried her mother, laughing at her daughter's outrage, in spite of sympathising with her plight.

'If I ever see them again, I'll kill them. They've cost me nearly fifty quid.'

Rebecca stood and paced up and down the room furiously, feeling like she had been taken for a fool and made to look silly.

Paul tried to calm her down, saying, 'Look, if you can find out where they're working now, I'll come along with a constable on their last night and try to catch them at it; I'm sure they must pull the scam everywhere they work.'

'I'll hold you to that,' said Rebecca, 'and I certainly will find them, even if they are working on the other side of the country ... the other side of the world, even.'

When Rebecca had finally calmed down, they all said their goodnights, and Paul escorted Margaret to his car.

'Don't do anything I wouldn't do,' Rebecca called after them.

The evening sun was low in the sky, and Paul put his sunglasses on as he drove.

'Is that your undercover look?' asked Margaret, but Paul just smiled.

When he drew up outside Margaret's house, he leaned over to kiss her goodnight, but Margaret put her hand to his lips and said, 'You're welcome to come up for a coffee, if you can stand to look at a woman with a bruised face any longer.'

'I would not only love to come up for a coffee, but I am quite willing to look at any bruises that you would care to show me,' he said, smiling.

'Well, you'd better come up, then. I have one or two in some quite interesting places. Unfortunately, they are quite painful, so you will have to be very careful.'

'Careful is my middle name,' said Paul, climbing out of the car.

The following day, Paul was sitting on the corner of one of the incident room tables, chatting to Derrick Jacobs about the mugging of Margaret and the fact that, although they were sure that the muggers had been into Richard's shop, nothing was taken.

Derrick voiced what Paul had previously keenly felt, asking if there could be a connection with the murder of Mrs Harper. It seemed that Richard was a link, in some way, between the two cases. First, there was his involvement with the bronze and then his shop being entered.

Paul said, 'I'm worried that the Harper brothers might be thinking that Richard is involved in their mum's murder, but I don't know how they would even know of his existence, let alone his connection to the bronze.'

He cast his mind back and remembered how puzzled he'd been by Kevin's reaction to his assertion that the bronze would be in their hands before the end of the day. Derrick had replied that people like the Harpers were privy to all sorts of information, from all kinds of random sources. He hadn't actually mentioned police sources, but Paul had caught his drift.

Just then, Reg came into the room, looking very pleased with himself again.

'I think we've got the bastards, Guv,' he said, excitedly, striding across the room.

Everyone stopped what they were doing and looked over at Reg.

'Well, you'd better fill us all in, Reg,' said Paul, anxious for news.

Reg walked over to the largest of the three notice boards that the team had been using and faced the room. Everybody gathered round and waited expectantly to hear what he had to say.

'As you know,' he began, 'the descriptions from one of our complainants and the description from Simon White were very close, and our quick-thinking Governor, here,' Reg nodded in Paul's direction, 'sent us to get CCTV coverage of cars matching the description of the assailants – a black or blue Mondeo.'

'Blimey, talk about sucking up to the boss,' Derrick said, and there was a general chorus of 'get on with it, Reg', followed by laughter from the back of the room.

Paul put his hands in the air, gesturing for silence, and told everyone to shut up and listen, but added, 'Get on with it, Reg,' which did little to hush the laughter.

Reg ignored the laughter and continued, 'Well ... we have footage of a black Mondeo Estate car, with a large roof-rack on CCTV, filling up with fuel. We made out the plate, and we came up with the owner's name, Jack Simmons, who lists his occupation as 'Antique Dealer'. Now, this Jack Simmons is known to work, on a regular basis, with one Alan Salter, who matches the description of the second man and is also an 'Antique Dealer'. But the very best news is ... their fingerprints are on file ... and they match the ones we lifted from the bronze.'

There was a smattering of applause and a cry of 'Way to go, Reg,' from somewhere in the room.

Paul quietened everyone down again and heartily congratulated Reg and the team on their fine efforts, however, he pointed out that, 'Now we know who the murderers are, or at least have good evidence incriminating our two prime suspects, the next job is to make it stick in court.'

Somebody from the team had immediately headed towards the DCI's office to let him know the good news, and he now stood in the doorway.

'Congratulations, everyone,' he announced, strolling over to centre stage, 'but Paul is absolutely right – let's make sure we've got all of our evidence together, dot the i's and cross the t's. We don't want it to slip away from us in court. We owe it to Mrs Harper, despite her sons, and, once we have these two in custody, the drinks are on me.'

Paul sat down in a chair with his feet hoisted up onto the table, with, what seemed to June Kelly, a rather satisfied-looking expression on his face.

The DCI walked over to him and shook his hand, as he struggled to get up, saying, 'Well done, Paul. Let's make sure we wrap this up properly. No mistakes now. It's a bloody good result and a good call getting the CCTV footage. I'm very pleased. Remind me what evidence we've got, besides the fingerprints and descriptions.'

'One of them has scratches on his face, so we should get a DNA match with the skin found under the victim's nails. I don't see how it can be anything other than air-tight.'

'I knew you could do it.'

'Thank you, sir. I'm glad I didn't let you down, but it's the team who deserve the credit.'

'You were never going to let me down, Paul, and, I agree, they do seem like a good team. Now, come into my office for a moment. I'd like you to tell me what's going on with this second body at Hilltop. Are there any developments?'

Paul followed his DCI to his office and took the seat that was offered.

'I've not had the PM report yet, sir, but it appears to be the body of a young male, possibly twelve to fifteen years of age, and the body has been in the ground for some time. I'm hoping the PM will come up with enough to check against missing persons.'

'OK, for the moment, at least, you stay on it, and let me know the moment you arrest our antique dealer friends. Do you think there is any connection between the two cases? It's a pretty weird coincidence.'

'I agree that it's weird, but there's no connection between Mrs Harper's death and our body in the garden. There's too big of a time gap, and we think Mrs Harper's death was accidental. But if you were to ask me if is there any connection between the body in the garden and our loveable twins? That's another question.'

'OK, well, I'll leave you to get on with it, Paul, but keep me in the loop on both cases, yeah? From what I hear about the Harper twins, it would be quite a feather in our cap if we could get them for something, especially murder.'

'As always, sir.'

Paul got up and left the office, wondering how on earth they were going to nail the Harpers for the murder of a yet-to-be-identified body, just because it was found at the house where they had lived as children. He was also wondering how many rounds of drinks he was going to have to buy at the pub when they made the arrests of Jack Simmons and Alan Salter.

Chapter 6

Sometimes, criminals who are well connected in the underworld and have been 'in business' long enough to build up a network of informants – often in the police force itself – are in a better position to make enquiries about who perpetrated a particular crime than the law enforcement agencies set up for precisely that purpose.

Kevin and Craig Harper were just such criminals. They swiftly contacted associates who dealt in stolen antiques and works of art. These associates then made enquiries on the twins' behalf. Information was also gleaned from certain police officers, who were finding it difficult to pay off various debts. The combined enquiries had led to the twins being informed that the police were interested in two dealers from Newcastle, who were working the area at the time of their mum's death and who had returned to Newcastle unexpectedly. More enquiries had been discreetly made on the brothers' behalf, and, although there were no details, it seemed that something unpleasant had occurred that had led to the dealers' premature homecoming.

Kevin and Craig, who, despite having never ventured further north than Birmingham, were well-known and respected, even in the Northern provinces. Thus, they called in a few favours, some of which weren't even owed. It was seldom worth arguing with the Harper brothers; they may not have been further north than Birmingham, but their reputation and influence certainly had.

One of the favours involved people who owned property in the north, but who often did business in London. These people operated freely in London, only because they had the tacit agreement of Kevin and Craig to do so and cut them a slice of any takings. The arrangement would have operated the other way around, if the twins had ever wanted to operate up north. They agreed to invite the said dealers to a meeting with Kevin and Craig at private premises, where issues surrounding their mother's death and the theft of property could be discussed in some detail.

In short, it had not taken the brothers long to establish that Richard Drake's involvement in the death of their mother was limited to possibly trying to fence 'The Night Watchman', but, for that alone, they had decided that Richard deserved to meet a sticky end, that, and the fact that they simply enjoyed hurting people. It was almost like a hobby to them, well, it certainly was to Craig, and it had earned them respect in the circles in which they operated or, if not respect, at least fear, and that was sometimes even more useful. Everybody knew not to mess with the Harper twins, even the hardened criminals that they mixed with were a little frightened of them, and if Kevin or Craig Harper asked you for something, you made damn sure you got it for them or you could find yourself taking an early bath, so to speak.

The twins decided to have a couple of days in Newcastle and attend the meeting in person, so they could mix family business with pleasure, for a change. The business with Richard Drake could wait a while. After all, they had already started the ball rolling by getting The Apostles to steal his assistant's handbag and keys. This had enabled them to find out a lot of useful information about Richard's friends, colleagues and clients, and returning the bag untouched must have given him plenty of pause for thought. The idea had been Kevin's. He liked to play psychological games with people. It had been brilliant the way that the inspector had turned up just at the right time to find the bag, especially as he had his new girlfriend with him to identify it – they couldn't have planned it any better. After they concluded their business in Newcastle, they could re-establish dealings with Richard. After all, there was no hurry, and, as yet, they hadn't decided exactly what his fate was going to be, other than that it would be extremely final.

When the brothers arrived in Newcastle, they drove straight to the *Holiday Inn*, where two rooms had been pre-booked for them, under the names Jones and Smith. The hotel receptionist who greeted them had taken the booking, and she had wondered then whether that was, in fact, their real names. But it was none of her business, and Smith and Jones were common enough names. Now they had actually turned up, one look at them was enough to tell her that a casual joke about their names would be extremely unwise. They looked very smart and presentable, even handsome, but had an aura about them that screamed, 'Caution! Handle with care.'

They had arrived late in the afternoon, so they showered and changed after their long journey and had an early dinner in the hotel restaurant, which turned out to be surprisingly good. Kevin and Craig were used to fine dining and had not been optimistic about what to expect, but after the meal, they sent their compliments to the chief and left a fifty pound tip for the rather plain-looking, but very attentive, waitress. After dinner, they called the people who were setting up their meeting for them. They wanted not just details of the venue, but the specific location of somewhere they could dispose of unwanted rubbish afterwards – probably two sacks of unwanted rubbish, they estimated – somewhere where it wouldn't surface for a very long time. Kevin and Craig were satisfied with the arrangements that had been made and so contributed handsomely to a local charity, by way of a 'thank-you'. Their friends were big supporters of charities; it was good for their image.

The day after Kevin and his brother arrived in Newcastle, Jack Simmons rung a couple of mates and arranged a rare round of golf. He enjoyed the game immensely, but not having the time to play that often, he still had a handicap of twenty-two – something he was determined to improve on. He pulled into the golf club car park, skidding slightly on the recently laid gravel and parking opposite the clubhouse.

He was just preparing to get his bag of under-used clubs out of the boot, when a black BMW with darkened windows pulled in alongside him. Jack, at first, assumed that this was simply more people arriving to play, but was quickly forced to reassess the situation. Two men in sharp business suits got out, and one held the back door of the BMW open, while the other approached Jack and told him that someone wanted to meet him, ushering him towards the car. It suddenly felt, to Jack, as if the air temperature in the car park had dropped by at least five degrees. He didn't understand what was happening and was about to refuse to get in, when the man ushering him towards the car discreetly opened his coat revealing the gun he was carrying underneath. Jack realised that he had no choice, other than to comply or to be shot where he stood. The man in front of him certainly didn't look as if he was making an idle threat.

As he slid into the back seat of the BMW, the armed man got in beside him, and his partner got in the other side, sandwiching Jack between the two of them. He could smell their aftershave and was convinced they both used the identical brand. The perfume was strong in the back of the car, and Jack thought it strangely feminine for armed men. The driver in front appeared to be dressed in a similar way, and, Jack thought that if they had been wearing sunglasses, they could easily have been mistaken for the Blues Brothers.

Despite the amusing appearance of the men and their shared taste in aftershave, Jack was undoubtedly scared. He had no idea who they were or what they wanted, but the fact that at least one was armed told him that the situation, whatever it was, was certainly no joke.

'What's this all about? Where are you taking me?' Jack asked, with a note of panic in his voice.

There was no reply to his question nor was there even an acknowledgment that he'd asked one. They drove for over an hour in total silence. Eventually, they pulled into the grounds of a remote farm, with a large house and several barns. When the car door was opened, Jack had expected the smell of manure and animals, but was, instead, greeted with the aroma of fresh-cut grass from an expanse of lawn at the front of the house and baking wafting from within. He was dragged out of the car and marched over to a small barn that looked, from the outside, as if it had been converted into some kind of studio or workshop. Unlike a working farm, the area was covered in smooth, clean tarmac, and there wasn't a trace of mud to be seen. The door to the barn was opened, and Jack was ushered through at gunpoint. He looked back at the main house, wondering who lived there, what they wanted from him, and why he was being taken into the converted barn, rather than the house itself.

At this point, Jack was oblivious to the fact that his associate and partner, Alan Salter, was already present; having had a knock on the front door of the semi-detached that he shared with next door's cats, at eight thirty that morning. Alan had been living in his house for nearly five years, and the previous owners had kept cats. He had never bothered to have the cat-flap sealed up, and it had only been a matter of weeks before next door's two Siamese had begun treating his house as a sort of cats' holiday home. The lounge had become their playroom, and, most nights, they slept at the foot of Alan's bed. Alan had no objection to the arrangement, as he had always been a cat lover, and, indeed, cats seemed to naturally take to him, seeking him out. This way, he had all the benefits of owning cats, with none of the vet's bills or other expenses, and he didn't have to arrange for anyone to look after them when he went on his business trips. For him, then, it was the perfect arrangement.

That morning, Alan had planned to look around the dealers for a new car. The Mondeo that was registered in Jack's name was still going well, but it had a great deal of mileage on the clock, and, after the recent unpleasantness, he felt it would be prudent to change it. Jack and Alan both had their own cars for everyday use, and they kept the Mondeo Estate for business only, although he knew that Jack was in the habit of using it privately, on occasion.

Alan had always been an early riser, and the knock on the door had interrupted his breakfast of toast and marmalade, so he was somewhat irked when he opened it and found himself shoved roughly backwards by a man in a business suit, who closed the door behind them with his foot. Alan was about to give the intruder a bloody good hiding, when the man raised the gun he had been holding and pointed it at Alan's head.

The first man was now joined by a second, who had somehow gained access through the back entrance. He explained to Alan, at gunpoint, that he was to accompany them to a waiting car at the rear of the house. Alan's pleas for information about why and where he was being taken fell on deaf ears, and he was forced to endure a journey very similar to Jack's – sandwiched between two men in the back of a BMW in complete silence, as a third drove them to their destination.

Once inside the converted barn, Jack's fear level rose dramatically, as, bound, naked, hand-and-foot to a chair in the middle of the room was Alan Salter, looking, if such a thing were possible, even more frightened than Jack felt.

The barn had been converted into some kind of office space, the purpose of which was unclear. The walls had been lined and painted and a suspended ceiling had been fitted, making the whole thing look like a huge, fixtureless office. There were heavy blinds on the windows, and these had been closed, cutting the room off from the outside world and necessitating the need for overhead lights to be switched on, giving the room a slightly eerie atmosphere.

There was another chair, positioned next to Alan's, and Jack was made to strip naked at gunpoint and was then tightly tied into it.

'What's this all about? What do you want from us?' screamed Jack, trembling, partly from being naked, but mostly from sheer terror.

'It's no good trying to get them to speak,' said Alan, 'I've been here a good couple of hours, and they won't say a bloody thing, other than somebody wants to meet us.'

'Who? Who wants to meet us?'

'I don't know! I don't know any more than you, but the signs don't look very bloody good, do they? I don't suppose they're friends.'

Both men sat in silence, cold and very scared. Occasionally, they looked at each other, for some kind of comfort that never came. Sometimes, they looked around the room, as if this would supply some sort of explanation of their plight, but, mostly, they just stared at their feet in fear, their thoughts running wild.

After half an hour, with still not a word spoken by the men in suits, two other men arrived. Neither Jack nor Alan could hear any exchange between the new arrivals and their abductors, but there was much whispering, shaking of hands and slapping of backs going on.

After a few minutes of this mutual back-slapping, the men in suits left the room, and their cars could be heard driving away.

The two new arrivals, who were dressed casually in slacks and open-necked shirts, brought up chairs and sat facing Alan and Jack in a casual and relaxed manner. It was an absolute contrast to the strict, threatening style of the men in suits, who had just left. These new arrivals didn't look hostile in any way, and it didn't look as if they were even armed, but neither Alan nor Jack felt that they could take any comfort from that fact. Indeed, in some strange way, it made the whole situation feel even more ominous.

Jack spoke first. 'Look, is someone going to tell us what this is all ...?'

He was unable to finish his sentence.

One of the new arrivals got out of his chair and slapped Jack so hard across the face that both he and his chair fell sideways onto the floor with a loud crash that echoed though the largely empty room. Both Jack and Alan were taken by surprise at the sudden and unexpected act of violence. Being slapped by a man was a new experience for Jack, and it was one that he didn't want repeated – it was a bit like being kicked by a mule.

'Only speak to answer a question,' the man said, tonelessly.

His companion got up and helped the first man to lift both Jack and his chair into an upright position again.

Then both men returned to their former, casual and relaxed positions sitting in the chairs, as if nothing had happened.

'Now listen carefully, both of you.'

The man's voice was quiet and almost soothing. 'My brother and I are going to ask you some questions. They're easy questions, to which you will know the answers, so there should be no need for any conferring between you. This is an interrogation, not a quiz. Just nod if that's clear.'

Jack and Alan were both fast learners, so they nodded in unison, without making a sound.

'Very good. You get the idea.'

The first question was aimed at Alan.

'You've recently been down in the Bristol area, I understand. Is that right?'

Alan, all at once, realised what this was all about. What was happening to them in this barn and the fact that they had accidentally killed a woman on their visit to Bristol had to be related somehow. If he had been scared before, he was terrified now.

'Yeah, we were there. Why?'

This time, it was Alan's turn to be slapped to the floor.

'We ask you the questions, and you answer them. I thought we had made that clear.'

As the two men lifted Alan back into an upright position and, once again, returned to their seats, Alan was desperately trying to think who they could possibly be and what their connection to the dead woman was. He feared that he was not going to leave the room as fit and healthy as he had entered it. Damn Jack and his bloody temper!

The next question was aimed at Jack.

'How did you come by those rather painful-looking scratches on your face?'

Jack thought long and hard before he replied, realising that an incorrect response would, most likely, be painful.

'A woman and I had a misunderstanding, and she scratched me.'

It was, in a way, both a truth and a lie.

'You killed this woman when you were down there. You pushed her down the stairs.'

This had been a statement of fact, rather than a question, and was not aimed at either of them, in particular, but an answer was still expected. Jack knew that it would be a waste of time to lie and that it would only result in more pain.

'It was an accident... I .... we didn't mean to kill her ... she attacked me.'

'So it *was* you, scar-face,' the man said, grinning at having given Jack a nickname and studying his face with interest. He reached out and turned Jack's face sideways, so he could examine the scratches more closely.

'The old girl always did have long nails,' he said to his companion.

Alan closed his eyes in despair. It was obvious, now, that these men were close friends or maybe even sons of the dead woman. He had never been a particularly religious man, but he prayed now.

'One more thing – and take your time, think your answer through carefully and answer honestly, because this is the big one – what was Richard Drake's involvement?'

Richard Drake?.. thought Jack. What's this got to do with him? He was the antique dealer whose shop they were in when Mrs Harper called that day. Suddenly, Jack saw a chance to shift some of the blame and, if he could do that, maybe some of the punishment, as well.

'Yeah, that's right – he's the bloke you want. He put us up to it. He gave us the woman's name and address, said she had some good stuff and that he'd pay us good money for it. It's him you want, really ... not us. It was an accident. She tripped. We didn't mean to kill her.'

'And so you sold the bronze cowboy to Richard Drake?'

Jack was confused, 'No! No, we were going to. That was the one piece he said he wanted, but we panicked when the woman died. We ended up in Bath and just sold it to the first dealer who offered us the money for it. It was all a terrible accident, but Drake put us up to it – he's the one you want. None of this would have happened if it wasn't for him.'

'Well, that's that, then. Not so hard, was it?' he turned to look at his partner, 'I think it's time to put the kettle on.'

Alan and Jack looked at each other in surprise and with a twinge of guarded relief. Jack wondered if their ordeal could really be over. Could it be that, after all the theatricals, all they really wanted to know was who had done it? Did they just want to know who had put them up to it? Were there to be no more consequences other than a couple of slaps? Alan, however, was still fruitlessly praying. He knew, instinctively, that the worst was still to come.

Jack's relief soon turned, once more, to dread, as the man standing in front of them took a gun from behind his back, where it had been tucked into the waistband of his trousers. He then placed ear plugs into his ears, retrieved from the pocket of his pants, and handed his companion a pair to do the same.

As soon as the ear plugs were in place, and without the slightest preamble or by-your-leave, the man pointed the gun at Alan's head and pulled the trigger.

Jack flinched at the sound of the gun going off; it was the loudest thing he had ever heard in his life, and his ears hurt as badly as if someone had jammed a pencil into each. He watched in horror as the back of Alan's head exploded in a cloud of blood, bone and brain, some of it spraying over him, almost causing him to vomit, and he lost control of his bladder.

Outside the barn, a passing cat had stopped dead in its tracks at the sound of gunfire. It then rushed away, as fast as its legs could carry it. Up at the main house, someone had peered curiously out of a window; they had been told that there was going to be some activity at the barn, but whatever was going on there was no business of theirs, as long as it didn't invite unwanted attention to the house.

Alan had been staring directly at the gun as the trigger was pulled, and it's possible his mind momentarily registered the flash from the muzzle. But, unlike his friend, Jack, who had been the cause of so much wretchedness, he never heard the sound of the explosion. The bullet had both entered and exited his skull and completed its mission long before the sound waves of the explosion reached his dead ears.

In spite of his possibly undeserved violent death, Alan had actually been the lucky one out of the ill-fated duo. His death, when it came, had been rapid and painless; Jack's, on the other hand, would be neither of these things. Jack would take several hours to die – hours when he would beg and plead for death. The kettle was boiling, and Craig went over to fetch it with a grin on his face and a spring in his step.

* * * * * * * * * * *

It was nearly two weeks now since Margaret had been brutally mugged, and, apart from the odd bruise that was still fading, she had mostly recovered from her ordeal and had now returned to work – something for which Richard was very grateful. Even a few days without her had brought home to him just how much he relied on her for the day-to-day running of the shop, and he had decided that she was worthy of a pay rise. Margaret had been delighted and had kissed him for the first time since her mother and father had died. Richard couldn't have been more pleased by her show of affection. He still thought of her as his second daughter, and he knew that Elizabeth felt the same. Perhaps this Paul fellow wasn't such a threat to their relationship after all.

He had been worried when she had started seeing Paul, firstly, because his chosen profession was a notorious marriage breaker, at least, according to all the police dramas he had seen on television, and then there was the substantial difference in their ages – eight years – to which, Elizabeth had said, 'Eight years? Oh, Richard, we've got meat in our freezer older than that.'

He had hoped that she was joking, but had got the message.

Then there was the fact that she now called Paul first for help or advice, instead of him, and that was taking some getting used to. Not for the first time, he thought, 'If I'm like this with Margaret, what am I going to be like when Rebecca finds the love of her life?'

Things did seem to be returning to normal, at last. The police knew who had been responsible for the death of Mrs Harper. Paul said that they now had CCTV footage of a car in the area that they had linked to a man in Newcastle. They had also linked his fingerprints to some that had been lifted from the bronze, so they were very close to arresting the culprits.

His daughter, Rebecca, was doing well, and she was expecting to start her new job as events manager at the *Holiday Inn* down by the city docks, any day. Judging by the number of new shoes and outfits she had brought home recently, the increase in salary was going to come in handy. She said that she would even have her own office that she didn't have to share with anyone else. Well, it was too small to share, she admitted, and it was slightly disappointing that it didn't have a window, but then that was because it had once been a linen closet, but, still, it was her very own office.

As Richard sat in the shop, thinking about normality and what that really was, the phone rang.

'*Richard Drake Antiques*,' he answered, automatically.

'Hello, Richard. Sorry I haven't been in touch earlier, but we have had some business to attend to up north; fortunately, that's all taken care of now.'

'Yes ... right,' Richard was trying to recognise the voice on the other end, but it wasn't familiar.

'Glad to see Margaret's back to her old self now and is over that terrible mugging. I'll bet you're glad to have her back in the shop now, aren't you?'

'Sorry ... but who is this?'

'Oh, sorry, how lapse of me. I didn't introduce myself, did I? I'm the man who returned Margaret's handbag, you know, on the front doorstep and all that.'

'Who is this? What do know about the handbag?'

'I thought about introducing myself then, but it was early days, and you had that nice inspector calling. What's his name now? Oh, yes, ... Manley?'

'Tell me who you are and what you want,' Richard demanded.

'Have the police got any closer to finding out who killed Mrs Harper yet? Bet they haven't. Incompetent, if you ask me – the lot of them.'

Richard could hear music in the background, and, unlike the man's voice, the music sounded familiar. It was someone playing the piano, but they were not playing it very well. It was a child playing, he realized, slowly. Suddenly, Richard's blood ran cold. He recognised the music and who was playing ... it was Rebecca! When she was around thirteen or fourteen, they had recorded her playing, and it was that recording which was playing in the background now ... there was no mistake about it. The recording had been on a CD, kept with others in his office at home. When they had fitted the new locks, Richard had checked everywhere for evidence of an intruder, but one thing he hadn't thought to check was the music and CD collection.

'Look, you've had your fun – been into my shop, my home – what more do you want? Why are you doing this? What have I done to you?'

'You have so many questions, Richard. Are you sure you don't know the answers to any of them?'

'No, I don't. You tell me – what's this all about?'

'In that case, let me ask you a question. Does Becky still play the piano? Probably not, I'd guess. She wasn't very good, was she?'

'Please, just tell me why you're doing this.'

'I spoke to your friends the other day, Richard – the ones you sent to Mrs Harper's house for the bronze. You won't be hearing from them again. They've retired, so to speak. We'll talk again soon, Richard.'

The phone went dead.

Richard sat and stared at the phone after hanging up the receiver, wondering if the man would ring back and say it had all been a joke, albeit in extremely bad taste. But he didn't ring back, and Richard was at his wits' end. Why was this happening to him? To his family? He had read about people who had stalkers following them around and messing with their lives, sometimes plaguing them for years. Was this what was going to happen to them? The bronze – why had he mentioned that? What had this got to do with Mrs Harper? Why did this man think that he was involved?

Margaret, who had overheard Richard's tense side of the conversation, was now standing expectantly in front of his desk, looking very concerned, 'Richard? Is everything all right? Who was that on the phone? What did they want?'

Richard tried, unsuccessfully, to put on a brave face, 'It's OK, Margaret ... it was just a prank call,' he lied.

'What on earth did they say to you, Richard? You look so worried, and you've gone as white as a sheet.'

'Really, Margaret, it was just someone playing a sick joke. Don't worry about it. It was just a bit of a shock, is all. Why don't you put the kettle on? We'll have a nice cup of tea. I'm fine, really.'

Margaret did as she was bid and made a cup of tea for them both, but she knew that Richard was keeping something important from her and that there was more to the phone call than he was letting on. However, she didn't pursue the matter any further, knowing that it would be pointless to press him anymore.

Paul and Margaret decided to have an intimate meal at Margaret's house, and they prepared it together.

'Is this all you have in the house to eat?' asked Paul, eyeing the contents of Margaret's fridge with little enthusiasm, 'some lamb chops and frozen veg?'

'I'm sorry. Would you rather we went out to eat?'

'No, I'll show you what my culinary skills can achieve,' he said, shaking his head.

While Paul prepared the meal for them both, Margaret told him about the worrying phone call that Richard had received. He tried his best to reassure her that everything was going to be all right, but, in truth, he was just as worried by the turn of events as she was.

'This all has to do with my mugging, hasn't it?' asked Margaret.

'The truth is, I don't know, Margaret. Your mugging, Mrs Harper's death – it all seems to be connected in some way. Did you manage to hear any of what the man said?'

'No, just Richard's side of the conversation, but he said that the man had been in his house and in his shop, so it has to be related.'

'Try not to worry, Margaret. I'll speak to Richard about it when I see him next. Now, let's eat.'

Paul had cooked an excellent meal, and, after they had eaten, Margaret said, 'That was a delicious meal. You never

cease to amaze me, Mr Manley. Who would have thought it –
a policeman who cooks! Who taught you?'

'My father was a head chef for years when I was
growing up, and he and my mum always encouraged me to help
with the cooking, which I enjoyed doing. They now run a little
tea room in Brixham, in Devon. I'll have to take you there one
weekend.'

'Have they got room to put us up?' she enquired.

'Oh, yes, even if my sister is at home.'

'You have a sister?'

Margaret began to realise how little she knew about the
man that she was now convinced she wanted to share her life
with, so the rest of their evening together was spent in a mutual
question-and-answer session that went on until it became far too
late for Paul to drive home, and he was forced, once again, to
spend the night.

Chapter 7

After the frightening phone call Richard had received, he decided to ring and get some much-needed help and advice from Paul, who suggested a meeting.

Paul was halfway out of the door of his office, on his way to the meeting, when the phone on his desk rang. He wondered, briefly, whether to leave it, but decided that it might be important, so he returned to his desk and took the call. It turned out to be Reg.

'Hi, Guv. Jack Simmons's car has been found abandoned at his local golf club, but there is no sign of Simmons himself. His house is under surveillance, but he hasn't been seen for a couple of days, according to his neighbours. The secretary of the golf club had, apparently, been sitting in his office overlooking the car park when Jack pulled in. He said that as Jack got out of his car, a black BMW pulled up, and Jack had gone off with two corporate-looking gentlemen in a BMW. He thought it odd at the time, and, when the car was still there in the evening, he called the police. Also, there is no sign of Alan Salter. Local police checked his house and found the back door open and signs that Mr Salter had been in the middle of breakfast when he left. In short, Guv, it looks as if someone has beaten us to them.'

'Blast and damn it!' raged Paul, 'It has to be the Harpers! It's too much of a coincidence to be anyone else. How on earth did they find out who it was? And how did they get to them so fast? Is somebody feeding them information? If they are, and I find out whom, I'll have them hung, drawn and quartered, so help me.'

Paul banged his fist down on the top of his desk in frustration, causing a coffee mug to tip over and spill the remainder of its contents onto some papers. He was angrier than he had been in a long time, and he needed to do something, anything, to break the mood.

Now that he had been delayed in leaving, anyway, Paul decided to ring the pathologist to find out if the post mortem report on the body that they had found in the gardens of Hilltop Cottage was ready, but he was told that it was still not finished.

'For Christ's sake, what's taking so long?' he demanded of the rather taken aback pathologist on the other end of the phone, 'it's only bones, for God's sake. Surely there can't be that much to do?'

As soon as he had uttered the words, he was sorry. They were doing their job as well as they could, in the same way that he was doing his, but he was angry and needed someone to take it out on.

'We're working as fast as we can, Inspector,' said the pathologist, who Paul had met a few times in the past, whilst working on various cases, 'but you wouldn't want us to rush and miss something, would you?'

'No, no, of course not. I'm sorry. I'm just a bit uptight at the moment. I'm sorry you were in the firing line.'

'That's all right, Inspector. We all get days like that. There is one thing I can tell you, though – my colleague is a bit of a dental expert, and he said that, judging by the dental work the boy had done, he reckons that he died at least twenty-five years ago, maybe more.'

'Thanks, that gives us something. And, look, I really am sorry about my outburst. I shouldn't take my troubles out on you.'

Paul hung up the phone and composed himself. He hated losing his temper; it never made a good impression.

Paul set Clive Pascoe and John Campbell the task of checking the files of missing persons, looking for boys between the ages of twelve and eighteen, who went missing between twenty and fifty years ago.

'Bloody hell, Guv, that's quite a time frame.'

'Then the sooner you start on it, the better. You get me a name, and I'll get you a bottle of Scotland's finest.'

Clive suddenly looked a bit more enthusiastic.

'Well, I suppose, in that case, Guv.'

He shoved John in the back and said, Get a move on, Campbell. There's booze on offer.'

They were all sitting in Richard and Elizabeth's lounge on the two large sofas that sat in front of the sofa table which had, briefly, been the home of 'The Night Watchman'. Richard and Elizabeth had Rebecca between them on one sofa, and Paul had a comforting arm around Margaret on the other.

Paul kicked things off by telling them the background and present employment of Kevin and Craig Harper.

He told them, 'They're career criminals from London, and it seems possible that they have the mistaken idea that Richard was, in some way, involved in the theft of their mother's bronze.'

'Why would they think Richard was involved? How would they know he bought it?' asked Elizabeth.

'I don't know, Liz. Probably, someone tipped them off.'

He went on to tell them of the girl whom Craig had been accused of raping and that she had later dropped the charges against him, but had left out an explanation of why she had done it and of her subsequent suicide. They were all very upset and frightened as it was, and he didn't want to add to it, if at all possible, but he needed them to appreciate what kind of men they were up against. Paul was worried for his new friends;

he was determined to get these Harper twins out of the picture, before they could do them any harm.

'You definitely think the phone call was from one of them?' asked Richard.

'I'm certain of it. Everything ties together – he mentioned Mrs Harper, the handbag and, most significantly, he said he'd spoken to your friends that you'd sent to take the bronze.'

'How far do you think they will go?' queried Elizabeth. 'If they were responsible for Margaret being mugged, what's their reason? They can't think she was involved.'

'I don't know how far they will go, Liz,' Paul lied, 'but they have been known to be violent in the past. However, I think they mugged Margaret simply to get Richard's keys.'

'How violent have they been?' Elizabeth persisted.

This wasn't going the way that Paul wanted, so he said, 'Look, we don't know what they intend to do. We don't know whether they just want to frighten Richard, like they did with the phone call, or whether they intend to go further, but they've tipped their hand now. I have informed my DCI, and he is virtually giving me a free hand in the matter.'

'You don't think they suspect Richard was involved in their mum's death, do you?'

It was Elizabeth, again.

'I don't think so, Liz. I think it's just about the theft.'

'Do you know for certain who did it?' asked Richard.

'We're pretty sure it was a couple of men down from Newcastle, knocking on doors trying to buy antiques. We think things got out of hand. She probably challenged them over something upstairs, they struck her and she fell to her death.'

'What makes you think it was these men from Newcastle?'

'We know they were in the area, because there had been complaints and their descriptions match the descriptions of the men who sold Simon White the bronze. We also have the registration of their car, and we matched it to two dealers in Newcastle, who, not only fit the descriptions, but whose prints were found on the bronze.'

'So you know their names?'

This time, it was Rebecca who spoke.

'Yes, we do. As soon as we identified the car, we had the name of one of them. We then discovered that he had a regular partner – his description fits as well – and with both their fingerprints found on the bronze cowboy that you had here, briefly, it's basically a cut-and-dry case.'

'So why haven't you arrested them? Surely when they are arrested for the murder, the Harper twins will stop their vendetta against Richard?'

Paul seemed hesitant.

'We can't locate them, at present. They may have gone to ground.'

Now it was Margaret's turn. She looked him in the eye and said, 'Paul, what aren't you telling us?'

Paul hesitated, again, 'Nothing, I'm sure they have gone to ground knowing that we are looking for them.'

This time, Margaret almost shouted.

'Come on Paul, what is it? What are you not saying?'

'All right ... we found their cars – one was in the garage of one of their homes and the other one appears to have been abandoned at a golf club.'

Margaret persisted, 'What do you think it means, Paul? Tell us. We have a right to know. I know you're trying to protect us, but, for Richard's sake, you have to tell us what you know. What exactly are we up against?'

Elizabeth reached across Rebecca and grabbed hold of Richard's hand.

'Well ... we have no way of knowing at the moment, but one possibility is that the Harper brothers have also managed to locate them. They may be holding them somewhere or they may ... '

'Go on, Paul. They may have killed them. Is that what you were going to say? Do these men kill people, Paul? Is that what you're trying to keep from us?' asked Elizabeth.

'We can't know for sure.'

'But *you* suspect they're dead?'

All eyes were on Paul, and he wished he could lie to them.

'Yes. I'm sorry, Liz. I think they probably are.'

'Oh my God! Do you think they might try and kill Richard?' screamed Elizabeth, now in danger of stopping the circulation in Richard's hand.

'We've no reason to think that they intend to go that far, Liz. If they are responsible for the deaths of our two suspects, then they know it wasn't Richard who killed their mum. And why did they mug Margaret, instead of trying to kill Richard? I think they're just trying to frighten him with things like that phone call.'

Although he told them that he thought the twins were just trying to frighten Richard, Paul was convinced his life was in danger, and he felt woefully inadequate to the task of protecting his new friends.

'What can the police do?' asked Elizabeth.

'We're looking into the disappearance of our suspects, obviously – they're wanted for murder, after all. And we're looking into trying to tie the Harpers to their disappearance. We know it was them, but we need to prove it, and, to do that, we need the bodies. So that's about all we can do, at the moment.'

'What can we do?' asked Richard.

'You all need to be vigilant, until this is over. Keep your doors locked and try not to be left on your own, especially you, Richard, but the same goes for all of you. It's not my place to suggest it, but I would feel happier if Margaret moved in with you guys for a bit. I don't think she should be on her own. I know she's not strictly part of the family, but she almost is, and she was the one who was mugged. They seem to know a lot about everyone, so they know how close you all are. I'm not going to be around enough to look after her if I am going to keep on top of the case and catch these people, so I'd be happier if she was here with you.'

'Now, that's a brilliant idea,' said Rebecca.

'No, I don't want to impose,' said Margaret. 'I'll be fine at my place.'

'I not only think it's a good idea ... I insist on it,' said Richard.

'They know where you live, Margaret. You can't stay there on your own. There has to be more safety in numbers.'

'I also think that someone should take Becky to work and pick her up,' said Paul.

'You don't think they would harm Rebecca? Why?' Elizabeth was close to tears.

'Rebecca is Richard's daughter; she has to be more at risk than Margaret. The fact is that we just don't know what they have in mind, but it could be anything that they think will hurt Richard, so that includes getting to any family members.'

Everyone sat in silence for a while, thinking about what had just been discussed.

Paul was upset at the way things had gone, he hadn't handled it the way that he had wanted or intended. His intention had been to both warn but also reassure them, and, instead, he had succeeded in frightening them. But he had to admit that it was better for them to be aware of the severity of the threat.

It was Richard who finally broke the silence.

'Anyone want another drink?'

Everyone did. They were all putting on a brave face for the sake of each other, but, in truth, they were all very frightened people.

Paul and Margaret were both invited to stay for dinner, and they gladly accepted. While Elizabeth prepared the food, Paul gave Margaret a lift home to collect the toiletries and clothes she would need, if she was to stay with Richard and Elizabeth. When they got back, the meal was all but ready. During dinner, there seemed to have developed an unspoken **agreement** amongst them all – any conversations would avoid the mention of police, the Harper brothers or anything to do with possible threats to the family. Only idle chit-chat was permitted.

After dinner, Elizabeth asked Margaret if she would give her a hand loading the dishwasher, and, as it was so obviously an excuse for girl-talk, the men made themselves scarce. Richard gave Paul a tour of the house and of some of the more interesting antiques he'd collected over the years. This included a Winchester rifle, like the one 'The Night Watchman' was holding, and an old Navy Colt percussion pistol, together with bullet mould and some percussion caps.

Richard explained that Elizabeth hated guns and that he was only allowed to keep them if the pistol was safely in its box in a drawer in his study, and the Winchester was confined to the wall. Elizabeth seldom, if ever, went in there.

In the kitchen, Elizabeth was asking Margaret about her relationship with Paul, and Margaret confided that she was embarrassed about the speed at which things had developed, confessing that they had already talked seriously about moving in with each other.

Elizabeth was delighted, and she admitted that the reason she had grilled Margaret about it was because she wanted to ask Paul if he would consider staying with them, until this awful business was concluded. Elizabeth thought it would be a good idea to have a police inspector in the house. It might just deter these Harper brothers from doing anything too dreadful.

'And Richard can take me to work, while Paul drops Becky off – it's perfect,' agreed Margaret.

Elizabeth smiled and said, 'Better let me tell Richard first. You know how he likes to be consulted, before we tell him what's happening.'

'Do you want me to put it to Paul or do you want to do it?'

'I think it might be better if we get Richard to do it. I'll tell him to make it sound as if it was his idea.'

Both women smiled broadly, for the first time that evening.

Richard spoke to Paul, after Elizabeth had explained her plan to him, and Paul thanked him for the caring offer to stay with them, but, mindful of the fact that they were all becoming more and more embroiled in a case that he was in charge of investigating, Paul declined the invitation, much to the dismay of Rebecca and, to a lesser degree, Margaret. She not only understood the position that it would undoubtedly put Paul in, but she was also a little frightened at the speed with which her feelings for him had grown. Paul also confessed to Richard that he felt that living in the same house as Margaret would distract him from his main aim of pursuing the Harpers.

They were just starting the fourth bottle of wine, when Rebecca shot up from her seat and announced, 'Oh, no! I almost forgot – I'm taking a boy on a date tonight.'

With Rebecca, it was always she who took the boy on a date and never the boy who took her.

'Is it a new boy again?' asked Elizabeth. 'None of the boys you take out ever seem to make it past the first date. Why is that?'

'It's because she sets the bar so high that none of them can possibly come up to scratch,' said Margaret.

'What criteria do they have to match?' asked Paul, curiously.

'Well,' replied Rebecca, thoughtfully, 'they have to be tall and good-looking, *obviously* ... witty, and it helps if they can play an instrument, preferably piano, but guitar will do. They have to love animals, and, most important of all, they have to be earning a minimum of thirty-five K a year. Apart from that, I'm pretty flexible.'

'Does this boy you're seeing tonight fit into that bracket?' asked Paul.

'I don't know yet. But, chances are, he'll just turn out to be "money in the bank" again, like so many of the others.'

'Money in the bank?' Paul enquired, puzzled by the reference.

Margaret cut in, explaining, 'As soon as she takes him out, she'll lose interest.'

They all laughed, but Richard was concerned and said, 'Look, I don't want to spoil things for you, Rebecca, but after all we've just been discussing, I don't think you should go.'

'I agree. Ring this boy up and make some excuse tonight,' pleaded Elizabeth.

'Look, he's picking me up. He'll be here any minute. I'll be in his company in a public place all evening, and I'll make sure he gets me home early. How's that? I can't stay confined to the house.'

Reluctantly, her parents agreed, with the proviso that she was to ring them when they got to the club and again when they were about to leave, no matter what the hour, and she wasn't to be on her own, at any time.

Miraculously, Rebecca got ready in twenty minutes flat – normally, she would never take a boy out without spending at least two hours in the bathroom and two hours getting dressed.

The doorbell rang almost as soon as she reappeared, so Rebecca kissed everyone goodbye and headed for the door. Richard went with her, determined to at least see what this young man looked like.

The conversation in the lounge eased away from Rebecca and her dates to Elizabeth's baking and her lemon meringue, with everyone agreeing that it was the best they had ever tasted, but the conversation was undeniably strained. There was really only one topic on everyone's mind.

It was nearly nine thirty the next morning when Inspector Manley and the team were all assembled in the incident room. Paul was updating everyone with details of the call that Richard had received. Paul's briefings were always casual affairs, normally conducted with Paul sitting on one of the tables and the rest of the team on chairs or tables facing him, with mugs of coffee in one hand and beacon rolls or cakes in the other, depending on the time of day. There was often a bit of light-hearted banter between them, but, this morning, everyone could tell that Paul was in no mood for triviality.

'Why should the Harper brothers think Richard Drake has anything to do with the case at all? They've, presumably, had no contact with him. And, anyway, I thought we were all agreed that the reason we're having so much trouble picking up our prime suspects is because we're all convinced that the brothers have somehow beaten us to it.' It was Constable Clive Pascoe who posed the question.

'What would make them think there was a link between Drake and our suspects?'

'Are we even sure that the phone call to Richard Drake was made by the Harper brothers?'

This time, it was June Kelly who raised the question.

Paul replied, logically, 'Who else would know about the bronze? It had to be one of them. We can only assume that they think he had some connection with our suspects. Maybe they think he was going to fence it for them? Maybe the brothers think that they were working for him. Whatever the reason, I am convinced the phone call was from them. I also think that they will try to get to Mr Drake and his family.'

'You're convinced they will try to hurt him? Maybe even kill him?'

'Come on, June, you were the one who found out the history of our friends, the Harpers, in the first place. What do you think they mean to do? Give him a slap and then forgive and forget? I don't think so. Tomorrow, I want to go and see the Harpers on their own turf, so to speak. Reg will come with me, and I'll get Blakey to set it up with our colleagues at the Met.'

For the first time, in what seemed like ages, the day had started out wet and murky, and now noon had arrived, the rain was coming down in torrents. Detective Inspector Manley and Sergeant Reg Evans were in conversation with Chief Inspector Hunt of the Met. in his office, which, despite the smoking ban, smelt heavily of cigarettes. Paul had rung and arranged the meeting soon after the team brief, the day before. He glanced at the office ceiling and noted that the top of the smoke detector was missing, and he suspected that the whole of Hunt's team were smokers. As upholders of the law, they obviously felt that they were above it. Paul was far from impressed with anything he had seen so far.

'So you want to have a word with our Harper brothers?' said DCI Hunt, leaning back dangerously in his chair and reaching in his pocket for a packet of cigarettes that he instantly replaced.

'Well, Ted, here, will take you to see them, won't you, Ted?'

The DCI indicated the Constable standing behind them, who didn't seem remarkably overjoyed at the prospect.

DC Ted Williams nodded, unenthusiastically, 'Sure thing, always enjoy a visit to the Harpers ... I don't think.'

Ted had been on the force for most of his forty two years, much of it in London, and he knew the Harper brothers well. Paul gave him the once-over and concluded that his manner and appearance definitely owed more to Columbo or Frost, than it did to Inspector Lynley or Kojak. He drove Paul and Reg to *Sparklers Nightclub* in the West End.

'Their club is in the West End!' exclaimed Paul, horrified.

'Nothing but the best for the Harper brothers, sir. What was it you expected? Some seedy little dive in a run-down part of town, was that it?'

'Yeah, I guess I did.'

'No, the brothers have a very up-market establishment. The people who frequent it have money to spend – lots of money – they get celebrities, footballers, politicians, all that sort in there. The likes of you and I can go in now, during the day, to see them, but we couldn't afford to buy a drink in there when it's open. Toffs and celebrities wall-to-wall ... makes you want to puke.'

Ted's tone of voice was almost sneering. He obviously had a real problem with the Harpers. Paul could certainly identify with that, but, at times, he sounded jaded and despairing, and that wasn't a good sign in a police officer.

They pulled up outside *Sparklers Nightclub* and got out of the car, pulling up their collars as a shield to the rain, which showed no sign of letting up. The front façade of the club was more like that of a grand department store, having six marble steps leading up to a pair of huge glass doors with gold-coloured frames and furniture. Despite the up-market address, one or two of the properties either side of the club had graffiti on them and a sprinkling of litter outside, which was now wet and clinging to the pavement. *Sparklers*, however, was swept clean of litter, and there was no trace of graffiti to be seen. On either side of the steps leading up to the doors were large blacked-out windows, behind which were photographs – both of the club's interior and of various celebrities, who had either performed there or been visitors. Paul instantly recognised several of the faces.

Once inside, they walked straight into the heart of the club, where cleaners were busy getting it ready for another night of fun and entertainment for the well-to-do. The air was full of the smell of hot vacuum-cleaner motors and spray polish. Kevin, who had been sitting on one of the many gold--coloured stools that surrounded a huge circular bar in the middle of the lounge, was chatting to the barman about paperwork that he was holding. He spotted them out of the corner of his eye. Kevin got off his bar stool in a leisurely fashion and strode over to them, with his hand outstretched.

'Ted ... nice to see you. How's the family? Well?'

'I've brought some people who would like a word with you both,' Ted replied, non-committedly.

Ted had not taken up Kevin's invitation to shake hands, so now he offered his outstretched hand to Paul.

'Inspector Girly, nice to see you again and ... Reg, isn't it. How are you both? Welcome to our little establishment. Have you caught Mum's killer yet?'

Kevin called out to his brother, who was deep in conversation with a young woman, dressed in jeans and a polo shirt. She was standing at the front of a large stage, with what looked like a song sheet in her hands. Paul guessed that she was an entertainer of some kind.

'Craig!' Kevin shouted, again, 'look who's come to see us. It's Ted with ... Inspector Manley, – that's right, isn't it? You must forgive my little joke before, it was very rude of me – and his sergeant ... now, give me a minute ... was I right? It is Reginald, isn't it? Reg to your friends. I hope you don't mind me calling you Reg?'

Craig had finished talking with the woman and came over to join them.

'Welcome. What can we do for you gentlemen? Do you need some help with your crime-fighting work?'

Kevin smiled easily at his brother.

Paul knew that this wasn't going to be easy, to say the least. The brothers knew they had nothing on them, and they were clearly mocking them. He decided not to play their games. After all, he did have one trump card – they wouldn't know that a body had since been discovered in Mummy's garden.

Paul told them that there were two things that they wanted to see them about.

'The first,' he said, 'is to clear up any possible misunderstanding about the involvement of Richard Drake in the death of your mother. Let me make it plain to you that he had no involvement, in any way, shape or form. I, therefore, expect all threatening phone calls to stop. We have two prime suspects for your mother's murder, and ...' he lied, 'we expect to be arresting them very soon.'

'Well, good luck with that, Inspector,' Craig smirked.

Paul went on to say that he suspected that they were involved in Margaret's mugging and that he would do his best to prove that, as well.

Kevin replied, 'Margaret? Oh, I expect you mean the lovely Miss Collins, Drake's shop girl. Do go on.'

Paul kicked himself for stupidly using Margaret's first name. These two were getting to him, and he was worried about the amount they seemed to know about everyone. He'd give anything to know where they were getting their information.

'Can you tell us what you were doing in Newcastle recently?' Paul asked, changing tack.

They, of course, had no way of knowing whether or not the twins had been to Newcastle, but Paul wanted them to think they knew more than they did.

'Newcastle?' Kevin frowned, then turned and looked questioningly at his brother.

'I think it's somewhere up north,' his brother replied, grinning from ear to ear.

'Oh, up north, you say?' he turned his attention back to Paul.

'Oh, no, Inspector, you've got it wrong. Why would we go up north?'

'So you deny you were there?'

'Really, Inspector, if I have to answer all your questions twice, this is going to take a very long time. Oh, well, here goes – my brother and I were not in Newcastle, wherever that happens to be. We have never been to Newcastle and, most probably, will never have reason to go to Newcastle.'

'You see, Mr Harper, we're investigating the disappearance of two men in the Newcastle area, and ...'

Kevin cut him short, appearing to be exasperated, 'Inspector Manley! My brother and I have never been to Newcastle! I hesitate to suggest that you need a hearing aid, but I believe I have already made that clear, so whatever you are investigating there has nothing to do with us.'

He gestured towards the door, indicating that the meeting was over, continuing, 'Now, unless you and your colleagues intend to arrest us on suspicion of making a phone call, I suggest you leave.'

'There are other questions that need to be answered before we go, Mr Harper.'

'Well, be quick, Inspector. My brother and I have enjoyed our little chat, but we really do have things to get on with.'

'Perhaps you could tell me the identity of the body we found in your mother's garden?'

Yes! Score one for Inspector Paul Manley, at last. That wiped the silly grin off his face. For a moment, maybe only a split second, there was concern written all over Kevin's face. He got it under control very quickly, but it had clearly been there, and it spoke volumes. It meant that Kevin and Craig were aware of the existence of the body and that almost certainly meant that they were the killers.

'A body, you say? Well, I really don't know what to make of that, Inspector. You don't think dear old Mummy and Daddy did something naughty, do you? Oh, surely not.' He turned to his brother, 'Craig, did you hear what the inspector said? It seems they've found a body in Mummy's garden. Did she ever mention anything to you about burying a body in the garden?'

'First I've heard of such a thing,' replied Craig. 'Not a dog or something is it? I wouldn't be surprised at the boys-in-blue making that kind of mistake.'

The concern was there, under the surface, on Craig's face, as well. He was slightly less in control of it than his brother.

'The body has been in the ground for some years, probably buried when you two were living at home,' continued Paul.

'Or maybe years before we were born, Inspector, but before our time or not, I can assure you that neither my brother nor myself had anything to do with burying any body. Is that clear, Inspector? I don't have to repeat it for you?'

'Rest assured, we will be speaking about this matter again,' said Paul.

'Well, until then, Inspector, Reg, Ted. It's been lovely seeing you again. Be sure and give my love to your family, won't you?'

Once outside, it was Ted who spoke first. 'Well, that went well. What exactly was the interview supposed to achieve?' he asked, as they returned to their car.

Paul was angry, both about how the interview had gone, but also about Ted's attitude, and he responded, sharply, 'I needed to see their faces when I mentioned the body that we've found, and I got just the reaction I was expecting. They knew of the body, and it's probably one of theirs, wouldn't you say so, Constable?'

'Yeah, probably, for all the good it will do you.'

'You've been in the police a long time, Constable. Lost the thrill of the chase, have you? Or perhaps you don't like bothering honest, upright citizens, like the Harpers? And tell me this, how is it that, apart from a suspiciously short spell inside, the brothers have apparently been allowed to build a mini-empire here?'

'They're nasty, Inspector, really nasty, and everybody knows what to expect if they cross them, so nobody does. Do you know what it is like trying to get someone to testify against people like them?'

'Sure, they intimidate people. It's always difficult to get witnesses to talk, but that's police work for you. You have to find ways around that. They must make some mistakes, leave some clues – they're only human, for God's sake. Has there never been any physical evidence against them?'

'If we ever do get evidence against them, it still won't go to court. Nobody will testify against them, and any physical evidence would simply disappear.'

'What are you talking about, disappear?'

'Listen, Inspector, suppose the person you care most about in the entire world is kidnapped, and you get a phone call one day, telling you that that person is going to be scalded to death, unless you "liberate" a certain piece of evidence. What would you do, Inspector? Ask yourself that.'

The rest of the journey was made in silence, apart from the noise that the heavy rain was making on the car windows, and Paul wondered if Ted had just made up the scenario about the kidnapping and the disappearing evidence or whether he had actually faced the situation for real, remembering how Kevin had greeted him in the club by asking about his family. What did the future hold for the people he was getting close to? And, honestly, what would he do in the circumstances that Ted described? Suppose someone was holding Margaret, in order to get him to do something? How far would he go?

Back in Bristol, Paul updated the team with details of the meeting with the brothers, but omitted the part where Kevin had referred to him as Inspector Girly; no doubt Reg would happily find an opportunity to do that at some point. The rest of the team had nothing to report on the search for their two suspects. A cloud of despair was descending on them. They all believed their suspects were dead, and, indeed, apart from trying to identify the body found in the garden, the investigation had become little more than a search for missing bodies.

Just as the team was about to call it a day, Clive Pascoe entered the room, beaming from ear-to-ear.

'Stephen Potter,' he announced, at the top of his voice.

Constable Pascoe now had everyone's attention.

'Stephen Potter was reported missing in 1980 and was never found. He, apparently, went out on his bike that he had just been given for his birthday and was never seen again. He lived in Long Barton and was a tall, clever lad – the same height as our body in the garden and the right age.'

'Have you got the file?' asked Paul.

'It was before everything was computerised, so there was only a hard-copy, as they say.'

'And where is the hard-copy, as they say?'

'Here.'

Clive held aloft a pale brown folder, which he opened and, with some ceremony, tipped its would-be contents onto the desk, but nothing fell out.

'Gone missing ... all of it, Guv. There is not one single piece of paper left. A missing boy ... there must have been boxes of statements alone, but it's all gone.'

Paul was reminded of what Ted had said about evidence going missing, and he thumped the table heavily.

'OK! So we open a new file – that one,' said Paul, indicating the empty folder that Clive had placed on the desk.

'Where did you get the information you gave us about the bike and knowledge that he was clever?'

'Newspaper reports of the time, Guv. There are lots of those, but they're mostly speculation on the part of the reporters.'

'I don't care. I want everything that was ever written about the case, and I want it on my desk, tomorrow. We are going to prove that Craig and Kevin Harper killed Stephen Potter and buried him in their parent's garden or nobody on this team gets a day off or holiday ever again.'

'That's a little harsh, Guv. And what happens if we do prove it?'

'Then I will personally treat one and all of you to the best end-of-case party the country has ever seen, and I will recommend every one of you for promotion. Well, what are you waiting for? Get the newspapers – tell me where he lived, who his friends were and how he fell afoul of the Harpers!'

'It's quite late, Guv. Do you want us to start fresh in the morning?'

'Yeah, I guess so. It's already thirty years late for poor Stephen Potter.'

The following evening, Richard and Elizabeth were watching the evening news with Rebecca, Margaret and Paul when the phone rang, and Richard nearly jumped out of his skin. It made him realise how on edge he really was. Reluctantly, he got up to answer the phone and then announced that he would take the call in the kitchen.

After a few minutes, Richard returned from the kitchen, with a rather perplexed look on his face.

'That was Michael,' he announced. 'He wants me to go over and see him tonight – now, in fact. He sounded a little upset.'

'But it will take you at least an hour to get there, Richard. Did he say what it was about? He's been coming to terms with Mavis' death a lot better of late, I thought,' said Elizabeth.

'He just said that he had something urgent to discuss in person that couldn't wait, and, strangely, he insisted that I come alone.'

'I'll bet one of his poker-playing friends has caught on to his little scam with the Vodka. I know he's started playing again, and I'll bet he's worried he's going to get beaten up or something.'

'Vodka scam? What's that?' asked Paul, curious.

Richard explained that Michael played poker on a regular basis with quite a serious card school – no multi-millionaires or anything, but Richard understood that one could win or lose as much as five or six grand in a night, so it wasn't small time, either. There were about twelve in the school, altogether, but they didn't always all turn up; mostly, there would be six or seven of them. They were supposed to take it in turns to play at one another's homes, but because Michael was the only one living alone now, they had started to have most of their meetings at his place.

Sometimes Michael would cook, because he enjoyed doing it, and sometimes they would send out for food. One thing they always did, however, was to bring their own booze, mostly beer or lager, but a couple of them would bring wine to drink. Michael was the only one to drink spirits, and his particular tipple was vodka. Obviously, the more they all drank, the worse they played, although one or two of them did keep a strict watch on how much they drank. Michael liked to give the appearance of being tipsy, whilst staying pretty sober, and, to this end, he diluted his bottles of Vodka with as much as eighty percent water. This had been his practice for many years, and Elizabeth – and Mavis, too, while she was alive – had often expressed concern about what would happen if anybody found out.

Paul said, 'This Michael friend of yours could end up in hospital if anyone cottons on. It's a risky game to play when money is involved.'

Elizabeth reiterated, 'Mavis and I were always warning him about the possibility of that.'

Paul asked, 'Would you like me to go with you, Richard? Just in case there's any trouble.'

'No, thanks, Paul. Michael specifically asked me to come alone. I expect he is just being melodramatic about something trivial, but he's a good friend, and he would make the effort to come to me if I asked ... so...'

He told Elizabeth that he would phone her when he reached the house, and again when he left, so she would know when to expect him. With that, Richard apologised to Paul and Margaret for leaving so dramatically, kissed both Elizabeth and Rebecca goodbye, grabbed his coat from the hall stand and was gone.

Michael Pegler's house was like a museum. Every wall in his rambling 1930's five-bedroom house was adorned with either a display of shields and swords or an array of pistols and rifles. Weapons of all sorts had been his hobby and passion in adolescence and his business in adulthood. The entrance hall of his home was a large wood-panelled rectangle that had an impressive wooden staircase leading to the five bedrooms and the two family bathrooms. There were four doors off the hall, two on the left under the overhanging landing, leading to a downstairs cloakroom and a well-stocked library, respectively. The other side of the hall had a door leading to the large, well-appointed kitchen and another leading to the equally large and impressive lounge that overlooked fields to the rear of the house.

When he had answered the front door bell, late that afternoon, he couldn't think who would be calling on him. Someone had once said that the most intriguing sound in the world was the sound of an unexpected door bell. They were right, of course, but not all surprises are good ones. It had taken a minute, even with all his experience with guns, to realise that the thing that the man at the door was pointing at him was just that ... a gun. This was no antique, either – it was a very modern and very dangerous-looking automatic.

Stunned and surprised, Michael stepped back into his entrance hall. Two men followed him in. At first, Michael had been too mesmerized by the muzzle of the gun just inches from his face to register the presence of the second man, but he was aware of him now and the fact that he, too, like his comrade, was armed.

'Is there anybody else in the house?' one of them asked.

'No ... I live alone,' Michael replied, 'What is it you want? Money?'

Despite Michael's assurance that they were alone, one man kept his gun trained on him, while the other did a quick tour of the house to ascertain the truth, or otherwise, of Michael's assertion.

Michael had occupied the house with his wife, up until her death only nine months earlier, but he was now the sole occupant. The unwelcome guests took him into his kitchen, where they – for some reason, unknown to him at this time – rolled up the left sleeve of his shirt to the elbow, securing him in a carver chair that one of the men fetched from the dining room. His ankles were bound to the front legs of the chair, with cord that the men seemed to have brought with them for precisely that purpose. They carefully secured his arms to those of the chair.

Since the men had first entered his home, they had had hardly spoken a word, despite his continued request for them to tell him what they wanted. This silence, on their part, had added to the menace that Michael felt. Why wouldn't they speak? While one of the men finished securing Michael to the chair, the other man retrieved a second one from the dining set and placed it in front of Michael, facing him.

'Just shut up and listen,' was the man's instruction, as he sat down in the other chair.

Leaning forward, he stared intensely into Michael's frightened eyes and told him that they wanted him to make a phone call.

'We want you to call your old friend Richard Drake and invite him over,' he said.

'Why? What's Richard got to do with this?'

'You just have to do as you're told, Michael. You don't have to know the reason.'

'And if I refuse? What then?'

Craig grinned, maniacally. He clearly liked this bit. He sauntered over to the sink, casually picked up Michael's kettle, filled it to the brim with water from the hot tap (he had always been an impatient man) and put it on to boil.

Michael watched the proceedings with mounting horror. They obviously weren't about to make tea, and why had they rolled up his sleeve? They couldn't possibly be planning to do what was running through Michael's head.

The kettle boiled in no time at all. Craig unplugged it and carried it over to where Michael was now squirming in his seat.

'OK, OK! You've made your point. I'll make the damned call; just tell me what you want me to say.'

'You need to learn a lesson first, Michael, and the lesson is to do what we tell you, without question and without hesitation. You also need to understand, firsthand, what the consequences will be, if you let us down.'

'Yes, yes, OK, I'll do anything you want. You don't have to do this ... *please*.'

Michael was now in a blind panic. This man was going to pour boiling water onto his arm, and there was nothing he could do to stop him, except plead and beg, and that didn't seem to be working one iota. In fact, looking into this man's cruel eyes, Michael realised, to his horror, that he was actually enjoying himself and that he was going to do this terrible thing, no matter what.

Michael, much to his dismay, had lost control of his bladder and urinated in his pants. These bastards had reduced him to this.

'If you do this, there's no way I'll make your damned call!' Michael screamed at him, in desperation.

'If you don't make the call, the next kettle-full will be in your lap, not on your arm,' was the chilling reply.

Michael began to cry then, and, a split second later, it felt as if a marine distress flare had been surgically implanted in his arm and discharged.

The pain was worse than anything that Michael, in his terror, could have imagined, and it didn't stop. After the first few millilitres of water made contact with his arm, the pain, unbelievably, got worse. The scalding water that followed was falling onto already severely damaged tissue, and, because Michael was restrained, he was unable to do any of the jumping around and flailing of arms that people normally do, in order to alleviate sudden pain. All Michael could do was scream.

Kevin had positioned himself next to his brother, and when Craig had begun to pour the water from the kettle, he had caught hold of his brother's arm and pulled it away before he could empty the kettle too far. He knew his brother well, and he knew that once he started hurting someone, it was difficult for him to stop. They wanted Michael to understand just how serious they were, but they also needed him to be in a good enough condition to fulfill the task they had in mind for him. Craig was initially disappointed by his brother's intervention, but soon understood, and, hey, so what? he reasoned, there was plenty more entertainment to come later.

They gave Michael an hour to recover from his ordeal and even helped him, by placing cold towels over his arm to ease the pain a fraction and to aid recovery. They had ensured that he would do as they asked. They now needed him calm enough to do it well and to be convincing on the phone.

They explained what they wanted him to do in more detail. He had to call Richard on the phone and say that he needed to see him tonight, on a matter of some urgency. He was not to be specific about the reason, but was to emphasize that Michael was in great need of his old friend. He was to tell him that the meeting needed to be kept a secret, even from Elizabeth, and that all would be explained to Richard when he arrived.

As well as being sisters, Mavis and Elizabeth had, in adulthood, been very close friends, and when they had married, it had become obvious that their respective husbands, Richard and Michael, also got on well. In fact, Richard and Michael had known each other slightly before meeting and marrying the sisters. They had played cricket together when they were younger and had common interests – they both had a fascination for old weaponry, they liked the same music, they supported the same football club and they voted for the same political party.

Michael had no doubt in his mind that Richard would come if he asked him, and he also had no doubt that these evil men would do him some harm, perhaps even kill him, for some reason. Michael had already proved, both to himself and to these men, that he was no hero, and of that, he was deeply ashamed. He had read many reports concerning resistance fighters and spies in the Second World War, who had endured horrible tortures under the Nazis to protect their friends and colleagues from discovery. Even the ones who gave up in the end, and supplied the asked-for information, held out as long as they could, in order to give their friends a chance. He, on the other hand, when faced with a similar situation, had caved in at the first threat of torture – he had wet himself and cried like a baby – and now, because of his cowardice, a dear friend would suffer.

Soon, now, they would want him to make the call, and he would do it – the searing pain in his arm and the smell of urine from his lap confirmed it. He began to try and think of ways that he might do as he was bid, but still warn Richard in some way. He remembered a scene in one of the *Star Trek* movies – another shared interest with his friend –where Captain Kirk and Mr Spock had a conversation that they knew was being monitored by the enemy. They had carried on a normal-sounding conversation that had, in fact, been in code. But Kirk and Spock had the benefit of pre-arrangement, which Michael and Richard didn't, and Michael knew only too well that if these men became suspicious, the consequences would be unthinkable.

But, then, what were the consequences of doing nothing? Although Michael had no idea who they were, neither of the men had made any attempt to conceal their faces, and so he would have no difficulty in describing them to the police or identifying them if they were caught. This ominous train of thought led Michael to the conclusion that unless he did something, neither he nor his good friend would survive the day.

The time had finally arrived. One of the men dialled Richard's house number on Michael's mobile, and, after untying his right arm, handed him the phone. Michael tried to stay calm as Richard answered, but there was a small, though noticeable, tremble in his voice. Michael had done as requested and, as expected, a curious and concerned Richard had readily agreed to come over. Michael had no idea what would happen when Richard arrived, only that it would be unpleasant and that, more than likely, neither of them would come to see the morning. Dear God! What had he done?

Chapter 8

Richard pulled his car onto the drive at the front of Michael's house, called Elizabeth on his mobile, to let her know he was there, then got out of the driver's seat and made his way to the front door, wondering why Michael hadn't put the outside light on, as he was expecting company. It was a couple of years since he had been there, and the sight of the house brought good memories flooding back, from when Mavis had been alive. He and Elizabeth had often been invited over for dinner or a barbecue. Many times in the past, after Michael and Richard had played cricket on a Saturday and Mavis and Elizabeth had done the teas, they would drop Michael and Mavis home and stay drinking and talking into the early hours. These days, although Michael still umpired matches, Richard found it increasingly difficult to find the time, and he now joined Michael just to watch the occasional home fixture. Mavis' death had hit them all hard, and Michael had stopped himself from giving in to depression, only by working on his book about antique weapons, continuing to support his cricket team and indulging his love of playing cards.

Richard knocked lightly on the door and was very surprised when someone other than Michael opened it.

'Michael's waiting for you in the kitchen,' the man explained and showed him through.

Richard followed, with an uneasy feeling growing in the pit of his stomach. When his eyes first fell on Michael, he was shocked to the core. He hardly recognised his old friend – his face was drawn and pale, and he looked, for all the world, as if he had been crying. It was only after the initial shock of seeing his friend in such a state that Richard began to register other things. Like the fact that Michael was tied to the chair that he was occupying and that one of his arms was badly burnt or scalded.

Realisation suddenly struck Richard, like a physical blow. My God, he thought, he's been tortured! Richard turned, in anger, to the man that had shown him in and was shocked out of his skin, for the second time in as many minutes, to see not just one man, but two – both of whom were smiling and pointing guns at his head.

The second of the two men had entered the room carrying a chair from the dining room, and he now placed it beside the one that Michael occupied, inviting Richard to sit.

'What's going on, Michael? Who are these men?'

Michael began to sob and blurted out, 'I'm so sorry, Richard. I shouldn't have called you, but these animals tortured me. Please forgive me – I'm such a coward.'

Richard was frantically trying to take it all in, and he soon began to realise that it was more to do with his own troubles, than with any of Michael's.

He looked at Michael's wretched demeanour and abused body and said, 'It's me that should be apologising to you, Michael. You mustn't blame yourself. This is about me, not you. There are things going on that you know nothing about. I'm really sorry you've become involved, and I'm truly sorry for what has happened to you.'

'I guess you must be Craig and Kevin Harper?' asked Richard, slowly turning to face the loathsome pair.

"That's right, Richard. Well done – very perceptive of you,' Craig clapped his hands in mock applause.

'It's good to meet you face-to-face, at last. Now, if you would be so good as to hand over your mobile,' he ordered, holding out the hand that didn't have a gun in it.

Richard did as he was told, and Craig turned it off, slipping it back into Richard's pocket.

'You must realise by now that I had absolutely nothing to do with the death of your mother. I never even got to meet her.'

'Maybe not, but you knew Jack Simmons and Alan Salter, didn't you. Richard?'

Richard didn't fail to notice the use of the past tense when the man spoke of the pair.

'No. Are they the names of the men who killed her? The police are looking for them.'

'Really?' Craig laughed, ''Well. I don't think they're going to find them.'

Before Richard had arrived, Craig and Kevin had come close to having one of their rare disagreements. Craig had wanted to give Richard one of his special 'hot baths', but Kevin had pointed out that they had exposed themselves too much for that. The inspector already knew that there was a link between their mum's death, Margaret's mugging and anything that might happen to Richard, because of the phone call, so they had to make his death look plausibly like an accident. The police wouldn't believe it for a minute, of course, but if it ever got to court, they had to give their barrister a chance to convince a jury that it could have been an accident. The scalding on Michael's arm could have been accidental, but if both men were scalded, and especially if one died as a result of it, it would be too implausible to believe anything other than murder. It would embroil them in a great deal of risky work and involve a lot of money to attempt to nobble a jury, so it had to be, at least, a plausible accident. Eventually, Craig had reluctantly agreed that Kevin was right, as he so often was.

'What's going to happen to us now?' asked Michael, having recovered a little of his normal composure.

'Well, as you ask, it goes something like this ...' said Kevin, 'You called Richard and asked him to come over. We shall never know why. Richard turns up, and two old friends start drinking together, have a bit too much, even. Well, then you decide that coffee would be a good idea, probably to sober up a bit, but, oh dear! Poor old drunken Michael has an accident with the kettle and scalds himself.'

Kevin glanced down at Michael's arm and continued, 'It looks like a very nasty scald. What can you do? It must be incredibly painful, but Richard is on hand and offers to drive you to Accident and Emergency. But, oh dear! Poor old Richard is pretty drunk, too, and, in no condition to drive, really, so the inevitable happens – he crashes the car, en route to the hospital, killing you both. It's all a terrible tragedy.'

Richard and Michael glanced at one another, and, although nothing could be said, there was a tacit understanding between them that if this was, in fact, to be the end, neither held the other to blame.

Kevin continued, 'Of course, other people may put forward a different interpretation of events. Certain people might even suggest that my brother and I were involved in some way, but then, the burden would be on them to prove it, and the accident theory's not a bad one – all the physical evidence supports it, and any good barrister could convince a jury of it, I'm sure.'

'You'll never get away with it,' said Richard.

'Forgive me if I disagree, Richard. I happen to think we have an excellent chance of doing just that. So, now ... what's it to be, gentlemen? Whisky? Brandy?' asked Kevin, as polite and smiling as ever. 'We have both with us, so what will you have for your final tipple?'

'If I am going to meet such an ignominious end, vodka would be my first choice,' said Michael, putting on a brave face for the first time that evening and seeing just the faintest of opportunities to turn the situation around. His brain was beginning to function again, and he hoped that Richard would realise why he had specifically chosen the vodka.

'Sorry, Michael, we didn't think to bring vodka with us.'

'I've got bottles of it in the drinks cabinet,' said Michael, 'I might as well finish it off, if it's going to be my last chance.'

Kevin was pleased at Michael's response. Unlike his brother, Kevin liked to see a man rally round and fight back with some backbone.

'Excellent! Now you're entering into the spirit of things,' he chuckled, 'Get it? Spirit of things, vodka ... oh, never mind. Richard, what can I get for you?'

'I'll help Michael finish off his vodka, if that's all right with you. Have one yourself, why don't you?'

Michael was pleased. Richard didn't like vodka, so he had obviously cottoned on.

'Oh, Richard! Good man – a response worthy of James Bond himself,' exclaimed Kevin, 'I really do appreciate the two of you taking it like this, especially you, Michael. You've really bucked up since Richard arrived. I do hope it's not because you're hoping for some last minute rescue by the cavalry, because there isn't going to be one for you, I'm afraid. Now, I didn't see you as a vodka man, Richard, but it's your choice. If there's enough for two, then vodka it shall be. I can't stand the stuff myself. Give me a decent single malt any day.'

Craig located the drinks cabinet in the dining room and returned with three bottles of apparently unopened vodka, unaware that Michael had perfected the process of opening and re-sealing the bottles, so that they appeared untouched.

'Wow! You like a drop of the hard stuff, don't you, Michael?', then, turning to his brother, 'You should see it, Kevin – it's like an off-licence in there.'

'In a glass or from the bottle, gentlemen?' asked Kevin, politely, 'Your choice, again, but one way or the other, you will drink it.'

Although Michael would have found it easier to be fed drink from a glass, he didn't want them to pour out the watered down vodka, in case they spotted something amiss. The mixture in Michael's bottles would hang around as dregs in a glass far longer than if it had been neat vodka, and it wouldn't make the characteristic curtains around the side of the glass. Although he thought it unlikely that they would pick up on these details, he felt it was better to be safe, than sorry.

'I'll take it from the bottle and save you both on the washing up later. What say you, Richard?' Michael replied, with as much bravado as he could muster.

'Brilliant,' said Kevin, truly pleased and, if he was honest, impressed with the way the men were now facing the prospect of a violent end. Craig liked his victims screaming and cowering in fear; Kevin much preferred the hero staring death in the face.

'Yeah ... whichever.'

Richard eyed the three bottles and wondered just how much Michael had diluted them or if he had diluted them at all. None of the bottles looked as if they had even been opened.

It took the best part of an hour for Kevin to force-feed the three bottles of 'vodka' to the two men. Both Richard and Michael would have done well in an amateur dramatics society, as they both put in a performance worthy of an Oscar, convincing Kevin that they were finding it increasingly difficult to drink, as well as finding it increasingly difficult to stay conscious. Michael was well-practiced at the deception, and Richard pretty much took his cue from what Michael was doing, with his head lolling about and the drink making him cough and splutter. When the three bottles were gone, the two men had consumed the equivalent of four or five large vodkas each and were, in truth, quite tipsy, but not yet paralytic and unconscious, as they pretended to be. Fear was helping to keep them sober.

Both men now hung their heads and, to any onlooker, appeared to be only semi-conscious, but Richard had one eye half-open and was trying to see what Kevin and Craig were up to. Kevin had brought a couple of glasses in at the same time as the bottles of vodka, and he now took Richard's hand and wrapped his fingers around one of the glasses, in order to make it look as if he had used it. He proceeded to do the same with the other glass in Michael's hand, after which, he poured the small drop of remaining vodka into the two glasses and placed them on the kitchen table. He looked at the table for a moment and then used the back of his hand to knock one of the glasses over, spilling the small amount of its contents. Kevin then went through the same fingerprint business with the three bottles, placed two of them on their sides on the table and dropped the other onto the floor, smashing it.

Craig was setting up the kettle and some mugs on the kitchen worktop, to make it look as if somebody had been in the process of making coffee and had dropped the kettle, whilst pouring.

Next, they untied Richard and Michael, and, while Kevin fine-tuned arrangements in the kitchen, Craig returned the chairs to the dining room. The cord they had used to bind their victims was neatly coiled and placed in Craig's pocket.

Thoughts were racing through Michael's brain. He began to regret choosing the vodka, thinking that if he was going to be in a fatal car crash, maybe trapped, in pain and bleeding to death or, worse still, trapped in a burning car, he would prefer to be drunk and unconscious. On the other hand, he owed it to his good friend to at least try and do something to save them both. He wished he could communicate surreptitiously with his friend and formulate some kind of plan with him, but it was clearly going to be impossible. When, he wondered, would be the best time to make a move? Should he try something now? They were, after all, untied, but, then again, they would have to be untied later, as well, to make the crash convincing. Perhaps it would be better to wait until they were in the car; at least, then, one of the men would be preoccupied with driving. But would the ensuing escape attempt then be the cause of a crash, in which they all died anyway? Michael's vodka-addled head was spinning, both from the drink and from agonizing over what to do and when to do it.

Very similar thoughts were racing through Richard's head. He, too, was considering what would be the best time to make their move and wishing that he could communicate with his friend, without the brothers realising. Richard, however, had decided that doing anything before they were in the car carried too much risk, simply because both men were armed. He found it very frustrating, that in a house full of weapons, they couldn't even lay their hands on something with which to hit their abductors over the head.

At last, Kevin and Craig appeared to be happy with the arrangements they had made in the kitchen, and they each got hold of the shoulders of one of their captives and proceeded to drag them to the front door and onwards, out into Richard's car. As he was being dragged across the driveway, Richard's left shoe came off, and it was only with a great deal of strength of will that he prevented himself from crying out in pain, as his heel made contact with the ground and was dragged across the concrete.

He found himself being bundled into the back seat of his Estate by Kevin and was aware of Michael being similarly bundled into the front passenger seat. Kevin disappeared briefly and returned with Richard's shoe, which he unceremoniously tossed into the back of the car. Going through Richard's mind was the fact that, at some time, they would have to transfer him to the driving seat, to make it look as if he had been driving, and he supposed that they would do that together and they would not be able to do it whilst holding guns. Would that present him with the opportunity he craved?

Something was going through Richard's mind, but he couldn't quite hold the thought in his inebriated state, even though, instinctively, he knew it was very important.

Kevin pushed Richard upright and leaned him back in the seat, knocking his head against the door, and, once again, Richard resisted the instinct to call out in pain. The bang on the head, however, may have been responsible for momentarily clearing his mind, and he began to consider what was happening in more detail. All four people were in his car, Michael's car was, presumably, still in his garage; where, then, was Kevin and Craig's car? They must have arrived at Michael's house in some sort of vehicle, but there hadn't been a vehicle on Michael's drive when he arrived. Richard began to work out what the brothers must have done. They would have taken two cars, he surmised, and left one unobtrusively parked, somewhere within easy reach of the intended crash site. The second car – which they must have used to get to Michael's – would now be parked somewhere secluded, but within walking distance of Michael's house. After they had succeeded in staging the crash, Richard deduced that they would use the car parked cannily near the crash site to return and pick up the one from Michael's. Richard was pleased that he had managed to work out their strategy, but none of this speculation helped with the formulation of an escape plan. If only he could recall his earlier thought, which was sneakily eluding him – he knew it was important, more than that, maybe their only hope.

Michael was slouched in the front passenger seat, desperately hoping that Richard would make some sort of move in the back seat, because the man beside him in the back was, he surmised, the far greater threat. As soon as Michael heard something from the rear seat, he would be poised and ready to stop the driver from interfering. He was determined not to let his friend down again.

Richard was thinking along the very same lines as his friend, realising that Kevin was going to be the most difficult to deal with, because he wasn't driving the car. Whether all the thinking he'd been doing was helping to make more solid connections in his addled brain or whether the effects of the alcohol were beginning to wear off early or whether it was just an adrenalin surge is unknown, but Richard suddenly remembered the important idea that had eluded him, earlier.

There was a weapon, of sorts ... and it was in the car! In addition to this, it was one which he was well-placed to get hold of easily. The paper knife, which he had bought for Elizabeth's birthday, was still in the map pocket behind the driver's seat, only inches from his knees. Richard's adrenalin was running in overdrive now, and his heart beat faster as he felt a sudden burst of hope and exhilaration.

Is this how men feel before going into battle? he wondered. Would the soldiers on ancient battlefields, lined up to face the enemy, or the troops in landing craft off the Normandy beaches, have felt the same emotions that he felt now? He had no doubt in his mind that if he had the knife in his hands, he could kill this man – this man, who was intending to kill him and his good friend; this man, who had cold-bloodedly organised for Margaret to be attacked, and who had invaded his home. He hoped and prayed that Michael would be ready to deal with Craig, because he was certainly ready to deal with Kevin.

The car was travelling smoothly along the road, but its motion was causing Richard to sway slightly, from side-to-side. Richard used the swaying motion to his advantage, and he slumped down between the front and back seats, as if the motion of the car had caused him to do this, in his drunken state. As he did so, he slipped his hand into the map pocket and was elated to feel the smooth, cool handle of the knife in his hand. He had no doubt that the action of pulling the knife up and out of the map pocket would also cause it to slide smoothly out of its scabbard, freeing the blade for its gruesome task.

As Richard slumped down between the seats, his head came into contact with Kevin's knees. Kevin leaned forward, regretting not having put the seatbelt on Richard, and grabbed hold of his shoulders with both hands, which effectively spread his arms wide, exposing his chest. With a mighty effort, Kevin heaved Richard back into position in the seat. At the same time, Richard brought the knife out of its place of concealment and thrust it, with all the strength he could muster, deep into Kevin's chest. The knife went all the way in with such ease that, at first, Richard thought he must have somehow completely missed. Eventually, however, his hand made contact with Kevin's chest, and he knew the job was done.

Initially, Kevin thought that Richard had just made a rather pathetic attempt to punch him in the chest, and he continued to try and haul him back into a more upright position. However, he was surprised by his sudden lack of strength and was forced to release his hold on him. Kevin looked down in some confusion and saw blood. Was Richard bleeding? He didn't understand, why did he suddenly feel so weak?

'Where the hell is all that blood coming from?' This futile question was the last conscious thought that Kevin Harper would ever have.

By midnight, Elizabeth was nervously pacing the floor, wondering why Richard wasn't home yet, and, even more importantly, why he wasn't even answering his phone. After Richard left, and everyone had finished their meal, Margaret and Paul had said that they would stay until Richard returned, because it was obvious that Elizabeth was worried. Margaret had tried her best to keep the subject focused on things other than the stresses of what had been happening of late, but she soon realised that she was fighting a losing battle.

At a quarter to one in the morning, Rebecca returned home from her second date with the boy she had 'taken out' the previous night, and, despite being worried about Richard and the late hour, Margaret wanted to know how her date had gone and what the boy in question was like.

Rebecca reported, 'His name is Daniel, and he has his own little music shop. He not only plays the classical guitar, but he actually makes them, as well. He's tall and good-looking, but, at the moment, he's still building his business and is only taking twenty-four grand a year from of it. The bonus, however, is that he is an only child, and both his parents died young, leaving him a detached house in the country, with half an acre of land. So, for the first time in ages, I have put a boy's number in my phone.'

'Well done, Becky,' said Margaret, 'he sounds really nice.'

'Bit mercenary, if you ask me,' said Paul, 'not exactly love at first sight, is it?'

Becky poked her tongue out at Paul, then looked around and enquired, happily, 'Where's Dad?'

They filled Becky in with the events of the evening, and the mood quickly sank again. Elizabeth was now looking at her watch every couple of minutes. She asked Paul if he thought she should ring the hospitals, just to check. By way of a compromise, Paul rang the station and asked to be advised on his mobile of anything involving a Volvo Estate or anybody called Richard Drake being involved in any sort of accident.

Eventually, they all fell asleep on the sofas in the lounge; Elizabeth and Becky on one, and Paul and Margaret in each other's arms on the other. The call, when it came, at five in the morning, woke them all with a start. Paul wandered into the kitchen to take the call; a feeling in the pit of his stomach told him that it would be bad news.

It was the duty sergeant, and he related to Paul that his friend's Volvo had been involved in a fatal accident and that the police, an ambulance and the fire brigade were on the scene.

'There seem to have been three or four people in the car, so the fatality may not be your friend, sir, but that's all the details I have at the moment, I'm afraid,' the sergeant apologised.

'Let me know the moment you have any more news,' said Paul, 'and find out what hospital they are being taken to, would you?'

When he walked back into the lounge, the three women were holding each other in a group embrace, fearing the worst.

'All we know at the moment,' said Paul, before any of them had a chance to ask, 'is that there has been an accident involving Richard's car, but we don't know if he's been injured or not.'

'Oh my God! I knew something was wrong,' cried Elizabeth, 'he would never be this late, without at least trying to contact me.'

'Try to stay calm. We don't know, yet, that he's hurt.'

'Where did it happen? How long ago? You have to drive us there straight away, Paul.'

Paul explained, patiently.

'Look, by the time we've located the scene of the accident, the ambulances will probably have already taken any casualties to hospital. It's far better to wait until we know whether he's been hurt and, if so, which hospital he's been taken to.'

Paul was trying to think of a scenario which would reasonably have three or four people in Richard's car. It didn't make any sense, and, most importantly, who had died?

They all agreed that it was best to go straight to the hospital if Richard was injured, and they waited anxiously for more news, with Margaret pacing up and down. Rebecca and her mother were hugging each other, as if, somehow, if they could do it long enough or hard enough, it would automatically make things better.

When Richard had plunged the knife deep into Kevin's chest, he called out to alert Michael that things were happening, confident that his friend would be waiting for just such a signal. He was right. Michael had been waiting for a sign that things were kicking off in the back, but he had decided not to act immediately, once he got the signal. He had reasoned that the driver would get the message that something was up at the same time as himself and that he would start to brake. Michael concluded that the slower the car was travelling when he made his move on the driver, the more chance he had of avoiding a serious accident.

His assumption was correct. As soon as Richard's call had been heard, Craig braked, slowing the car immediately. Michael watched him intently, and, as soon as he showed signs of reaching inside his jacket for his weapon, Michael lunged at him, catching him off-guard, because he believed Michael was still unconscious. Taken completely by surprise – by both the call from the back seat and the sudden attack from Michael – Craig lost control of the car. It was still travelling at some speed, and the braking caused it to begin skidding sideways. As its occupants were engaged in their life-or-death struggle, the car flipped onto its near-side. The car's momentum then took it over onto its roof, partially collapsing it. It skidded along on its roof for a short distance, before continuing over onto its off-side and back onto its wheels again. This whole process would have been repeated again, had the car's progress not been halted by a very large and substantial tree. The tree in question had occupied that particular spot for more years than the combined ages of all the car's occupants and stubbornly refused to be moved from it.

For a moment, the horrendous sound of the crashing and rending of metal was joined by the roar of a hundred birds, suddenly awakened and taking to the air. Soon, things quietened, and there was simply the silence of the night again, broken only by the sound of a small nocturnal animal scurrying in the undergrowth and the soft 'te-wit' of the owl that hunted it.

When Richard finally regained consciousness, he was soon aware that his body was hurting from head to toe, but he was unable to ascertain how badly he, or anybody else in the car, was injured. However, he discovered, to his growing horror, that he was trapped and, thus, unable to get free from what was left of his vehicle. He sniffed the air for the smell of petrol and was immensely relieved that he didn't sense any. He called out for Michael and was answered, not by his old friend, but by a young female voice, which he didn't recognise.

'Don't try to move. We'll soon have you out of there. Where do you hurt?'

'It hurts all over. How is my friend in the front ... in the passenger seat? Is he all right?'

'Let's just worry about getting you out, shall we? Your friends are being taken care of by others, so try not to worry.'

The sympathetic voice turned out to be that of a young paramedic, by the name of Becky, who kept reassuring Richard that he and his friends were in good hands.

'My daughter's called Becky,' said Richard, as the girl reached into the car to feel down his back for any ominous bumps and to ascertain where, and how badly, he was trapped.

She asked Richard lots of questions about where and how bad his pain was, on a scale of one-to-ten, and then announced, 'They're going to have to cut you out of the car, I'm afraid, so I'm going to put a blanket over you to shield you from the sparks. There will be a lot of noise, but don't worry, we'll soon have you out of there.'

Becky had been right about the noise. Richard's ears were still ringing when the ambulance finally arrived at the hospital. He kept asking the people around him about Michael, but he kept being told that they would keep him informed when they knew any more. He was becoming increasingly frustrated by the lack of information and was worried that his old friend may not have survived the crash. A little while after arriving, he was examined by a doctor, who gave him a pain-killer injection, for which he was very grateful, and he was soon asleep.

Paul's phone rang for the second time that morning, and everyone looked on anxiously, as he took the call. There was much yessing and nodding of his head, and Paul had to put his hand up to the three women to stop a barrage of questions while he was talking. Eventually, he hung up, and they all looked at him, with their faces pleading for information.

'Richard's alive and not too badly injured – just cuts and bruises.'

'Oh ... thank God!' cried Elizabeth, as she sank down onto the nearest sofa.

All three women burst into tears at the same time and were wracked by sobbing; they were so relieved.

'Blimey! What happens when you get bad news?' Paul asked, trying to lighten the mood, now that they knew that Richard was not just alive, but was relatively unscathed.

Some laughter tried to break through the crying, and Liz said, quietly, 'Thank you, Paul,' putting an affectionate hand on his shoulder.

'Which hospital?' asked Rebecca.

'He's been taken to Weston-super-Mare General. Are you coming or not?'

Paul was almost out of the door, catching them unawares, so the three women disentangled themselves from each other and joined him, still tearful.

On the journey to Weston-super-Mare General Hospital, they were all asking each other questions, to which none of them knew any of the answers, but this passed the time, and they were soon pulling into the accident and emergency bay. One ambulance was pulling away, leaving another parked with its back to the entrance, and its doors still wide open.

Paul wondered if it was one of these ambulances that had brought Richard in and just who had been the occupants of the other.

On arrival in reception, they learned that Richard had already been treated and taken to a side ward, but that Michael was undergoing surgery.

'What was Michael doing in the car?' asked Elizabeth, of no-one in particular.

'I'll see what I can find out,' said Paul, 'you go and locate Richard.'

Elizabeth, Becky and Margaret went straight to the ward to see Richard, while Paul went to locate any police that could give him some information about the crash itself and who, besides Richard, was involved? And, most importantly, who had died?

On reaching the hospital ward, the women discovered that Richard had been incredibly lucky – he was sitting up in bed, extremely pleased to see everyone and delighted to simply be alive. He had been removed from the car with only cuts and bruises, although some of them made Elizabeth wince when she saw them, and she had seen some pretty bad ones, as a nurse. Michael had survived the crash, but had not got off as lightly as Richard, having suffered breaks to both of his legs, one arm and a couple of ribs. There was nothing life-threatening, however, and he would be sharing the ward with Richard, after his surgery.

Some three hours later, Michael was wheeled in, propped up in a bed and looking like something out of *The Mummy Returns*, with a bandaged head and a leg in traction.

Despite the seriousness of his injuries, Michael was actually in good spirits and was delighted to see everyone, especially Richard.

The women listened in shocked silence, as the men recounted their story. Richard wondered how Elizabeth would take the news that he had deliberately killed another human being, but he needn't have worried.

'No human being would have treated Michael the way he did,' she said, gently taking hold of her husband's hand, 'so he really doesn't count as human in my book.'

She gave him a big, tight hug, and Richard, for the third time in the last twelve hours, once again, had to put on a brave face and suppress the instinct to cry out in pain.

'Well, I wish you had killed them both, Richard,' said Margaret, and, for a brief, fleeting moment, Richard was afraid he was going to be on the receiving end of another painful hug, but was saved by the timely arrival of Paul.

As Paul entered the room, he looked about for somewhere to sit and, seeing that all the chairs were taken, he made himself comfortable at the foot of Richard's bed. He announced that Kevin was definitely dead, as Richard had originally thought.

'What about the other bastard?' asked Michael.

'There was no sign of Craig at all, unfortunately. The crew on the scene said that they rigorously searched the area and found no sign of the driver. He must have survived the crash and managed to get out of the car.'

The room was silent as they all absorbed this unwelcome information.

It was Elizabeth who spoke first.

'He can't have got far, surely.'

'My team called in help, and they're searching the surrounding area, but, although it was late, he may have been picked up by a passing car.'

'So the scumbag's still out there somewhere,' announced Elizabeth, angrily. 'Well, I hope he is badly hurt and in a great deal of pain.'

'Amen to that,' agreed Michael, firmly.

Richard stared at his wife in blatant disbelief. 'Scumbag?'

Elizabeth shrugged her shoulders and sheepishly looked away from her husband.

After filling Paul in, with the details of their abduction and subsequent escape, the talk had turned to the extent of their injuries, and Michael complained that they didn't seem to have been dealt out very evenly.

'That's our Michael,' said Richard to Paul, 'he always finds something to moan about, even if it's simply that he's been abducted, tortured and nearly killed in a car crash.'

Paul grinned and wondered if he would be up to cracking jokes after the ordeal they'd just been through. These are remarkable people, he thought, not for the first time.

Paul climbed off Richard's bed and announced, 'Right! I'm taking Margaret home now. Anyone else requiring a lift had better come, as well.'

'I'll make arrangements to stay here,' said Elizabeth, reaching out and taking her husband's hand.

'No, Liz, that's a silly idea,' Richard argued, 'Michael and I are both going to need things from home. How will you get back? You might as well go with Paul now, and you can get things for both of us and then bring them down later.'

In the end, it was agreed that they would all leave with Paul, and Elizabeth would come back later with toiletries and other things that they might need in her own car.

Nobody had any idea where Michael's house keys were, and Paul announced that it would now be a crime scene anyway, so Liz said she would buy whatever he needed.

'So tell me what you both want,' she asked.

In the end, she left with a substantial list, compiled by the two patients, and jokingly suggested that she would arrange for it all to be delivered by a haulage company. Paul and Richard looked at each other and nodded happily, each acknowledging to the other that it was good to see Elizabeth coping so well with everything that had happened.

Elizabeth had, in fact, surprised herself, by being able to add a touch of humour. However, she was a little upset with herself, when she realised that her spirits had been lifted, not just by her husband's survival, but by the news of Kevin's death. Although it horrified her to acknowledge it, she was glad that he was finally dead and wished the same fate for his horrid brother.

Richard was not to be spared the pain of another hug from his wife, and, this time, there were two more to follow from Rebecca and Margaret. Because of his more extensive injuries, Michael enjoyed three farewell kisses, but was spared the discomfort of the accompanying hugs.

Just as they were leaving, Richard asked Paul if he would reconsider staying with the women that night, as there would be no man in the house, and he quickly relented, much to Richard's immense relief.

Chapter 9

Richard was allowed to return home the following day, but Michael had to suffer five more days of hospital food, before his doctors agreed that he could go home, with the proviso that he wasn't living on his own. Richard and Elizabeth had come to his rescue, on this front, by insisting that he come and stay with them during his period of convalescence, and they arranged for a hospital bed to be set-up in one of their guest rooms for him. So it was that the Drake residence now accommodated, not just the Drakes themselves, but Margaret and Michael, as well. Paul insisted that he couldn't stay there any longer or it would look unprofessional, career-wise, and, besides, he had to concentrate on the case or, rather, cases, as it now was.

Back at the nick, the incident room was a hive of activity. Craig had been located at the luxury flat that he had shared with his brother in London and had been brought to Bristol for questioning. The brothers had bought the flat as a base for their London operations, including the club, but they both owned other properties, some in their own names and some in others; however, they spent so much time together that a joint flat had been inevitable.

When questioned, Craig denied ever being in the car or anywhere near Bristol on the fateful night. In his interview, he had insisted that his brother had told him that Richard Drake had called him and said that he was to come to a particular house near Bristol, if he wanted to hear something of interest about their mother's murder. Craig said he had wanted to accompany his brother, but that, apparently, Mr Drake insisted that Kevin go alone.

'So where were you when your brother was at this alleged meeting?' Paul asked.

'Me? Oh ... I was playing cards with some friends in Camberley – that's in Surrey, by the way, just in case you were wondering, nowhere near Bristol. Normally, eight or ten of us get together every other week to play. Kevin would have been there as well, if it hadn't been for the call from Mr Drake. So, that night, there were eight people there, including myself.'

'And I suppose these friends will testify that you were there all night, is that right?'

'Oh, I imagine so, Inspector. Why would they lie about a thing like that?'

'Well, you will have to supply us with the names and addresses of all the people you say were with you that night, and we'll interview every one of them. You see, Richard Drake and Michael Pegler tell a somewhat different story, and there is a lot of physical evidence to support their version of events. They say that you kidnapped Michael and tortured him into calling Richard to the house; they say that you then tried to get them drunk, so that you could stage a car accident and, thus, kill them both.'

'My word! It seems that Richard Drake and Michael ... Pegler – did you say? – have very vivid imaginations, Inspector, because, as I understand it, the only person to be killed that night was my brother, and it was Drake who stabbed him to death, I understand. Has he been charged with that yet, by the way?'

'You'll find that it's called self-defence, Craig. You and your brother were trying to kill them, and I'm going to prove it.'

'Well, good luck with that, Inspector. I'll be interested to see how you manage it, because, as I keep telling you, I was playing cards in Camberley, and there are seven witnesses. As for my late brother, he was a dear, sweet man, who wouldn't hurt a fly, and now he's been murdered. I hope your department isn't going to try and sweep it all under the carpet, just because this Drake is a friend of yours. Can I go now?' asked Craig, brushing some imaginary fluff from his sleeve and turning to leave.

'No ... not quite yet. I've got some more questions for you, and I want our divisional doctor to examine you before you go. You seem to be in some pain, Craig. Have you been in an accident?'

'How very observant of you, Inspector. You really must be a very good detective. As a matter of fact, I have had an accident. I'm afraid I got rather drunk playing cards, you know how it is ... well ... the toilet at my friend's house is upstairs, and do you know what? It's rather a coincidence, I suppose, seeing as how Mum died and all, but I fell down the stairs, would you believe it? It's all very embarrassing. I don't normally let the drink get to me like that, but I paid heavily for my indulgence – cracked a couple of ribs, dislocated my shoulder, broke my collar bone, and I'm covered in bruises from tip to toe. Do you know, Inspector, the doctor who treated me – he was one of my friends that I was playing cards with, by the way – he said it looked as if I had been in a car crash. I was so injured.'

'Got it all worked out, haven't you, Craig? Well, we don't believe your version of events for a moment, and we're going to go over every single detail with a fine toothcomb, starting with our doctor checking you out.'

'Thanks for the offer, Inspector, but I have every confidence in my own doctor, and I have no desire for a second opinion, thank you very much.'

'It's not an offer, Craig. You're a suspect in an attempted murder inquiry – and a murder inquiry, as well, now that we have identified Stephen Potter as the body in your mum's garden. So, if I have to arrest you to get it done, I will, but then you'll be here for as long as I can keep you; if you co-operate, you can be out of here a good deal quicker.'

'Well, seeing as you put your case so charmingly, Inspector, how can I refuse the offer?'

'He'll want a DNA sample, as well.'

'Of course he will.'

'And then, we'll have another little chat.'

'In that case, Inspector, I think it's time I called my solicitor, don't you?'

'Yes, Craig, I do – I think you're going to need one.'

No more than an impressive forty minutes after Craig made his phone call, his solicitor turned up. He was younger than Paul had expected, probably no more than twenty-eight or so. He wore an expensive handmade suit and sported a diamond tie-pin. Paul wondered, perhaps unjustly, where the diamond in the pin had come from, as he was enquiring how he had arrived so quickly. Paul expected him to have travelled down from London, but he explained that the firm that Craig retained had offices in Bristol and that he was based there. He explained that any one of four solicitors could have turned up to sit with Craig in his interview. If he was to be charged, of course, Craig's personal lawyer would come down from London.

'OK, so, maybe, you bought the diamond yourself,' thought Paul, revising his earlier, uncharitable assumption, but it still irked him that a solicitor had turned up so quickly, at the snap of Craig's odious fingers.

Craig spoke to his solicitor for twenty minutes in private, after which, the interview continued in much the same fashion as it had started, to the extreme annoyance of Paul and John Campbell, who were conducting it. Craig was asked if he had ever known a Stephen Potter, to which he had, at first, replied no; however, after Paul pointed out that he lived within the same school catchment area, he thought for a moment and said that there may have been a boy with that name at the local school, but that he couldn't be sure.

'So he wasn't a friend of yours or your brothers, then?'

'No, Inspector, my brother and I had each other; we were very close, you understand – we didn't really need anyone else. I know that may seem strange to you, Inspector, but if you are not a twin yourself, it would be impossible for you to comprehend the relationship or, indeed, the enormity of the unbearable grief that I am suffering right now, at the loss of my beloved brother.'

Craig did look genuinely upset, as he spoke of his brother, but Paul was unimpressed.

'How would you explain Stephen's body being found in your garden?'

'My parent's garden, Inspector – you, yourself, said – it had been there for many years, and my brother and I would have been children when this poor Stephen-fellow was allegedly buried. In answer to your question, however, I can't provide an explanation for it, but that doesn't mean that either my brother or I had anything to do with it.'

Craig's lawyer cut in, 'Are you questioning my client about the death of Stephen Potter, Inspector, or about the alleged attack on Richard Drake and the death of my client's brother? You should confine your questioning to one or other.'

Craig smiled at the youngster, "Well said ... And on the subject of my brother, Inspector, has Drake been charged yet? Because it's about time; he's surely not going to get away with this absurd self-defence claim. If the law won't see justice done for my brother's death, than I shall have to,' announced Craig, leaning forward, menacingly.

Craig's lawyer put a restraining hand on his arm and nodded quickly, indicating that Craig should moderate his language and behaviour.

Craig looked back at his solicitor and shrugged his shoulders, compliantly.

Paul ignored the outburst, and, after a few more questions with no satisfactory answers, it was Craig's solicitor who suggested that things were obviously going nowhere, and Paul was forced, though reluctantly, to agree with him.

An hour after the interview with Craig and his solicitor, Paul was speaking to the divisional doctor, who had just examined him. He had caught up with the doctor at the coffee machine, located at the end of one of the many long corridors that criss-crossed the building, and they sat together on the hard wooden bench that faced it.

'Can we place him in the car, Doc?'

'He has injuries consistent with having been in a car crash, certainly; most significantly, bruising from a seat belt that probably saved his life, but I can't prove it was that specific crash. He only has to say that he had to brake hard in another collision in a car to explain the seat-belt injury. I could make an argument that it is likely that he was in the car, sure enough, but it would be easily disputed. If we had the jacket that he was wearing at the time of the accident, we might find matching fibres on the seatbelt, but, of course, we don't have it. Even if we find his DNA in the car, which I'm sure we will, we can't prove how it got there or when. Also, with the two of them being twin brothers, they would both have very similar DNA anyway, and the defence would have a field day with that fact. It's all circumstantial, I'm afraid. I'm sorry, Inspector; I know you were counting on something more positive.'

Paul thanked the doctor for his efforts and then went into the incident room, where he asked June if there was any more news.

'Nothing, Guv. I take it the good Doc couldn't help us much, judging by the expression on your face.'

'That's an accurate assessment of the state-of-play, June – no help at all, other than saying his injuries were consistent with being in a car crash, you know how it goes. He did, however, say that they would probably get DNA from inside the car. Let's hope Reg has more luck with our so-called witnesses. Do you know, Craig actually claimed that he fell down some stairs, just like his dear old mum, and that the doctor who examined him said that he was so badly bruised, he looked like he'd been in a car crash.'

'Oh, he does seem to have an answer for everything, doesn't he? I'll get you that coffee, Guv. You look like you could use it.'

As June turned away, she stopped and said, slowly, 'But, surely, Guv, if they do get his DNA from the car that would put him in it?'

'Yeah, but you know what would happen in court with DNA evidence, especially as there was someone in the car with very similar DNA. They will argue that it was contaminated and was really his brother's or that his brother had Craig's DNA on him and it was transferred in the crash or even that he had been in Richard's car some other time. It's good evidence, June, but it's just not enough on its own – we need a lot more than we have, in order to nail this guy. Who knows? He might even try to say we planted it in the car. Don't forget that the onus of proof is on us.'

Later in the day, the team got together for the usual briefing update, and Paul had just started to address them, when Chief Inspector Blake entered the room.

'Sorry to interrupt, Paul, but the team all need to hear this.'

He walked from the door to the area just in front of the notice boards, and the team parted like the Red Sea to let him through.

'Listen up, all of you,' he shouted, and everyone immediately turned their attention to the DCI.

'The investigation into the murder of Mrs Harper is now concluded. I have just had confirmation that the DNA obtained from the hair samples, taken from the hair brush of Jack Simmons, are a match to DNA obtained from the skin and blood found under Mrs Harper's nails. So it's not just the prints on the bronze any more, we actually have his DNA on the victim. So, congratulations to one and all, you have all done extremely well – we have the killer and his accomplice. Well ... we know who they are, and we have the necessary evidence, anyway.'

A general murmur of congratulations could be heard throughout the room, together with some mutual back patting, but it was obvious to everyone that there was more to come from the DCI standing in front of them.

'Now, normally, of course, the case wouldn't be closed until the killers were in custody, charged and found guilty, but as we have good reason to suppose that the two men responsible are no longer with us, there seems little point in wasting valuable resources trying to bring two dead men to account for the murder. The file will, obviously, stay open, but I have to tell you that unless something turns up very soon, the search will be called off. Now, I don't want anyone getting ideas above their station, but this was a murder by strangers, and, as you are all well aware, those are the most difficult cases to close, and this one was cracked very quickly by good basic police work – a fact that, I can heartily assure you all, will not go unnoticed higher up, I'll make sure of that.

'Now, it may, in part, be due to the team's performance, that it has been decided to keep you all together as a team, working from this incident room, until we can prove one of the following. Either that Craig Harper, along with his now-deceased brother, attempted to murder Richard Drake and

Michael Pegler or that they murdered Stephen Potter or that they murdered Alan Salter and Jack Simmons – take your pick.

'Obviously, we have the same issue of the missing bodies, with the last option. You can look on yourselves as a sort of 'Get Craig Harper Task Force', if you like. I'd prefer to have him for all three, of course, but, bear in mind, that they were probably minors for the murder of poor Stephen. So the attempted murder of Richard Drake and Michael Pegler seems our most likely possibility of a successful outcome. But let's get him for something, gentlemen ... oh, I'm sorry, and ladies.'

He smiled at June Kelly.

'The Met is going to co-operate in any way that they can; they want this man behind bars and his organisation closed down. The priorities, for us, are to convict Craig Harper of one of the crimes I've mentioned. The Met will concentrate on the Harper Brothers' businesses. With Kevin out of the picture, the Met think, and I agree, that this is the best opportunity anybody has had to stop their horrible little enterprises. The Met have assigned officers to gather evidence of their protection and extortion rackets; they believe the nightclub to be wholly legit, but they have confided in us that they have someone on the inside there. So, bear that in mind, if investigations take us down that path; remind yourselves what this man is like, and what would happen to any undercover operative, if their cover is blown.'

'Why is the Met so keen now?' asked June. 'After all, they've had the Harpers on their patch for years.'

'Quite right, June, but it seems that Kevin's death has weakened their organisation, and a lot of the support they could rely on before is melting away; other gangs are sniffing around, looking to take over, and the Met feel that Craig is at his most vulnerable. It would seem that Kevin was the brains of the two, and it's possible that Craig will make mistakes, without his brother to guide him. What's the latest we have on the attempted murders?'

Reg stepped forward and announced, 'We now have statements from all but two of the people that were supposed to have been playing cards with Craig on the evening of the crash, and the last two shouldn't be more than a day away.'

He looked over at Paul, expecting him to take over, but Paul nodded for him to carry on with his findings.

'There are a couple of very minor inconsistencies in the statements, but if you pull any of them up on it, they will just say, "Oh, yeah, that's right. Sorry, I was a bit drunk at the time." And, actually, if you put a group of people together, drinking for a night, and then ask questions about it the next day, there are going to be inconsistencies –it's a lack of inconsistencies that would be suspicious. The doctor who was there, who treated Craig after his convenient fall down the stairs, confirms Craig's story, and, would you believe, he's a consultant surgeon, with premises in Harley Street. And, get this, according to my source, he treated the Chief Constable's piles a few years back, but don't go bandying that information about; I was told in confidence, and I do not want to make an enemy of the Chief Constable.'

Everyone was amused by Reg's intimate revelation, but the DCI cut in, 'All right, all right, I think that particular piece of information should stay between these four walls, unless someone fancies pounding the beat again.'

June Kelly laughed and said, 'Chief Constables don't have piles, anyway, Reg – they have "haemorrhoids".'

'Not if I have to write the report, they don't,' replied Reg, 'how the bloody hell do you spell "haemorrhoids?"'

John Campbell, who had worked with Reg before, remarked, jokingly, 'What difference does it make, Reg? You can't spell piles properly, anyway.'

When the laughter had finally died down, Clive asked, sensibly, 'What's our next move, Guv?', and all eyes turned immediately to Paul.

'We keep picking away at the witness statements – interview them all again, see if they can remember to tell the same lies as the last time. John, Clive – you two can get on to that. We also need to try to place Craig in the driving seat of Richard's car on the night of the crash. It looks as if we will recover his DNA from the car, but we have to establish that it got there on the night of the crash to make it watertight. Now, let's think about how Craig and his brother planned to do things that night. How did they arrive at Michael's house in the first place? Presumably, they didn't walk, so let's speak to everyone in the general area – did they see any strange cars about, either parked up close or being driven towards Michael's? Where were they planning to stage the accident? If they were both in Richard's car on the way there, how did they intend to get back to pick up the car they had arrived in? and where is it?'

'That's quite a thought, Guv,' said Clive, 'if they had a car parked, ready for use, near where they were going to stage the accident, and they didn't arrive, perhaps the car is still there?'

'OK ... so let's get a map and pick spots where it would be reasonable to stage an accident.'

June Kelly got a map from the cupboard and started clearing a space on one of the large trestle tables. Clive Pascoe helped her, and they spread the map out, anchoring the corners down with coffee mugs.

'There must be loads of possible places,' said Clive. 'What sort of accident are we talking about, anyway? One like they actually had? Were they going to crash the car into a tree and burn it out with the victims inside? Or were they going to drive it over a cliff somewhere?'

John Campbell spoke up.

'Crashing into a tree and burning would be my choice – it would be easier to ensure that you killed them both. If you run the car over a cliff, unless it's a pretty steep one, you can't be certain it wouldn't get stuck on something halfway down; you can't be absolutely sure of killing the victims in the crash, you'd have to kill them first, and, in that case, a post mortem could definitely pick up on something.'

'That's all very true,' said Paul, walking over to look at the map, 'and it makes our task more difficult. There have to be many more places to crash and burn a car, than there are steep cliffs.'

Derrick, the office manager, who had been listening with intense interest, interrupted, 'Perhaps we're approaching the problem from the wrong angle, Guv. Instead of trying to find a possible crash location, maybe you should just find out what cars have been reported abandoned since the accident and then see if any of them are positioned near to a likely site for a crash or whether they can be linked to the Harpers in any way.'

June stepped in, 'They probably would have hired a car, Guv. If they used a stolen one, there would always be the possibility of it being spotted by uniform. I'll check all the car rental agencies and see if any cars are overdue for collection.'

Derrick began to assign them their tasks for the day, and Paul informed him that he wanted the team to concentrate on the attempted murders of Richard and Michael, as the DCI had advised, and that he would oversee it. But, in actual fact, he intended to investigate the murder of Stephen Potter, with June. Without bodies, he felt it unlikely that they would get anywhere with the murders of Jack and Alan, but he wanted to know if anybody on the team had any other thoughts about the situation.

'That's how I want to run things for now,' he concluded, 'if one investigation starts to look more fruitful than the others, we can, obviously, put more into it. Now that we've got three investigations going, I'll keep pushing the DCI for more personnel on the ground.'

He turned to June, 'Let someone else chase up the car-hire side of it, June. I want you with me. Let's find out what happened to Stephen Potter. Have you got the newspapers together yet?'

'*The Evening Post* and *The Western Daily Press* were the two local papers to cover it, Guv. There was very little in the Nationals, because Stephen went missing on the sixth December 1980.'

'And how did that affect the national coverage of a missing boy?' asked Paul, frowning.

'Because by the time the national press got to hear of Stephen's disappearance, it was probably the eighth.'

'And?' Paul queried, impatiently.

'Oh. come on, Guv! The eighth of December 1980? John Lennon was shot!'

'Oh, yeah, that would probably account for it.'

'But never mind, Guv – *The Evening Post* have sent over everything that they have on Stephen, so I have his parents' names – Susan and Derrick Potter – and their address – 59 Hill Street, Long Barton.'

'Well, that's definitely a start. I wonder if there is any point in visiting the house?'

'I would say it was well worth a visit, Guv.'

'And why is that, Constable? Is there something I should know?'

'Only that *The Evening Post* interviewed the next-door neighbours, at the time – a Mr and Mrs Clark, at 57 Hill Street. Well, I rang directory enquiries to ask if there was a number for a Mr Clark at 57 Hill Street, Long Barton, and, guess what? They're still there!'

Paul pointed to the door, indicating that she should follow him out, and said, 'Constable Kelly, I predict great things for you in the future, but if you persist in making me prise information out of you, grain-by-grain, I promise, I shall come up with an extremely embarrassing nickname for you and insist on using it in front of the team, is that clear?'

'Point taken, Guv. Shall I drive?'

'Yes, June, get me to Hill Street,' said Paul, and, then, turning back to the rest of the room, clapped his hands, barking, 'Well, don't just stand about people – let's get on it.'

* * * * * * * * * * * *

Craig Harper walked into the property letting agency, wearing an off-the-peg suit and sporting an open-neck shirt that he hoped made him look less memorable than normal, and introduced himself as Trevor Hunter. The real Trevor Hunter was born in 1968, the same year as Craig, but he had been a sickly lad, who had been born prematurely and, as Shakespeare would have put it, 'scarce half made up'. He had a hole in his heart and troublesome kidneys, which resulted in him spending as much of his twenty years in hospital, as he did out. In the end, he left the world the same way that he had come into it – prematurely.

Some years ago, after trawling through obituaries for likely names, Craig had obtained a copy of Trevor's birth certificate, and this had enabled him to resurrect Trevor – on paper, anyway. Craig now had a full range of documents in Mr Hunter's name, including a driver's license and a passport, both with Craig's picture on them. Mr Hunter had become, in death, quite well-off, money- and property-wise, with two well-stocked bank accounts, a not inconsiderable portfolio of shares and investments, a detached house in the country and a villa in Italy.

The rather attractive young lady, by the name of Sandra, who approached him, asked if she could help.

He replied, 'I'm going to be in the area, working for a couple of years, and I want to rent a house on the north side of Bristol, a few miles out. Do you have anything suitable?'

She offered him a coffee, which he accepted, and then regretted doing so, when he saw her heading for a machine at the back of the shop. She was very attractive and dressed to show herself off. Under different circumstances, Craig could have been tempted, but he had other things on his mind and was still finding some movements quite painful after the accident. He forced himself to sample the coffee, as she went through various files, eventually finding one that was more than suitable for his purpose.

'It's a three-bedroom house, with off-road parking for two cars and a detached garage,' she told him.

The property was situated in a road that was almost opposite the house owned by Richard Drake.

She explained, 'The property is owned by a man and his two sisters; they inherited it when their mother died, some time back. The siblings, however, can't agree on what to do with the property – one wants to sell it as it is, one wants to do it up first to get the best price and the other wants to buy her siblings out and live in it herself. Hence, the property is for rent at the moment, while the family sort out their differences. It is in need of modernisation throughout and is mostly unfurnished, but it is habitable.'

Sandra, who had taken quite a shine to the handsome Mr Hunter, with his casual manner and gold watch, offered to drive him to view the property herself. Craig was rather amused by Sandra's obvious flirting, and, under different circumstances, he may have rewarded her with the date she so obviously desired. However, he didn't want any complications, so he said, politely, 'That would be great. I'd certainly like to have everything sorted out, before my girlfriend arrives in a week or two's time.'

Sandra was disappointed by the reference to a girlfriend, and her smile all but disappeared.

The house, he decided, would suit his purpose perfectly, after he assessed the view from the bay window of the front bedroom. Richard Drake's property was clearly visible on the main road, just up from the turning. He paid the necessary deposit, together with the first month's rent and signed the contract, as soon as they returned to the agent's office.

Craig then visited John Lewis and purchased a dining room suite, an expensive single bed and bedding, some bits and pieces for the bathroom and kitchen and a very comfortable chair, in which he could sit and watch films on his new top-of-the-range television and DVD player. The fact that he wasn't at home, didn't mean he had to be uncomfortable, he reasoned. He also bought a couple of his favourite films to watch – *The Godfather* and *The Untouchables*. He loved gangster movies.

Everything was delivered, and he moved in, four days later. He made a couple of very discreet trips to his mother's house and picked up a few things – some because they would be of use to him at his new address and some because they were valuable, and, as he was not an executive for his mum's will (some firm of solicitors would end up happily making a small fortune out of that), he thought he would remove them, before probate.

The rented house would serve as a base of operations. He was near enough to the Drake's house, that he could keep an eye on the comings and goings there, yet it was shielded from the road sufficiently by extensive hedges, so that he and his car could stay unnoticed for some time. He had decided that Richard was to suffer before he died – first, mentally and, then, physically. He was rather good at making people physically suffer, and he looked forward to the challenge of applying mental torture. Kevin had always been good with that sort of thing, so he sat in his comfortable, new chair and pondered what his brother would have suggested in the situation.

After some hours of thought, a couple of whiskeys and a viewing of the Godfather, he had made some life-changing decisions. Firstly, he had decided on the first move in the 'Make Richard Drake Suffer' campaign. Second, he had decided to retire. Things were never going to be the same, now that Kevin was gone. He had to admit that Kevin had been the real brains behind their operations; he was the one who built the businesses up and made them what they were. Craig had been the brawn – the enforcer, who ensured that what Kevin wanted to happen, did happen, and that if anyone got in the way, they regretted it ... big time. Everybody knew not to mess with the Harper brothers and that had mostly been down to Craig.

Several people had already made offers for both the club and the other, rather more profitable, businesses. He would come out with a considerable sum, even if the offers were to be reduced, due to Kevin's recent demise. Then, there was the fact that he was Kevin's next-of-kin, as well as his mother's. There would be considerable taxes to pay, but he would still inherit an extremely large amount and that was just the stuff in his mum's and Kevin's names. Kevin had a duel identity, the same as Craig did, and they had set things up, so that they could each control the other's finances, just in case. That way, if one of them died, the other could simply transfer the funds from the deceased's accounts into his own. Similar arrangements had been made for the various investments.

Craig was a very wealthy man as Trevor Hunter, who owned a villa in San Remo on the Italian Riviera. When the assets from Kevin's other identity were transferred in, it would be enough to make most men's eyes water. All the assets he had as Craig Harper, together with the inheritance from Kevin and his mother, he would put into something easily transportable, such as diamonds, and he would arrange for those to be held in safety deposit boxes in England, Italy and Switzerland, so that he could dip into them if, and when, he needed, and Trevor Hunter would retire to his villa in San Remo.

Craig realised that, in retirement, he was going to be the richest man he knew, and that, in fact, he loved Italy – the weather was good, the food and the wine was superb and his money could buy him whatever his heart desired. As it happened, he also considered Italian girls to be the loveliest in the world – at least, while they are young, and the sun hasn't dried up their skin yet, and when they get older ... well ... never mind that, there are always lots of young ones, if you have money. Yes, first, Richard Drake, then, retirement in the Italian sun.

* * * * * * * * * * *

'There was no great damage to either the front or back of the vehicle, as there would have been, had it collided with another car, and it was obvious from skid marks on the road that the vehicle had braked hard, skidded and then tumbled sideways, until it hit the tree. This accounted for the majority of the damage being to the sides and the roof of the vehicle.'

'And, in your opinion, this would account for the fact that the driver of the vehicle was able to survive the crash and escape from the car?' asked the Coroner.

'That's right. We know that the driver was the only person in the car wearing a seat belt, so he would have been protected by that and the side-impact air bags going off.'

The Coroner's Court had been in session for over two hours. Richard and Michael had been questioned in great depth by the Coroner, who had wanted to know why Richard had taken the drastic action that he had. Had he really believed his own life, and that of Michael Pegler, to be in mortal danger?

After almost another hour, the Coroner spoke gravely to the Court.

'It is quite apparent to this court that Kevin Frederick Harper died as a result of being fatally stabbed in the chest by Richard Drake. Mr Drake's account of the events leading up to the stabbing – which involves himself and Michael Pegler being forced to drink alcohol by the deceased and his brother, so that they could stage a car accident and kill them – has been supported by both police statements and by much of the physical evidence that has been presented to this court. It is, therefore, the verdict of this court that Mr Kevin Frederick Harper died as a result of being "lawfully killed", by Mr Richard Drake, in an act of self-defence.'

Elizabeth had been holding her breath while the Coroner read his verdict, even though Paul had said that there had never been any doubt about the outcome. Nevertheless, she immediately rang Rebecca at work, to give her the good news. Paul had been hoping that Craig would attend the court, because it appeared that he had gone to ground, and everyone was eager to know where he was. They had recovered his DNA from the car, and Paul had decided that the case against him was strong enough to take to court.

'It doesn't look as if Craig is going to put in an appearance,' he said to Richard, 'which is a shame. I have men stationed outside the court, ready to follow him to his lair and arrest him if he puts in an appearance, but he's nowhere in sight.'

'Why would you follow him?' asked Elizabeth. 'If he shows up, why not just arrest him here?'

'We want to know where he has been staying, so that we can search it for any more evidence,' Paul replied. 'There's really no telling what incriminating stuff he may have with him.'

Sitting at the back of the court were two men engaged in deep conversation, and Paul recognised one of them as the solicitor who had attended Craig in his interview. Paul pointed out the two men to Richard, as they followed them from the court.

'Who is his solicitor talking to, do you think?' asked Richard.

Paul replied, 'The solicitor who I met was just a representative from *Holloway and Letts*, but I think the other man that he is talking to might be Craig's personal lawyer, down from London.'

They stood outside the court with Michael, who was now semi-mobile, but suffering from sitting on a hard seat in the court for hours. They were waiting for Elizabeth, who had paid a visit to the ladies room, after the long wait. The sun was warm on their faces, as they watched the two men get into their respective cars, after shaking hands. The solicitor who Paul recognised got into a black Audi 8 that looked as if it was polished every day and twice on Sundays, while his companion – whom Paul speculated was Craig's personal lawyer – got into a very smart, new Bentley Continental GT.

'Wow! Looks like being a gangster's lawyer pays well. Is that a car or is that a CAR?' commented Paul, shielding his eyes from the sun's rays with one hand, as he watched the two men depart from the parking lot.

'I think the term is limousine. Not jealous, are you Paul?' asked Richard, smiling.

'Me? Jealous? Well, maybe, just a little bit.'

'I didn't know you were interested in cars.'

'It's not the cars, as such – it's the trappings of wealth, in general. I wouldn't feel uncomfortable with a couple of wealthy trappings, if they were honestly come by.'

Elizabeth joined the three of them and caught sight of the Bentley, as it left the car park.

'Why have you never bought me a car like that, Richard?' she asked, sliding her arm through his.

'Because I didn't think it would be a good idea to re-mortgage the house just to buy a car, but if you really want one ...'

'No ... on second thoughts, my little Fiesta is fine; besides which, I think something like that would look a bit out of place in the hospital car park. I don't even think any of our consultants drive Bentleys.'

Richard was impressed that his wife knew the make of car and was going to say as much, but he noticed that Michael was beginning to wobble, so he suggested that they get a move on, before he keeled over. After a few more comments about how pleased they all were with the verdict, they said their goodbyes to Paul and headed home.

Chapter 10

June parked Paul's car outside number 57 Hill Street, and she and Paul got out of the car and looked at the two houses in front of them – 57 and 59. Number 59, where Stephen had lived as a child, looked as if it had been built the day before. The paintwork was fresh and new, and the roof looked as if it had recently been re-felted, and the tiles had since been replaced with more modern, stylish ones. The owners of 59 had obviously lavished all their love and attention on the house, because the garden, although not actually overgrown, looked somewhat neglected in comparison.

By contrast, next door, number 57 looked a little rundown, as is often the case when an elderly couple have occupied it for a long time and are growing older. It needed, as the estate agent would say, 'modernising', however, it was clean, and the paintwork was faded, rather than peeling or actually dirty. The garden, however, in stark contrast to next-door's, stood out from all the rest of the gardens in the street, and it was quite clearly somebody's pride and joy. The flower beds were pristine, with not a weed in sight, and the small lawn looked more like a bowling green.

They knocked on the door, and it was opened by a smartly-dressed gentleman, who looked surprised and more than a little anxious.

'Oh! I'm sorry,' he said, surprised, 'I was expecting my son; do forgive me. What can I do for you? There's nothing wrong, is there? Nathaniel hasn't been in an accident or anything, has he?'

Paul realised that June was already showing him her warrant card; it could be a shock to have the police turn up, just when you're expecting a family member.

'No! No, it's nothing like that. I'm sure your son is fine. Mr Clark, is it?'

'Yes ... that's right – Howard Clark and this is my wife, Ellen,' he said, indicating the equally smartly-dressed woman, who had just joined him at the door.

'I'm Inspector Paul Manley,' said Paul, showing them his warrant card, 'and this is Constable June Kelly. We would just like to have a few words with you about Stephen Potter, as we understand you were living here at the same time as the Potters; is that right?'

'Oh, yes, Inspector. We remember the Potters well, don't we, Howy?' said Ellen. 'Do come in and take a seat, both of you. Would you like a drink? Tea? Coffee?'

They followed the couple through to their sitting room, where they all sat on a rather old, but well cared-for, three-piece suite. The room itself looked as though it had been recently decorated, in contrast to the exterior, but in a style that was at least thirty years out-of-date.

Mrs Clark brought in a tray of tea for June and themselves and a mug of instant coffee for Paul, with enough biscuits to feed an army. Paul was just about to start asking them questions, when the doorbell rang. Mr Clark rose to answer it, once again, saying, 'That'll be Nathaniel now.'

'Nathaniel is our son,' explained Ellen, with pride. 'He's an army Major.'

Nathaniel came into the room, dressed in a hand-made pair of slacks and a smart white shirt, with collar and tie. He dropped the small suitcase he was carrying behind the settee and carefully folded the jacket he'd been carrying on top of it. He introduced himself to the visitors as just plain Nathaniel Clark, with no mention of any army rank.

Nathaniel's mother got up from the sofa, with some difficulty, to kiss her son and explained, 'These people have come to enquire about poor Stephen Potter.'

Nathaniel shook both their hands and said, 'So you want to know about Stephen Potter, Inspector? Does that mean you've found him at last?' he asked.

'Yes, we've recovered a body that we have positively identified as belonging to Stephen Potter. How well did you know him?'

Nathaniel smiled, as if recalling fond memories, and said, 'Oh I knew him very well, Inspector. We basically grew up together,' he said, taking up residence in one of the armchairs.

'I think I was about two years old when Stephen was born next door, so we got to know each other as toddlers, I suppose. Mum and Dad put a gate in the fence between our two gardens – to make it easy for us to play together as children, and we were the best of friends, until Stephen's disappearance when he was twelve. Well, actually, if truth be told, until just a little before Stephen's disappearance, I suppose.'

'What was he like?'

'Oh, Stephen was a good sort, Inspector. We became very close, in the few years that I knew him. We were both keen on football and played in the school team together, and we both liked shooting. Dad bought me an air rifle and set up a sort of firing range in the back garden, with bales of hay and everything to make it safe. I don't think Mr Potter was very keen on the idea to start with, but he soon came round, when he saw how good Stephen was at the sport. I turned out to be a pretty good shot myself – won a few tournaments in the army, that sort of thing.' Nathaniel pointed to a glass display cabinet, which stood to one side of the fireplace, 'But Stephen was much better than I was; if he hadn't gone missing when he did,

I think he might well have ended up shooting for his country – he was that good.'

Nathaniel's mobile phone rang, and, after excusing himself, he took the call in another room.

Paul stood up and walked over to the cabinet that Nathaniel had pointed to. It contained an assortment of photographs in silver frames – people in military uniforms; mostly group shots, with Nathaniel in most of them, but some single portraits of high-ranking officers. There were also two signed photographs – one of the former Prime Minister, John Major, and one of Prince Charles in uniform. On the top shelf, there were several trophies – some for swimming and running and three first-place medals for shooting, all awarded to Nathaniel at various stages of his career. There were also some medals and citations, one of which was 'The Conspicuous Gallantry Cross.'

'Mum likes to keep them on show,' said Nathaniel, returning to the room after his call, genuinely a little embarrassed by Paul's scrutiny of his awards.

'And why not?' replied Paul. 'She obviously has good reason to be proud of her son. Have you ever actually met the Prince?'

'On a few occasions. Tell me, what happened to Stephen, Inspector?'

'Unfortunately, we don't know what happened to him, yet,' said Paul, returning to his seat and taking a sip of coffee. 'We only now know where he ended up. Tell me what you remember about the circumstances of his disappearance?'

Nathaniel looked puzzled. 'Surely you have all that information on file, Inspector? We were all interviewed in some depth back then.'

'Well, it was a long time ago now, and I'm afraid the original case notes have been mislaid.'

'Mislaid? Well, now, that's an interesting interpretation, Inspector.'

'How so?'

'Well, my expertise has always been in communications and intelligence, Inspector, and I've had to deal with a great many sensitive files in my time. I can tell you that important files of that nature don't go missing, unless someone wants them to. Sometimes bits get shredded or deliberately lost to cover something up, but if the whole file is gone, then my guess would be that someone has taken it deliberately. It's been stolen, Inspector ... not mislaid. That would be my guess, anyway.'

'Well, that's as may be, but can you help us out with any information as to details of his disappearance?'

He turned to Paul. 'Where did you find Stephen's body, Inspector?'

'Well, I don't think I can divulge ...'

Nathaniel cut him short, politely, but firmly. He had an air of authority about him that was impossible to ignore.

'Come, now, Inspector, you came here looking for our help in the matter. I think you can trust me with a little information, don't you? And if you're worried, I have a security clearance in my wallet that is recognised by both NATO and the UN, so you can rest assured, Inspector, nothing of the matter will go any further.'

'Blimey! Are you a spook?' asked Constable Kelly, only half-jokingly.

Nathaniel laughed. 'No, I'm not a spook, Constable, although I know a man who is, so to speak. If I had been a spook, I would have told you I was in insurance or advertising or something, now, wouldn't I? Not everyone who works in intelligence is a spook, as you put it. You need to get out a bit more, Constable, and stop watching so much television.'

Paul considered the man for a moment and then continued, 'We were investigating a totally unrelated case and just sort of stumbled across Stephen's body in a garden.'

'In a garden, you say? And whose garden would that be, Inspector?'

Paul paused and considered the situation for a moment again. He was slightly irritated. He felt as if he was being interrogated by this army man, rather than the other way around. He was here to get information, not to give it out, but he had no reason to suppose Nathaniel wasn't what he seemed to be, and, besides, he reasoned, what harm could it do? So, he continued, 'Stephen was found in the garden of a Mrs Harper.'

Nathaniel's brow furrowed, and he appeared to be dredging something up from deep within his memory.

"Mrs Harper, you say? That name brings back memories. Did she have sons, by any chance?'

'Yes, she did, as a matter of fact – Kevin and Craig Harper. Why do you ask? Did you know them?'

'My God! That's right – Kevin and Craig Harper. Wow, fancy hearing their names, after all this time. Do you remember, Inspector, that I said that Stephen and I were the best of friends, until just before he went missing? Well, the reason we stopped being so close towards the end was because Stephen started to hang around with Kevin and Craig at school ... Yes, he must have been about twelve then, and I was fourteen. He seemed ... looking back on it now ... almost obsessed with them, and they played him along for laughs. You have to understand, Kevin and Craig Harper were not nice boys back then, Inspector. It's no good trying to explain how evil they were, because I couldn't convey it to you – one had to know them to understand. If Stephen was found buried in their garden, Inspector, then I have no doubt in my mind that they were, in some way, responsible for his death.'

'According to the newspapers, Stephen went out on his new bike for a bike ride on the day of his disappearance. Do you think it possible he would have gone to see the Harper twins?'

'Twins? Oh, yes, of course – they were both in the same class at school; they had to be the same age. I'd forgotten that. In answer to your question, Inspector, Stephen would almost certainly have wanted to show the twins his new bike, so I think it is very likely that their house was his destination that day.'

'Did you mention this to the police, at the time?'

'I'm sure I would have done, Inspector, and the Harpers would certainly have been interviewed. I was only fourteen at the time myself, but I seem to remember that everyone who knew Stephen was interviewed, and the police visited the school several times. I think the police were very thorough at the time, if that is what you were wondering?'

'Thank you, Nathaniel, you have been very helpful. We may want to speak to you again, if necessary.'

'If you don't mind me asking, Inspector, you say that you found Stephen's body while investigating an unrelated case, but that case brought you to the Harpers – how so?'

'Mrs Harper was murdered at her home.'

'Ah, I see, are we talking matricide here, Inspector? Because they would have been capable of it, I'm sure.'

'No, no, we do know who killed Mrs Harper.'

'And you've arrested them, I assume?'

'We will do, as soon as we can locate them.'

'As soon as you can locate them, you say? Have they gone missing, as well?'

Paul made direct eye contact with Nathaniel and said, carefully, 'Yes, they have.'

'And do Kevin and Craig know who killed their mother? Because, if they do, you had better find them, before

Kevin and Craig get to them, or you may not have anyone to arrest. Or do you think they may have already beaten you to your quarry? Inspector, is that the reason why you can't locate them?'

'Maybe ... who knows? It does look, at present, as if they may have been abducted.'

'Then God help them, Inspector. Tell me, what are my old school chums doing these days? Nothing honest, I suspect.'

'That's very perceptive of you, Nathaniel. As a matter of fact, they run a legitimate business – a nightclub in London called *Sparklers* – but we suspect most of their money comes from protection and extortion. However bad they were as children, when you knew them, Nathaniel, they're a damn sight worse now.'

Paul could hardly believe he was divulging so much information to a total stranger, even if he was a decorated army officer, with the Conspicuous Gallantry Cross, a NATO security pass and a signed photograph of Prince Charles.

'Extortion, you say? Oh, yes, that would fit the bill; they'd be good at that, all right.'

'Well, thanks again for your help,' said Paul, standing up to leave.

'The two men you are looking for, who murdered Mrs Harper, were they from around here?'

'Why would you want to know that?' Paul replied, irked, again, at being questioned.

'Just in case I can be of any further assistance to you, Inspector.'

'In what way? You think you might be able to find them, when we can't?'

Paul felt more than a little annoyed at the inference.

Nathaniel looked Paul straight in the eyes and just shrugged his shoulders, saying nothing.

Paul sighed and relented, once again; in for a penny, in for a pound, he thought. He was annoyed by Nathaniel's constant questioning, but could he really be in a position to help?

'They disappeared from the Newcastle area,' Paul said, at last, 'which is where they originate from, and, if it is Kevin and Craig who are responsible for their disappearance, they will have enlisted local help, in order to find them. They're not just evil anymore, Nathaniel; unfortunately, they have evil connections, as well.'

'Thank you for trusting me, Inspector. I know you must feel uncomfortable about divulging information, but I can assure you that it's safe with me, and if I can be of any further help, here is my card.'

Nathaniel smiled and handed the inspector a business card, with the inscription 'Nathaniel Clark' and a phone number, nothing more.

He then said, 'The men who are missing – you could save me some time and text me their names and addresses on that number ... if you want me to dig, that is.'

Paul had been, as Nathaniel intimated, uncomfortable about giving away the information he already had, let alone the names and addresses of suspects, but he had a funny feeling that this man could possibly be of help in the investigation and, having gone this far already, he said, 'I'll give it serious consideration, but I don't think your intelligence friends will have much information about our criminal fraternity. Aren't your lot too busy keeping an eye on terrorists and spies and the like?'

Nathaniel smiled, 'Even terrorists need to eat, Inspector, and bombs and guns cost money, as well – lots of money. I can assure you, they don't raise the kind of cash they need by running corner shops, and they're not all funded by governments. No, they have fundraisers, who indulge in criminal activities and are much more at home in your world, than you would think. So we like to keep an eye on the money, as well as the personnel. We regularly watch the key players in anything that involves large sums of money, especially if they have any foreign connections. Terrorism and crime, Inspector, have more in common than you might think.'

'OK ... one thing I don't understand, though, Nathaniel – you thanked me for trusting you with this information, but you also divulged your own line of work. Was that wise? You didn't even know who we were.'

'Didn't I? Well, at the end of the day, if you can't trust a man with the same name as oneself, who can you trust?'

'What? How could you possibly know that?'

June looked back and forth between the two men, trying to work out what was happening.

'It is ... Paul Nathaniel Manley, isn't it?'

Paul was shocked to his core.

Nathaniel smiled and said, 'It's no big mystery, really, Paul. I saw you and your lovely constable checking out the house as I got home, so I pulled in, just up the road, and did a quick check on your registration number, before I called in home. It's lucky for me that you use your own car – it didn't take long to find out a great deal about you. You're quite young to be an inspector, Paul. It's not unheard of, of course, but it makes you stand out from the crowd, so we found you quite easily, actually.'

'We?'

'My friends and I.'

'Are you saying you have a file on me?'

'Good Lord, no. We haven't got a file on you or anything like that. Why would we? But we do have quick routes to information about people. I knew who you were before I called in, and the phone call that I took earlier filled in some details.'

'What about the Constable, here, then – you don't know anything about her, do you?'

'The constable that was with you had to be June Kelly, because you only have one female officer on your team; added to which, of course, is the fact that we've had dealings with her brother in the Met. He was in a position to help out some of my colleagues a while back.'

'Peter! You know my brother, Peter? How?' exclaimed June, quite taken aback.

'No, I've never met him or anything, but, apparently, he helped us out once, so we do have a file on *him*, and, consequently, we know of you. It's nothing sinister; he's filed under 'friend'.

Paul turned to June Kelly, accusingly.

'You've got a brother in the Met? When were you going to let on about that piece of information? Oh, don't tell me, sources, right?'

'Sorry, Guv – I would have let on, in time.'

Paul and June said their goodbyes to Mr and Mrs Clark, and Nathaniel courteously showed them to the door.

'I meant what I said, Paul – Stephen was my best friend, until those two came along. I'll do a bit of digging myself, and if I find anything at all, I'll let you know. It's been nice meeting with you and lovely to meet you, June.'

They returned to the car in silence, but, on the journey back to the station, June asked, still puzzled, 'So is he a spook or isn't he?'

'Why don't you ask your brother? They seem to be acquainted.'

'Good idea, Guv. I think I will.'

'A little advice, June, not that I've had any dealings with people like that before myself, but even if he isn't a spook, as you put it, he certainly moves in strange circles, and he found out who we were pretty damn fast – too fast for my liking. So I should keep my head down, if I were you, Constable, and don't go mentioning it to anybody. However, he was certainly right about one thing, though.'

'Guv?'

'You do watch far too much television.'

Elizabeth was helping Michael sit up in the state-of-the-art hospital bed that they had hired for him. Although Michael could get about on his crutches now, getting out of bed and getting dressed and undressed were all still daily trials. Using the crutches also tired him out very quickly and was painful after an hour, so he still spent much of his day in bed, resting. He was being so well looked after, that he was beginning to believe he had died in the car crash and gone straight to heaven. Although, he quickly realised that it couldn't be heaven, because Mavis wasn't there.

Michael was about to tuck into one of Elizabeth's homemade curries, and it smelled delicious.

'They say the wheelchair will be here tomorrow, but I'm not convinced that it will be any better than the crutches,' said Elizabeth, arranging the pillows, so that Michael could sit up and reach the bed-tray she had placed carefully over his legs. 'You'll have one leg stuck out straight, so it will still be difficult to manoeuvre around the house.'

'Oh, I have no intention of staying up here bed-ridden for most of every day, no matter how good the room service is,' he said, determinedly. 'With a wheelchair, I shall be able to be up and about all day and be much more independent. If I'd had one on the day of the inquest, I wouldn't have been half the burden that I was.'

'You've never been a burden, Michael,' said Elizabeth, softly, as she made for the door.

Michael replied, gratefully,, as she was leaving, 'You know, I do appreciate all that you and Richard have done for me, Liz.'

'Of course, now stop worrying. You and Mavis would have done the same for us.'

'Ask Richard to come up, when he's finished eating, would you? I'd like a word.'

'I'll send him up to get your tray.'

After everyone had finished their meal, Richard went upstairs to see what Michael wanted, and he took him up a bottle of his favourite vodka.

'Well done, Richard, but does that lovely nurse know about it?'

'Oh, don't mind her, Michael. I intend to get her drunk tonight, as well. Now, what did you want to talk to me about?'

Michael explained, 'I've been thinking things over, and it's obvious to me that things are not concluded and that this Craig fellow is most likely going to have another go at killing you and maybe even me. You must have considered that your family is at risk, surely.'

Richard told him about the phone call, with the recording of the young Rebecca playing the piano in the background.

'My God, Richard, I can't imagine what you and Liz have been going through. But, listen, I know you want Rebecca and Margaret here, so you can keep an eye on them, but this Craig is going to know they're here. What if you and Paul can secretly move them to my place –Elizabeth, as well – he'll never think of looking for them there. Then it's just you and me against him, again, if he tries anything further.'

Richard poured both Michael and himself a drink.

'That just might be the makings of a good idea, Michael. Perhaps the bump on the head has done you some good. But I don't think your place is the answer. It's still a crime scene, anyway, so I don't think it's even a possibility.'

'Where else is there, then?'

'Do you remember Robert Powers? The film director at Mavis' funeral?'

'Yeah, what about him?'

'Well, he's in California at the moment, so his house in Bath is empty. I'm pretty sure he would let the girls use it, if he knew what the situation was. I'll call him now and find out for sure, then I'll call Paul and run it by him, see what he thinks. But even if Paul agrees, we still have to get the women to agree, as well.'

'One job at a time, Richard.'

Richard rang Robert Powers and explained their situation to him, while Michael rang Paul to put their idea to him.

'Well, Paul's up for it,' said Michael, after the call. 'He's on his way over to discuss it now. What did Mr Powers have to say?'

'He's more than willing to help us out. He said it was the least he could do, after all the help his daughter had from Mavis. He's e-mailing me the details as we speak. It couldn't be more perfect, actually – the security at the house is managed by a local firm, and they keep an extra set of all the keys and alarm codes. He is going to e-mail them with instructions, in order to allow us complete access. His cars are there, as well, so there's also a vehicle that the girls can use. It's perfect.'

When Paul arrived, he listened to their plan with interest and explained, 'If we do move the women to Robert Power's house for a while, they will also have to stay away from work, as well as home. Otherwise, Craig could simply follow them home and find out where they are staying. That would put them at even more risk than they currently are.'

'Well, they'll just have to take the time off work. Nothing is more important than their safety,' said Richard. 'Let's put it to them.'

In the end, Rebecca and Margaret agreed to go, but Elizabeth insisted on staying, 'I'll have to stay,' she argued. 'Michael's in no condition to cook, and Richard's a complete buffoon in the kitchen, so they'll both starve to death if I leave.'

Paul said, 'Just Margaret and Rebecca, then. I may be able to spare a man to keep an eye on the house for a while, but it won't be for long, and it definitely won't be 24-hour surveillance.'

Richard reasoned, 'I don't think it will take long for Craig to try something again, anyway.'

'How are we going to be sure that Craig isn't watching when the girls leave? He might follow them without us knowing and that would be playing right into his hands,' said Elizabeth, thoughtfully.

'You can leave that bit to me,' said Paul. 'I'll arrange for an unmarked police transit van to pull up on your drive and park short of the front door, directly outside the window to Richard's study, and covering it from view. Then Margaret and Rebecca can climb out of the window, totally unseen, and enter the van by means of the side door. Meanwhile, the driver can retrieve a package from the back of the van and bring it to the house. That way, if Craig is watching, it will just look as if you have had a delivery of some kind.'

'And when do we move?' asked Rebecca.

'No time like the present, really. Pack what you need and be ready to go when I say,' instructed Paul. 'Have you got the e-mailed instructions, Richard?'

'I've just printed them out.'

Margaret stood to attention and saluted, 'Yes, sir, Inspector Manley, sir,' she barked, causing one and all to laugh.

'Sorry,' said Paul, apologetically, 'I suppose I did sound a bit like a sergeant major.'

'A bit?' teased Margaret, slowly realising that Paul was just as worried about everyone's safety as Richard was and loving him all the more for it.

The girls went off to pack their bags, still giggling at Paul, and Michael asked for a quick word with Richard in private, before they left.

Paul used the phone in the kitchen to ring Reg at the incident room and told him of their plan. Reg said he would get Derrick to drive the van, because Craig hadn't seen him before, and he was familiar with transit vans. Reg would hide in the back.

Back at the station, Reg and Clive wrapped an old shoebox with brown paper and Sellotape, even putting the Drakes' address on it to make it look like a convincing parcel.

The women would be driven to the house, and they agreed that the only contact would be by phone, from then on. Margaret and Rebecca would have the use of a car, but they were to stay away from their usual haunts, keep a low profile and check-in by phone twice a day, both morning and evening.

Paul and the women were sitting downstairs, waiting for Reg to call, and Richard was sitting on the edge of Michael's bed, curious to know what was on his mind.

'What is it you wanted to speak to me about, Michael?'

'How do you envisage this whole thing with Craig turning out, Richard?'

Richard considered the question for a moment, before replying, 'In truth, Michael, not well ... not well at all, I'm afraid.'

'You must have considered your options by now. What have you decided? I'd half expected you to ask me the question long before now.'

Richard tried to smile, but only half succeeded, 'You did always know what I was thinking, Michael, but it's not an easy option to take. For God's sake, I'm not a killer.'

'You did all right by us both the other night, when the chips were down. Do you want to know or not?'

'It's my family that's at risk, Michael – of course, I want to know. Have you got one or not?'

'It's in my safe. That's half the reason that I suggested the girls went there. We'll have to think of another reason to go there now. I've written the combination down for you, but you'll have to be careful. Paul is no fool. You'll need a good excuse to go to the house, and, if you go, he's going to want to go with you, in order to keep an eye on you. If he sees you at my safe, you'll need a good reason for opening it. I have a bag under my desk in the lounge, put a few books in it for me to make it heavy and get some underwear and shirts for me, as well. If Paul wants to know why you've gone to my safe, tell him I want the photo album that's in there. It's quite a small one, and it has Mavis' wedding ring taped on the front. The gun and the bullets are on the top shelf.'

An hour later, Paul's phone rang, and Reg informed him that everything was now ready for the pick-up.

Paul had received a clip around the ear from Margaret and a verbal ear-bashing from Rebecca for suggesting that they were taking too much with them and voicing concern about the van's suspension.

'You may feel happy going away for an indefinite length of time without a change of underwear or deodorant, but I can assure you that we don't,' admonished Margaret.

Before the van's arrival, Paul gave the girls a list of do's and don'ts, which included staying away from their usual haunts and avoiding turning on lights at the front of the house.

'Always get the car out of the garage last thing before leaving and always put it back in the garage, as soon as you get back,' he warned and the girls agreed.

'Remember that the house is supposed to be empty, so it should look like it,' Paul said.

Rebecca smiled at Paul and said, 'You really have no idea about the house we're going to, have you, Paul? It's a mansion. It's been featured in magazines. There is no way it can be even seen from the road, so chill out, Sherlock. We'll be fine. Actually, I can't wait to try out the pool.'

'What pool? You need to stay indoors while you're there. You're not to go gallivanting around the garden.'

'Oh, really, Paul. As if Robert Powers would bother with an outside pool. I've seen photos of it – it's modelled on the Roman baths, and it looks incredible.'

'Sorry, I don't read the same mags as you, obviously,' said Paul, humbly.

When the van arrived, the plan went like clockwork, and they all agreed that even if Craig had been stood outside watching, he wouldn't have known that the girls had been smuggled out of the house.

Richard then turned to Paul and announced, 'Now that everyone is on the move, Michael wants some things from his house. He can't keep on buying new clothes, and there are some personal items he wants, as well as his mail.'

'That's really not a good idea, Richard.'

'Maybe not, but I'm going.'

Paul looked long and hard at Richard. He could see that there was no point in arguing, so, instead, he said, relenting, 'If you insist, Richard, but I'm coming with you. It's still a crime scene, after all.'

An hour after the girls left, Richard and Paul arrived at Michael's house, and Richard said, 'I promised to get a few books for Michael, and he wants some things from his bedroom. While I do that, could you check the kitchen and make sure there is nothing going off in the fridge or anything?'

'Sure, you carry on, Richard, but don't be too long, yeah? I'm supposed to be catching criminals, remember.'

'Thanks, Paul.'

As soon as he was inside the house, Richard retrieved the bag from under Michael's desk, slipped a couple of books into it from the bookcase and headed up to the main bedroom. On the wall opposite the window was an oil painting of a Battle of Britain Spitfire, done by an exceptionally good, but, unfortunately, unknown, artist. Richard felt behind the right-hand side of the picture and released a small catch. The picture opened, like a small door, and Michael's safe lay nestled behind it. Richard managed to open the safe after his third attempt, and, by that time, Paul called upstairs, enquiring what was keeping him.

'Be there in a minute,' shouted Richard.

He transferred the gun, the bullets and the photo album into the bag, closed the safe and returned the painting to its original position. Richard then quickly grabbed some pants and socks from the chest and a couple of shirts from the wardrobe. His heart was thumping away heavily in his chest, because he felt like some kind of burglar, who was about to be discovered at any moment. He had placed the bag on the foot of the bed and had just packed the shirts into it, when Paul entered the room, making him jump out of his skin.

'What's taking you so long, Richard? We need to be away from here,' urged Paul, grabbing hold of the bag and carrying it out of the room. 'Blimey! What did Michael ask you to get for him? A cannon?'

Richard laughed, nervously, 'Oh, just some clothes and some books.'

After getting back to the house, Richard took the bag up to Michael's room, where he put it within his reach and gave him the thumbs-up, before going back downstairs. He would transfer the gun to his study later, when Paul was gone. On returning downstairs, he found Elizabeth giving Paul a hug and realised that his wife had accepted him completely as a friend. Paul was definitely in their lives for the duration.

After Paul had left, Elizabeth gave her husband a hug and asked, worriedly, 'Do you really think Rebecca and Margaret will be safer at Robert Power's house, Richard?'

'Much safer than here with me, that's for sure. I wish you had agreed to go with them.'

'Oh no, you don't get rid of me as easy as that,' said Elizabeth and promptly started to cry.

Richard held his wife tight and, for the hundredth time, wondered if he really could go through with the horrible scenario he had in mind, if Craig should put in another unwelcome appearance.

Life was to go back to normal, as far as was possible, in the Drake house, so, the following day, Richard drove to the shop and opened for business. He had been reluctant to leave Elizabeth and Michael alone, but his wife insisted that they would be fine; the house was secure, and it was Peggy's day to be there, so they wouldn't be alone, and, anyway, Paul had a man posted, keeping a watchful eye, as well.

The next day, Rebecca and Margaret got one of Robert's cars out of his garage – a silver Toyota Avensis – and drove into Bath, intending to spend the day at the Bath Spa, swimming and being pampered with massages and beauty treatments at Richard's expense.

Elizabeth was running down the stairs at eight-fifty that morning to answer the door and let Peggy – her cleaning lady – in, but just as she reached the bottom step, her foot slipped on the last tread, and she twisted her ankle. Calling out in pain, she sat down heavily on the bottom step, took off her shoe and rubbed her ankle, in a vain attempt to stop it from hurting.

She heard a key in the lock and fully expected Peggy to come through the door. Peggy had a key to the Drake's house, because it was often empty when she turned up to work, but she always preferred to ring the bell before entering, as a matter of courtesy, just in case any of the family were still in bed when she arrived or were parading about in their underwear.

Elizabeth was surprised, however, when Louise – Peggy's niece – entered, and it was a minute or two before she remembered that this was the first week of Peggy's holiday and that she had previously arranged for Louise to take over in her aunt's absence.

When Louise heard the cry of pain from inside, she hurriedly got out the key that Peggy had given her and let herself in. She saw Elizabeth sitting on the step holding her ankle, and she instinctively rushed to her, asking if she was all right, thinking that Mrs Drake must have taken a tumble down the stairs.

'Oh, hello, Louise, I'm fine. I've just been stupid and twisted my ankle. Would you help me to the lounge, please?'

Louise took hold of Elizabeth's arm, helped her hobble into the lounge and sat her down on the sofa.

'Is there anything I can do to help, Mrs Drake? Can I make you a cup of tea or something?'

Elizabeth smiled and said that she would love a cup of tea and that Louise was to have one, too, and could she take one up to Michael, if he was awake? The British always think of tea in any sort of crisis, be it large or small, and Louise was no exception. Louise was about the same age as Rebecca, but Elizabeth thought she looked woefully thin compared to her daughter, especially in the thin summer dress that she was wearing that day.

When Louise returned with the tea, she said that she had left a cup on Michael's bedside cabinet, but that he was still asleep.

Elizabeth said, 'There is something you could do for me, if you're willing, Louise. But you must say no, if you don't want to do it.'

'What is it, Mrs Drake? What can I do for you?'

'I need to get the shopping done at the supermarket, and I need to pick up the meat that I have ordered from the butcher's, but I don't think I could drive at the moment. Could you do those things for me this morning?'

'Oh, I would, of course, Mrs Drake, but I came on the bus this morning, as my car is being serviced.'

'That's all right. If I give you the keys, do you think you could drive mine? It's an automatic, though. Have you ever driven one before? Don't be afraid to say no – I'll understand if you don't want to. I can always ring Richard.'

'I would do it, Mrs Drake, but I haven't driven an automatic before. I'm really sorry. Is it too far for me to walk?'

Elizabeth thought carefully for a moment, before answering. Rebecca's car was on the driveway, because they had gone to Robert Powers' home in the van, and they had the use of Robert's car.

'You could take Rebecca's little Clio. It's on the drive, and I know Rebecca won't mind at all.'

'Oh, well, OK, I used to have a Clio myself, so ... sure, I can do the shopping for you; all I need is a list and the address of your butcher.'

'That's marvellous, Louise. I'm sure that if I sit with my foot up for a bit, with a cold compress on it, it will be right in no time. Rebecca's keys should be on the hall table. I'll quickly make a list of what I want. Thanks again for doing this, Louise, it's very good of you. You're sure now? You honestly don't mind?'

Louise said, helpfully, 'No problem at all, Mrs Drake,' as she went back to the kitchen to return the cups and to get a cold compress for Elizabeth's ankle.

Elizabeth made a shopping list for Louise, trying to remember the important things that she wanted, without trying to hobble to the kitchen and look, and she wrote down the address of her butcher.

The sun was hot on Louise's face as she walked to Rebecca's car and when she got in, she made a few minor adjustments to the positioning of the driver's seat and mirrors, before driving off on her errands. Louise's first car had been a Clio, and it felt like driving an old friend, as she sped down the road into town.

Two hours later, Elizabeth was starting to get worried. She had deliberately not given Louise a very big shopping list, and the butcher was local, as well as the supermarket, so she would have expected her to be back long before now. She reasoned that perhaps the supermarket was particularly busy or perhaps it was just that Louise was taking a long time to locate things, because she was unfamiliar with the store's layout. She hoped and prayed that the car hadn't let her down or, worst of all, that she had had an accident; she was now regretting that she had asked Louise in the first place. Elizabeth eventually convinced herself that she was being silly and overreacting, because of everything that was currently going on, but after another agonising hour had passed, she decided to ring Richard at the shop and explained everything that had happened.

'Three hours? That is a long time. But she has probably got distracted or decided to go for lunch or something. Has she got a mobile with her?'

'Probably, but I don't have her number.'

'I'll bet there's no need to panic, but as you're so worried, I'll head round to the supermarket and have a look, see if I can spot Rebecca's car in the car park, and I'll go to the butcher to see if the meat has been collected yet.'

'Yes, please, Richard, if you would. I'm sure something has gone wrong. Louise seems such a sensible girl. She would have done the shopping and come straight back, I'm sure, and if there was a problem, she would have rung. She's a young lady; she must have a mobile with her, surely. Oh, wait! Why didn't I think of it before? I may have written her mobile number in the address book, along with Peggy's number. Let me have a quick look.'

Elizabeth painfully hobbled over to her handbag that was sitting on the hall table and got out her address book. She quickly looked up Peggy's number and, sure enough, written underneath was 'Louise - niece', with a number scrawled beside it. Richard hung on, while Elizabeth proceeded to call Louise's number on the house phone.

The phone rang for what seemed like an age, but then a man answered and said, in a tone that sent shivers up Elizabeth's back, 'Hello, Rebecca can't come to the phone just at the moment. She's a bit tied up, so to speak, but we'll get back to you soon. In the meantime, try not to worry – she's in good hands.'

The phone went dead.

'Oh my God! Rebecca! The man on the phone said Rebecca. Richard, I don't understand. Why is he saying Rebecca?'

Richard, who had answered his mobile when Elizabeth had rung, now picked up the shop phone and quickly dialled his daughter's number. He waited and waited, but there was no reply. He then called Margaret's phone – again, no answer.

'Elizabeth, I'm not getting an answer from Rebecca or Margaret's mobile. I'm coming home now; I'm on my way. Ring Robert's home number to see if they pick that phone up. If they don't answer that, then ring Paul and tell him what's happening. I'll be there soon.'

Elizabeth had just finished on the phone to Paul, when Michael entered the room, dressed in pyjamas and a silk dressing gown.

'Elizabeth, you look worried. What's wrong?'

Elizabeth had just finished explaining the morning's events to Michael, when Richard pulled into the driveway, and a police car followed him in. It was Paul and Constable Kelly.

Before they had even got to the front door, Elizabeth opened it and shouted at them, emotionally wracked, 'I still haven't heard from Rebecca or Margaret, and Louise is not back yet, either. What's happening? Where are they?'

She was in floods of tears, and Richard had to physically support his wife's bent frame, as they made their way back into the house.

* * * * * * * * * * * *

When they got to Bath Spa, Rebecca and Margaret changed into their bathing suits, as soon as they had checked in. They each put on one of the robes that were provided and went straight to the open-air rooftop pool. They alternated between there and the aroma steam rooms, forgetting all about gangsters, cops and robbers, and possible threats of violence. It was lovely, just drifting around in the rooftop pool overlooking the beautiful Georgian city of Bath, with the sun beating down on them. They felt like film stars, especially as they were staying in a film director's mansion and driving his posh car. They were determined to enjoy the day, and the spa was just the place to do it. For the first time in ages, they both felt completely relaxed. When they eventually decided to get out of the beautiful hot spring waters, it was partly because they were worried that they were going to emerge looking like human-shaped prunes and partly because doing nothing had made them ravenously hungry. Donning their robes again – like everyone else there – they went into the spa restaurant and had an equally relaxing lunch, after which, they forgot all about looking like prunes and decided to try out the Minerva thermal bath. Then it was time for a massage each, followed by a beauty treatment and an indulgent visit to the hair salon.

'Are you sure your dad knows we're putting all this on his card?' Margaret asked, worried by the amount of money they were spending in just one morning.

'Yeah, it's fine. Dad doesn't know that I know, but he has an account that is only used when he gives me the card. He just keeps the account topped up to what he is prepared for me to spend. So as long as the card doesn't reach its limit, I know that Dad is happy for me to spend it.'

'Are you sure that's how it works?'

'Yeah, trust me, I know how it works. He started doing it when I was fifteen, so that if I ran out of money when I was out, I wouldn't have to rely on anyone else or have to ask anyone for a favour, especially any boys. Now he lets me have it if he wants to treat me for some reason. Sometimes it really pays to be an only child.'

They had already been at the spa for several hours before they realised that it was now getting too late to do any shopping, so they had coffee and cake in the lounge, before getting changed back into their clothes to go back to the mansion.

Laughing and chatting excitedly, they returned to the dressing room, and it was only after getting dressed, that Rebecca saw that she had several missed calls on her phone; likewise, Margaret.

'I knew Mum wouldn't be able to resist calling,' said Rebecca. 'I'd better ring her back to let her know we haven't been shot or abducted or anything,' she said, smiling.

Paul had quickly organised a search party for Louise and had sent Reg and Clive to see what was happening, if anything, at Robert's house. Elizabeth was sitting right next to the phone when it finally rang, but she was too frightened to answer it, wondering if it was that same man again, maybe, this time, with news of Rebecca that she didn't want to hear.

Richard grabbed the phone from beside her, put it to his ear and cried, almost instantaneously, 'Oh, thank God! Is Margaret with you? Are you both OK? Your mother has been frantic with worry. Why haven't you been answering your phones?'

Elizabeth tore the phone from her husband's hand, needing confirmation first-hand that it was, in fact, her daughter, intact, on the other end. When all the crying and relieved sobbing had died down, Paul asked to speak to Margaret and questioned her about their day; had anything out of the ordinary happened? Had any strangers spoken to them? Were they completely sure that they hadn't been followed to the spa?

'No, everything has been fine. We've had a wonderful relaxing day. Why? What's happened? Why is everyone so concerned all of a sudden?'

He instructed her, briefly, without giving anything away, 'Go back to Robert's straight away and make sure the place is secure.'

Margaret was desperate to know what had been going on and pleaded to be let in on the situation.

He explained, 'Louise – the cleaning lady's niece – has gone missing in Rebecca's car, and when Liz tried her phone, it was answered by a man, who seemed to think that it was Rebecca's phone that he had.'

'Do you think this man took Louise, thinking that it was Rebecca? Do you think it was Craig?' Margaret asked, alarmed.

Paul tried to reassure her, but without much conviction. He had never met this young girl, Louise, but his heart ached at the thought of what she might be going through at that very moment, in the hands of the sadistic monster that he knew Craig to be.

Not long after Paul put the phone down, his mobile rang. It was Derrick Jacobs, calling from the incident room.

'Rebecca's car has been located in the supermarket car park, and it was unlocked, with no sign of any shopping in it. It would seem likely that something happened to Louise just as she got out of the car, before she had a chance to lock it. John Campbell is at the supermarket now, and he is checking over the car park security cameras, but it looks as though the car has been parked in an area that the cameras, unfortunately, don't cover.'

Paul and Richard looked at each other, grimly, with growing foreboding, and Elizabeth had begun crying again, both with relief that Rebecca was all right and fear of what terrors Louise could be suffering.

Michael sat on one of the sofas, wishing there was something he could do, but resigning himself to being a helpless bystander, as potential tragedy unfolded around him.

* * * * * * * * * * * * *

Louise's sudden disappearance had changed the priorities of the whole operation. Extra police were now available, and the existing incident room was far too small to cope with the increase in the size of the team. The room had been assigned to the team, in order to investigate the murder of Gladys Harper, and, although that was effectively over, the team was now investigating the murder of Stephen Potter, the attempted murders of Richard and Michael, the disappearance and possible murders of Alan Salter and Jack Simmons and, now, the abduction of Louise Brown.

Paul was in a meeting with Sergeant Derrick Jacobs and DCI William Blake, and they were trying to figure out the best way for things to proceed. DCI Blake had been investigating the murder of a shopkeeper by young thugs, when he had confronted them over shoplifting, but this was now all but concluded, as the culprits had been arrested and charged, so he had more time now to give to the current investigation.

The DCI began, seriously, 'I think it would be best if we set up another incident room, and I can run the investigation into Louise's disappearance with a completely new team. Obviously, there will be a considerable overlapping of the cases, because both teams will be looking for Craig Harper. I take it that nobody has any doubt that he has abducted Louise?'

Paul and Derrick both nodded their agreement.

'Doing things that way will allow you, Paul, to continue investigating the other aspects of what is an increasingly diverse case. It also means that I will be able to put together another much larger team, completely independent from yours, Paul, and, therefore, the manpower on the ground will be considerably increased.'

Paul agreed, and Derrick assured them both that he would make it his personal responsibility to ensure that any information acquired by either team, with regards to the whereabouts of either Louise or Craig, would immediately be communicated to the other.

'Right, then, gentlemen, there's lots of work to do. Let's get on with it.'

Chapter 11

The house that Craig had rented was perfect for his purpose. Richard's house was situated on a main road, and two houses down from it, there was a turning on the opposite side of the road. It was in this road – Hawthorn Avenue – that Craig had managed to rent a detached house, only one up from the corner – number four. This meant that from the upstairs front-bay window, he had a remarkably good view of the front of Richard's house, that, although set back from the road with a large drive, was clearly visible from the road. From this vantage point, Craig was able to monitor all of the comings and goings of the Drake residence in relative comfort. Both Margaret Collins and Inspector Paul Manley were frequent visitors, although he hadn't seen Margaret for a day or two. The inspector, however, was beginning to look more like a family friend, than a policeman who was investigating a case. He was also, now, screwing the delightful Margaret, as well, and who could blame him for that? She was quite a looker. He was even considering it himself. However, the daughter, Rebecca, would be a much better target, from the point of view of hurting Drake. As yet, he had not had the pleasure of seeing the daughter. He seemed to keep missing her appearance on the scene, but he could be patient. Well ... up to a point, anyway.

* * * * * * * * * * *

Louise got into Rebecca's car and adjusted the seat and mirror angles to suit her driving position. It was a beautiful, warm day, and she was looking forward to doing Elizabeth's shopping, because it would make a welcome change from being inside the house cleaning. She didn't dislike her work, and it earned her good money, being in business with her aunt, but she did sometimes get a little bored with housework and cleaning, especially on glorious, sunny days like today, when she thought she would rather have been a gardener, surrounded by the aromas of flowers, rather than polish and disinfectant. She had started helping out her aunt when she had simply needed an extra pair of hands on occasion, but as her aunt's business had grown, they decided to go into partnership together and to call their firm *Dusters*. It was proving a great success; they were even talking about the possibility of taking on an employee. The next couple of weeks were going to be hard, though, with her aunt on holiday, but they had managed to rearrange some customers' times, and Louise was going to work some evenings, as well, so that they didn't let anyone down.

Driving the little Clio was fine, but she was aware that she would only be covered by third party insurance if there was an accident or something of that sort, so when she pulled into the supermarket car park, she decided to park well away from most of the other cars, which effectively meant as far away from the store entrance as possible. Her own car had been scratched a couple of times, by people opening their car doors carelessly or without looking, and sometimes cars were damaged by people not being careful with their trolleys. Being relatively early on a Monday morning, the store wasn't very busy, and she could probably have parked closer than she did, but, even so, another car had followed her in and seemed intent on parking close by. She got out of the car and was about to get the bags out of the boot, when she became aware that the driver of the other car had come up behind her.

The next thing she knew, the driver had put one arm around her body, pinning one of her arms to her side. He then brought the other hand, which was holding some kind of rag or handkerchief, up to her face and held it tightly across both her mouth and nose. She struggled instinctively, but he was a well-built, extremely powerful man. Even so, just before the chloroform took effect and she drifted into unconsciousness, she had the distinct feeling that the exertions of holding her struggling form were causing him some pain.

Craig had taken a sleeping pill the night before. What with missing his brother badly and still being in quite a lot of pain from his injuries in the crash, he was finding sleep difficult to come by. That morning, he hadn't woken until just before nine o'clock, sleeping right through the alarm. He was infuriated with himself. He had started watching the Drake's house from the upstairs front bedroom window, as soon as he had made himself a cup of coffee and quickly dressed, which, by that time, was around ten minutes past nine. He had missed the usual early morning signs of a household rising. Both the upstairs and downstairs curtains were open, and the hire car, that Richard was using, was gone from the drive.

Richard accumulated so much stuff in his line of work, that even though the Drake's house boasted a double garage, there was never enough room in it for even one car. Fortunately, the drive was big enough to accommodate Richard's Estate, Elizabeth's Fiesta automatic and Rebecca's little Clio, together with enough space for one other vehicle.

Craig expected to see Rebecca's car gone by now, as well, but perhaps she had a day off work or something. He was pleased that he hadn't missed her, because, as yet, she was the only member of the Drake family that he hadn't seen. He was also surprised that the cleaning lady hadn't parked her car on the drive, because his understanding was that she worked for Elizabeth Drake on Mondays, Wednesdays and Fridays, without fail, and he assumed that she would arrive in a car.

Perhaps she was ill or on holiday, he mused, thoughtfully. He kicked himself, once again, for getting up so late and missing so much.

About ten minutes after Craig started watching the house, the front door opened, and a young girl came out and slid carefully into the front driver's seat of Rebecca's car. Craig was watching through his binoculars. So that's Rebecca Drake, he thought. She's plain, rather than attractive, he decided, and she hasn't inherited her mother's natural elegance or poise, either. In fact, now that he studied her face more closely, he concluded that there wasn't a great deal of family resemblance at all. Perhaps Richard isn't the real father, he chuckled to himself. As he didn't find Rebecca all that appealing, Craig again began to wonder whether he could find time to fit in a session with the lovely Margaret, but quickly decided against it; he really did want to get things wrapped up now, so that he could enjoy his retirement in sunny Italy, and there just wouldn't be time for such an indulgence.

Seeing Rebecca get into her car was just the opportunity that Craig had been hoping for. Everything he needed was in the car, ready, so he was down the stairs, out of the house and into his car as quickly as he could, so as not to miss her. He had hurried, because he assumed that Rebecca would simply climb into her car and drive away, probably to work. But he was more than a little worried that if work wasn't her destination, he might lose her in traffic, unless he was following her closely. Well, as it turned out, he had worried unnecessarily. He was in his car, with the engine running, long before she was even out of the drive; she must have been fiddling with the radio or something, he pondered.

If Craig had stayed at the window – watching, rather than rushing down to follow Rebecca – he may have wondered why she needed to adjust the driving seat and mirrors of her own car, before driving off, but, as he didn't, he was pleased to slot into the flow of traffic, only two places behind her. She had turned in the wrong direction for work, which reinforced Craig's earlier suspicion, that she had a day off, and he was intrigued to know where she was going.

If the opportunity presented itself, he was well prepared to kidnap her, there and then. He had chloroform in the glove compartment, rope, cable ties and duct tape in the boot, and, once again, he reflected, with pleasant anticipation, that it had been a long time, since he had 'entertained' a woman. When she had pulled into the supermarket car park, his mood had sunk – not only was shopping the most boring activity on the planet, but a busy car park was no place for a kidnapping; there would be far too many witnesses, for one thing. For some reason, however, she drove to the far end of the car park, well away from the usual hustle and bustle, as well as from the CCTV cameras, he noted, with growing interest. This was shaping up to be a different situation, after all. The car park was uncharacteristically quiet, as well. As she was parking well away from the other cars and cameras, he decided to take a chance, even though he knew that Kevin would have strongly disapproved of the spontaneity of his actions. 'Patience, brother',' he could hear him cautioning.

He drew into the space next door, but one, to her and swiftly took the chloroform out of the glove compartment, before casually emerging from the car, so as not to alarm her. He walked around to the nearside of the car and opened the back door, as if to retrieve something from in there, and, as he was doing this, Louise walked to the back of the Clio and was poised to open the boot. It was not as easy as he had expected. He was behind her quickly enough – putting an arm around her tightly and placing the chloroform rag to her mouth and nose – but he had inadvertently trapped one of her arms at her side, and this seemed, somehow, to give her some leverage.

He was much stronger than his small female opponent in the struggle and was soon able to subdue her with the chloroform and bundle her into the back of his car, after only a brief struggle, but not without considerable pain. He had underestimated how much his injuries would affect his ability to overpower her, and without the chloroform, he would have been in some difficulty, as his ribs were still very painful.

Once he had her in the back of the car, he looked about him, pleased that nobody appeared to be taking any notice of what was happening in that part of the car park. The few shoppers who did happen to be about were concentrating on packing their cars with their groceries and getting home before their recently purchased food began to defrost and so that they could have a much-needed cuppa. He considered just getting in and driving her back to the house as quickly as possible, but if he took longer to get back than expected, there was a chance that she could come round, and that would be embarrassing, especially if there were people about to witness it. So he bound her hands behind her back with long cable ties, stuffed a small piece of rag in her mouth and taped over it carefully with duct tape. Then he threw a blanket over her to keep the nosy parkers at bay and drove her to his lair.

Louise felt as if she had been boozing for a week and had woken up with the granddaddy of all hangovers. There was something laid over her that felt more like an old blanket, than her usual soft duvet. Then she began to remember the events that had unfolded at the car park and realised, in horror, that she wasn't tucked up in her cosy bed. Somebody was pulling her out of a car and forcing her to walk to God knows where. Her head really throbbed, and she wanted, more than anything, to take some tablets to make the pain go away.

As she was dragged hastily from the car, the blanket that had been covering her fell off, and she was able to vaguely take in her surroundings. She was obviously on someone's driveway, and she was being roughly dragged towards the house, but she had no idea where it was. She had no way of knowing how long she had been unconscious and, therefore, no way of knowing how far they had travelled from the supermarket car park.

She felt very thirsty, her hands were tied tightly together and there was something in her mouth that was making it difficult to breathe. She was very, very frightened. Whoever her abductor was, he dragged her up a flight of stairs and sat her in a wooden chair, with her hands still tied firmly behind her back. She was very uncomfortable and became progressively more so, as he proceeded to tie her into the chair, by looping thick rope around her chest and securing her ankles to the chair legs. She was scared, thirsty and still woozy from whatever he had used to subdue her. She longed for her abductor to remove the gag, so she could tell him how thirsty she was and how much her head was hurting.

Craig was very pleased with himself. Despite the pain he had suffered during the abduction, he had managed to kidnap Richard's daughter and transport her to his temporary accommodation, unseen. The fact that the house had a driveway, where he could park off-road, and a five-foot hedge, that prevented unwanted attention from the street, had served him well in his endeavours. Getting the girl out of the car and upstairs had been an effort, even though she had started to come round, and he had managed to get her to walk in the direction he wanted, after a fashion. He left her securely bound to a chair upstairs, while he made himself a well-earned drink and took some painkillers.

Although he had decided to kidnap Rebecca, in order to hurt Richard, he had not made up his mind, yet, exactly how to best use her to that end. The first thing, however, was to let Richard know that he had her and that he was in a position to do whatever he wanted to her. Kevin had always said, 'Don't tell victims exactly what you intend to do, because their imagination will always come up with something much worse', and it was good advice. Kevin always had good advice; Craig missed him terribly.

As Craig placed the painkillers carefully back in the cabinet, he suddenly knew what his first move would be and decided he would need to do a bit of shopping. But, he reasoned, if he was to leave the house, Rebecca would have to be tied even more securely than at present. It was surprising how much noise people who were tied in chairs could make – bouncing about and falling sideways. He didn't want any of that going on while he was out. To this end, he took the mattress off the iron-frame bed that had been left in the upstairs spare bedroom and securely tied Louise to it, with a combination of cable ties and duct tape. He checked her bonds one last time before he left, reflecting that he could probably have secured her to the bed just as effectively, leaving the mattress in place, but then, making Rebecca comfortable formed no part of this plan.

Louise was now fully conscious and terrified. She had been abducted by a strange man and tied to an old bed for God knows what reason. All sorts of thoughts were racing though her mind, and none of them were very pleasant, to say the least. The most likely reason for a man to kidnap a young woman, she thought, was to rape her, so why had he immediately gone out and left her there? She had heard the front door slam and his car pull away. Perhaps there was more than one of them? Was another man about to enter the room and do horrible things to her? Or was it something else? Was it something even more terrible than rape? Was she to be kept a prisoner and slave for years, never to see her family again? She had read about that kind of thing happening.

Then, a glimmer of hope occurred to her. Could it be that they were going to hold her for ransom? Stupid girl, she thought, almost straight away, why would anyone hold her to ransom? Nobody in her family had any money. Perhaps they had mistaken her for someone else? Was that a good or bad thing? Would they let her go, when they realised their mistake? Or would they simply kill her if she was of no use to them? A multitude of thoughts and fears were racing through her brain, but she was finding it difficult to concentrate, because she was so thirsty, and the bed he had tied her to was not just uncomfortable, but downright painful to lie on. If only he would take the gag out of her mouth and speak to her; perhaps, then, she could discover what this was all about.

After a while, the pain in her head began to wear off, and she started to think more clearly, but although the pain in her head was thankfully subsiding, she had all sorts of other bodily pains quickly developing. The iron framework of the bed was digging painfully into her back and buttocks, and the way she was tied left very little room for movement. Whoever this man or men were, they had no thought for her comfort whatsoever, and the rag, or whatever it was, in her mouth was becoming a real threat to her ability to breath.

She began to think longingly about escape. Was it possible? Certainly, if she was to attempt it, now would be the best time, while he was out of the house. But her bonds felt very strong, and struggle as she might, all she managed to do was to make herself even more uncomfortable. She began thinking again about the possible motive for her abduction. If it was rape, why hadn't he done it? No, that seemed less likely to her now, which brought her back to the possibility of a ransom demand. Perhaps it was a case of mistaken identity; she had been driving Rebecca Drake's car, after all, and the Drakes certainly had money. How well off they actually were, Louise didn't know, but they weren't poor, by any standards. The more she thought about it, the more it seemed to be the most likely explanation for her current predicament. She reasoned, also, that when her abductor finally removed her gag, she would be better playing along and pretending to be Rebecca Drake. Her aunt Peggy had always spoken very highly of Mr and Mrs Drake, and Louise was sure that if they received a ransom note, they would pay up, even if they knew that the kidnapper had mistakenly taken Louise, rather than the intended Rebecca. They wouldn't just leave her to her fate, she was sure of that.

Craig got into his car and drove back to the supermarket, where he had abducted Louise. He remembered spotting a large DIY store on the same site. This time, he parked as close to the store as possible; he didn't want to leave her alone for any longer than he had to. Once in the store, he headed straight for the tool section and began examining the various pincers, pliers and cutters, but, once faced with the selection, he couldn't make up his mind about the best kind of implement for the task that he had in mind. Then, all of a sudden, he spotted it. It looked, for all the world, like a pair of garden secateurs, and, for a moment, he wondered if perhaps he might have had more luck in the gardening section. The cutters that had caught his eye were, actually, he discovered, for cutting the plastic water pipes that plumbers seemed so fond of installing these days. He decided that they would also be ideal for the task that he had in mind.

He purchased the cutter, along with some more duct tape, and then visited the supermarket pharmacy and purchased a first-aid kit, some antiseptic and some extra bandages. The supermarket also had a section that sold greetings cards and wrapping paper, and, from there, he bought a small gift box, some wrapping paper and a stretch of ribbon. After all, he had read in Richard's diary that it was Elizabeth's birthday on the tenth of July, and he wanted to give her a birthday present that neither she, nor Richard, would ever forget.

On returning to the house, Craig immediately went upstairs to check on his guest. It was obvious that she had been struggling, but it was just as obvious that the bonds had held fast. She was watching him closely, and he wondered if she knew who he was and what he was capable of. Well, she would discover that later, he thought. There was no other furniture in the room, so he fetched a couple of chairs from downstairs and, having placed one beside the bed, he methodically laid out the contents of the first-aid kit, together with the antiseptic and the pipe cutter.

Louise turned her head and watched the proceedings, with mounting dread. She tried to speak, to plead with the man not to hurt her, but only muffled moans escaped her lips. Her heart began to race, and her eyes bulged, as she saw him take the cutters and felt him grab hold of her hand. She was struggling furiously and rocking her head from side to side, but was unable to prevent him from pulling her ring finger up and placing the cutter around it. She closed her eyes and prayed to God that the pain would not be more than she could bear. She was overcome with gratitude to the Almighty, when her prayer seemed to be answered.

She felt the razor-sharp blades slice easily and quickly through the flesh of her finger and then registered a terrible crushing of bone, but she felt no real pain, as such, and, for that, she was grateful. However, she knew that it would only be a temporary respite and that the pain would set in before too long. The man tended to her wound and bandaged it very professionally, forcing her to wonder how many times he had deprived people of their fingers and bandaged them up for ransom. She was now convinced that this was his purpose in holding her. He was obviously going to send her finger to the Drakes, along with the ransom note. How could the Drakes fail to pay up, after receiving her severed, bloody finger in the post? Her ordeal would surely be over soon.

She had thanked God for saving her from the pain that she had expected, but it was beginning to feel as if he was going to renege on the deal and then some. The wound where her finger had been removed was beginning to throb horribly. She felt strangely calm in the circumstances, however, and was now keenly aware of her surroundings and the range of strong smells in the room. She could make out the unmistakable hospital smell of antiseptic and blood, presumably from the dressing of her finger, the musty, damp smell of a house long since empty and the distinctive aftershave of her captor, which she knew she would never forget, as long as she lived.

She wished, mostly, that he would remove her gag, because her mouth was now very dry and sore. She wanted to ask him for a drink and some painkillers – she had never been so thirsty – surely he wouldn't begrudge her those few, small things. She also wanted to ask if she could be tied in the chair again, because the bed springs were now cutting into her deeply, hurting far more than even the wound, where her finger had once been.

She turned her head to watch him, as he wrapped her finger in some tissue paper and placed it in a small box – the kind you put little presents in for birthdays and Christmas. He took great care in wrapping it in gift paper and even went to the trouble of expertly tying a neat little bow. Craig complimented himself on a job well done, and the timing was perfect, too – if he put the finger in the post today, it should arrive on the Drake's doormat on Elizabeth's birthday. How much more perfect could it be?

After her abductor left the room with his grisly package, Louise realised, to her increasing horror, that, in all the time he had spent with her, he had not once tried to conceal his face. Louise wasn't a stupid girl; she knew what that meant – she could identify her kidnapper. It dawned on her that there was no way he was ever going to let her go, and she couldn't hold back the tears.

* * * * * * * * * * * * * * *

When Paul arrived at the station, he realised that he had forgotten to get a birthday card for Elizabeth, and he was about to put a reminder on his phone, when Constable John Campbell approached him, carrying two cups of coffee. As he handed one to Paul, he said, 'We've had a bit of a result with the cars, Guv.'

'Go on, John, we could do with some new evidence. What have you got for me?'

'We found a car belonging to A1 Car Rentals abandoned a short walk away from Michael Pegler's house. It's been brought in, and they're checking it to see if we can place Craig or Kevin in it.'

'Whose name was the car hired under?'

'It was hired out to a Mr Colin Winters.'

'And have you managed to trace him?'

'Yes and no, Guv. He died in 1978, aged ten.'

'So we can assume that Colin Winters is either Craig or Kevin, then. Well, let's see if we can find out where this Colin Winters has been staying. Has he rented a house or apartment somewhere? Or is he staying in a hotel? Check the more upmarket ones first, actually. I can't see our friend slumming it, somehow. I take it the car is being checked for prints? It will be very useful if we can place Craig in it. See what you can find out. What about the other car? The one that we think they must have left near to the intended crash site? Has there been any luck with that?'

'No, Guv, not yet. But I've been thinking about that. Craig was driving Richard Drake's car to the intended crash site, so if the actual crash happened near to the intended crash site, Craig would have realised that they were close to the vehicle, and, when he managed to get out of the crash, he could have easily made his way to where the other car was waiting. I'll bet that's how he managed to get away from the scene with no one seeing him, if he was still in a fit enough state to drive, that is.'

'Yeah, you could well be right. Good work, John. Let me know if they get prints or DNA from the car that we have got, as soon as possible.'

'Will do, Guv.'

* * * * * * * * * * *

The morning following the amputation of her finger, having managed only the odd, troubled doze during the night, Louise was now suffering the torments of purgatory. She had been lying on the metal springs of the bed, without even a blanket between them and her, for most of the day before and the whole of that long night. Her back and buttocks felt as if they were on fire; the thin, cotton dress that she was wearing had provided no protection at all, and she felt it sticking to her in places, where she was sure that she was bleeding. It felt as though she'd been flogged with a bullwhip. She had been gagged since her abduction took place, and her mouth was now swollen and painful, as well as incredibly dry. She was still finding it increasingly difficult to breath. Added to this was the fact that the hand, which was now minus a finger, was throbbing so intensely, she was convinced some infection had set in, despite Craig's competent doctoring skills. To add humiliation to her plight, she had needed to empty her bladder in the night. She would have cried, but there was no longer enough moisture in her body to make any tears.

Craig had worried the whole time that he was away from Rebecca that she would find some way to either escape or alert someone to her situation, so he was reluctant to leave her again. He had wondered about keeping her for a while and then sending her back to her parents, piece by piece. That idea certainly appealed to him, but the risk of keeping an increasingly injured person captive in a house near a busy main road was too great. So, after all his great plans and ideas for Rebecca, it was looking as if his best course of action would be simply to kill her and send a hand or other body part to the Drakes, so that they would know their daughter's fate. He had also planned to do other things with Rebecca, but he could hear Kevin, as clearly as if he had been standing next to him, telling him not to take risks simply for a bit of fun – money, maybe, but not a woman. There would be all the women he could possibly want in Italy. Craig was now increasingly anxious to bring things to their conclusion, so that he could relax and simply enjoy his retirement.

* * * * * * * * * * * * * *

Nathaniel Clark was sat at his rather imposing desk, with a memo in one hand and a rapidly cooling cup of coffee in the other, when there was a firm knock at his door.

He looked up and replied 'come in,' automatically checking his desktop for any sensitive material that might be immediately visible and above the security clearance of whoever was about to enter his office.

As it turned out, he needn't have bothered with

checking, as the person who entered was Susan Cummings, and, she, despite not having an army rank, was his immediate superior – his boss, in effect.

'Good morning, Nathaniel, how are you?' she queried, with a genuinely warm smile.

'Good morning, Susan. I'm fine, thanks. To what do I owe the honour of a visit this morning? You normally summon me upstairs if we need to chat. Is everything OK?'

Susan sat herself down, facing Nathaniel.

'Yes, I hope so, Nathaniel. Did you enjoy your spot of leave? I hope your mum and dad are keeping well?'

'Oh, yes, they're fine, Susan, thank you for asking. They asked after you, of course,' he lied.

'Of course they did,' she answered, knowingly, 'I'll come straight to the point, Nathaniel. You've been asking around if anybody has information about a couple of low-lifes missing in the Newcastle area on a particular date. Was that connected to any on-going operation you are involved in?'

Nathaniel looked at Susan a little sheepishly. 'Probably not, actually. You might say that it's more of a police matter, and I will be completely open with you and declare a personal interest. An old friend of mine was murdered when I was just a youngster, and there seems an outside possibility that his murderers could now be caught. If I can manage to find out anything, I would very much like to pass it on to the police.'

'Well, from your point of view, Nathaniel, I have some good news. But you need to be careful with it, for both of our sakes.'

Nathaniel looked at his superior with interest. They had worked together closely for many years and made a good team. They liked, and trusted, each other, on both a professional and personal level, and they had covered each other's backs so many times in the past, that it was almost as if they shared the same one.

'As you probably know, we keep an eye on a location called Little Copse Farm, just outside Newcastle. You will also know that the fact we do so is a well-kept secret, and it needs to stay that way. We are certainly not the only agency with interest in its comings and goings. Now, I'm sure I don't have to remind you that if anything you do compromises our position, regarding Little Copse, you'll be for the high-jump. That is clearly understood, Nathaniel?'

'Of course.'

Nathaniel couldn't believe what was happening. If he wasn't mistaken, Susan was about to trust him with information that could effectively end her career, as well as his own, if he wasn't very careful with it. He had never had any dealings with Little Copse himself, but he knew of its importance.

'If I tell you what I know, and you screw it up, it's basically curtains for both of us, you know that, right?'

'Why would you tell me, then?'

'We've worked together for a long time, Nathaniel. Why ... you could almost call us friends, right? I trust you when you tell me it could help bring murderers to justice, and I've always like to see murderers get their just desserts.'

'You know I'll be careful.'

'OK, then. At the moment, there are a couple of our Russian friends staying at the farmhouse. We don't know why, yet, but we suspect that they are here to meet someone, and we'd like to know who that is. On the day that you are interested in, there was some suspicious activity at the main outbuilding that appeared to be totally unconnected with our visitors.'

'I'm all ears.'

'Two black cars turned up, about an hour apart. Four men got out of each car – three in suites and one dressed quite casually in comparison. Our man on the ground couldn't be certain, but it is possible that the casually dressed men were not there by choice. In the early afternoon, a hire car turned up, and two more men got out of it. These men were greeted very warmly, and, after a short time, the six men in suits left in their two cars. About half an hour later, a gunshot was heard, coming from vicinity of the barn.'

'Just the one shot?' interrupted Nathaniel, surprised.

'Apparently, though I see where you're coming from. There was no more activity there until well after dark, when the two late arrivals were seen loading a couple of crates or boxes into one of the farm's vans. They then drove away in the van, but returned a good four hours later, got straight into the hire car and left, never to return.'

'And the two casually dressed men were never seen to leave? Is that right?' quizzed Nathaniel.

'Our men say that they never left on foot. So they are ether still there ...' Susan tailed off, suggestively.

'... or they were in the crates!' finished Nathaniel.

'What do you propose to do now?'

'Well, obviously, I can't tell the police where all this took place, but it does fit the bill of the situation that I'm looking for, if you'll forgive the pun. In other words, it's the right time-frame and the right location. In a way, it's good that they took the bodies away from the farm, actually.'

Susan Cummings stood up and prepared to leave. 'Well, that's my good deed of the day done. Oh, there is just one other thing to bear in mind.'

'What's that?'

'You now owe me, big-time.'

Nathaniel smiled, broadly. 'When was it ever not so?'

Susan smiled on her way out, after saying, 'Oh, and, actually, I'd forgotten that you even had a mum and dad.'

'Well, that's all right, because they didn't really ask after you.'

Grinning, she closed the door behind her.

Later that day, Nathaniel walked into the office of Joe Good – another colleague, with a debt outstanding.

'Afternoon, Joe, how's tricks?'

'No, absolutely not. It's out of the question, so don't even bother to ask me,' said Joe, immediately, putting his hands up in the air defensively, as if fending off a blow.

'What? I haven't even asked you for anything yet. Really, is that any way to greet an old friend?'

'You're not an old friend, Nathaniel. You're not any kind of friend. You just got me out of a spot of trouble once, is all, and I've paid you back with favours, time and again. It always gets me into trouble. I could have been head of this department by now, if I hadn't kept helping you out on the side.'

One last favour, and I promise the slate is wiped clean. In fact ... I'll owe you, how's that?'

'Honestly? It doesn't sound good. It sounds as if you want something big, maybe even something that could lose me my job or even my liberty, so, no, I'm not doing it, whatever it is.'

'Joe, I'll write you an official authorisation.'

'Yeah, OK, so where does the favour come in, then?'

'Well, I need it done ASAP. It can't wait to go through the usual authorisation channels – it will be too late by then.'

'What is it you want, exactly?' asked Joe, concerned as to the way things were heading.

'You know Little Copse Farm ...'

'Yes, I do, and I'm not touching anything to do with that place, unless it's been though the right channels and duly authorised by the man, so that's that.'

'I was going to say that there is a field some way from the farm that used to be part of it at one point in time, but is not anymore. All I need is an aerial photograph of the field – one quick, low-level pass should be enough. There's a small aerodrome nearby, so there must be light aircraft flying over all the time. There's no need for anyone to be suspicious or get nervous.'

'You swear that this is legitimate and that the slate will be wiped clean?'

'On my mum's life.'

'What? You had a mum? I'll bet she was burnt at the stake years ago. So, what sort of photo do you need? What is it, exactly, that you are looking for?'

'I think there may be a couple of bodies buried in the field, and I need to locate them as soon as possible.'

'All right, I'll see what I can do. And then you owe me, right? That's what you said.'

'Absolutely, I promise.'

Nathaniel left Joe's office, wondering if he would still have the same rank, or even a job, in a couple of weeks' time; he was really going out on a limb with this job.

* * * * * * * * * * * * *

As soon as Louise saw the expression on her captor's face when he entered the room, she knew that she was going to die. She was as certain of this fact, as she was that the sun would rise in the morning, and she wouldn't be there to see it. It was so unfair, she suddenly thought, plaintively. She had never done anyone any harm, and she was young and healthy, with her whole life before her. She wanted to meet a nice young man and fall in love, raise a big family, see the world and grow old with those she loved, but, now, she would do none of these things. She began to cry, which only made breathing even more difficult, and, once again, she prayed to God that whatever happened wouldn't hurt too much. If she hadn't been so tightly gagged, she would have swallowed her pride and furiously begged for her life, offered him anything so as not to kill her, but the fact of the matter was that she was gagged and bound, and, deep down, she knew that all the begging and pleading in the world wouldn't divert this sadistic man from his path; she could read it plainly in his face. Why? Why her?

She began to wonder how he was actually going to do it – how he was going to kill her. She tried to tell herself that at least it would end her unbearable suffering; the pain she was suffering now was almost too much to endure. She hoped and prayed that he would be merciful and do it quickly, just shoot her in the head, maybe. At least, that way, it would be relatively quick and painless, wouldn't it? She thought she could brace herself for that, maybe. As he moved closer to the bed, her heart began to beat even faster; she could feel it pounding away in her chest. She furiously hoped that he didn't have a knife – she didn't want to be stabbed or, worse, have her throat cut. She didn't think that would be very quick at all, and she'd always hated knives. She started to panic. Dear God, not a knife. She knew she wouldn't be able to be brave if it was a knife. She lost control of her bladder again, but, this time, she didn't even care. What did it matter now? What did anything matter now?

As he stood beside the bed, she looked down at his hands. To her horror, he wasn't carrying a gun or a knife - it was a plastic bag. She stared into his face and pleaded with her eyes as a hopeless last resort, but to no avail. He was going to suffocate her by placing a plastic bag over her head. Oh, God, no, please, she didn't want to go like that – that wouldn't be quick at all. By this time, she was screaming frantically inside. She struggled furiously and shook her head from side to side, oblivious, now, to the pain that it caused in her back, but it made no difference. He easily and deftly slipped the bag over her head and held it firmly closed around her young neck.

In those moments, God had let Louise down. She had prayed that it would be painless, but, instead, when her cruel captor had put the abhorrent bag over her head, and she had taken a breath, no air entered her lungs. It felt as if someone had cut open her chest with a blunt saw and ripped her straining lungs from her breast. The last few moments of Louise's young life were spent in complete terror and agony.

Craig was always morbidly fascinated by how long it actually took people to die, and he often wished that he could be aware of what was going through their minds in those last few seconds. He remembered reading a book, once, about pirates. The hero and his companion were being made to walk the plank – something which only ever happens in popular fiction and Hollywood films, he knew, as there is no historical evidence that anyone was ever executed by pirates in that way. In this particular book, the hero's advice to his companion had been to breathe out and empty his lungs before being pushed into the depths of the sea, because the suffering would be over far quicker that way. He wondered if Rebecca would have followed the hero's advice, if he had told her the story before he covered her head with the plastic bag. He didn't think so; she held her breath as long as she could, and the terror and pain that he'd seen in her eyes had been amazing to witness.

The next problem that he faced was what to do with the body. Perhaps he would buy a chest freezer and just leave it there in the house, until it was time to leave for Italy, at which point he could dump it somewhere out-of-the-way, before he finally left. If he dumped it in one of the usual places, it should stay undiscovered for quite some time, certainly enough for him to leave the country and disappear. He would remove a hand to send to Richard and Elizabeth in a couple of days, but he would give them a fighting chance to get over the initial shock of the severed finger, first.

He had been in the house for a few days already, and he was getting impatient to kill Richard now, so that he could conclude his business, once and for all, and finally go abroad. He would have to open an account in his own name, once there, so that he could transfer the money that he was due to inherit from both his mother's and his brother's estates. He had hoped that things would be concluded and neatly tied up before he left, and he had a very acceptable offer for both the club and the other businesses, from a new acquaintance based near Newcastle. He was pleased that he didn't have to sell to a London crew, because they had tried to muscle in numerous times in the past, and this would be one in the eye for them. So he had decided to go earlier than he had originally planned and let things conclude in their own time over here. His lawyer was well aware of his dual identity and had handled a lot of questionable, and some downright illegal, business dealings for him in the past, so he could definitely be trusted to look after matters at this end. After all, he would do very well out of it.

First things first, though – how to deal with the body. He dismissed his first idea of purchasing a chest freezer; no, he would dispose of it properly. He needed to get a few things, first, and then he would pay a visit to the woods, in order to pick a good spot in which to bury it. It would not be the first body he had disposed of, by any stretch of the imagination, but he thought that, perhaps, it might just be the last. Deep in woodlands or forest is a good place to successfully get rid of a body, because not many people will venture in these areas at nighttime, or, indeed, even during the day, even if they do happen to hear some strange activity occurring. The mistakes that most amateurs make concern not burying the body deep enough and doing it on open ground, where it can often be found and dug up by wild animals. All too often, the inexperienced killer will underestimate how difficult it is to dig a grave and will start doing so with wildly inadequate tools. They also make the mistake of bringing the body with them during the digging process. This not only makes them rush the task, for fear of discovery, but also leaves them vulnerable and in possession of incriminating evidence, if any busybody does turn up.

No, the first, and most important, thing to do is to pick a good spot, and this is best done in broad daylight – all sorts of things can be missed under the cloak of night, as Craig well knew. He knew of a case where a man had killed his wife and buried her in nearby woodlands at night, only to discover – to his cost – the next day that he had dug a very shallow grave, right next to a busy bridle path, which he had simply missed in the dark. How Craig had laughed when he heard the story. What an idiot!

The next thing, is to have the right tools – not just a shovel, but a pick-axe and a chainsaw, as well, so that you can dig deeply and easily cut away any roots that threaten to stop proceedings. If the grave is to remain undiscovered, then it has to be as deep as possible. Lastly, Craig knew that it was crucial to never have the body with you, when you are digging. If you happen to arouse somebody's suspicion, if you are overheard or if you are just unlucky enough to have a late-night dog walker pass by the area, the last thing you want is to be found in possession of a dead body. So, the golden rules are: carefully pick a spot in daylight; dig deep and do this at night time, then cover the grave and conceal the earth mound with twigs or leaves while unattended and then take the body to the grave and fill it in the next night. Craig could have written a best-selling 'How To' manual on body disposal. The last two bodies that he and Kevin had disposed of were buried, uncharacteristically, in an open field near Newcastle, because they had not chosen the site. However, he was still very confident that they would remain undiscovered, simply because he knew that the job had been done properly.

He had spotted a large tool shop the last time that he had gone into town, so he was confident that he could get everything he needed locally, without having to return to where he had bought the pipe cutter. Returning to the same place too many times gets you noticed – another one of Kevin's little jewels of wisdom.

Chapter 12

July the tenth was Elizabeth's thirty-ninth birthday, and, while it would normally be celebrated in grand style by the whole family, with both Margaret and Rebecca banned from returning to the family home until Craig Harper was safely behind bars and with young Louise missing, it had been quickly agreed to put the celebrations on hold for the time being. Nobody was in the mood for celebrating anything, other than the safe return of Louise or the welcome incarceration of Craig Harper.

Richard had bought Elizabeth a gold pendant, to replace the paperknife that had effectively saved his and Michael's lives, and he had given it to her, with a cup of tea, in bed that morning. Normally, Richard took a great deal of time looking for just the right present for his wife. Either that or, as was the case with the paperknife, he would put something away, if it presented itself during normal trading, but it had to be just the right thing. The pendant, however, he bought as a sort of stop-gap, intending to get something really special for her, when their present situation finally resolved itself. Margaret and Rebecca had arranged for flowers to be delivered, and they had arrived promptly the day before, and, although Elizabeth had loved them, they had made her think of funerals and whether or not poor young Louise was still alive. She had certainly shed her daily quota of tears. Rebecca had also bought her mother some clothes, as she often did, because they both had such similar taste and style, but these were in Rebecca's wardrobe, so she planned to give them to her mother when they next met.

Elizabeth was a big Agatha Christie fan, and Michael had managed to find her a first edition of *Death on the Nile*, which was currently having a little restoration work done on the rather fragile binding. It was supposed to have been ready before her birthday, but with all the unpleasantness, Michael had been unable to pick it up, so he had to resort to describing it to her, instead. Elizabeth had always wanted to own a first edition, and so she was delighted with the gift, but complained that it was too much.

Michael was continuing to make good progress with his recovery and was now making a nuisance of himself, hobbling around the house on his crutches, although he still needed a lot of help navigating the stairs. The wheelchair, which they, at one time, thought he might need, instead of being returned to the shop where they had purchased it, had since been donated to a local charity for injured soldiers – one which often benefited from Michael's kind patronage. He argued that he had never been called upon to defend his country or fight in a conflict of any sort, and the reason why he had never been called upon to risk his live in that way was because there were always plenty of brave, young men who were willing to do the fighting for him. He was immensely grateful to them, for that, so if he could do something to help them, occasionally, he was more than glad to do it.

Richard had pretty much made a full recovery from his injuries in the crash and was completely pain-free, according to him, although Elizabeth said that he still looked a bit like an artist's palette in the shower. She had joked, when he first arrived home, that she would keep a photograph of some of his bruises, so that they could match the colours next time they decided to decorate their house.

Elizabeth's mood seemed to alternate between reasonable good humour and downright depression. She was still unsure as to whether she should ring Louise's parents or not, because she didn't know them at all, and she didn't even know whether her family had contacted Louise's Aunt Peggy on holiday, in order to tell her what had happened. She felt guilty that they had allowed Louise to come to the house, when all this business was going on with that awful man. She should have realised the potential danger to visitors and cancelled the damn cleaning. Both Michael and Richard had repeatedly told her that there was no way any of them could have known that there was any unlikely danger for Louise. Elizabeth had to promptly excuse herself and ran upstairs crying again, something that she had begun doing at least twice a day since Louise had gone missing, and which was causing Richard a great deal of anguish. He honestly feared that his wife was on the edge of a breakdown, but she had stubbornly refused to let him call the doctor.

The three of them – Richard, Elizabeth and Michael – had been having breakfast in the kitchen, when Elizabeth had started crying again and promptly disappeared back upstairs. Richard confided in Michael and told him of his fears for his wife's emotional health, to which Michael replied that he, too, had seen the signs, but that if she wouldn't see the doctor, all they could do was to try to support her as much as possible and hope and pray that Louise would be found alive. They would try to shield her from stressful situations, they agreed, but, of course, avoiding stress, at the moment, was very difficult for all of them, if not downright impossible.

Elizabeth had finally composed herself and returned to the kitchen after about twenty minutes, apologising for being so weak and crying so easily. Richard had just put the kettle on to make everyone another cup of tea, when the door-bell rang.

'Somebody must have sent you a present or a card that's too big for the letterbox,' said Richard, who immediately turned to answer it, hoping that the newly arrived birthday mail would brighten his wife's sombre mood.

The postman held a handful of cards, some inevitable bills and a small package. The cards and package were all addressed to Elizabeth, and the bills to Richard.

'It's always the same, Michael,' said Richard, in mock frustration, handing the cards and the small package to his wife, 'Liz gets the pretty, coloured envelopes, and I get the brown ones. Now, tell me, is that fair?'

Elizabeth started to brighten up a bit, while she was opening the birthday cards from friends and family. She purposefully left the little package till last.

After opening and reading each card, she passed them over to Richard, who dutifully read them and passed them over to Michael to read. Now, they both looked on, in anticipation, as Elizabeth used a small pair of scissors to cut the neatly tied ribbon and unwrap the small parcel. Inside the wrapping paper was a small gift box.

'Who is it from?' asked Richard, intrigued.

Elizabeth looked back over the wrapping paper that she had just removed, looking for a tag or something that would indicate who the surprise gift was from, but she found nothing.

'Whoever has sent it has forgotten to put a gift label on it, so I won't know who to thank. That's annoying.'

'Maybe there is a clue in the box itself?' suggested Michael, helpfully.

Elizabeth carefully opened the lid and took out the present, meticulously wrapped in a piece of clean, white tissue paper. She laid it on the kitchen table in front of the three of them and gently unfolded it. At first, they thought that it must be some kind of sick practical joke, but then the sickening realisation that it was a real finger fully hit them.

Elizabeth screamed and made to run from the table, but Richard grabbed hold of her and held her tight, cradling her head into his shoulder.

Richard and Michael both stared in complete horror and disbelief at the heart-rending object on the table before them, instinctively knowing that it was Louise's finger, but also realising that it was meant to be Rebecca's.

Richard escorted his sobbing wife upstairs, almost carrying her weak body the last few yards, and laid her down on their bed, unable to comfort her or prevent the awful sobbing that racked her frame. He tenderly covered his wife with a blanket from the chest at the foot of their bed, kissed her gently on the cheek and told her to try and get some sleep, even though he knew there was absolutely no chance of it. Seeing his wife in such a state almost made him cry himself; he felt so helpless.

He went to the top of the stairs and shouted down to Michael, who was also, now, close to tears.

'Michael, will you ring Paul from the kitchen phone and tell him what has happened? I'm going to call the doctor for Liz.'

When the doctor finally arrived, he gave Elizabeth a sedative to help her sleep, and, after he left, Elizabeth thankfully managed to doze off. Richard, Paul, Sergeant Reg – as he had become known to them all – and Constable June Kelly were all in the kitchen with toast and mugs of tea and coffee, courtesy of Michael, who had now mastered the art of standing stationary at the kitchen worktop, without the aid of his crutches.

'How is Liz?' asked Paul, worriedly, as Michael deposited a steaming, hot mug of coffee before him.

'She'll be fine in a bit,' Richard lied. 'The doc gave her a sedative to help her sleep, but I'm afraid this has been building for a while. The finger just brought it to a head. She's a strong woman, though – I'm sure she'll cope,' he said, praying that what he was saying was true.

'We really just need to find Louise alive, now. What do think are our chances, Paul?'

Paul finished examining the severed finger, that he was holding gingerly in a gloved hand, and asked June to take it back to the station for a proper examination.

'We all know that it's Louise's finger, of course,' he replied, matter-of-factly, 'but we had better check, just to be certain. Now, I'm no expert, but my guess would be, just from looking at it, that she was alive when the finger was removed, so ... horrible though that fact is ... it means that there is hope that she will still be found alive.'

He turned to June, 'Get the doc to confirm that, as soon as possible, and have all the packaging checked for prints and DNA; let's hope that Craig's been careless, for once. When you've done that, can you bring the car back for Reg and I?'

June carefully put the grisly present back in the box and placed it, together with the wrappings, in an evidence bag, leaving soon after for the station.

'Reg, I don't suppose they saw anything other than the postman delivering mail, but can you please check with our surveillance teams anyway?'

Michael and Richard turned, in unison, to look at Paul, and they both said, simultaneously, 'Surveillance team?'

Paul took a sip of his coffee and said, 'Sorry I never said anything, Richard, but it hasn't been for long. DCI Blake is running the investigation into Louise's abduction, and he organised the teams, knowing that she had been mistaken for Rebecca and that Craig would almost certainly be in touch, one way or another. We didn't want the knowledge that you were under surveillance to influence your behaviour in any way, as it could possibly tip Craig off. But the fact is that your home, the shop and Robert Power's house have been under constant surveillance for the past two days, and they will continue to be, until we nail this bastard and find Louise. Whenever Elizabeth or you or the girls have gone out, you have been followed by our men.'

'All three properties, Paul? Don't get me wrong, I'm grateful that so much effort is being put in to the investigation, and it's good to know that the women are being carefully watched, but I thought that you said you were short of both manpower and money.'

'We are, Richard – desperately short, in fact – but a young woman is now missing and that changes everything, including the budget. It's also the reason that the DCI is totally onboard now.'

At this point, Michael chipped in. 'If the girls are being watched, how come no one knew where they were when Louise was taken? That would have saved some heartache here, I can tell you.'

'Until Louise was taken, we only had someone driving by occasionally. At that point, we didn't have the manpower to follow anyone constantly, but, as I say, it's different now.'

'And nobody has any idea where Craig might be holed up?' Michael asked, incredulously.

'None, unfortunately. We've been looking to arrest him, since his brother's inquest, but Craig beat us to it and has gone-to-ground somewhere, probably the same place that he's now holding Louise.'

'So you have no idea where to start looking, even?' asked Michael.

'None at all, at the moment, Michael. We are doing our best, and there are a lot of people involved in looking now. The London boys will let us know if he turns up at the club or at any of his London haunts, but, personally, I think he's close by, maybe even in this area – somewhere that he can easily keep tabs on Richard and his movements.'

Richard and Michael looked at each other, as the significance of Paul's last remark slowly sank in.

After the police had finally left, and Richard had sneaked in to check that Elizabeth was sound asleep, he and

Michael sat talking in the lounge, with a couple of rather large, stiff drinks.

'Tell me what you would do, now, if you were Craig?' asked Michael, thoughtfully.

'How do you mean?'

'Well, you have kidnapped a young woman, and you may or may not have discovered that she is not the person that you originally thought. You have brutally cut off her finger and sent it as a sick gift to the person that you want to suffer. Do you kill her now? If so, why didn't you kill her straight away? Is there any good reason to keep her alive? Most importantly, how are you going to adequately keep track of your quarry and their movements and, at the same time, avoid the attention of the police? I think Paul is right. I think Craig is based around here, somewhere.'

'Whoa, slow down, Michael, you're going way too fast for me. Where is all this leading, anyway?'

'We both know that this whole thing is only going to be concluded in one of two ways. Either Craig is going to kill you or a family member or one of us is going to kill him. Don't get me wrong, I like and respect Paul as much as you do, but I can't see the police resolving this particularly satisfactorily ... can you, really?'

'Oh, well, I don't know ... the police may manage to catch him and lock him away for a long time. Remember, they have found a young boy's body in the garden now, so it's not simply the attempted murder of us anymore – it's actual murder and abduction of Louise, as well.'

'Yes, OK, granted. But they don't hang murderers these days – more's the pity – and you and I can surmise that a man like Craig, with all his nasty connections, can reach out from inside prison. He could easily –what's that term? –"put a contract out on us." He'll find a way to make life extremely unpleasant, even if he is incarcerated, and you know it.'

'So you're actually suggesting that I kill him, knowingly, in cold blood?'

'We've talked about this, Richard! I don't suppose there will be anything very cold about it, but, honestly, can you look me in the eye and tell me you haven't come to the same conclusion? You knew it, the moment you picked up the gun from my safe you knew it wasn't just for self-defense. I still have to show you how to use it properly, too. Why don't you go and get it now, while Liz is still asleep?'

Richard obediently returned to his study, where he had carefully hidden the gun in the top drawer of his desk. Retrieving it, he held it in his hands, testing its weight and wondering whether he could actually point it at someone and pull the trigger. He had held guns before, of course, but they had always been revolvers of one sort or another, including his own Navy Colt. He even had powder, a bullet mould and percussion caps for it, and Michael had once offered to have it proof-fired for him, in order to see if it could still safely be used. But Richard had not been willing to chance damaging the weapon, so it still lived contentedly in its own polished oak box, with all its accoutrements, on a shelf in Richard's study.

After fetching it from his study, Richard handed the gun and ammunition over to Michael, who said, seriously, 'Watch and listen carefully, Richard. This is a Barrette 92 double-action semi-automatic pistol. Now, it's very important that you don't get confused with the term double-action. With the revolvers that you are familiar with, single and double action refers to the actions that take place when you pull the trigger. So, for instance, with a single action revolver, the gun has to be manually cocked first, and then pulling the trigger performs the single action of firing the gun.

'With a double-action revolver, pulling the trigger both cocks and fires, making two actions. However, things are a little different with a double-action automatic. With an automatic, pulling the trigger the first time both cocks and fires, as you would expect – hence, double action – but the recoil on this weapon, both ejects the spent cartridge and cocks the gun, ready for the next shot. This effectively makes it a single-action pistol, after it is first fired.

'It is possible to cock the hammer manually, for the first shot, but I don't recommend it, if you're not practiced with the weapon. I certainly don't want you shooting your foot off, by firing the first shot prematurely. So, remember, Richard, the first time you pull the trigger, it will be harder, because it has to cock the gun first, but any subsequent shots will only require minimal pressure on the trigger, because it will already be cocked and ready. Are you OK with that? Do you understand?'

'Yeah, yeah, I got it – first time, hard; second time, easy.'

'That's right. It's the same as what they say about killing someone – the first time is hard; the second time, it's easier. It's a shame we haven't got anywhere for you to fire the gun properly, so that you can get used to the recoil and the different trigger pressures, but a dry-run will just have to do.'

Michael went on to show Richard how to load and unload the gun and how to check and make sure it was unloaded, by removing the clip and checking the breech.

He also wanted to show Richard how to clean and look after the gun, but Richard had stopped him, saying, 'For God's sake, Michael! I'm not going to keep the damn gun if I use it! I'm never going to want to clean the bloody thing, that's for sure.'

'OK, OK, point taken. But there is one more thing that you need to remember – get in close and aim low. The first shot will require extra pressure on the trigger and that will raise the barrel, so your shot will go higher than you think. After that, you won't need so much pressure, but the recoil will still tend to raise the barrel as you fire, so make sure that you always hold the gun with two hands, just like I've shown you, and like you've seen on the television, and, remember, aim low.'

Michael made Richard go through the actions of holding and firing the gun several times, until he was satisfied that Richard at least stood a chance of hitting a target, if it wasn't too far away. After the tuition, Richard put the gun back in the drawer of his desk, and, although he had been a little impatient with Michael for making him go through the motions, he had to admit that he did feel just that little bit more comfortable and sure in handling the gun now.

On returning to the lounge, he discovered that Michael was not yet finished with his questions.

'Now, do you have a decent telescope or pair of binoculars, Richard?'

'I have some binoculars somewhere, I think. Why?'

'Look, if I was this Craig fellow, I'd want to go to ground somewhere close to my quarry, so that I could keep an eye on them. The best way to do that would be to move into a house that overlooks the quarry, even Paul said he thought he was close by. Have there been any places close by that have recently been up for rent and that are now occupied? Has any neighbour taken a lodger lately? Or gone on holiday?'

Richard went and retrieved his pair of binoculars and helped Michael upstairs and into the bedroom he was occupying, during his period of convalescence. Once there, they closed the curtains tightly, so that only a crack remained. They eagerly scanned the front of all the houses that they could immediately see from this window. There was no sign of anything out of the ordinary, but they agreed to repeat the performance from the bay window in Elizabeth and Richard's room twice a day, until Craig was safely located.

'What am I supposed to be looking for, exactly?' Richard asked, peering through the slightly open curtains.

'Well, I don't know, exactly, but maybe an upstairs room, with the curtains pulled, like we've just done, you know, with just a crack left open, maybe the glint of sun off another pair of binoculars, perhaps a house that looks largely empty, but has a car in the drive, just anything out of the ordinary, really.'

'Won't the police be doing all of that already?'

'Probably, but we really need to find him first.'

Richard was a little sceptical about what Michael was proposing, but Michael was convinced that Craig was watching them from somewhere close by, and, if he could see them, it stood to reason that they would probably be able to see him, too.

* * * * * * * * * *

Paul had just been into the Chief Inspector's office, keeping him updated with the unfolding events and to see if the London boys had any more news of Craig's possible whereabouts, but there had been little to report, either way.

On returning to the incident room, however, Reg immediately informed him, 'June's been doing some more digging into the Harper family's affairs, Guv. She has discovered that the workshop that was owned by the late Frederick Harper still forms part of Mrs Harper's estate. June has just rung the council, and, apparently, Mrs Harper was still paying rates on it. It's not rented out, either – the council have it listed as currently unoccupied.'

'So it was never sold?'

'That's right. Apparently, the old guy had a heart attack in 1980 and never worked again. The then-foreman – a Mr

Alan West – ran the business for a few years, but when he eventually left, the workshop was closed down. However, as you say, it was never sold.'

'Well, where is it?'

'It's on a little trading estate in the Fishponds area, and I'll bet the keys are the ones that we found in the desk at Mrs Harper's – the ones that we couldn't identify.'

'Right, June can drive me to Hilltop Cottage to retrieve the keys, but I want you at the workshop asap, in order to judge the lay of the land. Get John or Clive to inform the DCI of this information and get his team, and themselves, to meet us at the trading estate. If Craig has keys for the workshop, it might just be where he's hiding Louise. Better get armed response there, as well, and make sure that everyone knows to make a silent approach. If Craig is there, I don't want him alerted to our arrival.'

Paul, with June Kelly driving, visited Hilltop Cottage and retrieved the keys that Reg. referred to. From there, they drove to the Fishponds trading estate and located the entrance to Frederick Harper's workshop, where Clive, John, the DCI's team and the armed police were quietly waiting.

Paul made sure everybody was thoroughly briefed, before Reg put the most likely looking key into the rusting padlock that secured the outer gates, managing, after a slight struggle, to open it. He unhooked the padlock from the chain, which was tightly looped though the handles of the large and somewhat rotten gates and, with a little help from the others, pushed them wide open, so that an armed team could enter easily.

'I don't think Craig, or anyone else, has been here in a while, Guv. Not for a long time, I'd say – that gate hasn't been opened for years,' said Reg.

The party of police stood in the open gateway, surveying the scene beyond and feeling a little as Lord

Carnarvon and Howard Carter must have felt standing at the entrance to Tutankhamen's burial chamber, unseen for countless years. But they, unlike Howard Carter and Lord Carnarvon, saw nothing remotely wonderful.

Inside the ageing gates, the yard was strewn with the overflowing rubbish and leftovers of a once-thriving business. There were rusting metal benches and several long abandoned templates and jigs, which had once helped to make essential components for industry, maybe costing thousands of pounds. On the opposite side of the yard was the building itself – a two-storey, brick-built structure, with a double-pitched tiled roof, which now looked in dire need of repair and through which pigeons could be seen entering. The elevation facing them had a row of matching windows to both floors, the only difference being the fact that the ground-floor windows had steel bars over them, whereas the upper floor had a sort of metal grill covering.

One of the upper windows could obviously be opened from the inside, in case of fire – a fact that was indicated by the metal fire escape leading down from it, on which two armed officers were currently ascending. Two windows, along from the left corner on the ground floor, was a pair of large sliding doors, inset into one of which was a single personnel door, which the rest of the armed police were in the process of opening.

After a depressingly short period of time inside the building, the armed men returned with their officer, gesturing that all was clear and that it was perfectly safe to enter. Paul's heart sank. Even after seeing the condition of the rusting padlock on the front gates, he had still hoped that Louise was here.

Inside the workshop, there was a large open area, dotted about with various old benches and broken machines. Some of the benches had items on them that looked as if they were still in the process of being manufactured, but the whole place smelled of damp, decay and fetid pigeon droppings.

'Good Lord!' exclaimed Paul. 'If it wasn't for the putrid smell and the thick layer of dust over everything, you could imagine that the place is just closed for the weekend and that the workforce will be back in to continue with their work on Monday, as usual.'

'It's kind of eerie,' said June, suppressing a shudder.

'My information was that the factory simply closed when the foreman left. I had just assumed that everything had been sold off, but obviously not,' said Reg. looking around. It was almost as if he could see the men still working hard at their workbenches and hear the dull mechanical noise of the machines and the monotonous hum of the men's conversations.

'There are machines and tools everywhere,' he said, thoughtfully, 'It's like an Aladdin's cave in here. It's a wonder that it was never broken into. Some of these things must be worth a lot of money, surely.'

DCI Blake dismissed the armed response team and wandered over to Paul, exclaiming, in frustration, 'Damn! I really thought we had a good chance of finding her here. I'll leave you to check things out, Paul. Let me know straight away if you find anything of interest. Oh. and, Paul? Don't beat yourself up about it; it was a good shout.'

'Thank you, sir, but it is incredibly disappointing. I really thought ...' Paul stopped mid-sentence and walked away, suddenly overcome with emotion and not wanting the DCI or his team to see what might be regarded as weakness.

June Kelly had witnessed Paul's reaction, and she walked up to him, putting a hand on his shoulder, 'We'll find her, Guv.'

'Well, we'd better do it quickly, June. I can't stop thinking about what that bastard's doing to her.'

Chief Inspector Blake left with the rest of his team, and Paul returned to his team, having recovered his composure.

'Well,' he said, 'I have no idea what we can expect to find here, so look for anything that might indicate that somebody has been here recently. Remember, there's a young woman missing, so check very carefully. We can't yet rule out the possibility that she may have been here and then been moved elsewhere. I'll check out that door over there,' he said, pointing, 'it looks like it could be old offices. The rest of you, spread out and get searching.'

'Well, judging by the state of the front gate, I don't think anyone has been here since it closed for business, Guv,' Reg, concluded.

'I think you're right, Reg, but let's have a good look, anyway. We might get lucky.'

As Paul walked towards the offices he had spotted, his mobile rang. It turned out to be Derrick, calling from the incident room.

'Are you still at the factory, Guv?'

'Yes, we've only just started to have a good look around, why?'

'No sign of Louise, then, Guv?'

'No.'

'Sorry ... I've been checking into a bit more of the history of Frederick Harper, and I've discovered a rather interesting coincidence. It would appear that he had his heart attack, after returning to the factory after hours one night. It seems that he was there all alone, and it was lucky for him that he was able to call 999 when he was taken poorly. The emergency worker who took the call wasn't sure which service Mr Harper wanted, so she alerted all three. The ambulance arrived first and radioed the fire service to cancel the appliance. Then the police arrived, but they took no interest in the matter, because there was no crime or break-in involved, so, apparently, the foreman who was called out as a key holder was the last to leave and lock up.'

'OK, I've got the picture so far, but what was the interesting coincidence?'

'Well, this all happened on the evening of the day that Stephen Potter went missing. So, my question is ... what was so important that meant Fred had to return to the factory that night?'

'And a very good question it is, Derrick. Why did he return to the factory, I wonder? We'll get together and talk about it in more depth, after we've finished up here, OK?'

Paul snapped closed his phone and then let the others know what Derrick had said, after which, he thoroughly searched the offices, only to find that any paperwork – unlike the dusty tools and machines – was long gone. He was just finishing looking around, when there was an excited call from Reg.

'Guv! What do make of this?'

Paul found Reg and June at the far end of the factory, in what appeared to be one of two large, spacious storerooms. When he entered the room, Reg was pointing at the wall behind the door that Paul had just come in through. Paul turned to look, and it took a moment for him to register which of the many items hanging there had been the cause of so much excitement ... but then he spotted it. Hanging in full view, minus its wheels, was a bicycle.

Paul caught the eyes of the other two in the room and laughed, dismissively, 'No ... there is no way. It can't be that simple, surely?'

'What else would he be doing here that night, Guv? If he had just buried Stephen in the garden, then the only other thing left to get rid of would be the bike; so why not bring it here? He could cut it up, maybe even melt it down or something of the sort. I'll bet you a tenner that's Stephen

Potter's bike and that Frederick Harper brought it here that night to get rid of it. He was just unfortunate enough to have a heart attack, before he could get the job done.'

'So you think the foreman hung it on the wall in here the next day or something, when clearing up, and that it's been hanging there, ever since?'

'Why not?'

'Guv, over here!' called June, excitedly, who was looking under one of the two tables that constituted the only furniture in the room. 'I've just found the wheels!'

June stood up from where she had been crouching, and Reg and Paul stared at her, both smiling broadly. Her uniform was covered with dust, and she had a streak of what could only be oil smeared across her left cheek.

'What?' she demanded, seeing their amused expressions, then looked down at herself, 'Oh damn!' and did her best to brush the excess dust from her clothes.

'Right, get a team down here, then. If Fred did bring Stephen's bike down here to get rid of it, then perhaps he brought the gun, as well. Get the bike tested for DNA – Stephen's and any of the Harper's ... Oh, and June, as soon as we get back to the incident room, I want you to track down Fred's old foreman, if he is still with us. Oh, and did people put postcodes and that sort of gaff on possessions back then? Perhaps Stephen's parents marked the bike in some way ... Remember, it's just a bike, until we can prove it's Stephen's.'

Both Reg and June left the factory feeling a little more upbeat about the situation that was unfolding, but Paul's mood didn't seem to match theirs at all.

'You don't look all that happy at finding possible evidence, Guv.'

'Well, I was hoping that we would find Louise or at least something that would say that she was still alive. I just don't think we stand a chance of getting Craig for Stephen's murder, no matter how much evidence we happen to uncover. I'm seriously considering packing in this enquiry, in favour of the others – for one thing, it's far too time consuming.'

Reg and June both frowned, and Reg asked, worriedly, 'Why, Guv?'

'Well, because there are too many other possibilities that he could realistically put forward. All the evidence we have at the moment points to his dad as the killer, as much as one of the boys. Remember, they were only ... what? Twelve, perhaps? Stephen could have called at the house when the twins weren't there, and, for some reason or other, their mum could've killed him, maybe by accident, and their dad just got rid of the evidence to protect her. Or perhaps it was Kevin that killed him, nothing to do with Craig at all? No ... without an eyewitness, I don't think we have a chance of pinning it on Craig. It's obvious that one of the Harpers did in poor Stephen, but three of the possibilities are dead, and Craig could easily argue that it was any one of them. And, on top of that, none of this gets us any closer to finding Louise.'

The incident room was a hive of activity. June was busy trying to track down Frederick Harper's foreman from the factory. Clive Pascoe had been assigned to try to discover who sold Raleigh bikes in that area around 1980. John Campbell had discovered that Stephen's mother, Susan Potter, had divorced her husband in 1984 and permanently relocated to New Zealand. She had recently been informed, by the police unit in New Zealand that Stephen's body had been finally discovered, but she had decided that she would not be returning to the UK. Therefore, John had given the local police a list of questions, concerning the bike and Stephen's precise movements on that fateful day, and they would interview her, when she was ready. Stephen's father had died in 2001, at the age of 59, from a long-standing liver problem, probably brought on by excessive drinking, prompted by Stephen's disappearance.

Paul informed his team that he believed their best chance of putting Craig Harper safely inside was to prove that he and his brother had attempted to murder both Richard and Michael and that Craig had abducted, and possibly murdered, Louise, mistaking her for Rebecca Drake.

Clive replied, confused, 'I thought Blakey and his boys were dealing with the specifics of the Louise abduction?'

'They are,' said Paul, 'but the investigations are so closely linked that any evidence which has turned up for one team is likely to be of interest to the other – that's why Derrick is making sure everything is shared. Both teams are unified in that they're looking for Craig, don't forget.'

Paul shared with them his feeling that there was little chance of convicting Craig for Stephen's murder and that, unless some bodies began turning up, the same was true for the murders of Alan Salter and Jack Simmons. The main thrust for them, now, must be the attempted murders.

Paul's mobile rang shrilly, but it didn't show a number on his screen. When he answered it, he recognised the voice straight away and was very intrigued.

'Inspector Manley,' he said, surprised.

'Hello, Paul, it's Nathaniel here. Can you talk?'

Paul wandered casually out of the room and took the remainder of the call in the privacy of the corridor.

'Hi, Nathaniel, I was wondering if I would hear from you again. What can I do for you?'

'Can we meet?'

'When?'

'Well, I'm sitting in the lounge bar of The Bear and Rugged Staff, just down the road from you. If you tell me what you'd like to drink, I'll have it waiting for you.'

'What? You want me to come now? You haven't given me very much notice! We are right in the midst of something serious – a young girl has been abducted.'

'I'm very sorry to hear that, but I can assure you that you will want to hear what I have to say, Paul.'

Paul made his excuses to the team and decided, on a whim, to take his car to meet Nathaniel at the pub. He could easily have walked the short distance – the pub was so close – but even though it was a warm, sunny day, he wasn't in the mood for strolling, and he was anxious to hear what Nathaniel had to say.

Nathaniel was at the bar when Paul entered and, when he recognised him, he nodded towards a table in a quiet corner and mouthed the word 'coffee', to which Paul put his thumb up and quickly grabbed a seat at the suggested table. Nathaniel joined him with the two cups of coffee and sat down facing him. There were only a couple of other people in the bar, and they were sitting well away from the two men, so Paul and Nathaniel felt at ease talking openly.

Paul looked at him questioningly, and Nathaniel began to explain.

'There is a farm, just outside Newcastle, that was broken up, subdivided and sold off as three lots, about ten years ago. One lot encompassed the farmhouse and barns, together with about ten acres of land; the other two lots are just farmland and grazing, with no attached buildings. Now, you have to do a great deal of digging, in order to discover that two of the lots ended up being effectively owned by the same people – people who have connections to the Russian mafia, as well as to certain drug families in Columbia. In a nutshell, all people you wouldn't ever want your daughter to meet. The farmland and grazing are hired out to a local farmer and, to all intents and purposes, are completely separate from the house and the grounds with the couple of barns. It seems that the new owners use the house and barns for all sorts of meetings, parties and as accommodation for visiting friends from abroad.'

Nathaniel paused, to take a sip of coffee, and Paul did the same.

'Some people that I know keep a close eye on the farmhouse, because there are occasions when some very interesting groups end up staying there. The barns, on the other hand, are used for all sorts of gatherings and activities, if the house has guests and is unavailable. There are a couple of Russians staying at the house at the moment, as well as some staff, a cook and what have you. Now, according to my very reputable sources, there were some comings and goings to one of the barns on the day that your suspect mysteriously went missing from the golf club.'

'I'm impressed. You really have been digging. I didn't mention a golf club in our conversation the other day.'

'I said that I would, and thanks for giving me the names of your suspects, by the way. That certainly speeded matters up for me, and it couldn't have been an easy decision for you to make.'

'It wasn't, Nathaniel, but you're welcome.'

'Now ... I overstepped my authority a bit, the other day, and had some aerial photographs taken, which show the rented block of farmland in question. I then had a friend of mine, who is an expert at interpreting such photographs, look them over carefully for me, and he tells me that one particular corner of one of the fields has been disturbed very recently. Now, when I say disturbed, I don't mean it's been ploughed for planting. We are talking about just one slim corner of the field – about seven foot by six foot or, if you'd prefer, about the size of a double grave. Now, if I were in your shoes, Paul, I would be quite anxious to see just what was buried in this particular spot, because it could well be the two men that you're looking for.'

'Bloody hell! That's a bit of a leap, don't you think?'

'Is it? We both agree that Kevin and Craig would have contacted local firms for help. These local firms have access to the barn where activity was confirmed on the day that your two suspects go missing, and that activity involved the disappearance of two men. You're convinced the brothers killed them, and two graves turn up on land that is connected with the barn. So, in answer to your question, Paul – no, I don't think it's a leap at all. I believe that your suspects are buried in the corner of that field.'

'Just where is this farm and adjoining field?'

'There is no need for you to know precisely where the farm is, just the field where the digging has taken place.'

'And the activity that you describe definitely involved two men disappearing?'

'As I said.'

Nathaniel passed a thick envelope across the wooden table. 'Now, these are the photographs, together with the precise coordinates of the field. Obviously, my name is not to be associated with any of this, and, I can tell you – or warn you, more like – that if anyone, including you, goes anywhere near the farmhouse or barns, they will find themselves up to their eyes in more shit than most people will ever see in a lifetime. They will also be minus a career and, possibly, even the prospect of any future career. Added to which, it wouldn't do my prospects a lot of good either. Please take my word for the seriousness of the consequences of poking into the affairs at the farm, Paul – I'm not joking about this.'

'I don't know where it is, anyway.'

'And it has to stay that way, so don't go making any enquiries. The only digging that you need to do is in that field.'

'Well, that's all well and good, Nathaniel, and, believe me, I am grateful for your help – this is fantastic, case-altering information, if it's correct – but I can't just go digging up fields without a warrant, and I don't think I'm going to get one, because someone – who must remain anonymous – tells me that there are bodies buried there.'

'Also in the envelope is an untraceable anonymous letter addressed to you, stating that your suspects have been buried in that field. If that's not enough, and I can't think why it wouldn't be, there is also the name and phone number of a judge. This is a judge who friends of mine have found very helpful in the past in these sorts of matters, and who, I am sure, will look very favourably on any request from you. Now, I'm sorry, but I have to go. Keep in touch, Paul.'

'Don't tell me you've got a corrupt judge in your pocket, as well?'

'No, Paul, he is not corrupt, more the opposite, in fact. He is a true patriot and a friend of this country, who likes to see real justice achieved in these sorts of cases, unlike some of the judiciary, who seem to think their role is to protect the guilty.'

'OK ... but tell me again, why are you so keen to help with this? Why would you risk what you keep telling me you're risking? It doesn't make sense.'

'As I've said before, Paul, Stephen was my best friend back when we were young, and, if he hadn't met the Harpers, I think we would have been friends for life. Friends are important, don't you think?'

Paul returned to the busy incident room, where he banged his coffee mug on his desk to get the team's attention.

'Listen up, everyone – forget what I said earlier. I have just been given some crucial information, albeit from an anonymous source, telling me where the bodies of Alan Salter and Jack Simmons are buried. My source has also supplied an aerial photograph and matching coordinates of the site.'

Paul pinned the photographs to one of the investigation boards.

'Bloody hell, Guv,' said Reg, impressed, 'We could all do with informants like that. How reliable is it?'

'Well, to be honest, I don't really know. As I said, it's completely anonymous, but I have a gut feeling that it's extremely reliable.'

'Doesn't work for an insurance company, by any chance, this informant of yours, Guv, does he?' queried June, knowingly.

Paul gave her a sharp look that clearly said, 'Don't even go there.'

The team looked at each other and shrugged their collective shoulders at June's enigmatic remark, while Paul finished updating the noticeboard and quickly headed for the DCI's office.

Paul ran everything past DCI Blake, who said, with utmost confidence, that they would never manage to get a warrant to dig up a field, simply on the word of an anonymous informant, but that it was, nevertheless, worth a shot, and he would see what he could do in the matter.

Paul handed him the judge's card that Nathaniel had just given him and said, 'You might want to try this man, Justice Hatcher. I'm told that he might be sympathetic to our cause.'

'Justice Hatcher? I know that name,' said Blakey, scratching his head, 'Yes, I remember, a couple of years back, there was some controversy over a freedom of information issue – a journalist or an action group or something took the government to court to get them to release some crucial documents, but this Justice Hatcher found for the government, and everyone started saying that he was in the government's pocket. It was something along those lines, anyway. Well ... we'll see, I'll certainly give it my best.'

Chapter 13

The DCI called Paul into his office and announced, baffled, 'I don't understand it, but we've been granted a warrant to search the field that your informant has put us onto.'

He proceeded to pick up the warrant from his desk and handed it over to Paul.

'I've already spoken to our boys up there, and you will be liaising with an Inspector Barrett – first name, John. They have arranged for a team to go in to the site first thing tomorrow morning, so you need to get up there, bright and early. Now, who do you propose to take with you?'

'Reg and June are the obvious choices, sir. I'll take the DNA profile of our boy up with me, so as to save some time if we do happen to unearth our prime suspects, and, obviously, I'll keep you informed of our progress.'

'Good luck, Paul,' said DCI Blake, genuinely, 'I hope this informant of yours has got his finger on the money, otherwise, this is going to be a very expensive red herring. Is he a pilot or something, your man? I took a look at the photos myself, and, I must say, they look very professional for a civilian.'

Paul looked straight at his DCI, as earnestly as he could manage, and, totally ignoring the last question, said, 'Don't worry, sir, I have a gut feeling that this is going to work out just fine. Trust me.'

'In that case, it's a shame that he can't help us to locate poor Louise.'

'Yeah ... I know. None of the breakthroughs that we've had brought us any nearer to finding her.'

A somewhat more subdued Paul updated the team about the warrant that had been obtained and told Reg and June to bring overnight bags in the morning and to be ready to go at 5 a.m. which earned substantial groans from both of them, but neither spoke up to disagree.

'Oh ... June, you watch it, if you're staying somewhere overnight with those two. Remember, Paul is spoken for now,' said Clive, teasingly.

And before he could get a chance to say anything more, Derrick hastily cut in with, 'Yeah, and Reg is well past it.'

'Hey! Not so much of the Reg-is-past-it thing, you lot. I can still hang my hat on it.'

'Yeah ... but not your umbrella anymore, eh, Reg?' countered Clive, cheekily.

Reg good-naturedly gave up, accepting defeat in the light-hearted ribbing and realising that he was only digging a deeper hole for himself by continuing to comment.

'Oh, hell! I haven't got any pyjamas to wear, either,' said June, laughing at her colleague's comments.

Paul was happy to see the team back in good spirits, even if his own were still low, believing that the prospects of finding Louise still alive were now pretty small. The prospect of finding their suspects' bodies, however, had changed everything, and, for once, they could be relatively optimistic about being able to put Craig away for a long time. Paul crossed his fingers and prayed that his instincts were right about the mysterious Nathaniel Clark.

Paul, June and Reg put their overnight cases in the boot of the car and set off at 5 a.m. the next morning, as they had arranged. They made good time, as the roads were clear from work traffic until around 7.30, and it was promising to be another bright, sunny day. They stopped briefly to change drivers and fill up with petrol, so they arrived at ten forty-five am to find things already well under way at the now cordoned-off site. A large tent had already been erected in one corner of the field, from under which two body bags were being carried out and placed in the back of an unmarked hearse to be taken directly to the morgue.

'Blimey, Guv,' said June, stretching, to ease her muscles after the long car journey, 'Either they started very early this morning or those photographs pin-pointed the spot dead on, but either way, it looks like ... you know who ... was spot on with his information.'

'Fingers crossed, June. We don't know who or what they've dug up yet.'

Detective Inspector John Barrett greeted them rather tersely upon their arrival.

'Glad you could make it at last. Traffic bad, was it?'

Paul was about to reply, but the inspector continued without pause. 'Anyway, we've located your bodies for you, and they're on their way to the morgue now. I'd like to know who the hell took those photographs and how you got hold of them? And, while we're at it, how did your team make the connection between this burial site and your prime suspects? Just what's going on here, Inspector?'

Paul was profusely apologetic, sensing the suspicion that he had caused.

'I'm really sorry, John, but I honestly don't know anything more about the circumstances surrounding the photos being taken. They were sent to me anonymously, along with a letter, which detailed that our suspects were buried here and, really, that's as much as I know about the matter.'

He could sense that John Barrett wasn't at all happy with how events had unfolded at the field, and he could understand his feelings perfectly. Supplying a team and equipment to dig up the bodies was coming directly out of their budget, and they were getting nothing in return – not even, in John Barrett's eyes, important information. Murder victims had been located on their patch, and they were, effectively, being kept out of the loop. It was fairly obvious that John Barrett thought that Paul had organised obtaining the photographs himself and that he was purposefully keeping the local police in the dark, trying to grab whatever glory was going for himself. Paul was sympathetic to the inspector's plight; he would be pretty upset, too, if their roles were reversed, but Nathaniel's warnings had been succinct and steadfast.

After they had left the site, they briefly visited the local police station, where they were informed that the autopsy would be performed later the following morning, by a Doctor Roland Phelps at ten am. The three of them decided to book into a local Premier Inn for the night and dined out on police expenses at a rather posh restaurant. Over dinner, Reg tried, unsuccessfully, to milk them for more detailed information concerning Paul's mysterious informant. It was obvious that June knew more than she was letting on, but what was just as obvious was that he would have to resort to pulling her fingernails out, in order to discover what it was that she knew.

The next morning, Paul, Reg and June – now well-fed and well-rested – arrived at the morgue twenty minutes late, having got hopelessly lost on the way there, only to discover that the autopsy had started much earlier than they'd been told it would. So, somewhat to their joint relief, they were to be spared most of the more upsetting elements of the autopsy or so they foolishly thought. Although all three had attended numerous autopsies before throughout their careers, they all preferred to give them a miss, if at all possible. Reg always said that if he had wanted to see meat cut up, he'd have become a butcher, not joined the police.

When they entered the autopsy room, they found that Doctor Phelps was, in fact, overseeing both of the autopsies, which were being performed simultaneously on twin autopsy tables by two younger doctors, who were part of his team – one male and one female. Doctor Phelps introduced them as Doctors' Williams and Elton.

Paul strode over to the twin autopsy tables, 'So, what have you got for us so far, Doctor Phelps?' he asked.

Doctor Phelps indicated the body nearest to them, which was modestly covered from the waist down with a white sheet and laid out on one of the two stainless steel autopsy tables.

'Obviously, we haven't had all the necessary test results back yet, but we have managed to positively identify this particular body as belonging to the late Mr Alan Salter –one of your prime suspects in a woman's murder, I believe. So it would seem that you do, indeed, reap what you sow,' smiled Doctor Phelps, calmly.

'Yes, that's right,' said Paul, thinking that the good doctor's manner was a little on the jovial side, considering the circumstances. 'Have you managed to identify the other body, as well?'

'Oh, yes ... he's your other suspect, all right, but we'll get to him in just a minute.'

'The cause of death for this man was not difficult to identify, largely due to the bullet hole just here,' said the doctor, pointing to the middle of Alan Salter's forehead, just above the eyes. 'And, of course, the fact that a significant part of his skull at the back is missing, if you look here,' he made to lift up the victim's head, but Paul stopped him, hurriedly.

'No ... that won't be necessary, doctor. I think we can happily take your word for it, but, please, continue,' rushed Paul, trying, and failing, to warm to the good doctor.

'Very well ... just as you like. He was definitely shot at close range, but we don't have the bullet in question, I'm afraid, so we can't tell you anything specific about the murder weapon that was used. There are pronounced restraint marks on the victim's wrists and ankles, and the bullet appears to have been angled down from close range, so I believe he was tied to a chair when he was shot, and the murderer was likely to have been standing in front of him, like this.'

Dr. Phelps adopted a slightly open-legged stance and, modelling the position, held his hands out in front of his body, as if he was holding a gun.

'We've taken some measurements, using the downward trajectory of the bullet, and if the killer was standing close in, as I believe he was, then that means that the killer was a little over six feet tall. I can also tell you that this man's death was definitely quick and painless; he wouldn't have known a thing, except, of course, he must have been looking straight at the gun as it went off, so I suppose he half expected it when it happened.'

'Just the facts will be fine,' said Paul, growing even more irritated by the doctor's nonchalant manner.

'Certainly, Inspector, if you would follow me, then,' Doctor Phelps almost skipped over to the second autopsy table, where this body was completely covered.

'Now, victim number two is much more interesting. His death was anything but quick and painless; in fact, I've never seen it's like before.'

He pulled away the covering sheet, with what could only be described as the kind of flourish that a magician might use on stage, in order to reveal the climax of a trick. All three were truly horrified at the sight that met them. June stepped away, as white as the discarded sheet and steadied herself against one of the many stainless steel cabinets lining the walls.

Paul looked at her, concerned, and asked, considerately, 'Would you like to go outside and get some fresh air, June? You're not going to faint on us, are you?'

June composed herself quickly, 'No ... I'm fine, Guv. I'll be all right in a minute or two.'

Paul glared fiercely at the doctor and said, angrily, 'That was completely unnecessary. This isn't some kind of a bloody side-show. That's a human being lying there, and, no matter what he may have done, he didn't deserve to die like that, and he certainly doesn't deserve you using his body as if it was some kind of exhibit in a grisly side-show.'

The two doctors, who had performed the twin autopsies and who were now standing behind Doctor Phelps, appeared remarkably unsurprised by Paul's sudden outburst, possibly having witnessed similar displays of shock from several other unfortunate observers of the doctor's somewhat bizarre manner.

Doctor Phelps was suitably repentant, however. 'You're absolutely right, of course, Inspector. Please accept my profuse apologies for my inappropriate behaviour.' Slightly shame-faced, he turned kindly to June, 'Constable Kelly, isn't it? I do hope you are all right? I am profoundly sorry. Please believe that it wasn't my intention to upset you in any way.'

'That's OK. I'm fine now, Doctor,' replied June, looking at Paul and Reg with an expression that conveyed her displeasure. 'I haven't come across anything quite that bad before. I wasn't prepared, that's all. Please, continue. How exactly did this man die?' she asked, calmly.

Paul was impressed at the speed with which June had recovered her composure. He returned her gaze with a look that clearly said 'well done' and a smile that implied that he knew that when she had remarked that she hadn't seen anything that bad, she had been referring to the doctor's behaviour and not, as he clearly believed, the state of the body on the table.

'Well, basically,' the doctor continued, 'this man was scalded to death.'

'Jesus!' exclaimed Reg.

Doctor Phelps resumed his explanation, unperturbed, 'Yes ... but the truly gruesome part is that it looks as if it was carried out over a period of some hours.'

'Why do you say that?' asked June, curiously, steeling herself to examine the body more closely.

'Because, quite simply, if this amount of scalding had occurred all at once, he never would have survived the trauma.'

'And what makes you think that he did?'

'Well, quite a large volume of water was used – far more than just one kettleful – so, unless they had some other means of boiling the water, they would have had to boil it several times.'

'Unless they had more than one kettle,' offered Reg.

'That's right, of course, Sergeant. But, surely, the whole point of killing a man in this bizarre and sadistic way would be to make him suffer, so I am pretty sure that it took this man a long time to eventually die.'

'What actually killed him in the end?' asked June.

'I think it went something along these lines. Firstly, there is considerable scalding to the legs and feet. The feet are known to be a favourite target for torturers, because they have a large proportion of nerve endings, which is why, in some countries, it has been common practice to cane people on the soles of their feet as punishment. From what I understand, it's extremely painful. You can see that the arms and the back have received a lot of attention, and the body would have needed time to get over the initial shock of the scalding, before it could take any more.

'Then attention seems to have turned to two more areas that regularly get torturer's pulses racing – the genitals and the eyes, but which of these two got it first, I can't reliably say. There is a substantial tuft of hair missing from the back of the head, so I think that the torturer pulled the head back, in order to pour hot water into the eyes, and the victim must have then jerked forward, with so much force, that it pulled his hair out by the very roots.'

All three were feeling extremely queasy again and were finding it difficult to imagine how one human being could do such evil things to another. Paul asked, 'What finally killed him?'

'That's a first for me, as well. Again, the victim's head must have been held back, and his mouth somehow held open, or perhaps the nose was pinched, thereby forcing the victim to breathe through the mouth, then he was, effectively, made to drink boiling water. I know he was alive when this was done, because there is evidence that he attempted to swallow, but it is clear that he would have died quickly after that, from either the trauma of the experience or simply the damage to his airways, making it impossible to breath. The men who did this, Inspector, and I am sure that there must have been at least two of them involved, are the most sadistic bastards I've ever come across. I sincerely hope and pray that you get them both, soon.'

'Can you help us with that, Doctor?'

'Yes, actually, I believe I can. The bodies were wrapped tightly in blankets, before being put in the ground, and whoever buried them, probably dug the graves as well, because they were extremely hot and perspiring, so there is a great deal of their perspiration evident on the surface of the blankets and some hair strands, as well. In fact, there is DNA all over the place, and the first thing we did was to match it to your suspects – Craig and Kevin Harper – and that's one result that we have already got. Is that the sort of help you wanted, Inspector?'

Paul was elated, 'Yes, Doctor! That's exactly what I wanted.' Paul turned to June and Reg with a triumphant look on his face, 'We've finally got him!'

Doctor Phelps interrupted, 'Excuse me, Inspector, but you have them both. We recovered DNA for both Kevin and Craig Harper.'

'Yes, I know ... forgive me, Doctor, but Kevin Harper is dead.'

The doctor looked thoroughly bewildered and then said, 'Bloody hell, Inspector, do you ever get to arrest any of your suspects? Or does murder always come in the domino fashion with you lot down in Bristol?'

'How do mean, domino fashion?' asked Paul, quizzically.

'Well, as I understand it, a woman was first murdered at the hands of these two, then these two get sadistically murdered and now you're telling me that one of the men that killed them is also dead! Your prisons must be the least crowded in the country!'

'Well, our prisons are soon going to have one more inmate, Doctor, and I shall dine out on that day, believe me.'

As they were leaving, Paul allowed Reg to get ahead of them, just out of earshot, and quietly remarked to June, 'Don't you just love the irony of it?'

'What irony?' asked June, puzzled.

'Don't you realise? We've managed to get the evidence that we need to convict Craig for murder, from crucial information, supplied by the best friend of Stephen Potter. If Craig and his brother hadn't killed Stephen, all those years ago, he would probably have got away with this one, too.'

'You're right, Guv ... that's irony for you.'

* * * * * * * * * * * * * *

Lately, Richard had been mostly working from home, and he was coming to the swift conclusion that not only did he prefer working there, but that the shop was largely unnecessary these days, as so little of his business was actually conducted on the premises. A small lock-up storage facility would effectively do exactly the same thing Elizabeth had booked some holiday time off work at the hospital, because she was feeling so depressed and was unable to concentrate on the needs of the ward and her patients, partly because she was missing the daily contact with her only daughter and partly because she couldn't help thinking about the fate of poor Louise. Sometimes she found herself hoping that Louise was dead, because, at least that would mean that she wasn't suffering some unthinkable torture at the hands of a sadistic monster.

It was only by spending time with her husband and dear Michael that she was managing to stay relatively sane. They both seemed to have an uncanny ability to smile through adversity, which she severely lacked, but at least when she was with them, some of it seemed to rub off on her, and she was able to make it through the day. She knew her husband was worried about her precarious mental state. In turn, she was worried about her husband's safety and her daughter's and, indeed, Margaret's, for that matter. Damn this awful man! She found herself wishing, many times over, that he was dead.

Elizabeth was in the middle of having a short nap, upstairs. The tablets that the doctor had prescribed often made her sleepy mid-mornings, and it had become a kind of routine. She didn't bother getting undressed for her naps; she just kicked off her shoes and snuggled down peacefully under the quilt. Richard was in the kitchen reading the morning paper and wondering when politicians were going to develop some good old-fashioned common sense, when Michael returned from his morning walk. He had decided that it was high time that he took a look at the outside world again and was now so proficient on his crutches, that he could even manage the stairs on his own, although Richard or Elizabeth insisted on standing alongside him, just in case. But the only time he had been outside the house since the accident, other than the garden, had been when he had accompanied Richard and Elizabeth to the inquest. He was slowly going stir-crazy and had decided to take a much-needed stroll up the road.

'Anything interesting in the paper today, Richard?' Michael asked, cheerfully, slamming the front door closed with his backside and then sheepishly remembering that Elizabeth would be upstairs sleeping.

'Sorry,' he whispered.

'No, not really, just the usual doom and gloom – another firm laying off workers, someone else moving production abroad. The only people making any money these days seem to be the bankers, who caused all the misery in the first place.'

'Yeah, you're right there,' said Michael, accepting the hot mug of tea that Richard handed him, 'I'll bet that the bloke I just saw going into your neighbour's house is a banker, judging by the car he was driving – a beautiful new Bentley.'

'Another Bentley? Wasn't it a Bentley that we saw at the inquest the other day?'

'Oh my God! How stupid, am I?' Michael almost fell over in his excitement, 'Oh, wow! You're damn right, we did. I thought I had seen another one lately, but I didn't twig as to where precisely. It was Craig's lawyer at the inquest, remember? Yes ... thinking about it now, I'm sure it was the same man; it was certainly the same car, that's for sure. Oh my God, Richard! Don't you see what this means? I was right – he has been watching the house, and now I know where he has been doing it from. We've got him! Richard ... we've got him!'

Michael was almost dancing with joy over his discovery, holding his crutches aloft and in imminent danger of crashing into the kitchen table.

'Slow down, Michael, slow down. We don't know for certain that it is the same car, and, even if it is, we don't know that he is visiting Craig.'

'But what are the odds of it, Richard, eh? How many new Bentleys have you seen this year? And it's the same colour and everything. You know it's him ... same as I do. It's just that there is a very human part of you saying that it's wrong to kill him – to kill anyone, no matter what they've done. Well, that's OK, Richard ... I'll do it.'

'You? No, it's my family that he is threatening. He thought it was Rebecca that he was kidnapping when he took Louise, remember? No, if anyone is going to do it ... it has to be me. I can do it ... I have to do it.'

'But can you do it, really? It will be very different to stabbing Kevin. You were in fear of our lives then. This will be, as you said yourself the other day, in cold blood.'

Michael carefully propped his crutches against the kitchen worktop and slowly rolled up his left sleeve. He held his arm up in the air for Richard to see. The disfigured flesh still looked raw and angry.

'You weren't there when he did this, Richard, so you have no way of knowing what he put me through or how often I still wake up at night, dreaming that it's happening again. I know I could kill him, Richard, and I could smile while I did it.'

Richard's heart went out to his old friend, realising that although Craig's wrath was aimed squarely at him, it was Michael who had suffered the most physically from the situation – being tortured and then enduring horrific injuries in the car crash. Then there was poor Louise, of course – what had the bastard done to her? He had got off relatively lightly so far, compared to them.

Richard replied, 'Anyway, knowing where he is, is one thing, getting to him unobserved is quite another, so how do we manage that successfully? He's got a gun, as well, don't forget.'

'Well, now that we know precisely where he is located, I can give that question some serious consideration. Tell me, what you know about those houses? Are they all double-glazed, do you think?'

'Why would you want to know if the house is double-glazed or not?'

'Oh, Richard, you have so much to learn house breaking and so little time to learn it in. First, another cup of tea is needed, and then I would propose a quick trip to a tool warehouse to purchase some necessary goods, so that you can 'go equipped', at least, I think that's the expression that police use.'

Richard shook his head in disbelief, as he put the kettle on to boil, 'There is definitely a side to you that would shock Elizabeth, Michael. Did Mavis know about your criminal tendencies?'

Richard had, in fact, been into a couple of the houses in Hawthorn Avenue, and so he drew Michael a plan of both upstairs and down, from what he could remember.

'The best points of entry seem to be the downstairs dining room or kitchen, because the windows are big enough to allow a man to climb through fairly easily, if they haven't been changed,' volunteered Michael.

The idea was for Richard to simply walk up the front drive and around to the back of the house, passing between the side of the house and the detached garage that was set slightly back from the road. This would be achieved in the early hours of the morning, when it was safe to assume that Craig would be asleep in one of the upstairs rooms, probably, they guessed, the front one, with the expansive bay window. He would have a tool bag with him, containing a trammel-head glass-cutter with a rubber sucker at the centre, a sharp, heavy-bladed Stanley knife, a rubber-headed mallet, a chisel and a glazier's suction tool for holding panes of glass.

Richard would then have to play it as he saw it, because there were so many variables – there could be patio doors to the dining room at the rear; there could be French double doors; there may be a conservatory; the back of the house could be double-glazed, the same as the front, and that double-glazing could be internally or externally glazed. It might even be easier to get through the back door, rather than one of the windows. So Michael spent an hour giving Richard a crash course in breaking into houses.

'How do you know all this stuff in such detail?' Richard asked, baffled. 'Perhaps it would be better for me to just reconnoitre the place one night – you know, case the joint first, see what I'm actually up against.'

'The answer to your first question is an interesting combination of a misspent youth and conversations in cards school; as for the second suggestion, that's entirely up to you, but it gives Craig another day to either disappear or get to one of us before we get to him or, worst case scenario, decide to kill Louise, if he hasn't done that already.'

'I shall want Elizabeth out of the way when this happens. She would never agree to it for a second, and I can't go sneaking out in the middle of the night, without the possibility of her waking up.'

'How are you going to arrange that?'

'She has been missing Rebecca terribly, since she moved to Robert's place, and you've expressed an interest to see it.'

'I have?'

'Yes ... so I am going to suggest – and you are going to back me up on this – that you and she go to visit, stay a night or two, at the very least.'

'It's a good idea, in one way, but I don't like the thought of you not having me nearby for back-up, should anything happen. What if something goes wrong? I think I should just drop Elizabeth off there and then return here.'

'No, Michael, either it's my way or I ring Paul and tell him that we know where Craig is. Maybe it's best if we do that anyway.'

'If you've got cold feet, I told you, I can do it.'

'I still can't quite believe that we are talking about breaking into someone's house and killing them in cold blood while they sleep. We can talk all we want about his ability to still get to us from inside, and dress it up as some form of self-defense, but it's not actually self-defence, is it? Quite frankly, it's murder.'

'Yes ... OK, it's murder. But it still comes down to the same question that we've been over, again and again – is he going to kill you? Or are you going to get in first and kill him? You have to decide, Richard.'

'I know.'

A short while later, the kitchen door opened softly, and Elizabeth came into the room, refreshed from her nap. 'What are you two conspirators up to? Not hatching any plots, I hope.'

'No, of course not. Michael's been complaining that he's getting itchy feet stuck at home, and he feels like he needs a change of scenery for a while. He mentioned that he would like to see the Power's residence – he's heard so much about it from Rebecca – so I suggested that you drive him over there and maybe stay a night or two with the girls.'

Elizabeth desperately wanted to see the girls, but was not sure that it would be safe for Richard to be alone at the moment.

'Oh, I don't know, Richard. I'd love to see Rebecca and Margaret again, of course, but I don't like the idea of you staying here on your own. Anything could happen.'

Richard and Michael reminded her that the police were watching them around the clock and that they couldn't go on living in the cautious way that they were for much longer, anyway.

Eventually, after they had pointed out the unmarked police car parked up the road, they persuaded Elizabeth to take time out for the short trip, and she had gone upstairs straight away to pack an overnight case; she really was missing Rebecca terribly.

While she was safely out of the room, Michael said, hurriedly, 'Ring me on my mobile before you leave on your mission, and if I haven't heard from you again within forty-five minutes, I'm dialling 999, OK?'

'Forty-five minutes isn't long enough ... let's say sixty.'

'OK, sixty minutes, then. If you haven't managed to break in, get upstairs and locate and shoot Craig during that time, then I can assume that something's gone wrong, and I'm ringing Paul.'

'Agreed.'

The two men solemnly shook hands.

When Elizabeth returned, she seemed happier and brighter than she had for days, but she still expressed great concern about leaving Richard on his own.

Richard reminded her, again, 'Remember, the house is under constant surveillance, and I am going to ring Paul and tell him what we are planning on doing, so I will be more than all right, I promise. Give Rebecca my love.'

'I will.'

Elizabeth explained that she had gathered up Michael's things while she was upstairs, so as to save him the climb. She hugged Richard for a long time, before she and Michael left, driving away in her car. Getting Michael into Elizabeth's car had been a bit of a struggle, but with the passenger seat pushed right back, he had just managed it, with a little help.

As good as his word, a little while after Michael and Elizabeth had left, Richard rang Paul and informed him of what they were doing.

Paul had replied that not only was that perfectly fine, but that he had wonderful news on the investigation-front.

'I've just got off the phone from telling Margaret, actually. We've found the bodies of Jack Simmons and Alan Salter, and, better even than that, Kevin and Craig were uncharacteristically careless and left their DNA all over the bodies when they buried them. They must have been very confident that the bodies would never be found. All we have to do now is to find the bastard, and we can, at last, put him away for a very long time. I intend to charge him with the murders of Jack Simmons and Alan Salter and the attempted murders of both you and Michael. I'm confident that we can now get a conviction for both. Isn't that the news that we've been waiting for?'

Richard was silent on the other end of the phone, his mind now in turmoil. All he had to do was to tell Paul that he knew of Craig's whereabouts, and they would have him in custody; and, in Paul's words, there was little doubt that he would be convicted. But Michael was right, he knew, that this wouldn't be the end of the matter. Realistically, even if he was sent to jail for a long stretch, he would still have plenty of dangerous contacts on the outside. He would still be able to get to his family if he so wanted, and Richard had no doubt in his mind that Craig would want to. It might not happen soon, but they would have to live the rest of their lives wondering, whenever one of them was late or couldn't be immediately contacted, whether something horrible had happened at Craig's behest.

'Richard, are you still there? Did you hear what I just said? We just have to find him now, and then it will all be over.'

'Yes, Paul, I heard you ... that's great news. I was just ringing to tell you that Elizabeth has taken Michael to see the girls at Robert's house and that they are going to stay there for a couple of nights; she's missing the girls terribly.'

'Yes, you said, Richard, and thanks for letting me know. As I said, that's perfectly fine; the place is still being carefully watched. You're repeating yourself, Richard –is everything all right? I have to say, you don't sound as happy about the news as I expected you to be. We'll get him soon, Richard, count on it, and you'll be able to put all this terror and stress behind you, once and for all.'

Richard hung the phone up, his mind racing with conflicting thoughts. Should he have told Paul what he knew? What if things went wrong tonight and Craig managed to get away?

Suddenly, Richard had had enough. He was done with it – no more messing about and no clandestine breaking and entering, either. He was going to have it out with Craig right now, face-to-face, and the whole business would be over for good, one way or another. There was only one policeman watching the house now, as the other was following Michael and Elizabeth in the car. He went to his study and took the gun from its drawer. He checked that it was loaded, just as Michael had taught him, and put it in his pocket with steely determination. The policeman watching the house was sitting in a car, parked a few houses up on the opposite side of the road, where he had a good view of the Drake's front door and most of the front of the property.

Richard slipped carefully out of the back door and walked to the five-foot high fence at the very bottom of the garden. He kicked a substantial hole in the fence and pulled away several lengths of overlap strip, so that he could simply walk straight through into his neighbour's garden. He was quite prepared for a confrontation with his neighbour, but it appeared that no-one was at home at present, so he proceeded to drag their wooden patio table across to the back wall of the garage, and, once standing on top of the table, he was able to climb onto the garage roof, walk to the front and jump down into his neighbour's front garden. He then let himself out of the front gate and into the road that ran parallel to his own. From there, he resolutely walked two blocks down and then across, back into his own road. The police car would be facing him as he walked back up the road, but it was a reasonable bet that officer inside would not bother to take much notice of a man approaching from that direction on foot, especially as he would be turning off into another road, before he got to the house that was currently being watched. As Richard got steadily closer to both Hawthorne Avenue and, consequently, the police car watching his house, he became acutely aware of the gun weighing down his pocket. The weight of it was pulling his pocket down considerably, so he put his hand in his pocket and held it, supporting its weight.

Richard had no real plan other than to confront Craig, shoot him and make good some kind of escape. As he turned into Hawthorn Avenue, his heart was beating twenty to the dozen, and he kept repeating to himself Michael's instructions, over and over, 'get in close and aim low.' Once he was in the driveway of number four, his mobile rang, making him start suddenly. He quickly retrieved it from his pocket and turned it off, afraid that it may have already alerted his quarry. He took the gun from his pocket and banged on the door ... his heart racing with fear and anticipation.

The door opened within seconds, and Craig, politely, stood back to allow Richard to enter the house. Richard had the gun raised and held firmly in both hands, pointing it at

Craig, just as Michael had instructed. The situation struck Richard as somewhat surreal, with Craig still backing away into the hallway and himself following him readily into the passage. Richard wondered why he hadn't fired already. That had been the idea, after all, and he was close enough ... but then, suddenly, the realisation came to him ... there was still the unanswered question.

'What have you done with Louise?' he shouted, with his voice trembling noticeably. 'Is she here?'

Craig looked puzzled for a minute, but quickly caught on to his mistake – he must have kidnapped the wrong girl.

'Louise?' He slowly raised one hand up to his mouth, his fingers pressed against his lips, the way that young children do when caught out. 'Oops. Was that her name? Well, well, what a silly mistake. I did wonder about the lack of family resemblance. It actually occurred to me that she might not be yours and that you didn't realise. But don't let's stand here idly chatting in the hall. Do shut the front door after you, Richard. I assume that I'm right in thinking that you don't want the police around here ... any more than I do.'

Richard put his foot to the door, slamming it shut, without ever taking his eyes off Craig.

'Come into the kitchen, Richard. I'll make us both a nice cup of tea, and we can have a proper chat. You can tell me what ... um ... what's-her-name was doing in Rebecca's car.'

Craig turned and walked confidently into the adjoining kitchen. Richard followed, not once taking his aim off Craig. As Craig turned to walk away, Richard noticed, for the first time, that he, too, was holding a gun, only Craig's was held casually at his side, as if he didn't have a care in the world. Richard kept telling himself that he should just shoot him now – in the back would do nicely. Louise was almost certainly dead by now. But there was always that chance, and, even if she was, in fact, dead, where was her body? Her grieving parents would need her body for some sense of closure.

'Put your gun on the table,' he ordered Craig, forcefully.

Craig simply shrugged his shoulders, 'And if I don't, will you shoot me? What about poor what's-her-name? She could be still alive, and she could be anywhere; how will you ever find her, if you kill me? I assume that is your intention, and that this is not supposed to be some kind of ridiculous attempt at a citizen's arrest?'

'Put the gun on the table,' Richard ordered, louder this time.

'Oh, very well ... if it makes you happy,' sighed Craig and brought his hand up very slowly, placing the gun that he was holding on to the tabletop.

'Well, now, Richard, the ball appears to be in your court. So, where do we go from here?'

Richard couldn't shake off the nagging idea that Craig was more in control of the situation than he was, even though he was the one with the gun in his hands. It was almost as if Craig was actually enjoying the predicament that he was in.

'You tell me what you have done with Louise, and I call the police, otherwise, I just shoot you now.'

Richard's hand was beginning to shake, not so much from nerves, although they were certainly playing their part, but from the strain of holding the gun up for so long. Craig was actually beginning to smile at him.

'Oh, dear, poor Richard, you're not really very seasoned at this tough guy business, are you? Look ... why don't you put the gun down for a bit? It must feel like it weighs a ton by now. Just rest it at your side for a moment; you'll find that the ache in your arms will go quite quickly if you do, and I promise that I will give you fair warning if I intend to make a grab for mine. Now, I can't say fairer than that ... can I?'

The bastard is playing with me, thought Richard, furiously. He should just shoot him and have done with it, but if they later discovered that Louise was locked away somewhere and starved to death, while waiting to be rescued, all because he had shot Craig, he would never be able to live with himself. So, instead, he ordered Craig to go upstairs, and he followed close behind, still holding the gun in both hands and aimed at Craig's back. Richard had decided to check, first, if Louise, or her body, was somewhere in the house.

They ascended the stairs, and as Craig reached the landing, he began to play the cocky role of an estate agent, pointing out to Richard the features of the house – where the bathroom was and indicating that the upstairs boasted three bedrooms. It was as if he was engaging in some kind of bizarre role-play game that cast Richard in the role of potential buyer. Richard began to wonder if Craig was actually mentally ill in some way.

Richard ordered him into the first bedroom. Craig opened the door in mock-politeness and gestured for Richard to enter first.

'You first,' ordered Richard, 'stand over by the window.'

Craig did exactly as he was bid, and Richard entered, surveying the room to make sure that Louise wasn't there, without physically getting too close to Craig. His arms were, now, not just aching, but painful and tense, so he lowered them slightly in front of his torso, while still keeping hold of the gun with both hands. He was confident that if Craig tried anything, he would still be able to raise the gun and shoot in good time.

Craig's smile broadened, when he saw Richard lower the gun.

'Told you,' he said, 'most people don't realise just how heavy a gun can be. To hold it up in that position for a long time is a big mistake, but you'll learn. Oh, no, I'm sorry ... you won't, will you? Because, of course, you'll be dead soon.'

Richard raised the gun again. Craig's casual manner was unnerving him. As he backed out of the bedroom, he ushered Craig out onto the landing and into the next bedroom. Craig again entered first and took a couple of steps inside, in order to allow Richard access to the room.

Richard entered the bedroom behind Craig and almost broke down when he saw the pathetic sight on the bed. Louise's body was still tied down on the bed. Richard couldn't even begin to take in the full horror of the grisly spectacle laid out before him. One hand was bandaged and bloody, and he was, thankfully, unable to see the expression on her face, because the plastic bag that covered it was misted up inside, with the remains of Louise's last breath.

As Richard visibly struggled to bring his emotions under control, Craig lunged at him and caught him totally off-guard and unprepared. The two men slammed up against the wall of the room, hard. Richard took the full impact and was completely winded. At the same time, Craig brought his right hand, palm uppermost, up under Richard's chin with considerable force, slamming the back of his head hard against the wall and knocking him unconscious. Richard slumped to the floor, and Craig knelt beside him, removing the gun that Richard still clutched uselessly, in his hands.

* * * * * * * * * * * *

Elizabeth's spirits soared when she finally arrived at the mansion and saw Rebecca and Margaret. It had seemed an age since they had last held each other, and all three were so excited, and there was such a babble of questions and answers, that Michael took himself off to the enormous kitchen to make a pot of tea for them all. This was going to be the longest day of his life. He was desperately worried about Richard and how he would fare with Craig. He had to resist the temptation to phone him, but it was hard going, to say the least.

He reluctantly turned his attention to finding a teapot to make tea. The kitchen, he thought, looked more like the bridge of a spaceship, and Michael was still looking for anything remotely resembling a kettle, when Elizabeth came running in, ecstatically.

'Wonderful news, Michael!' she gushed, 'Paul has just rung Margaret to tell her that they now have the evidence they need to convict Craig for murder. They have recovered some bodies and have DNA and everything –isn't it wonderful? All they have to do now is to find him, and it will all be over, finally. I have to ring Richard to give him the good news.'

Michael briefly wondered how the news would go down with Richard and thought that perhaps it would convince him to confess to Paul that they had located Craig's hiding place. He told Elizabeth that he wanted to speak to Richard, as soon as she had given him the good news. They all gathered round Elizabeth, as she excitedly rang their home phone, but, oddly, there was no reply.

'That's odd. Richard's not answering the phone,' she told them, a little alarmed.

'Perhaps he's in the loo reading the paper? You know how long he spends in there, Mum,' chipped in Rebecca, jokingly.

'I'll try his mobile,' said Elizabeth, dialling the number quickly. When she had no joy with his mobile, she turned to them, with a confused expression, 'Now I'm really worried. His mobile was ringing, and then it just stopped. I think someone might have turned it off, and Richard wouldn't do that, especially if he saw that it was me who was ringing him.'

Michael was in a quandary. He couldn't think of a valid reason why Richard would not want to answer his phone, but he didn't want to interfere, if Richard was doing something to advance the plans that they had made. Then there was the additional fact that Paul would probably have tried to contact Richard with the good news after speaking to Margaret, and if Paul failed to contact him, he may call by the house in person and that could put a definite spanner in the works, if Richard had decided to go and confront Craig earlier than planned.

Turning to Elizabeth, he said, 'Ring Paul and see if he has managed to have contact with him.'

Paul confirmed that he had spoken to Richard just after speaking to Margaret, but because Elizabeth was concerned, he assured her that he would drive out to the house himself to check on both him and the surveillance team.

When Elizabeth relayed Paul's response, Michael crossed his fingers superstitiously.

Chapter 14

Craig estimated that Richard would remain in an unconscious state for at least a couple of minutes, so he took the opportunity to pop quickly into the front bedroom and look out of the bay window, to see if there was any activity at Richard's house. All seemed very quiet, so he went back into the second bedroom to consider his options. He would dearly like to spend some time with Richard and make him suffer properly for killing his brother, but everything was coming to a head now, and if Richard had found him, the police surely couldn't be far behind. He was now just anxious to get this business quickly concluded and start his new life in Italy.

Craig walked over to the bed and began to cut Louise's body free, just as Richard was stirring. He then sat in one of the two chairs in the bedroom and waited patiently for him to come round properly. Richard regained consciousness by degrees, remaining slumped against the wall facing Craig and hazily wondering if his jaw was broken. Craig was now pointing Michael's gun at him, with the seemingly ever-present smile still plastered on his face.

'When you're ready, Richard, you can pick up ... ah ... what's-her-name and carry her downstairs for me, there's a good fellow.'

'Her name was Louise, you bastard!'

'Oh, sticks and stones, Richard.'

Richard put his hand round to the back of his head to feel for damage and found a rapidly growing, egg-shaped bump, but, luckily, no blood. He was angry with himself for letting this nasty excuse for a human get the upper hand. He thought the most likely outcome now, would be that Craig would torture and, finally, kill him. He was truly sorry that he had let everybody down, not just his family, but Michael and Louise, as well.

Craig instructed Richard again, 'Come on. Richard, pick up what's-her-name and carry her downstairs.'

'What if I say no? Do it yourself.'

'That's fine, Richard. I am getting sick and tired of playing our little games now, anyway. It's been fun, but time is running out, as they say, so if you don't do what I asked, I shall simply shoot you in the gut, and you can stay up here dying, slowly and agonizingly, while I carry her down. From what I am told, it's an extremely painful wound. It's up to you; I really don't mind either way when it comes down to it. Perhaps you'd like to flip a coin for it?'

Richard heaved himself up off the floor of the bedroom with some difficulty, as he was still more than a little woozy from the bang on the head. He crossed, tottering, over to the bed. Once again, as he stooped to pick up the lifeless body of Louise from the bed, he was overcome with an immense sense of grief for a life cut so tragically short. He started to remove the plastic bag that covered her head, but Craig stopped him.

'Leave it on, Richard. If you see her face, you'll only start blubbing or something, and I can't abide seeing a grown man cry, can you?'

Richard cradled the lifeless body with some difficulty, but he managed to carry her downstairs, as Craig had instructed him to. As he did so, the hopelessness and despair that had overwhelmed him when he first came round began to ebb away, and he realised that as long as he had breath in his body, there was still a fighting chance that he could make this man pay for killing an innocent young girl and torturing his old friend. Anger was giving him much-needed strength. Once downstairs, Craig opened the front door and prudently checked to see if anyone was outside, before unlocking his car with the remote and ordering Richard to carry Louise's lifeless form over to the vehicle. He instructed Richard to place her body in the boot of the car and then to get into the driving seat. He closed the front door of 4 Hawthorn Avenue and got into the back seat of the car, right behind Richard.

'Start the engine and drive where I tell you,' instructed Craig, 'and, remember, I still have the gun trained on you.'

He knew that he was going to be taking a huge risk by both disposing of Louise's body and killing Richard in broad daylight, but the site that he had selected to be Louise's last resting place was very remote, and he was confident that the chances of anyone being there during the day was minimal.

Two days earlier, he had spent several hours driving in, and around, Leigh Woods, using detailed maps of the area, which he had previously downloaded from the internet. Once he had selected a spot on the map that appeared to be deep in the woods and away from any major paths, he reconnoitred it on foot, so that he could see if it was possible to carry a body to it and to evaluate how difficult it would be to dig a deep-enough grave. Consequently, he had found what he considered to be a perfect spot – a place where the ground was firm enough to let him drive off the road for the first part of the journey and where the trees were far enough apart to allow him to drive almost right up to the grave site itself.

He had committed the details of the route to the grave site to his memory, so that he would be able to find the spot at night with no difficulty, and the next night he had done just that. Craig had driven along the road at night and, after identifying a particular tree that had fallen against its neighbour, knew that the turn-off was just yards ahead on the right. Once off the road, he knew that he had to pass two tall trees on the left, then one on the right, turn slightly left, pass two more on the right and so on. He had committed the whole route to memory, and so he found the site with no difficulty at all. That night, he had taken the necessary tools with him, together with a flask of coffee, and had spent several hours digging the grave. A couple of times, he had been driven to use not just the sturdy pick-axe, but the petrol-driven chainsaw, in order to get past some substantial roots. The noise of the chainsaw, when he started it up, had seemed incredibly loud to him in the dark silence of the night, together with the screech of hundreds of birds taking to the air in unison. But even at the nearest point of habitation, if anybody had been awake and taking the time to listen, it would have been but a distant hum, muffled a hundred times over by the dense foliage and stifling fronds of the thick woodland.

After he had dug the grave to the required depth and size, he had relaxed with his second cup of coffee of the night, and then set about the task of covering the grave, hiding it from prying eyes, in case anyone did happen to stumble upon the site. He achieved this with broken branches and foliage; he also took the time to put leaves and twigs over the mound of earth that his evening labours had produced, so as to render it less obvious. He surveyed the scene by torchlight and was happy that what he had done would successfully conceal the gaping hole, until he returned and utilised it for its grisly purpose. All that remained to be done, then, was to bring the body itself the following night and finally inter it in its final resting place.

That scenario would have to change slightly, now, because of Richard's impetuous actions, calling at the house. At first, when he realized that the man walking up to the front door was Richard, he had assumed that the police had somehow managed to trace him, and Richard had either managed to acquire the information or that the police were using Richard, in some way, so as to draw him out. However, he soon realised that Richard must have spotted him somehow; perhaps he had recognised his lawyer's car, parked outside on the driveway, which he may have seen and noted earlier, at the inquest. Craig thought that had his brother still been alive, he would have had a sneaking admiration for Richard Drake. For his own part, however, Craig loathed the man that he was preparing to kill, and he regretted not finding the time to do it with more aplomb. He and Kevin had certainly underestimated him the other night, to Kevin's cost, but nothing changed the fact that he was, in fact, going to die.

Craig gave Richard the directions for the grave site, and they drove towards the point on the road where one tree lay against its neighbour. Here, Craig ordered Richard to pull in to the side of the road, because he wanted to make sure that the road was clear of all traffic, before turning into the woods. With the way clear, Richard steered the car off the road and followed Craig's instructions, weaving the car this way and that between the trees, until he was told to stop.

Richard wasn't sure what Craig intended to do. He had assumed that he was taking them somewhere to get rid of Louise's body, but surely he couldn't be intending to just leave it in the woods. Was he simply going to execute Richard there, as well, leaving their bodies for animals to finish off? Richard was also afraid that Craig intended to kill him in some grisly way, rather than just shooting him; he certainly seemed to like that sort of thing.

Craig ordered Richard out of the car and instructed him to take Louise's body out of the boot and to carry it, once again – this time, further into the woods. After a couple of minutes of walking, Richard was beginning to falter. It was difficult enough under foot anyway, without the added complication of carrying a dead body at the same time. He wondered if now would be a good time to make his last ditch attempt for freedom. He could pretend to stagger and drop Louise, making a grab for Craig in the process, much like he had done to Richard, back in the bedroom. But Craig had been successful in overpowering Richard, because Richard had been shocked at seeing Louise's body for the first time. Craig was very much alert and watchful, almost expecting some kind of attack, which reduced Richard's chances of success considerably.

The decision was effectively taken out of Richard's hands, as they arrived at their destination.

'Stop here,' ordered Craig, tonelessly, 'Put what's-her-name down.'

Richard was glad to be able to finally put down his sorrowful burden, as his arms were very weary.

'Clear away those leaves and branches over there,' Craig ordered.

Richard did as he was bid and was both surprised and disheartened to discover a large hole that he almost fell into. He had been hoping that Craig would need to still dig a grave and that he had not thought it through carefully, because it would be difficult, if not near impossible, to dig one here, with all the networks of roots and undergrowth. It was devastating to discover not only that one had already been successfully dug, but that the grave that he was looking at looked almost as good as one dug in a proper cemetery, by a mechanical digger. He marvelled over the fact that Craig had managed to achieve all of this.

Richard realised that time was very short and that if he was going to do anything, it would have to be in the next few minutes. He didn't want to die, especially not at the hands of this animal. He was ashamed to realise that he was literally shaking with fear.

'Climb in, Richard,' commanded Craig, using the gun to indicate the grave.

Richard was looking about him desperately for something that he could use and, in an almost pathetic attempt to give himself more time, he said, defiantly, 'And if I refuse?'

Craig's answer made his blood run cold.

'There are two ways this can go for you, now, Richard – either you climb into the grave, I shoot you in the head, put the body of what's-her-name in on top of you and bury you both or I shoot you in both legs, drag you into the grave myself and then finish the job. So it's up to you ... you can be buried dead or you can be buried alive –your choice. But you have to decide now or else I will make the choice for you, and I don't think you'll like it.'

Richard slowly moved towards the open grave, with his heart thumping in his chest, and his whole body trembling in fear. His eyes were focused on the open grave before him – it was over three feet wide, but it looked no more than five feet deep. He could see where tree roots had been cut and sliced away with some kind of saw.

It was then that he saw it – just the smallest of straws for him to clutch at as a last resort. When he got to the very edge of the grave, the fear he had previously felt melted away and was replaced by steely determination.

Instead of crouching down slowly and climbing in to the gaping hole, as Craig would expect, he swiftly leapt into the grave, turning on the spot as he leapt, so that he ended up facing the edge that he had just been stood up on. He reached out with his hand and picked up the cricket-ball sized rock that he had spotted before his jump. Hurling the rock at Craig's head as hard as he had ever thrown any cricket ball in his life, he hoped and prayed that the years had not diminished his perfect aim.

Craig was stood no more than four yards from the open grave, watching and smiling contentedly as Richard walked towards it, having made the decision that Richard would, in fact, breathe his last under the weight of Louise's dead body and a ton of earth. He wondered briefly if Richard would still be screaming when he finally padded down the last clod of earth.

Craig cocked the gun that he held in his hand, preparing to shoot Richard in the legs, but he was taken completely by surprise when Richard did some kind of pirouette into the grave. He was even more surprised when what felt like a guided missile hit him squarely between the eyes. He staggered drunkenly backwards, stunned and completely disorientated, tripped over an exposed root and fell backwards onto the ground, dropping the gun in the undergrowth. When he came to his senses, he sat bolt upright and was just about to extradite himself from the undergrowth, when his eyes focused on Richard looming before him, in possession of the gun once more.

When Richard hurled the stone and watched it strike Craig straight in the face, he experienced such an immense rush of adrenaline, that all his incumbent aches and pains vanished in an instant, and he felt like a twenty-year-old once again. Seeing Craig stagger and fall, Richard climbed, not without some difficulty, from the grave, using the cut off ends of tree roots, as if they were the rungs of a ladder. He saw Craig drop the gun and knowing that he, undoubtedly, would soon recover his composure, even if the stone had caused him injury, he immediately rushed to the spot where it had landed.

By the time Richard had successfully located the gun and pointed it at his adversary, Craig had almost recovered from the effects of the blow, but there was blood pouring from his nose and an ugly gash starting between his eyes, and extending up his forehead.

Craig dazedly got to his feet, and the two men stood facing each other, like gunfighters on the main street of Dodge, but with only one of them armed. It was Richard's turn to smile; in fact, he laughed hysterically out loud, unable to control his overflowing emotions.

He stared at Craig, trying to work out what it was that was different about him, and then he realised that it was the first time that he had seen him without that damned smile stuck across his face. He suddenly remembered the joke that Sandy had cracked, the fateful day that Richard had bought the paperknife from him, and, now, he repeated it to Craig.

'Have you heard the one about the man who had a cricket ball just miss his left ear by four inches. It hit him right between the eyes.'

Craig just stared back at him, blankly, his eyes darting between Richard's face and the gun in his hand.

'What's the matter, Craig? Don't you find that funny? Lost the ability to smile now, have you?'

Richard was euphoric, knowing that he had bested his opponent when the chips had been down and knowing that he was not going to make the mistakes of earlier in the day. He held the gun tightly in both hands and pointed it at Craig's lower chest. Then he stepped in closer and squeezed the trigger.

The noise of the gun going off in the quiet of the woods was shocking, and wildlife took sudden flight, for hundreds of yards around them. Craig looked as if someone had physically lifted him off the ground and thrown him backwards. He lay flat on the ground, moaning and clutching at his chest. Richard calmly walked forward and stared straight into his eyes, both of which were closed, due to blood pouring into them, from the gash over his eyes. So Craig never saw Richard aim the gun a second time – this time at his forehead and very close.

The noise from the gun was just as shocking the second time, but Michael had been right about the amount of pressure required on the trigger – the second squeeze had been much easier. First time, hard; second time, easy, Richard reflected. Now there could be no doubt that Craig had gone to meet his maker, whoever, or whatever, that had been.

Richard sat down heavily on the ground and took stock – a full house of emotions coursing through his still body. He felt fear – fear at the enormity of what he had just done; he felt extreme elation that he had emerged victorious from a life-and-death struggle; he felt joy over the fact that his family were now free of the threat that had hung over them; he felt proud that they were safe, because of his protective actions; and he felt bewilderment about what would happen next. Surely the whole world had heard the gunfire, and the place would soon be swarming with police and dogs and helicopters, he thought. So Richard sat on the remains of a fallen tree and waited for the inevitable.

After what seemed like an eternity, but was probably no more than twenty minutes, Richard began to realise that even if someone had heard the shots, they would have little idea where they had come from and may have casually dismissed them as the result of a car backfiring or a farmer's shotgun. He started to wonder what he should do next. He had a ready-made grave, of course, so body disposal was no problem. But what was he going to do about poor Louise? A callous man would put her in the grave along with Craig – the way that he had planned to do with Richard – but Richard knew that the anguish her family was feeling now would be infinitely worse if they were never to discover what had happened to their precious daughter. No, Louise would have to be discovered and given a decent burial, not simply be discarded in a hole in the ground.

Richard decided that manual labour would aid his thought process, so he dragged Craig's body over to the grave and rolled him into it. He then steeled himself sufficiently to be able to remove the plastic bag that had covered Louise's face for so long. He wiped aside a few strands of hair from her eyes and gently closed her lids with his palms. He then threw the bag into Craig's grave, along with the gun. He vaguely remembered that there had been a shovel in the boot of the car, which he had noticed when he had placed Louise's body there. He realized that it would now be required, but where was the car? He retraced their steps through the woods with some difficulty, but eventually found it and managed to get back to the gravesite again without too much bother and with the much-needed shovel.

Richard filled in the grave, making sure that the roots that had been dug out went back in, and then he covered it over, as Craig had intended, with copious amounts of twigs and leaves, using a broken branch with leaves attached to sweep the surrounding area where the mound of earth had been. In fact, a great deal of earth was still left over, even though he had stamped down hard on the earth as it was put in. Why is it, he wondered, that not all the soil which you dig out of a hole will ever go back in again? When he was finished, and he looked over the site, he concluded that he had done a pretty decent job of concealing it and was confident that within a very short period of time, there would be little, if any, sign of the extreme disruption that the ground had suffered. He and Craig had done a good job between them, he reflected, ruefully.

He then had the pitiful task of, once again, carrying poor Louise to the car. He searched the boot this time and found a pair of almost new gardening gloves that Craig must have worn, so he carefully put them on and wiped any area of the car that he may have touched, in order to remove his prints. Richard, once again, lifted Louise gently into the boot of the car and closed it, firmly. He was just about to get into the car, when he realised that his shoes and trousers were caked in soil and debris from the grave site, as would be the back of Louise's dress, where he had laid her down. Realising that the police might well have the technology to be able to discover where precisely the soil had come from, he tiredly opened the boot of the car again and, holding back tears, he removed Louise's dress, stripped to his underpants, rolled Louise's dress and his trousers inside his shirt and placed them carefully behind the front seat of the car. He opened the driver's door, sat sideways on the seat and removed his shoes, before sliding in and tucking the shoes behind the seat on top of the bundle of clothes, trying not to spill soil on the carpet.

He heaved a sigh of relief at finding the keys still dangling in the ignition. He was not sure that he could have faced digging Craig up again, if they had been in his pocket. He knew that he still wasn't thinking very clearly. Richard drove the car back to 4 Hawthorn Avenue, feeling very exposed, driving the car through town in his underpants. But, he reasoned, it was a summer's day, and he simply hoped that anyone noticing him would assume that he was just shirtless and not almost naked in the car. He parked the car on the driveway, directly outside the front door, so that the car itself would help shield the front door from any prying eyes, and, when he was absolutely sure that the coast was clear, he quickly exited the car and approached the front door.

Damn! The door was locked, and *those* keys must be lodged in Craig's pocket still. Why hadn't he thought of that? He'd been lucky with the car keys, but his luck had clearly just run out. He returned to the car and took out the bundle of clothes, which he then placed on the ground. After locating his wallet from among them, he removed a credit card and returned to the door, where, with surprising ease, he managed to open the door latch with it. He made a quick mental note to buy Michael a large bottle of his favourite vodka, so as to thank him for his tutorial on burglary methods and techniques.

He glanced at his watch. It was almost four in the afternoon, and he had to get back to his house, without being noticed – a somewhat difficult task in just his underpants – and he also had to dispose of Louise's dress. He went upstairs to search the remaining bedrooms and found, to his relief, that Craig had an almost-full wardrobe of clothes at the house. He picked out a clean outfit. All the clothes in the wardrobe appeared to be made to measure, including the shirts, but they were a reasonable fit. Feeling much more confident now that he was fully clothed again, Richard thoroughly explored the rest of the house, wiping down every surface that he had touched, and every surface that he may have touched, the last time he was there, with a clean dishcloth retrieved from the kitchen. He also explored the garden area and found a garden incinerator that looked unused. He assumed that Craig had bought it with the disposal of evidence in mind, so he lit a fire, using some spare newspaper and an old broken wooden chair that was stowed away in the shed, and burned Louise's dress and his own soiled clothes, except for the shoes. They had cost a great deal of money, and Elizabeth would undoubtedly miss them. No, they would have to be cleaned and kept.

He finally thought that he was ready to head home, but he kept thinking that he must have forgotten something, so he went over things carefully, one more time in his head. He had disposed of the soiled clothing; he had wiped all traces of his fingerprints, both from the house and the car; he had disposed of Craig's body and the gun; the spade, he had thrown further into the woods, just before leaving. Michael was not expecting him to take any action until much later that night, which was why there had been only the one call from Elizabeth. He still had to think of an excuse for turning off the phone and not bothering to ring her back, as he normally would.

Well, he mused, if he had overlooked something, then that was too bad, because he was anxious to be in his own home again. He walked out the front door and returned to his house in the same way that he had left it, although he found it much harder scaling his neighbour's garage from the front yard, because there was no patio table to stand on, to boost him up. However, his mood was such that he felt, in those moments, that he could achieve anything. Once he had dropped heavily back down into his neighbour's garden, he returned the patio table to its former location and tidied the fence, as much as was possible under the circumstances. He thought he would probably tell his neighbour that he had been working in the garden and had accidentally taken a fall against the fence. Although his neighbour would really have to be a fool to believe that a simple fall would result in that amount of damage, he failed to see what he could do about it, especially as Richard would obviously offer to pay completely for the repairs.

Back in his own environment, Richard showered and changed into his own clothes, putting Craig's into a plastic waste sack, with the intention of taking it to the local tip, before the day was out. But what if the local tips were closed already? It was now gone four-thirty, and he had an idea that was just the time that they closed for the evening. He didn't think the police would suspect him of anything, but if they did, they would certainly search the house thoroughly and, in that case, would naturally find the clothes. But then, he thought, carefully, if he simply hung the clothes in his wardrobe, why would they suspect them of not being his? Was he now just becoming paranoid about making a mistake? He thought perhaps that he was.

That was it, he thought, tiredly. What would be, would be. He was going to mix himself a stiff drink, ring Elizabeth and then ring Paul and tell him that he knew where Craig was hiding out. It was all nearly over; surely, nothing could go wrong now.

Richard was just about to pick up the phone and dial Elizabeth's mobile number, when it began to ring.

'Richard Drake,' he answered.

It was Elizabeth, calling again to check on him.

'Where on earth have you been, Richard? Paul called at the house and said that there was no reply. He thought that you had sneaked out, so as to have some time to yourself for once. We were all frantic with worry, though. How dare you put us all through that?' And, with that, she promptly began to cry.

Richard apologised for his errant behaviour, making the feeble excuse that things had finally got on top of him, and he had had to get out of the house and get some fresh air – to be on his own, in order to think things through. He told her that he had just discovered where Craig was hiding, and he was about to ring Paul and tell him. Elizabeth wanted details, and Richard promised her that he would explain everything later, but that the sooner he rang Paul, the better for everyone involved.

Richard was beginning to feel much more relaxed; things seemed to be going according to plan, except, of course, there was no plan – he was flying by the seat of his pants, so to speak. After briefly reassuring his wife, Richard asked to speak to Michael and informed him that the situation had come to a head quicker than they had planned, and that he would explain soon enough.

'In the meantime, Michael, don't worry about anything. It's all turning out much better than could have been expected. Just play things by ear, until we have a chance to speak alone. I'm going to ring Paul now and tell him about the Bentley that you saw. I'll tell him that I've only just put two and two together and have finally remembered where we saw a Bentley recently.'

'Well done, Richard, I can't wait to hear all the details. I'll see you soon.'

Soon after, Richard rang Paul on his mobile, 'Hi, Paul, it's Richard. You're not going to believe it, but I think I know where Craig is hiding out. Michael managed to go out for a walk this morning, and when he came back, he made some casual remark about having seen a new Bentley on an adjoining street. Well, something about it has been nagging at me all day, and I have just this minute remembered where I saw one recently. Do you remember seeing one outside the coroner's court? Craig's lawyer got into one after the inquest. Don't you see? It has to be the same one, I'm sure of it. The driver was visiting someone in number four Hawthorn Avenue, just opposite my house. That has to be how he mistook Louise for Rebecca; he was watching the house from inside number four when Louise took Rebecca's car that day.'

'Whoa, slow down a tad, Richard. You're telling me that you think Craig is staying in a house on the opposite side of the road to you? What did you say? 4 Hawthorn Avenue?'

'That's right! You have to get over here, right now!'

'OK, I'm on my way as we speak, Richard. We'll check it out straight away. Who is in the house with you at the moment?'

'No one, it's just me. Michael took Elizabeth over to visit the girls this morning.'

'Oh, of course, that's right. Well, you make sure that you lock all your doors and stay in the house, OK? Don't open the doors to anyone, but me, Sergeant Evans or Constable Kelly, is that quite clear, Richard?'

'Quite clear, Paul, please, just get here as soon as possible.'

Richard couldn't stop himself from playing the day's events over and over in his mind. Had he overlooked something crucial that could tie him in with Craig's disappearance? Could he have done anything differently to ease the pain that Louise's family were naturally going to suffer, when they learnt of her gruesome death? How much should he tell Elizabeth?

He went upstairs to look out for the arrival of Paul and his team, and the first thing that he noticed was that the car that had been parked up the road, keeping a close eye on his house and family, had now moved, so that it was parked directly outside, where it could closely observe 4 Hawthorn Avenue. Richard found himself pacing the room, backwards and forwards, for what seemed an eternity, until he eventually saw Paul's car, driven by June Kelly, pull onto the driveway of number four, along with two more police cars, which parked outside. Two men, whom Richard had not seen before, got out of the car that had been watching his house earlier, and they casually started to walk towards Hawthorn Avenue. Paul waited at the door, to be joined by several armed officers – all of whom held their guns in a remarkably similar manner to that which Richard had employed, earlier in the day. He empathized with them, knowing something of what they must be feeling, armed and ready to enter into an unknown, and potentially dangerous, situation.

Paul stood to one side of the door and knocked, loudly. Another officer stood by, with what looked like a battering ram, ready to knock down the door, if there was no answer to their knocking. Paul knocked again and followed up by calling out, telling the would-be occupants that the people standing at the front door were armed police and that they had to come out of the house, with their hands on their heads. It was just like in the television shows that Richard and his wife watched on a Saturday night, except that now, Richard was resisting the urge to open up the window and shout over to the police that everything was all right – that Craig wouldn't, in fact, be opening the door, because the evil bastard was dead, and it was he, Richard Drake, that had rid the world of him and avenged poor Louise.

Suddenly, Richard's emotions shifted. He felt sickened and took stock of himself. This isn't me, he thought, I've now killed two men, and I feel a sense of triumph, rather than remorse. What have I become? Will things ever go back to the way they were? Will I ever feel normal again? He was close to tears – tears of sadness and relief, all rolled confusingly into one.

Richard watched as the policeman with the battering ram smashed it hard against the door, on a level with, and very close to, the lock. He smiled, thinking how easy it had been to open the door earlier in the day, with no more than a credit card, and without causing all that needless damage. For some reason, this thought instantly caused him to stop smiling, and he didn't quite know why. There was something, but he couldn't put his finger on it.

He stayed at the window, watching with interest as 4 Hawthorn Avenue slowly turned into a crime scene, with police blocking off the area of pavement outside the house and an army of men and women in overalls going in and out. Eventually, interest naturally turned to the car standing in the driveway, and there was a flurry of increased activity, when the car boot was finally opened. A white tent was hurriedly erected over the car and the surrounding area, and it was no longer possible for Richard to continue to observe proceedings.

Richard called Robert's house to let everybody there know that Craig's hiding place had been discovered and he said to them that he wanted, more than anything, to have his family home again.

It was almost seven in the evening by the time that they finally all arrived home. Margaret had rung Paul to find out what she could, but Paul was too busy to say very much at that point in time, other than Richard had been right about Craig's hiding place. Craig had, in fact, been staying at the house, but they had not found him there when they entered, but that they had recovered the body of a young girl in the boot of the car, who they believed was Louise.

Elizabeth had broken down and cried when she heard that, and they had all tried to comfort her as best they could, even though they, too, shared her despair.

Partly to try to break the morose mood, and partly because it was true, Rebecca suddenly declared, 'Well, I don't know about anybody else, but I'm starving, and I think I'll rustle something up in the kitchen. Does anybody else want anything?'

'I think that everyone is probably hungry, Rebecca,' said Richard, gratefully, 'why not ring for a takeaway instead?'

'Yes, that's a good idea, Richard. Let's do that,' said Elizabeth, and everyone else agreed.

'Well, what does everyone want, then? Shall I order a Chinese or would you prefer Indian?'

Everyone agreed that a Chinese would be fine, so Rebecca was elected to ring the nearest Chinese takeaway and order a set meal.

'They probably will do set meals for four, six or eight people, which shall I order?' she asked.

'Eight!' everyone shouted, in unison.

Richard told her to put the cost of the meal on his card and reached into his back pocket to take out his wallet. Even before he had pulled it out, that nasty nagging feeling that he had experienced earlier returned with a vengeance ... and he knew that his credit card wasn't going to be there.

He vividly remembered using it to open the front door of Craig's house and pushing the door open. He remembered going back outside to retrieve his dirt-clogged clothes and Louise's dress from where he had placed them on the ground. But, for the life of him, he couldn't remember where he had put the card down. It has to be either in the house somewhere, he realized, with growing dread, or on the ground outside, and with the police swarming all over the place, they were sure to find it. After all he had gone through, for it to end with him being arrested seemed more than harsh, but then, on the other hand, it had almost ended, on two occasions, with him being killed, so perhaps he shouldn't grumble too much at his fate. A few years inside was much better than a hole in the ground, he reasoned, tiredly, and at least his family was safe – he had done well by them, which was the most important thing to remember.

He wondered, fleetingly, whether he would be better off pleading innocence of everything, except for confronting Craig at his house, because, as he saw it, the only thing that the discovery of the card would prove was that he had been inside the rented house. On the other hand, he had no doubt that a court would be lenient towards him for killing Craig, because of the nature of what he had been through, even though, this time, it would be extremely difficult to argue self-defence, with a body shot twice and then buried. No ... let them try and prove whatever they thought that they could.

He suddenly realised that they were all staring straight at him, wondering what the problem was.

'I think I have mislaid my card somewhere. Have you got yours on you, darling?'

Elizabeth swiftly retrieved her card out of her handbag, and Rebecca proceeded to order the takeaway food. Four hours, half a bottle of vodka and four bottles of wine later, the girls had all retired, exhausted, to bed, leaving Richard and Michael to finish cleaning things up in the kitchen.

'So what exactly happened? And where is Craig? Do you know where he is?' asked Michael, intrigued.

'What actually happened is a surprisingly long story, as a matter of fact, but the significant highlights are that Craig is finally dead and buried, and I have, unfortunately, left incriminating evidence at his house.'

Over the rest of the bottle of vodka, Richard slowly recounted the whole story of his confrontation with Craig – both at the rented house and the makeshift grave site – finishing with him missing his credit card, some hours earlier.

'My God! Richard, you've been to hell and back. It must have truly been a nightmare for you. But well done, my friend, I'm very proud of you. Not many men could have endured all that and come out of it, as you have.'

'What? Getting arrested and sent to prison, you mean?'

'Well, like you say, Richard, all the card proves is that you were at the house. In fact, if they happen to find it outside on the driveway, you could say that you sneaked up to the front window of the house to look in the window or something like that.'

'And took my credit card out to do what, exactly?'

'I suggest that we go up to bed and sleep on it, Richard. We'll see if we can come up with more a plausible explanation in the clarity of the morning.'

The next morning over breakfast, everyone was in a remarkably more positive mood than of late. Richard had successfully convinced them all that Craig would now be long gone, knowing that the police were on to him and that they had now recovered Louise's body. He declared that he intended to open up the shop the very next day and that it was high time that Rebecca got stuck into her new position.

Despite the fact that he truly expected to be arrested at any moment, Richard was happier and more relaxed than he had been since he first learned of the existence of Craig Harper and his brother.

Elizabeth phoned Louise's grieving parents and sympathetically offered to help, in any way that she could. They told her that Peggy had come home from her holiday and was staying with them until after the funeral – whenever that would be – and that they were very grateful for Elizabeth's kind offer of help, but felt there was little she could do at this stage. Although Elizabeth felt utterly helpless in the circumstances, she was pleased that she had managed to speak to them and that they didn't blame or resent her for the foolish mistake that Craig had made, thinking that Louise was Rebecca. Elizabeth desperately wanted to find a way to help them, but Richard gently assured her that it was best to leave them, so that they could grieve in their own way.

Both Richard and Michael spent the day expecting an unwelcome visit from the police at any moment, but, surprisingly, they didn't put in an appearance. The following day had been almost back to normal – Richard and Margaret spent it at the shop, rearranging items to make it look fresh and open for business. Elizabeth had gone in to the hospital to explain that she was now able to return to duty on the wards, and Michael had spent the day practicing being able to walk without his crutches and booking a much-needed holiday in a warm, exotic location.

Rebecca phoned home, late morning, to say that they were all invited to the *Holiday Inn* in Bath, that coming Saturday night. Her magician friend, Carl, who had previously conned her out of nearly fifty pounds from the hotel till, was giving his final performance there that Saturday, and Paul had agreed, not only to take Margaret to see the show, but to have a couple of plain clothes officers there, so as to keep tabs on the sticky fingers of Mr Magic.

When Richard heard about the event, he insisted on making it a family affair.

'Let's all go,' he suggested, cheerfully, 'we'll see the illusion show and have a slap-up meal – both to celebrate your birthday properly and to celebrate the welcome fact that we won't be hearing from Craig Harper, anytime soon.'

'Are you quite sure that we are rid of him for good?' Elizabeth asked, unconvinced.

Richard took her in his arms, looked her straight in the eye and said, firmly, 'Yes, Elizabeth, I personally promise you, that we will never hear from that man again.'

'But how can we be absolutely sure that he won't be back in a year's time or five years' time? I don't think I shall ever feel completely safe again. Oh, Richard, I've never wished anyone dead before, but I do that man, more than anything.'

Richard hated seeing the pained anguish in his wife's face, and, in that moment, he decided to confide in her.

'You do trust me, don't you, Elizabeth?'

Elizabeth was both puzzled and a little shocked by the directness of the question.

'Of course I trust you, Richard. Why should you need to ask that?'

'Then I am going to tell you something in the strictest of confidence, and we will never speak of it again, not even between ourselves. No questions once I've told you ... none at all. Is it agreed?'

Elizabeth scanned her husband's face, keenly, aware that he was going to say something monumental, but with not the slightest notion of what it could be. 'Yes, Richard, I agree. We won't even discuss it between ourselves, I promise.'

Richard kissed her full on the lips, as if sealing a bargain between them, and then quietly whispered, 'I know, beyond any shadow of a doubt, that Craig Harper is dead and buried, and that his body will, hopefully, never be found.'

'How could ... ? You.'

Richard put a finger to his wife's lips, to remind her of the promise that she had just made with him.

There was silence between them for a while, as the enormity of what her husband had just admitted slowly sunk in. She was full of questions, some of which she wasn't exactly sure that she wanted the answers to. She could only think of one way in which her husband could be so sure that Craig was dead, and it dawned on her that that was exactly why Richard had elicited the commitment from her that she was not to mention it again.

She was shocked to think what her decent, kind, loving husband was capable of, but also, she realized, immensely relieved. Whatever he had done, he had done for his family and for poor Louise, and she loved him more in that moment than at any other time during their lives together.

They stood holding each other closely for some time, before Richard said, 'How many people shall I book a table for?'

'Well, let's see,' said Elizabeth, her mood now completely changed, but still unwilling to physically let go of her husband. 'You and me, obviously, Michael, Margaret and Paul and Rebecca and Daniel – that's seven in total.'

'Daniel?'

'The young man that she took out the other week –you know, the one with the music shop, who inherited his parent's house and plays the guitar. Oh, Richard, don't tell me you've forgotten already.'

'Right, of course, seven it is. I'll ring and book.'

'Oh, did you happen to find your credit card, by the way?' she asked, curiously, 'you will need it, when we go to the hotel for the show on Saturday. Are you treating everyone?'

'Yeah, I guess so.'

'If you haven't found your card, then you should cancel it straight away. You can use mine on the night, instead.'

Richard had been in an upbeat mood, but talk of his missing credit card had suddenly taken the edge off it. The fact that he had not yet been approached by the police made him vaguely hopeful that he had lost it in one of the streets on his way between Craig's and home, but, deep down, he knew that wasn't the case. The only other possibilities, as he currently saw it, was that it had been knocked under something, maybe a piece of furniture, and it was still there waiting to be found or perhaps one of the police officers who were searching the house had picked it up casually, without checking the name, and had automatically assumed that it belonged to Craig. In which case, it would be in an evidence bag somewhere, along with other items of his, and, sooner or later, he felt sure that someone was going to notice the name on the card. Either way, he felt like he was living on borrowed time. A family party, then, was just what the doctor ordered.

* * * * * * * * * * * * *

The music was definitely too loud, but the cabaret was very good and included not just 'Carl – Man of Mystery', but a very talented female vocalist and a near-the-knuckle local comedian, who everybody thoroughly enjoyed. It was a far cry from the last few weeks, and, although Craig was not actually physically behind bars, everyone was happily convinced that they had seen the last of him. Even Paul seemed pessimistic that he would ever be found or charged with anything. Talk inevitably centred around the events of the past few weeks, since Mrs Harper had been murdered, even though everyone was trying hard to avoid it.

Richard had found that he actually liked Rebecca's date for the evening, and he discovered that he was, in fact, quite a musical historian. He was interested in hearing about how musical instruments had changed and developed over the years, deciding that it was a new field that he might take an interest in. Perhaps he could take the time to study them in prison, he thought, wryly. Elizabeth also seemed to take to Daniel, as did Margaret and Paul, so he fitted into their little celebratory group with ease, and, when the cabaret had finished, he danced with not just Rebecca, but with Margaret and Elizabeth, as well. It seemed like an age since Richard had seen his wife and daughter so happy and relaxed.

Michael was also in good form, but in danger of having too much to drink, as usual. As they were all booked in to stay the night at the hotel, he would have retired to his bedroom, if it wasn't for the fact that he was curious to see if the magician was arrested.

The cabaret had been over for quite a while, and the ballroom was thinning out of dancers. The conversation between them had peacefully subsided, and Michael was all but asleep, when Rebecca pointed out to Paul that the 'Man of Mystery' was chatting animatedly to the barman, and his assistant was standing watching, close behind him. Paul swiftly stood up and nodded to someone positioned near the exit, who also looked a little tipsy. The subdued lighting in the room made it difficult to see exactly what was happening, but, after the space of a few minutes, there was some commotion at the bar. Rebecca leaned over and gave Paul a hearty kiss on the cheek, as she saw the magician and his assistant being escorted out of the hotel by two burly plain clothes officers – one of whom had been the tipsy-looking guy by the exit.

Another young man strolled over happily and rested his hand on Paul's shoulder. 'Thanks, buddy, I owe you one.'

'Not me,' said Paul, grinning from ear-to-ear, 'that's the little lady who cracked the case of the reappearing fifty,' he said, pointing to Rebecca.

'Well, well done, young lady. I expect Paul will be willing to take a personal statement from you, so as to save you coming in, and he can pass it on to me. Is that all right with you, Paul?'

'Yeah, that's OK, Jack,' said Paul, sarcastically, 'I'll do your job for you, as well as my own, shall I?'

'Good man, Paul, see you around.'

'A couple of friends from Bath that I know,' explained Paul, after they had gone. 'I tipped them off about Carl and his dealings, and now they owe me one. Life can definitely be sweet sometimes. And now that's concluded, and we are all together, I think it is the perfect time to make an announcement.'

All eyes turned to Paul, as he got to his feet, gave Michael a quick nudge to make sure he was fully awake and said, 'I am happy to tell you all that Margaret has finally succumbed to my good looks, charm and sophistication and agreed to be my wife.'

'Wow! That's fabulous news,' cried Richard, truly delighted. The life-threatening events of the past few days had well and truly put his earlier concerns into perspective.

Everyone congratulated the happy couple and then Richard announced, jovially, 'I think we need a bottle of champagne to celebrate properly.'

'Good idea, Richard,' replied Paul, happily, 'I'll come with you to the bar to order it.'

The two men got up and walked over to the bar, now as old friends. Paul proceeded to order a bottle of their not inexpensive champagne.

'I'll get this,' said Richard, charitably reaching for his wallet.

Paul watched, smiling, as Richard produced his wallet and then he said, slowly, 'You'll need this, then,' holding out a credit card for Richard to take.

'No, no, seriously, I'll get it. It's my treat,' he repeated, reaching for Elizabeth's card that was in his wallet.

Paul continued to hold the card out for Richard, 'Seriously, Richard, you should use this one.'

Richard stopped rummaging in his wallet and stared at the card in Paul's hand, not knowing what to think about the gesture. He stared hard at it, for some time, thinking that he'd got it wrong, but there was no mistake. It was, indeed, his card – the one that he had used to open the front door of Craig's house! He didn't know what to do or say, so he just stood still, staring blankly at it. The barman was waiting for the payment for the champagne, so Paul handed the card to him, instead. The barmen inserted the card into the machine and handed it over to Paul, asking him to enter the pin.

Paul politely declined and, indicating Richard, said, carefully, 'Sorry, mate, it's not my card...... it's his.'

Richard said nothing, as he dutifully punched in his pin number, accepting the card and receipt in return.

He stared at Paul, but was still utterly speechless, so it was Paul who finally broke the silence between them, 'You really ought to have been more careful, Richard. Anybody could have picked it up.'

'Where ... Where did you find it?'

'Somewhere that it definitely shouldn't have been, but that doesn't matter. What matters is that I found it, and nobody else knows. I think it would be in both of our interests if it stays that way, don't you agree?'

'Oh, yes! I'll drink to that, Paul ... and I'll drink to your marriage. I hope Margaret has explained to you that I'll be giving her away.'

'Yes, that was made abundantly clear, Richard. I do just have one nagging question, though.'

'What's that?'

'Is there any possibility – any at all – that Craig will put in an appearance, at any time in the future?'

'There's no possible chance of that, whatsoever, Paul. Is that a problem?'

Paul shrugged his shoulders, 'More like the end of a problem, if you ask me,' he replied, smiling.

The End

* *

The Author:

Colin Holcombe, was born and raised in Bristol. A former Antique Restorer, he has also been a Cabaret Entertainer, Adult Education Tutor, and Kitchen Designer.

Colin, has tried his hand at various sports, including, gliding, tennis, badminton and golf, and has written several reference books.

First Time Hard, is his first work of fiction.

Lightning Source UK Ltd.
Milton Keynes UK
UKOW05f2038020414

229314UK00012B/645/P